TALES FOR A
NEW MILLENNIUM

Beverly R. Sherringham

iUniverse, Inc.
Bloomington

Tales for a New Millennium

iUniverse books may be ordered through booksellers or by contacting:

iUniverse
1663 Liberty Drive
Bloomington, IN 47403
www.iuniverse.com
1-800-Authors (1-800-288-4677)

ISBN: 978-1-4759-1524-2 (sc)
ISBN: 978-1-4759-1525-9 (e)

Printed in the United States of America

iUniverse rev. date: 10/05/2012

To the Georgetown University English Department

Contents

STARCHED SHEETS

The Turner exhibition at the MET did not disappoint. Brightness illuminated the room. How could it not? Beams of radiance flowed like arrows through the air causing a prism of light that reflected every nuance of color in the room. Hushed tones marveled at such refractory genius. How could a brush and a few dollops of paint elicit such sublime splendor? Did not the high-ridged mountains overpower the tiny specks of people surrounding them? This was the sublime in all of its glory. Evan Centinel stepped back and gasped slightly at the sight of the Houses of Parliament burning amidst a crimson-orange glow. He did not know why he shuddered. It was involuntary and the mark of an overwhelming sensation within his being. Evan felt a sense of relief at the sight of the gift shop signaling the end of the exhibit. His sensitive nature could not endure another moment of such sublimity. For certain, he would return next week for another glimpse. Evan returned the earphones and the recorder to the attendant. He was oblivious to the sounds emitting from the recorder. The majesty of the exhibition spoke for itself.

Of course, it was not the first time Evan had witnessed Turner's glorious talents. He observed them in full at Tate Britain in London, where Turner's spectacular works enjoyed their own wing. How amenable of the English to lend a sizable portion of the masterpieces to the MET so that Americans could grasp a bit of culture. If the poor wretches won't go in search of culture, culture must come in search of them. Perhaps it would make the world a better place, and why wouldn't it? A rather disheveled young man approached Evan. He wore a tee shirt which seemed to have acquired a stain or two since Evan saw it last.

"Pleasant lunch, was it?" asked Evan noting the stain.

"It was OK," said the young man ignoring the stain and his father's disapproving countenance. "Hey, listen, we want to go to the park for awhile. Would it be all right? I mean, you could finish up here, and we could meet you in say an hour or so."

"I thought that this trip to the museum would be informative and enjoyable for you and your friends. I take it you're not enjoying yourselves?"

"We're having a great time, Dad. We went to see the dead shark. Amazing!"

"Fine," said Evan with a twinge of disgust. "I will meet you at the front entrance in an hour."

The young man and his adolescent friends scurried down the magisterial staircase and exited the luxuriant museum with great aplomb. Evan wondered what he would do with himself for an hour. Perhaps he could relax on a bench in the park and take care of a few important matters on his BlackBerry before the office phoned demanding a quick response to whatever matter was pressing at the moment. The park was certainly large enough to avoid hindering the rambunctious curiosity of the adolescents.

Evan made himself comfortable on a bench adjacent to the Great Lawn and checked his BlackBerry. The red light was flashing, as ever. "London Calling...," the email began. She always began her emails with *London's Calling...* Evan surmised that it was a song of some popularity. The only familiarity he had with it was in the episode of *Billy Elliot* when scores of uniformed policemen armed with nightsticks beat them methodically upon shields as they waited to pounce upon Billy's brother, Tony. Tony wasn't very likable, so he deserved it, Evan reasoned. "Promotion ensured," the message announced. "Come and join the celebration." Evan wished that there had been more details, but the message was scant, as always. A quick check of his schedule indicated that he would not be able to take off this week or even the next. He would miss yet another celebration.

She was always celebrating. Life was one long celebration of one kind or another. Ah, the mark of the young. In point of fact, she was only slightly older than his son. What an odd couple they were. Winter and spring, but was he really winter? There were a few gray hairs here and there, but he kept his youthful, well-toned body, and his genes contributed an endless supply of youth serum, which penetrated every pore on his face and seemed to mask any advance of age. Winter, indeed. It was more like spring and Indian summer. "That would make a great title for a book," thought Evan absent-mindedly. Books were always on his mind. As senior editor for a major New York publishing company, books and reviews swirled intermittently within his mind alongside thoughts of her at all hours of the day and night.

There were sprinklers spraying the Great Lawn. If she were with him, she would, surely, run through the sprinklers in her bare feet laughing and reveling in the cool, blissful waters. Evan remembered their trip to Paris, where she jumped into the fountain near the plaza across from the Eiffel Tower. He stood aghast as she spluttered around in the waters. No one seemed to mind. Parisians knew how to enjoy life and expected everyone else to enjoy it as well. He couldn't imagine such a thing occurring in England. England was calm, clean, and observant of the decorum necessary for civilized living. Paris, on the other hand, was grimy and somewhat truculent. Blast civility. Embrace life through the grime and make a memory that will bring pleasure through the years. Evan checked his schedule again on the BlackBerry calendar. Perhaps he would be able to rearrange a few appointments and make a quick trip to London for the celebration. "New York Responding," read the subject line of his email. All right, he was not witty or informed of the email responses that indicated that one was aware of the latest trends in social networking. It was the best "Old Winter" had to offer on a bright and glorious summer afternoon in Central Park.

The Barnes and Nobel patrons were exceedingly chatty. Evan sank in the upholstered easy chair and tried to concentrate.

"What on earth are you reading?" asked Mindy, his wife of twenty-four years.

"It's David Sedaris's new book," said Evan enjoying a witty line.

"Well, I hope that you don't bring it home. That skull won't go with anything in the living room."

"If I had a den," said Evan reasonably, "I wouldn't need to disturb the décor of the living room."

"Are we going to discuss this now in front of strangers reading books?" asked Mindy.

"No, Dear, we are not," said Evan standing. The chair was comfortable, and he did not want to remove himself from its warm tentacles, but he did not want to disturb the other readers. There were swarms of young children running around asking questions and making their presence felt throughout the store. An hour ago, there was silence as Evan settled into the easy chair. He thought it remarkable that the suburban Barnes and Nobel stores had easy chairs and appropriate lighting. The ones he frequented in the city seemed to have an aversion to chairs. Patrons stretched out on the floor reading as best they could. Surely, suburban parents had one retreat on a cheerful, sunny Sunday morning – Barnes and Nobel, where children could run around endlessly and, perhaps, select a book or two. Evan tried to remember whether there were children running around the Barnes and Nobel bookstores in the city. If there were, they were confined to the children's area. The suburban children seemed to have free rein of the store. Evan wished that someone would direct them to the children's area.

"What kind of book is that?" asked Mindy of a teenage girl approaching them.

"Dad?" appealed the young girl to her father.

"Leave your father out of this," said Mindy. Her voice seemed unnecessarily shrill. "Why can't you get an intelligent book? Why is it always those teenage girl books where everyone sleeps around and goes to a private school?"

"Dad?" insisted the girl with exasperation.

"Here's a copy of *Les Miserables*," said Evan anticipating the inevitable brouhaha. "Take the books to the checkout line. We'll meet you there."

The girl took the books with a smile and walked to the checkout line.

"You know that she won't read *Les Miserables*," said Mindy. "You just did that to annoy me."

Evan placed his arm around his wife's shoulder. "Minifred, why ever would I want to annoy you?" They walked slowly to the checkout line. "Did you select a book, Dear?"

"You know that I don't like to read," said Minifred. "What do you have there? Is that another travel guide? Who do you think you are, Rick Steves?"

Mindy enjoyed watching the PBS Create channel. It was filled with home improvement projects, sewing projects, famous chefs, and her all time favorite, Rick Steves, the travel expert. Rick Steves' travel escapades fascinated Mindy; in fact, she kept a list of places of interest that they should visit when the children were out of the house and off to college. Samuel was a freshman this year, but there were two others, Gretchen and

Hans. Gretchen had no interest in college, and Hans was at that impressionable age when dead sharks were of keen interest.

"I may take a trip to London next week," said Evan. "It will be a short trip. Do you remember that new author that we are trying to lure? I think that we are on the verge of making an impact."

"Why is it always you?" asked Mindy.

"Because I must get away from you in order to keep any semblance of sanity," thought Evan, but he said politely, "This is a big deal, or else I would send one of the associates. I must handle this personally." Evan paid for his books and Gretchen's books.

"Can I come with you, Dad?" asked Gretchen wistfully.

"No!" said Mindy. "You have softball practice. You must keep up with these sports for your college applications. They want to know that you are active and not the couch potato you are."

"Perhaps next time, Sweetie," said Evan diplomatically. For once, he was grateful for Mindy's intrusion.

Evan looked around the terminal, but he did not see her. There was no one waiting; in fact, Gatwick was practically empty. He waited his turn to show his passport. The clerk checked the passport of a young woman ahead of him and inquired as to the nature of her visit. The woman stated that she was presenting a paper on the sublime at one of the universities. The clerk asked for more specific details and asked questions about the paper. Evan wondered what the clerk knew about the sublime. Of course, it was her job to question people entering the country, but, surely, this was absurd. The woman began to explain the key points of her paper. Satisfied that the woman was, indeed, a scholar, the clerk granted her admittance. Evan approached the clerk's desk. The clerk yelled out to the woman, "Hey, this is reality not the sublime! The exit is over there." The woman changed her course and walked meekly out of the check-in area. Evan viewed the clerk with derision. Such rudeness was unnecessary. He waited to be quizzed and determined to tell the clerk that his business in her country was none of her concern. She did not quiz him. Perhaps she had a special dislike of scholars, or perhaps he looked like an editor on assignment. For whatever reason, he was given a smile, a stamp on his passport, and polite directions to the exit.

Evan read his David Sedaris book with the skull on the cover as he waited patiently for her to arrive. An hour later, she appeared. He stood and greeted her with a kiss on the cheek.

"Sorry I'm late," said the young woman. "Peter had a class."

Evan noticed a young man standing behind her. He had dirty blonde hair and wore jeans and a tee shirt that seemed equally dirty.

"Peter, this is Evan. Evan, Peter," said the young woman making quick introductions.

Evan extended his hand. "Pleased to meet you," said Evan.

"Peter will be joining us," said the young woman. "You don't mind, do you?"

Evan smiled. "Welcome, Peter."

Peter's grin was wide and genuine. He really seemed happy to be in their company.

"How do you know Peter?" asked Evan lifting his bag and proceeding towards the taxi area.

"We're old college chums. Peter is working on his doctorate. Guess what he's working on?" asked the young woman.

"The sublime?" answered Evan sardonically.

The young woman laughed. Peter considered the suggestion with interest.

"Funny you should mention that," said Peter beginning to make a connection between his dissertation topic and the sublime.

"I wasn't serious," said Evan stopping him in mid-sentence.

"Peter is very serious," said the young woman. "He's going to be a professor, aren't you Peter?"

"Yes." The answer was simple. Peter seemed to be contemplating the relation of the sublime to his research. "Now that you mention it…"

"I told you that he is serious about his work. Now, he'll be thinking of your comment the entire day," said the young woman.

"Prentice," said Evan, "perhaps I can have a word privately?"

"Uh-oh," said Prentice, "I feel a storm cloud brewing. We'll be right back Peter."

Peter did not seem to notice them. His thoughts were interweaving the possibility of the sublime within an engineering context. Evan led Prentice to an area near the ATM. Her short, dark pixie cut made her look even younger than her twenty-three years. Her dark eyes were oval and filled with light. Evan always thought that she wore too much blush, but once he saw her without any and realized that she was quite pale and needed a bit of color on her cheeks. Her lips were adorned with red lipstick, though not startling. She wore a suit that seemed to be gray herringbone, a white blouse, and black pumps. In her heels, she only reached his elbow. Evan was quite tall, 6'5" to be exact. His height always made him feel young and quite energetic. This morning, however, he felt old and tired.

"Why is Peter here?" asked Evan gently. "I thought that we were going to celebrate your promotion. You must tell me all about it."

"Peter is living with me temporarily," said Prentice matter-of-factly. "His roommate moved out, and he couldn't afford to keep the apartment alone, so he moved in with me."

"I see," said Evan. "You have one bedroom; where does Peter sleep?"

Prentice laughed. "Peter doesn't sleep. He eats and breathes his dissertation. You'll have to be careful where you tread. His papers are all over the living room."

"So then your relationship is purely platonic?" asked Evan. "Is he gay or something?"

Prentice looked at Evan with wonder. "No, he's just preoccupied. He won't be a problem. I thought that we'd be staying in your hotel with all the fancy amenities; although, with my promotion, I can afford my own amenities now. Not on your level, of course, but perhaps I can afford to pay for M&Ms in that fancy hotel."

"Then, you're staying with me?" asked Evan.

"Of course," said Prentice. "unless you want to maneuver around Peter's papers. He has a dog also, Reginald, a lovely Irish setter with a reddish blonde coat that sheds everywhere."

"It sounds as though Peter and Reginald are planning to stay," said Evan with concern.

Prentice kissed his cheek and then wiped the red lipstick off with her fingers. "I'm helping a friend. Is that allowed?"

"Of course," said Evan. "I wish that you had mentioned it sooner. How long has Peter been living with you?"

"Not long. Would you rather that I told you while you were in New York? You would have jumped to conclusions, as you're doing now. I see the furtive looks you're giving him."

"I just want you to be safe and happy," assured Evan.

"You sound like my father," laughed Prentice. Evan shuddered.

"Come on, let's drop Peter off, and then we'll check into the hotel," said Prentice.

"And where are we dropping Peter?" asked Evan.

"Home, of course," said Prentice. She led Evan by the hand to Peter, who was now perched in a chair in lotus position. Evan observed him carefully. Was he some kind of hippie? Were there still hippies? What nerve to bring a shedding dog with him. Prentice loved dogs. Peter opened his eyes and smiled at the pair.

"Ready?" asked Peter.

"Ready," reassured Prentice. They walked towards the taxi stand – one contemplative other-worldly being, one youthful professional embarking upon a new career, and one middle-aged man too tall to fit comfortably within the taxi.

Evan wanted to take a nap, but he didn't dare broach the subject. Prentice hung her suit carefully over a chair near the desk.

"How do you like it? It was the first thing I purchased when I heard about the promotion. Now I really look professional, don't I?" asked Prentice. "Of course, I don't wear it to work. I only wore it today to impress you. Usually, I wear it when I visit potential clients. They love the traditional look. It's Brooks Brothers, you know."

"No, I didn't know," said Evan sitting on the bed in his shorts.

"I saw the label in most of your suits. I figured if it's good enough for you, then it will impress our clients. Most of them are around your age."

Once again, Evan shuddered.

"Of course, Peter says that I look ten years older in it, but that's the point. No one wants to hire a company that looks young and inexperienced. Am I right?"

Prentice folded the bedspread to the end of the bed. "They say these spreads have germs of some kind. I think that they are right. That's the first place people sit, isn't it? They take off their clothes and sit on the bedspread."

"Have I become predictable?" asked Evan.

Prentice sat beside him in her white camisole and bikinis. "What's troubling you? It's Peter, isn't it? Don't let it bother you. He's a friend, that's all." She moved a couple of strands of hair from Evan's forehead. "I want to tell you about my new position. I have been assigned to the innovative design department."

"And what do you innovate?" asked Evan.

"It's like a think tank for merchandise. We think of innovative ways to sell products."

"It sounds intriguing. Tell me more," said Evan. Slowly, he was losing his desire to take a nap. Prentice chirped on about her new position with much enthusiasm. He loved watching her speak. Evan wasn't really listening. He was watching her lips form words and smile simultaneously. He was noting her incessant gestures and the way her pixie fluttered as she moved her head from side to side. She was like glitter, and Evan felt as though he had gained ten years of lost youth. From what he could gather, the position was quite frivolous and unstable. He wanted her to return to the university and attain an additional degree. Competition was steep in all fields. An advanced degree couldn't hurt, but she was determined to work for a small but lucrative cyber company. Evan had seen these companies skyrocket to fame and fortune, on the one hand, or plunge into dust, on the other. The CEOs were inevitably young, ambitious dreamers with nothing to lose. Stability and job security were not the goals they sought. The thrill of the unknown seemed to keep this generation moving towards an unsteady but happy future. Evan didn't know how they did it, but he could certainly understand how Peter could end up without a roommate with a steady job. The problem was that if this company folded, Prentice would be out of a job as well. How would she pay the rent for her apartment or for her new herringbone suit, obviously expensive and of excellent quality?

"How many people does this company employ?" asked Evan.

"Twenty-five or twenty-six, twenty-seven if you include Peter," answered Prentice.

"Why would I include Peter?" asked Evan curiously. "Is he a part-time employee?"

"Silly, Peter owns the company. He started it a few years ago but decided to work on his doctorate instead. He checks in from time to time, but he lets us run it."

Evan sat incredulously on the unmade bed with pristine white, cotton sheets. Soft, flexible sheets that seemed to caress every inch of their bodies and offered no resistance as they moved within them. Evan wondered about the thread count of the sheets and determined that the luxury hotel had not been forthcoming about the quality of the room, certainly not the sheets, which seemed rather thin. Didn't anyone value quality anymore? As he lay next to Prentice, gently slumbering with red lips, although not startling, he thought of his parents' insistence upon starched sheets. Each week, the laundry would return a neatly wrapped, brown paper package, which contained white, starched sheets. Starched sheets – a sign of quality, genteel upbringing, and good taste. Smooth and forthright, starched sheets provided a sense of stability and well-being in an ill-governed world. Mindy detested the idea of starched, white sheets and refused to allow anything other than floral sheets that had the smell of fabric softener on their bed. Starched sheets – the end of an era.

The travel brochures were spread out on the bed, and Mindy checked the itinerary carefully.

"What is this?" asked Mindy noting a destination to a rather non-descript place in Latin America. "We can't go here. I can't even pronounce it. Besides, Rick Steves doesn't have a brochure for this place."

"Heaven forbid that we should travel to a place where Rick Steves hasn't trodden," said Evan brushing his thinning hair. Too many strands lay embedded within the hairbrush, and they were all gray. Graying hair and shrunken bones; yes, he felt that he was shrinking. He didn't seem as tall, or was it the approach of his fifty-eighth birthday? The advancing years were a threat proclaiming the end of his youthful vitality. It had been years since he had travelled anywhere. Since his retirement, he sat around the house most of the day working on his posters. He had taken up a hobby. Evan designed posters of faraway places. It was a lifetime ambition to see the world; the time had arrived, now that all of his children were college graduates. Samuel went on to pursue a Master's degree in architecture from a Midwestern university; Gretchen, after a tumultuous beginning at the local community college, was able to transfer to New York University and graduate with a degree in journalism. Hans graduated with honors with a degree in oceanography from the University of California. Their bedrooms were empty. Evan contemplated selling the house and moving to a warmer climate, perhaps Nevada. As anticipated, Mindy disapproved. Never having visited Nevada, she concluded that there were too many gamblers in the area. The entire state was, in her opinion, a mammoth Las Vegas casino. The compromise was the world-trip that they promised themselves they would take when the children were grown and out of the house. A world trip seemed like a grand idea, but Evan would rather take the trip with Barney the dinosaur than Mindy the grouse.

"Fine," said Evan. "Cross it off the list. Where are my sketch pencils? I can't find them in the den."

"Check the kitchen counter," said Mindy finalizing the itinerary. "I used them to make a shopping list."

"You needed an entire box of pencils to make a shopping list?" asked Evan.

"Why are you so protective of your pencils? Ever since you made Hans' room into a den, you act like it's off limits. You don't want me in there, and you don't want to share anything in there. I used a pencil, so sue me."

This was the general tone and content of their daily conversations - petty bickering about insignificant topics, only the topics were not insignificant to Evan. The den was his sanctuary, and his hobby was his relief from days of endless boredom.

"Gretchen's driving us to the airport tomorrow in her new car," said Mindy proudly. "Did you remember to pack your eye drops? You know you get red eyes when we travel on a plane."

"Yes, I packed them," said Evan tediously. "What time is Gretchen coming? I want to run on the treadmill at the gym before we leave tomorrow."

"You won't have time to run tomorrow. Why don't you run today?" asked Mindy searching the travel brochures. "Where's Italy? What did I do with Italy?"

"Perhaps you're right," said Evan. "I'll go to the gym today. I should be home around dinner time."

"All right," said Mindy packing *Rick Steves' Italy* into her suitcase.

Evan packed his sneakers into his gym bag and gathered his car keys. It was his last chance to say goodbye to Ann, his latest mistress. Evan had been involved with three women during the past five years. The first was Ethel, a single mother in the next town. He met her at a book reading at Barnes and Nobel. Mindy did not attend, and Evan, quite happily, ventured out alone. He sat beside an attractive woman with a young son. They began a harmless conversation about the author, which led to coffee in the café and dinner the following week. Ethel did not mind that Evan was married; she preferred married men. She did not want to become too involved. Her son was her priority, and she did not want anyone to mar their close relationship. The affair ended soon after when her son began to establish a father/son relationship with Evan. That was prohibited. No one would ever abandon her son again, which Ethel knew would be inevitable, so she broke off the affair. The second woman, Halley, was a dance instructor. She taught ballet, jazz, and tap at a dance school in Hauppauge, a few towns over. Halley was single. She saw prospects in Evan and hoped that when Hans graduated that Evan would leave Mindy and marry her.

The idea was, of course, preposterous. Evan never mentioned marriage. Halley lived in a fantasy world, which would, sooner or later require engagement with reality. Evan circumspectly ended the relationship when Halley purchased an engagement ring for herself and gave him the bill.

Ann was different. She, too, was single, but she harbored no fantasies about the relationship. It was what it was — companionship and occasional passion. Neither of them was too emphatic about the passion element. Both enjoyed playing croquet at a small croquet field in a secluded corner of Central Park, and they shared a high regard for one another. They also shared the same interest in books, music, and art. Evan met Ann at a film event at the Metropolitan Museum of Art, another invitation that Mindy declined. Evan felt no remorse for his philandering. He was a human being with an indifferent wife.

Gretchen arrived in a shiny blue convertible. She wore a scarf around her head like a Hollywood actress in the nineteen sixties. She parked in the driveway smiling broadly. Mindy hastened to the driveway admiring the car's sleek design. Evan followed observing the tires, speedometer, and inquiring of the gas mileage. Gretchen's friend wore a tweed cap and looked like someone out of a fashion magazine for the country club set.

"Mom, Dad, this is Professor Blenleigh. He's going with us to the airport."

The young man did not look like a professor; in fact, he seemed quite debonair. Evan wondered if he had anything to do with Gretchen's purchase of such an expensive convertible on her salary as an entry-level staff writer at his former place of employment.

"Do you teach journalism?" asked Evan.

"Goodness, no," said Professor Blenleigh. "I teach English literature."

"Professor Blenleigh was my English instructor," said Gretchen proudly.

"Well, Professor," said Evan, "what brings you to these parts?"

"He's going with us to the airport, Dad," said Gretchen with that look of exasperation she saved for her parents when they seemed incognizant of some great truth.

"I don't understand," said Evan. "Are you travelling?"

"Dad!" shrieked Gretchen.

"Shall I help you with the bags?" asked the professor calmly.

"Evan!" yelled Mindy, "We forgot to take Harold to the kennel. It won't open for another two hours. We have to get to the airport. What are we going to do?"

Harold, the beagle, stood in the doorway looking curiously at the bewildered humans.

"I'll take him, Dad," said Gretchen.

"How will he fit in the car? This is a small convertible. He won't fit with all of these bags," cried Mindy.

"He can sit on my lap," responded the professor. "Come along, boy." The professor led Harold to the car and positioned him on his lap in the back seat.

"All right, then, it's settled," said Gretchen. "Come on, let's go."

"I want to check the windows," said Evan.

"Dad, I'll check on the house. Don't worry. Come on or you'll miss your flight."

Mindy sat in the front, while Evan, Harold, and the professor sat in the back. The convertible sped off down the tree-lined street.

After saying goodbye to Gretchen, Professor Blenleigh, and Harold, Evan and Mindy entered JKF Airport in search of the group with whom they would be spending the next four weeks. The group was just as Evan had imagined - middle-aged, graying retirees in search of a world-wide fling with life. The tour guide was a tall, thin humorless man named Gil, who wore a navy blazer, white pants, and brown boat shoes. Gil looked as though he should be commandeering a boat somewhere off the Aegean coast. The only thing missing from his ensemble was an ascot around his neck, a nautical cap, and a pipe extending from his pursed lips. Gil spoke with an affected accent, but Evan could not place the location. It was as ineffectual as Gil beneath his haute exterior.

Mindy formed an alliance with a couple from New Jersey, who seemed similar in appearance and spoke with the same inflections. Evan wondered if people noticed similarities between himself and Mindy. It was an horrific thought but plausible. When two people spend every waking moment together, something is bound to rub off. They were called Edward and Judy and seemed to be the typical suburban New Jersey couple. Of course, Evan did not know any New Jersey couples, but they were as he imagined New Jersey couples. There was a certain snobbery attributed to people living on Long Island. They thought themselves superior to people living in New York City and the surrounding boroughs, and they certainly breathed a different air than people from New Jersey, but Edward and Judy seemed harmless, and it would be nice to share the world travel experience with an agreeable couple. There were a few single travelers, who seemed to relish their solitude and made no attempt to attach themselves to anyone in particular; most of the sojourners were married.

Marriage was an admirable institution. Mindy had her faults, but if the truth be told, Evan would marry her again if he had the opportunity. She rarely complained, took whatever adversity life sent her way, and moved forward without a backward glance. She had her good points. When she was stricken with breast cancer and underwent a mastectomy, chemotherapy, and radiation treatment, she was courageous and undemanding. She did not feel sorry for herself, nor did she expect any special treatment. When the reconstructive surgery left her disfigured with one hard, gargantuan breast without a nipple and twice the size of her remaining breast, she took it in stride. At least she had two breasts and not a stitched line where her once youthful breast, a breast that nurtured her children and enticed her husband, had been. Evan watched his wife speaking with animation to Edward and Judy, and he felt remorseful that he considered her a grouse just one day prior.

Gil led the group aboard the plane to their assigned seats, where they reviewed their itineraries, brochures, and coupons to various estabularies in Rome, Athens, and Singapore. Evan checked his watch, which displayed the time in most European cities. It was a new acquisition purchased especially for the tour.

"It will be twelve twenty-two PM when we arrive in London. You should try to get some sleep," advised Evan.

"How can you sleep?" asked Mindy. "We'll be in Ireland in a few hours."

"No, London is the first stop. Ireland is Thursday," informed Evan. "Here, look at the itinerary." Evan pointed to Monday's destination.

"I don't care what *that* says," insisted Mindy. "Gil says that we're going to Ireland first."

"Don't be ridiculous," chided Evan. "Ireland's out of the way. Why would anyone go to Ireland first?"

"What do you have against Ireland?" asked a male member of the group sitting in the seat ahead of Evan. He turned around and looked inquisitively into Evan's eyes.

"I have nothing against Ireland. It's a lovely country. I'm merely stating a fact. The itinerary states very clearly that our first stop is London."

"Well, the itinerary is wrong," said the man turning around and relaxing his head on the headrest. "We're going to Ireland first, and that's that."

Evan raised his hand like a school boy to get Gil's attention.

"Excuse me, but the itinerary states that our first stop is London. Has there been a change?"

"Oh, yes," answered Gil cheerfully, "our first stop is Dublin."

The man in the seat ahead of Evan turned around and smiled menacingly then returned to his restful position against the headrest.

"You might have warned us," said Evan.

The entire group looked at Evan with annoyance and disgust. They whispered amongst themselves. Evan was certain that they were talking about him.

"What are you doing?" asked Mindy quietly. "Why did you say that?"

"I don't know. It just came out," said Evan.

"Well keep it in," whispered Mindy. "Why would you say such a thing? How would you like it if somebody wanted to be warned before they entered the United States?"

"I'd like it just fine," said Evan. "We have too many people as it is."

Evan opened his newspaper, and Mindy pretended to read the brochures. Edward and Judy averted their eyes when Mindy tried to make eye contact. The world tour was off to a tremendous start.

"Did you notice how Harold took to the professor?" asked Evan placing the newspaper on his lap. "It was almost as though he knew him."

"We just met him. How could he know Harold?" asked Mindy arranging her brochures to place Ireland first.

"There's something about him. Did he seem foreign to you?" asked Evan.

"No," answered Mindy.

"It seemed as though he was trying to disguise an accent or something," insisted Evan.

"Maybe he was born in a foreign country but lost his accent

when he moved to America. People do that all the time. Maybe we'll come home with an accent," suggested Mindy.

"Don't be absurd," said Evan. "We won't be in any country long enough to acquire an accent."

"Maybe we can extend our trip," said Mindy wistfully. "We can stay longer if we like a country and meet the group later. Gil says that it's possible to do that."

"We won't be staying longer," assured Evan. "I'm sure I know that professor from somewhere."

"Maybe he was a client or looks like a client," intoned Mindy. "You've travelled all over the world, Evan. I'm sure that a lot of people look familiar to you. This is my first trip abroad, and I'm going to savor every minute."

Evan leaned his head against the headrest and watched the plane ascend into the sky.

"I never forget a face," said Evan.

"You forget lots of faces," corrected Mindy. "You forgot your cousin Gerald from Cincinnati."

"Gerald's face is unremarkable; whereas, Professor Blenleigh's face is familiar. I can't place him."

"Here," said Mindy handing her husband the brochure of Ireland. "You should brush up on your facts of Ireland if we're going to land in Dublin first."

"Shannon," said the woman next to Mindy. She was one of the single women travelling alone. "We will stop in Shannon for inspection, and then we'll proceed on to Dublin. I've flown here many times."

"Really?" asked Mindy. "I'll bet you know all the fun places to see."

"What do you mean we won't stop in Dublin first?" asked Evan.

"Planes to Dublin stop in Shannon first so that they can inspect our bags," said the woman. "You never know when a terrorist might be onboard."

"This is the last straw!" said Evan. "Why doesn't anyone

know where we're going? First, I'm told that we're going to London. Then, I'm informed that the plane will arrive in Dublin. Now, you're telling me that we're going to Shannon, wherever that is. What kind of operation are they running here?"

"Calm down, Evan," whispered Mindy. "People are staring again."

"I will not calm down!" insisted Evan. "I demand to be told where we are going before we arrive. Is that too much to ask?"

A flight attendant approached them.

"Is anything wrong?" asked the flight attendant.

"My husband forgot his medication, and he's upset," said Mindy. "Do you think that I can get a vodka and tonic for him?"

"Instead of his medicine?" asked the flight attendant.

"It's six o'clock in the morning," said Evan. "I will not drink vodka and tonic at six o'clock in the morning. I would like to see the pilot. Perhaps he can give me a clear indication of where this plane is heading."

Evan unfastened his seatbelt and climbed over the passengers in his row.

"What are you doing?" cried Mindy. "Where are you going?"

"Sir," responded the flight attendant, "you must return to your seat and fasten your safety belt."

"I will do no such thing," persisted Evan. "I will see the pilot!"

"He's lost his mind," said one of the group members.

The flight attendant called for help. Two male passengers, who were not a part of the group, grabbed Evan's arms and wrestled him to the floor of the moving plane until Evan was restrained. An unknown man emerged from the back of the plane and placed handcuffs around Evan's wrists as he lay on the floor face down.

"Wait," said Mindy. "He didn't get to eat breakfast, that's

all. He get's cranky when he doesn't eat breakfast. Wait. Where are you taking him? Evan!!"

"We'll go next year," comforted Evan as the car left the JFK parking lot. Mindy clutched the travel brochures to her breast and looked straight ahead in a state of bewilderment. "It's all for the best," continued Evan. "Obviously, they didn't know what they were doing. First London, then Dublin, then…"

"And they thought that you were a terrorist?" asked Gretchen incredulously.

"No, they thought that I was deranged," said Evan. "They kept me under observation for twelve hours. When I was released, I found your mother in this state. She hasn't spoken a word since the incident."

"It was her lifelong dream," said Gretchen sympathetically. "She had been planning this trip since I don't know when."

"We'll go next year," said Evan confidently. "Next time, I'll arrange everything with a reputable travel agent."

Gretchen stopped by the kennel to retrieve Harold, and the family returned home, where the kitchen window was left open and a squirrel was racing frantically around the house trying to escape. Harold, of course, gave chase. It was a homecoming in keeping with the spirit of the Grand World Tour.

After a week's interval, Mindy, still not uttering any words to anyone, ventured out of the house. She drove to the Barnes and Nobel bookstore and purchased several audio language guides. When she returned home, Mindy began a cursory study of French, German, Italian, Russian, Greek, Spanish, Chinese, Hebrew, and Portuguese. She even purchased a British English audio language guide in order to improve her English. Determinedly and methodically, she practiced each language until she became fairly fluent. So keen was her interest that she enrolled in language classes and began reading foreign language newspapers. Mindy changed the language preference of her iPhone and her computer to match the language she was studying. Curiously, she only spoke to those around her in the language she was learning. It was her form of immersion. All notes were written in the language of the moment, and she began to adopt the customs of the country to help with the immersion. Food, clothing, and entertainment were enjoyed in the language of choice. It was most remarkable. Mindy changed her name to the equivalent in each of the foreign languages, and she went so far as to replace their cleaning lady with women whose origins complemented the language she was studying. In this way, she was able to converse with others in her new language. Of course, people around her thought that she had become unstable since the Grand World Tour fiasco, but Mindy did not mind. She determined to learn the necessary languages and visit the countries on her own. Evan was not invited to join her. Mindy thought that she might take a cruise to the countries and approximated three years of immersion before she would be ready to set sail.

At first, Evan was annoyed with this change of behavior; however, his wife became quite interesting. Her change of lifestyle, language, and manner were intriguing. Soon, he broke all ties with Ann in order to remain home with the fascinating French woman, German woman, Greek woman, and so forth. Evan purchased small items which he thought would add to the international intrigue – French perfume, an Italian handbag, a Spanish scarf. His wife had become fascinating. He loved watching her prance around in costume speaking foreign languages, cooking and eating foreign foods, and making foreign statements that he could not decipher. It was like having new women in the house. Evan's existence was blissful.

One morning, Evan awoke and found that Mindy was not at home. This became a pattern of behavior. Mindy was out of the house more than she was in, and her absence was a disconcertion. When he inquired as to her whereabouts, she would respond in the language she was studying. Evan, of course, could not understand; in fact, he was unable to determine which language she was speaking. It became a formidable problem. To add to the disconcertion, strange people began visiting Mindy – couples speaking languages Evan could not understand. He sat with them at the dinner table and listened to them converse. He sat in the living room after dinner drinking wine and smiling politely as they continued their discourse. This had to be stopped. Mindy, or whatever she was calling herself that week, was leading a double life. She was rarely at home during the day, and she returned home, more often than not, with friends who were not a part of his world. Evan did not know what to do. He could not discuss the matter with Mindy, for she only spoke the language she was studying. Evan knew that this was her form of revenge for the collapse of the Great World Tour.

Professor Blenleigh made a logical suggestion when Evan joined him and Gretchen for lunch.

"Why don't you wait until she begins to study British English. You'll be able to speak with her at that time," said the professor.

"That's ridiculous," asserted Evan. "Am I to wait until she decides to study British English before I can understand what she's doing or saying?"

"I think that this entire matter is ever so interesting," said the professor laughing slightly. "I must say, I've never experienced anything like this. Have you any idea when she will begin her foray into British English? I may be able to introduce her to a few people."

A reddish-blonde Irish setter ambled into the living room and sat near the professor.

Evan's eyes met Professor Blenleigh's. "Of course!" remarked Evan. "Now I know where I've seen you."

He had only spoken a few words at that time, and his long, dirty blonde hair hid most of his face, but Evan recalled him vividly. The hair was now clean and closely cropped. The clothes were no longer dirty jeans; they were tailored and hung superbly on the professor's trim body.

"Where?" asked Gretchen entering the living room carrying a small tray with three glasses of port. Professor Blenleigh and Gretchen shared an apartment in the East Village. Apart from the fact that there was an endless stream of pedestrian traffic in front of the building, the apartment was quite nice. It was small and cozy and furnished in Mediterranean décor.

"Yes, Evan," said the Professor Blenleigh, "where have we met?"

"Nothing," said Evan. "I thought that you reminded me of someone else. Let's have that port, shall we?"

"Cheers," said the professor lifting his glass. The others followed suit. Evan and the professor exchanged glances as they lifted their glasses to their lips.

It was three weeks before Evan summoned the courage to call Professor Blenleigh and arrange a meeting. They met at a coffee house. Neither ordered coffee.

"I wondered how long it would take," said the professor.

"You're Peter," said Evan at last. "I never forget a face."

"That's implausible," said Peter. "Gretchen informed me that you forgot your cousin Gerald from Cincinnati once and caused quite a furor within the family. You seem to do that sort of thing frequently, Evan."

"Never mind that," said Evan. "What are you doing here? You were studying architecture, weren't you?"

"Engineering," said Peter. "I discovered that I had a passion for English literature. I can thank you for that. Do you remember your comment about the sublime?"

"Vaguely," said Evan. "I was being facetious, as I recall."

"Well, as it happened," continued Peter, "I began researching the sublime and its connection to modern society. I found the notion intriguing, so I wrote my dissertation on the sublime and its impact upon modern engineering and architectural design in the United States. I have been travelling around the

United States gathering research for five or six years. I decided to remain in New York, where I met Gretchen."

"You owned a company, as I recall," said Evan ordering tea.

"I sold it years ago," said Peter. "I made a tremendous profit. It allows me to survive here in New York on a professor's salary."

"What happened to Prentice?" asked Evan.

"Ah, Prentice," said Peter. "Prentice is happily married and living in London. I thought of marrying her once."

"Did you?" asked Evan remembering her red lips and pixie haircut.

"She was a bit flighty. Don't you agree?" asked Peter. "Gretchen is more my type."

"And what type is that?" asked Evan.

"Gretchen is down-to-earth, logical, and focused," said Peter.

"Gretchen? My daughter Gretchen?" asked Evan incredulously.

"Oh yes, when she is not around you or her mother, she is quite a different person."

"I see," said Evan. "Well, what are we going to do about this uncomfortable situation?"

"I'm not suffering from the least bit of discomfort," assured Peter. "I am pleased that we can speak candidly now."

"Neither my wife nor my daughter can know of our previous encounter," insisted Evan.

"Of course not," said Peter. "That would be grievous, wouldn't it? I must tell you that I am thinking of asking Gretchen to marry me. Perhaps we will live in London."

"Yes," said Evan. "Move to London. That's an excellent idea."

"Then I have your approval?" asked Peter.

"I see no reason why Gretchen shouldn't marry you and move to London. You should be able to obtain a position within one of the universities, and you're financially secure. The important thing is that you move to London. The change would be good for her," reasoned Evan. "How soon can you arrange it?"

"I must propose first," said Peter. "There is always the possibility that she will not accept."

"What do you mean?" asked Evan. "Why wouldn't she accept? You're already living together."

"There is another variable, which I have not mentioned," confided Peter.

"What variable?" asked Evan anxiously. "Come on, man, out with it!"

"Please calm down, Evan," said Peter. "You're ruffling my shirt."

Evan noticed that his hands were grasping the buttoned collar of Peter's oxford shirt.

"I'm sorry," said Evan placing his hands against his forehead. "I've been under a lot of pressure lately, and now this revelation. It's just too much. What variable can prevent you from marrying my daughter and moving away?"

"You see," said Peter carefully, "now don't become irate, but the fact is that I've grown quite fond of your wife."

Evan removed his hands from his head and looked at Peter quizzically .

"She came to me in her distress," said Peter earnestly. "I was the listener she needed, and she began coming more frequently to discuss her problem."

"She spoke to you in English?" asked Evan with astonishment. "She didn't try to converse in Chinese or Hebrew?"

"My dear fellow, she only does that with you," said Peter. "You see, you hurt her quite severely when you cancelled the world tour; in point of fact, I suggested that she begin learning new languages in order to give her self-appraisal a boost, and I introduced her to some of my colleagues fluent in various languages. They have been visiting your home."

"It was you? How treacherous!" bellowed Evan.

"You may hold yourself accountable, Evan," said Peter. "Minifred was deeply hurt. She wanted to embark upon the venture with hopes that you would lose interest in your mistress. She says that you have had several. Of course, I could not confirm anything to the contrary. Minifred feels that you instigated the entire episode on the plane in order to return to your mistress."

Evan's hands returned to his forehead. "I wasn't aware that she knew."

"They always know," assured Peter. "Be that as it may, I promised to accompany her on her cruise as tour guide and companion – strictly legitimate. I don't want to see her roaming around the world alone, and she certainly won't go with you or any other member of her family connected with you. She wants a fresh start. That's fair, isn't it?"

"Have you taken leave of your senses?" asked Evan. "You plan to accompany my wife on a world tour without me?"

"I assure you, my intentions are quite honorable" said Peter.

"It's out of the question," remarked Evan.

"It is in my best interest to help this family remain intact," said Peter. "My parents were divorced when I was quite young. It was a hellish existence being transported from one to the other. I would like to rear my children within a stable family. If you and Minifred suffer strife, it will impact Gretchen adversely. Minifred will not attend the wedding if you are there; if you stay away, there will be no father to give the bride away. Holidays will be negotiated by one parent's absence. Tensions will mount; your marital discord becomes our marital discord. Soon, Gretchen will take her worries out on me and our children. I've experienced this, Evan. I have no intention of reliving it."

"Does Gretchen know about any of this?" asked Evan.

"Of course, not," responded Peter. "She will find all of this unsavory, and that is not the way I want to begin our engagement. You must speak with her, Evan, and convince her that I should accompany Minifred on her world cruise; she is determined to sail alone. I can assure you that if Minifred travels alone, she will align herself with some chap with designs on your financial holdings. He may even insist upon moving into your house after the divorce."

"What divorce?" asked Evan.

"Surely, you don't expect her to remain married to a philanderer, do you?" asked Peter matter-of-factly.

"I don't understand your involvement in this," said Evan quietly. "Why did she come to you?"

"I know that this comes as a bit of a shock," said Peter. "Why don't we table the item until we have had an opportunity to digest it thoroughly? Shall we meet again next week?"

"You haven't answered my question," persisted Evan. "Why did she confide in you?"

"Women find me agreeable. I listen to them, and I don't judge them. They're delightful creatures, aren't they?"

"Stay away from my wife," said Evan heatedly. "And stay away from Gretchen also."

Peter smiled. He always smiled when confronted with an irate husband, a frustrated student, or an unscrupulous business partner. His smile was an unaccountable part of his tranquil charm. It was a charm that was unassuming, yet ever so intoxicating. Peter breathed charm, gentility, and sincerity. He was one of the world's creatures gifted with the undeniable ability to bring out the best in every person he met. People needed him and desired him, and no one thought poorly of him when he moved on. It was his special gift.

"We'll talk again," said Peter. "You're upset now. Shall we meet again next week to discuss the engagement? I've already purchased the ring."

Peter produced a gorgeous, oval-shaped diamond ring from a small, red Cartier box. The ring glistened and gleamed and seemed to sing arias. Evan could not remove his eyes from it.

"I hope that she likes it," said Peter. "I'm going to propose tonight, so be prepared for a phone call of exuberance from Gretchen. You're a lucky man, Evan, with so many beautiful women in your life. They are remarkable creatures, aren't they?"

Evan sat silently as Peter paid the bill and exited the coffee house. The only thought that garnered his attention was Minifred and her knowledge of his other women. How long had she known? She did not give any indication that she suspected his infidelity. Peter's words, *they always know*, haunted him. He could fix this. Peter was right. A broken family extends through many generations with broken holidays, broken birthdays, broken graduations, and broken lives. He would fix it before it was too late.

The phone rang at 9:35 PM. Evan assumed that it was Gretchen. Mindy responded in German. Evan did not know if Gretchen spoke German. Mindy gave the phone to Evan jubilantly; Evan listened to the news in English.

"Yes, I suppose we can celebrate tomorrow evening. What time do you want us?" asked Evan. "All right, see you then. Yes, I'm very happy for you. No, I think I'm coming down with a cold, that's all. We'll see you tomorrow."

Mindy took the phone from Evan and continued to converse in German. Evan was truthful. He did feel the onset of a cold. Stress always made him catch a cold. He watched Mindy climb the stairs happily. He watched her dress for bed wearing the pretty cotton nightgown he bought her last Christmas. Holidays together were important. Evan could not bear the thought of spending holidays apart from his family. Soon, there would be grandchildren, and he would be excluded. Gretchen would side with her mother. Infidelity was a serious bonding issue with women. He would be ostracized. Peter was right. The family must be preserved.

When Mindy folded the bedspread to the end of the bed, Evan noticed something curious. There were no flowered sheets on the bed; in fact, it looked like...yes, Evan was certain that his eyes did not deceive him. He stopped buttoning his pajama top and walked to the bed. He touched the sheets – white, starched sheets. Evan looked at Mindy blankly. He did not comprehend. Mindy smiled, took her husband's hand, and lay with him on the smooth, starched sheets. Evan was ecstatic. It was a sign of forgiveness. Somehow, she knew that he knew that she knew, and all was forgiven. Mindy would sacrifice her own desire for comfort and sleep with him on the sheets he had been denied for their entire married life. It was a sign. She forgave him. Mindy said something in German and began kissing her husband passionately. Evan's bliss could not be surpassed.

When Evan awoke, Mindy was gone, as usual. This morning, Evan did not mind. He lay upon the starched sheets and thought of all of the wonderful times he would share with his wife. Forgiveness was a beautiful thing. It was a floral bouquet in the desert. It was a stream gliding through a fragrant, sunlit meadow. It was sheer heaven.

Gretchen phoned and said that Mindy would meet him at the apartment. She noted her father's lifted spirits. There did not seem to be any trace of a cold in his voice. Gretchen could not wait to show him her new engagement ring. Evan brought his breakfast to the bedroom on a tray and ate in bed. The starched sheets brought such joy; he did not want it to end. He was young again. The world was his oyster, as it was in his youth. It stretched before him like a rippling lake leading to exotic lands and experiences. Evan began to look forward to the new world tour. He would begin gathering travel brochures and share the experience with Mindy step-by-step. How exciting everything was again. It was the way he felt when embarking on a new relationship. Evan put the thought out of his mind. His philandering days were behind him. It was only Mindy now, and she was enough. Soon, there would be grandchildren to take fishing and hunting. What if they were girls? It would not be a problem. If they lived in England, Peter would see to it that the children hunted. It was the English way, wasn't it? Evan had seen movies where English women hunted alongside the men wearing spiffy hunting regalia. Life was good.

The evening arrived too quickly. Evan took the train into the city, which meant that he and Mindy would return on the train rather than in the car. It was all part of his new, romantic way of embracing life. There would be no worries of parking spaces or traffic. They could see a Broadway musical or have a drink or walk hand-in-hand through the village with the other lovers.

Evan climbed the stairs to Gretchen and Peter's apartment. Gretchen bubbled with excitement as she showed her father her engagement ring. Evan pretended to be astonished. Quite frankly, he was astonished. He had never seen a diamond ring like the one on his daughter's finger. It was large yet dainty and elegant. Gretchen asked her father to make cocktails while she dressed. Peter had secured tickets to see a Broadway musical, and they would all celebrate and dine exquisitely before the show. Evan made himself a martini and sat in the large, green leather wing chair near the window. A small fire glowed in the fireplace. For the first time, Evan noticed the delicacy of the apartment. Surely, it was Peter's doing. Gretchen had not been trained in the art of delicacy, but she seemed to be learning. Evan noticed little things that indicated that his daughter was becoming a refined young lady. Little touches like the way she held her glass or the manner in which she tilted her head when speaking. The little touches meant a lot. The doorbell rang.

"Will you get that, Dad?" asked Gretchen from the bedroom. "It's probably Mom."

Evan opened the door. A delivery man stood smiling holding a brown package.

"It's a delivery man," said Evan. "Are you expecting a package?"

"Oh, it must be the laundry. Will you pay him for me, Dad?"

Evan paid the delivery man and instructed him to keep the change. Evan placed the package on the sofa and returned to his drink. Gretchen emerged from the bedroom wearing a chic, black dress. Her father helped her with the clasp of her pearl necklace.

"You look stunning," said Evan.

"Thanks, Dad," said Gretchen.

"I placed the laundry on the sofa. They charge a lot to clean shirts nowadays, don't they?" asked Evan. "Your mother always washed and pressed my shirts. I didn't have to use a laundry. Perhaps someday you'll take care of laundering Peter's shirts. It will save you a bundle, no play on words."

"Don't be ridiculous, Dad," said Gretchen. "I won't have to do laundry. Peter's fabulously well-off; besides, those aren't shirts. Those are our sheets. Peter won't sleep on anything but white, starched sheets. I think it's something he learned in England. He thinks that plain cotton sheets are an abomination. Peter can't understand how anyone can sleep on them. Peter is very particular, Dad. When he *woos* a lady, as he calls it, the first thing he does is introduce her to the concept of these white, starched sheets. Then, the woman is his," laughed Gretchen. "I told him that once we're married, if any of my friends begin adorning their beds with white, starched sheets, he's going to be in big trouble. Dad, why are you shaking?"

The End

BIO-CHEMICAL PICNICS

The high-pitched sound of chirping crickets and considerate birds making soft melodies in the late afternoon were certainly consoling. The air-conditioner had been taken out of the window, and a breeze blew in through the screen. The air was better without the air-conditioner; in fact, without it blocking the view of the sunlit leaves, the world seemed a friendlier place. It was a peaceful Saturday before Labor Day. Summer was over, or so it seemed. The air was certainly cooler, so much so that one needed a blanket at night in order to be comfortable. Where did summer go? It ended abruptly, as though it had other business and no desire to wait around for an official parting. The seasons were like people – always leaving or always changing. When would they get it right? Looking through the third eye, Preston envisioned a field of green with swaying blades of grass. The doorbell disturbed his calm, tranquil meditation.

Preston signed for the UPS parcel and placed it gingerly upon the sofa. He had almost forgotten that he ordered it. Surely, it must be the English picnic basket that he ordered at the beginning of the season. That it would arrive at the end of the season seemed commiserate with everything else that involved any reference to the untimely affair. She urged him to order it. No, she begged him to order it. It was not the

35

usual run-of-the-mill picnic basket. Leave it to the English to design a picnic basket that invoked feelings of elegant outdoor dining under skies of blue or gray. Preston opened the box and unwrapped the package. There it sat waiting to be greeted with civility and warmth. Preston had none of those feelings to share. She left him alone and empty. Perhaps, he was not entirely alone and empty. Now, he had an exquisite picnic basket complete with four porcelain dinner plates, four crystal wine goblets, four linen napkins, a silver place setting for four, a cork screw, a cheese knife, a cheese board, and a blue-plaid blanket rolled neatly and attached to the side of the basket. Yes, it was elegant, but Preston was now alone. He had no idea where to picnic with this new basket with all the trimmings. Was he to spread his blanket and dine alone amongst the young beauties clad in bikinis stretched out on the sun-drenched grass of Sheep Meadow? Certainly not. Perhaps he would drive to the country and enjoy nature with his new *friend*. One thing was certain — he would not sit gloomily bemoaning the past or the lack of her presence. If she could not see the value of a fine, upstanding man of impeccable taste, then good riddance. Summer may have been coming to an end, but fall was right around the corner. An autumn picnic could be just as festive as a summer picnic. Preston closed the lid of the basket and contemplated his elevated mood. Suddenly, there was new hope in every breath. A smile creased his lips. This brown, wicker basket was his reason to begin anew. It offered fresh opportunities of promises fulfilled. Other men had charming smiles or unlimited bank accounts or toned bodies or all of the accoutrements needed for modern day courtship, but Preston had something far more valuable. With a bit of imagination, this stately picnic basket would bring him the life he deserved and a person upon whom its splendor would not be wasted.

He packed the picnic basket with grapes and things within his refrigerator that seemed befitting of such a fine specimen of wicker. Perhaps he could pick up a few things on the way. Preston checked the LIRR train schedule. The trains were running on holiday schedule. It did not matter. He was in no rush. It was a day for exploring and reconnecting with everything positive that the city had to offer. The basket was not made for Long Island use. It must make its debut in New York.

The picnic basket occupied the seat next to him on the train to New York, which was practically empty. People were remaining home on this last holiday weekend of the summer season. Lexington Avenue was empty as well. Preston noticed a bull dog sitting in a baby's stroller. Its owner pushed it proudly down the street. It occurred to him that he would need a dog, a small dog that wouldn't mind accompanying him on his outings and wouldn't require its own transportation. As he walked up Lexington near 65th, he pondered the choice of breed. Not a dainty terrier or a husky bull dog - something in-between would be nice. While contemplating life with a new, furry creature, Preston stepped carelessly off of the curb into the path of an oncoming bicycle. The rider swerved to keep from hitting him. "Sorry," muttered Preston inaudibly.

He passed a fruit stand and purchased an array of fruits and vegetables. Was it his fault that he was a vegetarian and had no desire for meat? Now for the wine. He continued to walk up Lexington until he found a wine store and purchased a bottle of merlot. What about cheese? He had a cheese board and a cheese knife. Cheese must occupy a place within the basket. The best he could find was a package of cheese sticks at one of the delis. Not exactly a lunch fit for a king, but Preston was no king; he was not even a knave. He was a man in search of a spot of grass upon which to place his wares and display his new life – a new and desperate life, so it seemed.

It was now time to leave the avenue and walk towards the park, where there would be grass and festive people. It never ceased to amaze Preston that there were always people walking around in Central Park. Even if it rained and the grass and benches were wet, there were always joggers running, cyclists riding, skaters skating, and lovers whispering under trees. Each section of the park had its own personality. He was approaching The Great Lawn. It wasn't really his favorite spot, but he usually found himself there amongst the residents of the city. It was far enough from the sections with hordes of tourists to be a respite for city dwellers. Preston opened his blanket under a shady patch of green. He could see the top of the castle. Yes, this was the spot. Something wonderful would happen here. Good Grief! Was that his supervisor? What on earth was he doing here? Preston could not imagine him anywhere but in the office or driving around Suffolk County. Oh no, was he coming towards him? Preston began unpacking his picnic basket as though he were anticipating the arrival of another person. He looked up and smiled when his supervisor walked near him.

"Preston, is that you?" asked the supervisor.

"Mr. Graley, what an unexpected surprise," said Preston.

"What are you doing here?" asked Mr. Graley looking at the picnic basket on the blanket. "What are you having a picnic or something?"

"Yes," said Preston simply.

"Oh, look at that fancy place setting," said Mr. Graley's wife. "How lovely, you must be waiting for someone special. Isn't that lovely, Dear?"

"Yes, lovely," said Mr. Graley. "We're here watching our son play for his company team. They're playing over there." Mr. Graley pointed to the baseball diamond several yards away. "We should start a team at Blonelfield's. We could play some of the other corporations in the area. What do you think, Preston? Do you play baseball?"

"Not really," said Preston, "but it sounds like a great idea."

"So, where's your friend? You're not out here alone, are you?" asked Mr. Graley.

"I expect she'll be along soon," said Preston pouring the

merlot into the crystal wine goblets. "She's taking classes downtown. The buses are slow today."

"Let's go and leave him in peace," said Mrs. Graley. "Enjoy your picnic."

"Thank you," said Preston placing the cheese sticks on the porcelain plates.

"That really is a nice picnic basket, isn't it, Dear?" asked Mrs. Graley.

"Really nice," said Mr. Graley. "See you Tuesday."

"Right," said Preston waving at them as they sauntered away.

This was an interesting development. Did they believe his story, or were they being kind? Preston mulled the idea over in his mind. Suddenly, another idea occurred to him. Would it work? Anything was possible in a city filled with unending resources. He had told one lie. Perhaps he could resolve the problem by telling the truth. He looked around for a likely couple nearby. Leaving his picnic, he approached them.

"Excuse me," said Preston. "I'm sorry to disturb you, but I seem to have lost my keys somewhere in the park. I think that they may be by the Delacourt Theater. I was trying to get tickets for tonight's performance, and I must have dropped them. Do you think that you could watch my picnic basket for me while I go check? There's wine, cheese, and fruit. Please help yourself to anything you like. My girlfriend was supposed to meet me, but she called and said that she couldn't make it, so I'm stuck with all of this food, and now I can't find my keys."

The couple looked at him without suspicion. They agreed to wait at the picnic site until he went to look for his keys, and yes, they would love a glass of wine and a bit of the cheese. They moved to the blanket and sat down before the feast. Preston hastened away towards the Delacourt Theater in search of the imaginary keys. He observed the couple sipping the wine and nibbling the cheese and the grapes. He smiled feeling grateful that someone was enjoying the festive occasion. All right, it wasn't the truth exactly, but it could have been if she hadn't left him. It was all her fault. Now she was making him become a liar. After an appropriate interval, Preston returned to the picnic site waving his keys.

"They were right where I left them," said Preston. "No, don't leave. Please stay and finish your meal. It's the least I can do to repay your kindness."

As they ate, they enjoyed an amiable conversation. Rich and Miriam were visiting Miriam's mother, who lived in NY. They were from Houston, Texas. Miriam was a native New Yorker, who transferred to Houston when her firm relocated. She met Rich, a native Texan, and they were married. Now they were visiting New York for the holiday and returning to Houston tomorrow. Miriam's mother, sister, and nieces were visiting the MET, not far away, but they would probably love to come and join the picnic. Miriam phoned her mother on her cell phone, and she agreed to meet them. In a half an hour or so, Miriam's mother, sister, and adolescent nieces appeared at the blanket. They phoned for delivery from a nearby deli. Soon, the delivery man rode up on a bicycle carrying a parcel of food, sodas, plastic cups, and napkins. The picnic was underway. Everyone ate and enjoyed the company. Miriam's mother told many amusing stories, which made everyone laugh. It was as though they were old friends enjoying a holiday picnic. Preston felt elated that everything was going swimmingly.

As expected, Mr. and Mrs. Graley sauntered by again. This time, their son and a few men from the baseball team, still in uniform, followed behind them. Mr. and Mrs. Graley smiled and waved as they passed, happy to see that Preston was in the midst of whom they believed to be his girlfriend and her joyous family.

"See you Tuesday," shouted Mr. Graley as they passed.

"Yes, see you Tuesday," answered Preston waving cheerily.

Preston's new *family* waved at the Graleys as they continued down the path.

"What do you do, Preston?" asked Rich.

"Call me Nigel," said Preston. "My real name is Nigel. Preston is sort of a nickname. To answer your question, I work for a small insurance firm on Long Island. We insure priceless works of art."

"Nigel sounds like a British name. Are you from the UK, Nigel? You don't have an accent," said Miriam.

"I was born in London, but my parents moved to New York when I was a baby. That's why I don't have an accent. They still live in London. I go to visit them a couple of times a year. What about you two? What do you do?" asked Nigel.

As Nigel listened to Rich and Miriam describe their career paths, he realized that he was beginning to assume a new identity, a false yet palatable identity. With his new identity, Nigel felt empowered. His speech became more direct, and he seemed more focused. Nigel wondered how to continue the charade. Was it a charade if one really believed it? Perhaps he was really a bloke named Nigel. Perhaps Preston was the true alien. He certainly felt more attractive as Nigel, and his picnic basket indicated a person of exquisite taste and sophistication. Run-of-the-mill people do not carry around crystal wine goblets and refined porcelain dinner plates. Nigel shifted his focus back to the conversation. Miriam's mother was telling another story. Nigel wondered if her stories were as authentic as his new identity.

"Nigel, you must come to dinner tonight," said Miriam. "It's our last night in New York before we return to Houston."

"You should come on down to Houston," said Rich. "We've got parks bigger than this one. You'll love it."

"Yes on both accounts," said Nigel. "I would love to come to dinner tonight, and I would like to visit Houston at some point, if I can bring my dog, that is."

"What kinda dog you got?" asked Rich happily. "We've got two German Shepherds back home, Brick and Brac."

"I have an English bulldog," said Nigel. "His name is Edgar."

Rich laughed. "Well, bring Edgar along too. We've got plenty of room."

The afternoon was progressing beautifully. Nigel tried earnestly to remember all of the deviations from the truth that he had uttered. He made a mental note to make a category on his BlackBerry for pertinent facts about his new identity. The identity did not end with the chance meeting in the park. Nigel found it necessary to expand his falsehoods to his office as well. What choice did he have? Mr. Graley had already seen his *girlfriend* and her *family*. Slowly, he began using the name Nigel within his office. He said that it was his nickname, short for his middle name, Nicholas. That part was true. His middle name *was* Nicholas. Perhaps on some planet Nigel was the equivalent of Nicholas. *Who's to say thou art not a poet?* People adopt pen names all the time. Nigel decided that guilt was unnecessary. Life was complicated, too complicated to have one name and one identity. Besides, Nigel's life was certainly more interesting than Preston's. Nigel began applying for credit cards under his new name; surprisingly, it worked. He began signing his name as Nigel P. Hornsby. Establishing a new life was an exciting excursion into the unknown. Slowly, Nigel updated his wardrobe from milk with cookies to champagne with strawberries. He began reading more British books and subscribing to British magazines. Why, he even began carrying a long, serious, black umbrella with a curved, wooden handle rather than the fold-up umbrella that he always kept in his briefcase. Nigel purchased a black bowler hat to match his black pinstriped suit. These items replaced the baseball cap and khaki pants, which he usually wore to the office.

It wasn't long before the corporate heads began taking Nigel more seriously. His confidence grew, and he spoke with more assurance at the morning meetings. Nigel was given more responsibilities, which were appropriate for a man in a black, pinstriped suit. Nigel sold the small ranch house he inherited from his mother on Long Island and moved to an apartment with a terrace on the Upper East Side of Manhattan. The building had a doorman, who sometimes walked Edgar, a sturdy bulldog and Nigel's new companion.

Nigel visited Miriam's mother, who lived with her daughter and granddaughters, several times since Rich and Miriam returned to Houston, and she always called them when Nigel was there for a group chat by way of the computer's web camera. Bric and Brac even made an appearance on the computer screen. It was agreed that Nigel and Edgar should visit Houston during the Christmas holidays. This was delightful news. Nigel always felt out of sorts during the holiday season since his mother passed away. He was an only child, and his nearest relative lived in Pittsburg, a town he did not relish visiting, but he made the journey each year so as not to be alone during the holiday season. *She* would always visit her family without him.

It had been quite a while since Nigel thought of her. In point of fact, he hadn't thought of her for several weeks. The thought of the holiday season brought thoughts of her to mind. The holidays had a way of forcing people to make connections they would ordinarily refrain from making. Perhaps he would call or send a Christmas card. Did people still send Christmas cards through snail mail? Everything was done impersonally online nowadays. Why bother? She was his past. Let the past die in peace. He was off to Houston for the Christmas holidays. It would be interesting to visit a warm climate during the holidays. Nigel pondered what type of gifts to get for Rich and Miriam. Perhaps he should purchase something for Bric and Brac as well.

Nigel commuted to Long Island to work each day, but the commute was tolerable; most commuters were going in the opposite direction. He always found a seat on the train, and he was able to enjoy an hour of leisure as the train wended through the Long Island suburbs. As the small red light flashed on his BlackBerry, Nigel checked his messages. There was an unknown email address, but the subject line bore Miriam's name. Quickly, Nigel opened the email. It was from Miriam. She wanted to discuss a matter privately with him before he embarked on a journey to Houston. To his surprise, Miriam and Rich were in the throes of a very unpleasant divorce. They were both still living in their house amicably until a final settlement could be determined. Nigel felt downhearted at this news. He liked Miriam and Rich. The divorce would inevitably mean the end of the family gatherings. Miriam and Rich were like family to him. Once again, change occurred to upset everything in an ordered world. Perhaps the world was not meant to be ordered, but Nigel wished that it could be, if only for the holiday season. Reluctantly, Nigel phoned the number that Miriam included within the email. Miriam's voice recording announced that she was unavailable, but the caller should leave a message. Nigel began his message when Miriam interrupted. Her voice was welcoming, and Nigel felt at ease. Miriam explained the details of the divorce. There was infidelity on both sides, and a divorce seemed the most logical solution. Nigel expressed his condolences and wondered how to proceed. They still expected him to visit, and Miriam wanted to assure him that he was still a part of the family and welcome at their gatherings. Her male companion would be there, and Rich's female consort would attend also. Miriam continued as though this arrangement was perfectly normal. She inquired as to Edgar's health and reassured him that the canine was welcome.

"I must say, Miriam," said Nigel carefully, "this does seem rather unusual."

"Don't be silly," laughed Miriam. "People bring their dogs here all the time."

"No, I meant the, well, the guests," said Nigel uncomfortably.

"Oh, you mean Trevor and Angela," said Miriam. "There's no point in hiding the truth, I always say."

The word *truth* made Nigel shudder. It had been awhile since he and *the truth* made a connection. It had gotten to the point where the lies were intermingling with the truth to such an extent that he was having a difficult time distinguishing between them. If one lives the lie, is it still a lie? If the lie becomes truth, is it still a lie? What hybrid form of reality is it?

"You'll still come, won't you?" asked Miriam.

"Yes, of course. Edgar and I will be departing on the 7 AM flight to Houston on the twenty-third. That isn't too early is it?"

"Of course not," assured Miriam. "Trevor will pick you and Edgar up at the airport. We're all anxious to see you."

"How will I know Trevor?" asked Nigel.

"Don't worry, Trevor will know you," said Miriam.

Nigel wondered how Trevor would notice him in the crowded airport. What did Miriam consider so remarkable about his appearance that Trevor would spot him in a crowded area? The answer was soon forthcoming. As Nigel entered the waiting area, a policeman approached him. His smile was radiant, and he extended his hand.

"Nigel, welcome to Houston. I'm Trevor."

Nigel shook Trevor's extended hand. "I wondered how you would recognize me in such a crowded area," said Nigel. "I suppose you're accustomed to finding people."

"I just looked for a man with a bulldog named Edgar." Trevor patted Edgar's head. "You're Edgar, aren't you?" The dog barked. "Come on, Nigel. I'll drop you off before I go to work."

Nigel and Edgar followed Trevor to a grey SUV parked in the lot. Nigel tried to observe Trevor as they drove through the traffic. He was certainly younger than Miriam, but Nigel expected that with a name like Trevor. The name was indicative of a tall, slim man with light brown hair balancing himself on a surfboard. Trevor wasn't far from the mark. He was tall, but his build was solid. His muscular frame was evident through his uniform. Trevor's hair was one shade from being light brown. Nigel thought that he might be thirty years of age.

"How was your flight?" asked Trevor making polite conversation.

"It was a comfortable flight," answered Nigel. For some reason, the policeman's uniform made him nervous.

"I see you like to read," said Trevor noticing the book on Nigel's lap. Nigel forgot that he was carrying the book. "I read that back in high school. It's about those rabbits, right?"

Nigel looked at the cover of *Watership Down* and wondered why he needed to look at the cover before he could verify the subject of the book. "Yes."

"Great book," said Trevor. "Me, I go for books about foreign places with lots of mountains and snow. I like cold places."

"It doesn't get too cold down here, does it?" asked Nigel.

"Naw. That's why I'll be heading for Alaska next year," answered Trevor.

"Alaska?" asked Nigel. "Will Miriam like the cold?"

Trevor laughed. "Miriam can't stand to even look at an ice cube. That's why she moved out here to get away from the cold."

"Then, you don't plan to, I mean…," said Nigel hesitantly.

"Don't be shy, Nigel. Ask your question," said Trevor.

"I thought that you and Miriam might be getting married at some point," said Nigel.

"After her divorce from Rich you mean? Well, we talked about it, but we haven't decided yet. Who knows, I may not like Alaska and come high-tailing it back here to Houston."

"Forgive me for saying, but it doesn't sound like much of a future for Miriam, does it?"

"I'm all about the truth, Nigel," said Trevor. "I've put my cards on the table with Miriam. I haven't hid anything, and I haven't pretended that it is what it ain't. Do you know what I mean?"

"I suppose so," said Nigel. "It just doesn't seem like Miriam is getting anything out of it."

"Well, what are you supposed to get out of it?" asked Trevor. "You mean life, right? Well, we get out what we put in. As long as we are honest and put everything out there, then nobody gets hurt."

The words *honest* and *truth* kept intruding upon the conversation. Nigel wondered if Trevor knew about his name change and secret identity. As a police officer, Trevor would surely have the means to investigate him. Was this his polite way of telling him that he knew all about him and his pretense? Edgar stirred restlessly in the back seat.

"He doesn't get car sick, does he?" asked Trevor.

"I don't know," answered Nigel. "He's never been in a car."

"I think that we'd better stop and let him get some air." Trevor turned off at the nearest exit and pulled into a diner. "How's about we get ourselves a cup of coffee while Edgar settles his stomach. Was he sick on the plane?"

"I don't know," said Nigel. "There was a special section for animals. No one said anything to me." Nigel felt like an inept schoolboy in Trevor's company. First, he was reading what Trevor considered to be a high school book, and second, he seemed incognizant of the ways of the world or the ways of his immediate environ. Nigel imagined that Trevor thought that he lacked muster. They purchased their coffee and sat at a picnic table outside of the diner. Edgar relieved himself and then made himself comfortable by Nigel's foot.

"It's rather warm, isn't it?" asked Nigel.

"This ain't nothing," said Trevor. "It gets really warm in the afternoon. It must seem strange to you coming from New York."

"Not really," said Nigel.

"I visited New York once," said Trevor. "It was in July, and it must have been ninety-five degrees. I don't know how you stand all of that humidity. People packed against each other—I don't know how they breathe. They got some pretty nice sights though. I went to the Statue of Liberty and took a boat ride around Manhattan. I've seen the Christmas tree on TV. That's a great sight, too. How long you been living in New York?"

"My parents moved to New York when I was a baby," said Nigel. "We lived on Long Island for many years. I moved to Manhattan when my mother died." It was the truth, well, as near the truth as Nigel could depict.

"So, then, you're English," said Trevor. "I always liked the English. Proper people, and they speak really nice. Well, I guess we'd better head on over to Miriam's. Rich is fixing a Christmas dinner that will set your mouth to watering."

They entered the SUV and started down the road. Nigel felt impending doom circling him. He did not know why, but he was like *Fiver*, always able to forecast catastrophe.

Rich and Miriam lived on a street filled with upscale, rather ostentatious homes all marked with the obligatory built-in swimming pool. The aroma of seasoned beef filled the air. As they approached the back of the house, a domestic dressed in a black uniform with white apron and hat offered to take Nigel's bags. It had not occurred to him that Rich and Miriam were people of means. They certainly acted like ordinary people. A young girl was petting Edgar. There were several children running around the area playing and frolicking in the warm, December air. Christmas decorations were all about; cheerful, bright red bows and candy canes hung on outstretched silver garlands that dressed the patio area. Rich and Miriam approached Nigel simultaneously. They were as effervescent as ever. Two or three adults followed them and shook Nigel's hand. He wondered if one of them was Angela. He was led into the house by Rich and Miriam to get settled before joining the

Christmas barbecue. A Christmas barbecue was a novel idea to Nigel but a good one. Edgar romped through the house with Bric and Brac. They became immediate cohorts. It was obvious that they had run of the house, and they soon disappeared out of sight.

"How was your flight?" asked Rich as he led Nigel into a rather large, spacious room with a festive balcony overlooking the patio area and what seemed to be a large expanse of land. Nigel was impressed. He had no idea that they lived in such luxury.

"It was adequate," responded Nigel. He wondered why people always asked how the flight was. How could it be? Most flights did not offer meals anymore, charged for bags, and the flight attendants seemed a bit harried and disgruntled.

"I told Rich to ask our neighbor, Dennis, to fly you in, but you know Rich," said Miriam. "Dennis has his pilot's license and a beautiful plane that just sits in that airport. He wouldn't have minded one bit."

"Do you know how much it costs to fire one of those things up? You know that the economy is tight right now. We shouldn't impose that kind of expense on Dennis," said Rich.

"He could always say no," countered Miriam.

"You know he won't refuse," said Rich impatiently.

Nigel felt that a storm was brewing. He hadn't known Rich and Miriam to be quarrelsome, but then, how well did he really know them?"

Trevor entered the room and kissed Miriam's cheek. "I'm off to work. Nigel, I'll see you when I return. I told Chester to stop overcooking those steaks, Rich. He cooks all the blood out of them. You'd better go down there and tell him what to do."

Trevor exited as abruptly as he entered.

"It's so hard to find a good cook nowadays," said Rich impatiently as he left the room in a huff.

"Don't mind him," said Miriam cheerfully. "He lost a lot of money when the economy crashed, and he let most of our staff go. We hired cheaper employees, but they don't seem to know what they're doing. Be thankful you don't have that problem, Nigel."

"I was surprised about the divorce," said Nigel bringing up the subject gingerly.

"Well, these things happen," said Miriam. "We've been having problems for years; we just gave up trying to work things out. Money does that to you. When you lose a good part of it, you lose yourself. Do you know what I mean?"

Nigel nodded, although he had no idea of what she meant.

"Will you remain here?" asked Nigel.

"No, we're selling the house. We haven't put it on the market yet, but it's in the works," said Miriam.

"I had no idea you and Rich had all of this," said Nigel looking at the lush acreage outside of his window.

"It doesn't matter, does it?" asked Miriam. "I never felt that it was mine. This is Rich's parent's estate. His father died a few years ago, and his mother insisted that we move in to help her run the estate. There are horses in the stable. Do you ride?"

"I'm afraid not," said Nigel.

"Well, we must teach you. Come, let's join the others," said Miriam. "I want you to meet our friends."

"Miriam?" asked Nigel insistently. "Please don't find me intrusive, but I must know. How does Rich feel about Trevor, and how do you manage with the thought of Angela?"

Miriam smiled. "So that's what's troubling you. Well, it *is* an unusual arrangement, I admit, but we all get along. Trevor is an old friend of Rich's, and Angela is my hair stylist. She's worked for some really famous people, you know. Rich met her when she came here for my weekly manicure, pedicure, and hair treatments."

"It is hard to believe that it doesn't bother you," said Nigel. Bric, Brac, and Edgar entered the room, each chewing on some sort of bone.

"Take that outside, you scamps," said Miriam playfully. "You'll get the carpet dirty." The dogs took their treasures and ran down the hall. "To answer your question, Nigel, yes, it bothered me at first, but you have to take life as it comes. Enjoy the good things and realize that the bad things can make you more resilient and bring new opportunities. I'm going back to college. Did Trevor mention it?"

"No," said Nigel.

"I'm getting my M.B.A.," said Miriam. "By the time I finish, the job market should be back on its feet. See what I mean? New opportunities wait at every corner of some unpleasant experience, if you look for them. Come on, let's go down and meet everyone."

Miriam led Nigel to the patio area. The house was amazing and filled with artwork and relics. The décor was Southwestern, but the interior was decidedly Sotheby's. Some of the replicas looked genuine, but that could not be possible. Only the finest museums in Europe housed the priceless pieces Nigel observed. He estimated their value. It was difficult to completely divorce himself from work. It was difficult to imagine what these works of art would be worth if they were the originals. Perhaps it was not difficult at all. Nigel totaled the estimate in his mind. If they were the real thing, he would be standing in the midst of an incomprehensible sum of money. The thought excited Nigel, and he wanted to continue the game and explore the various rooms he passed on the way to the patio but decided to concentrate on meeting new acquaintances. The young girl who greeted him and Edgar when they arrived appeared again. She seemed to be nursing a bruise on her knee. A young woman applied a bandage and kissed the girl's red knee.

"Nigel, this is Angela and Serena, her daughter," said Miriam.

Serena, face covered with tears, pointed to her knee.

"I see, you've suffered an injury," said Nigel. "Perhaps Edgar can help to make it better." He looked around for Edgar, but he was not visible. Nigel called him.

"Don't bother," said Angela. "I saw that pack of he-wolves runnin' towards the front. I think they're chasing a cat or something. Come on Serena, be brave. Momma will get you a nice, cold soda. You want one Miriam?"

"None for me," said Miriam pleasantly. "How about you, Nigel?"

"No, thanks," said Nigel. "I'm fine.

"Well, it was nice meetin' you," said Angela. "Why don't you come on over to the grill and watch Rich put his special barbeque sauce on the ribs? You'd better bring a gallon of water, Nigel. They're the hottest things this side of Texas. You don't look like a rib man to me. Maybe you'd better stick with the salads over there on the small table."

Nigel was confused. Was she casting aspersions on his manhood? He could eat a rib with the best of them, hot or cold. It just so happened that as a vegetarian, he preferred the salad bar. Was that a crime?

"You go ahead, Angela," said Miriam. "We'll meet you over there."

Angela and Serena walked to the grill greeting guests along the way.

"That was your replacement?" asked Nigel.

"Don't be unfair. She's a nice person once you get to know her. She's a whiz at taming cuticles, and look what she does with my hair," said Miriam. "You don't find stylists like that just anywhere."

Nigel followed Miriam to the grill, where Rich was *holding court* in a large, white chef's apron. He was laughing loudly with a group of men, all fighting to keep the saliva in their mouths as they awaited his special sauce. Rich seemed pleased to see Nigel approach.

"Here's the man from New York," announced Rich. "Now, I warn you, Nigel, these ribs aren't for city folk like you, so I've got another sauce over here for people with tender palettes." Nigel took humbrage.

"Are you suggesting that I can't tolerate your special sauce?" asked Nigel.

The men surrounding the grill laughed heartily.

"I think he's throwin' down his *gauntlet*, Rich. You'd better be careful," said one of the men playfully. The others laughed.

"Don't take offense, Nigel," said Rich good naturedly. "This special sauce was handed down by my great-grandfather, and even *he* had trouble keeping his tongue in his mouth."

"I will have some," said Nigel determinedly. People began to crowd around the grill as though there was to be a gun fight at the OK Corral. Rich placed a rib on a paper plate. He poured a small amount of his special sauce on the rib.

"Give him a *real* one," said Rich's mother nibbling a large rib covered with the special sauce. "That's not enough to even get his juices started."

"This is good to start," said Rich. "Don't forget, Nigel is our guest. I don't want to have to call the fire department if his tongue starts burning."

Rich passed the plate to Nigel. Nigel took a breath and reached for a plastic fork.

"What's he doin'?"asked one of the men. "Eat it with your hands!"

"That's enough," said Miriam. "Come on, Nigel. I want to show you around the estate."

"I will eat this first," said Nigel determined not to be intimidated by one woman and saved by another. He lifted the rib from the plate with his bare hands and took a small bite as everyone watched.

"Take a *real* bite!" yelled Rich's silver-haired mother.

Nigel chewed the beef, which was quite tasty. There was no immediate response. All of a sudden, Nigel's tongue was aflame. His eyes watered, and his tongue struggled to keep the beef in his mouth. As a vegetarian, it was not easy. He would not be viewed as a fool. Nigel swallowed the beef quickly hoping to relieve his tongue and mouth of the burning, but now the burning was slowly sliding down his inner-being. He gasped and held his chest.

"Get him some water!" yelled Rich as the other men laughed. The women were sympathetic, apart from the matriarch and Angela. They guffawed like men. Serena held Nigel's arm as he took a quick swig from a bottle of cold water. Even after consuming half of the bottle, the fire within still burned, and he felt nauseous. Miriam and Serena led Nigel into the house away from the laughter. His eyes were tearing, and his vision was blurred. His brain felt as though it was on fire as well.

"Sit in here for a while," said Miriam leading him to one of the sitting rooms. Nigel held his stomach as he ingested more water.

"What's in that sauce, anyway?" asked Nigel.

"Who knows?" answered Miriam. "It's been in Rich's family for years. Every time one of my relatives visits from New York, they go through this ritual. I'm sorry. They think it's funny."

Nigel coughed spasmodically and finished the bottle of water.

"I'll get you some more," said Serena running from the room.

"Why don't you lie on the sofa and rest awhile," said Miriam. "If you go outside now, they'll just tease you."

Nigel stretched out on the sofa and tried to gather his wits, which were seared by the special barbeque sauce. Serena returned with a fresh bottle of ice-cold water; Nigel drank hurriedly.

"What makes them behave that way?" asked Nigel. "They seemed to enjoy watching me suffer."

"They don't know any better," said Miriam. "Life out here is different. Serena, why don't you go outside and see if you can find Edgar to keep Nigel company."

The young girl ran out of the room forgetting about her bruised knee.

"Nigel, when you return to New York, I want to go with you," said Miriam.

Nigel looked askance at his hostess. Suddenly, the pain in his throat and chest was replaced by a new type of discomfort.

"What do you mean?" asked Nigel.

"I mean I want to leave this place as soon as possible," said Miriam.

"What about Trevor? What about Bric and Brac? I don't understand. You mean you want to just pack a bag and leave?" asked Nigel.

"Precisely," said Miriam.

"You'll stay with your mother, I presume?" asked Nigel.

"I will stay with you," answered Miriam matter-of-factly.

Nigel's discomfort increased. "With me?"

"With you," affirmed Miriam.

"What about your mother and your family? Wouldn't you rather stay with them?" asked Nigel hopefully.

"No, they won't agree to it. They're a staunch Catholic family. They refuse to accept the divorce."

"I don't know about this, Miriam," said Nigel. "I need time to think about it. What about Trevor? What will he think? He has a gun."

"We all have guns, Nigel. You're in Texas," informed Miriam. "We'll leave tomorrow night."

"But that's Christmas Eve," said Nigel astounded. "We can't leave on Christmas Eve."

"Why not?" asked Miriam.

"Because it's Christmas Eve," said Nigel. "Who does that?"

"We do," said Miriam.

Nigel took a deep breath as Edgar, Bric, and Brac raced into the room. They were still playing and frolicking about.

"How can I do that to Rich and Trevor?" asked Nigel. "They've been really nice to me."

"Rich just humiliated you in front of all of his friends," answered Miriam. "It will only get worse. When he and Trevor are together, they're like a couple of frat boys. Trevor will be off tomorrow, so he will be here all day. When he finds out about your reaction to the special sauce, there'll be no stopping the pranks. We can leave as they're trimming the special tree. No one will miss us. We'll take Bric and Brac with us."

Things were not going as Nigel had planned. He would need a new plan for a woman replete with special sauces, special trees, and a plethora of guns.

Rich placed the six-foot red velvet ribbon atop the special eleven foot Christmas tree.

Everyone stood around the tree adoringly. He had outdone himself this year. The ornaments were the special bubbly percolators that made the sound of an aquarium as colorful bubbles *percolated* inside each glass tube.

"All right, Miriam, turn off the lights," said Rich. "Let's see how bright these babies shine this year."

Everyone waited for the room to darken. "Miriam, turn off the lights!" yelled Rich.

There was no response.

"I'll turn them off," said Angela. The room became dark. Rich plugged the extension cord into the socket. The tree lit up in a spectacular dazzle of colorful, bubbling lights. Everyone was agog.

On the plane, Nigel sat beside Miriam. Bric, Brac, and Edgar were safely stowed away in a separate section of the plane.

"Right now, they're lighting the tree," said Miriam smiling.

"Won't Rich come for you, or at least Trevor?" asked Nigel.

"Trevor won't come to New York. All he can think about is going to Alaska, with or without me. Rich won't come. What's the point? It's over. We both know that," said Miriam.

"I'm a bit unclear about all of this. Is that why you invited me? Are you using me to get away from Rich and Trevor?" asked Nigel.

"Don't be silly," said Miriam calmly. "I don't need help getting away from Rich or Trevor. Neither one cares if I leave Texas."

"But you barely know me," said Nigel.

"I know you," answered Miriam applying her lipstick without a mirror. "You are Preston Hornsby, insurance adjustor for a small company on Long Island, but in reality, you work for the government. Preston Hornsby is your real alias. You really *are* Nigel Hornsby, and the picnic basket was just an excuse to infiltrate our little family business. I placed a few items within the lining of the picnic basket when we met. That is why we kept in close contact with you and why I am here now. I'll retrieve the items when we get to New York, and then I will be on my way."

"I cannot allow that," said Nigel. "The stolen artefacts are not the priority. That recipe for the special sauce uses herbs and spices which are illegal within the United States. The government wants the *spices*. They have been treated with toxins that are being developed for chemical warfare."

"Chemical warfare? But, we've all eaten it," said Miriam. "We've been eating it for years."

"Yes," said Nigel, "the effects are indeterminate. It may take several years, but there will be a serious reaction. I don't think anyone has ingested enough for it to become fatal. At any rate, we will be monitoring all of you closely for the next few years to test the effects. We'll return the artefacts that you took from the house in order to avoid suspicion. They will think that we have run off together and continue their daily routines. You will enter the special hospital we've set aside for you and others who are a part of our research."

"You mean you will let them eat that poison knowing what it will do to them?" asked Miriam astounded.

"We appreciate their sacrifice," said Nigel.

"But you ate it too!" shrieked Miriam.

"I had to be certain that the chemicals were present in the sauce. You see, we all make sacrifices that will benefit mankind," said Nigel.

An armed guard took a stunned Miriam to the back of the plane. Nigel sipped his wine and thought how lovely his special picnic basket would look in the spring upon the verdant grass of Hyde Park.

The End

BAYSIDE LOLITA

It was the best of times; it was the best of times. Blast Dickens! The icy January wind pierced Christopher's face. He tightened his scarf around his neck. The economy was experiencing an horrific downturn, but it was a good year. Christopher had an esteemed position as a tenured professor at one of New York's most prestigious universities. His baby face fooled many people, particularly his students. He celebrated his thirty-fifth birthday last month, but he looked like a twenty year old. His lean, tall structure and unruly chestnut hair made him appear to be one of the students on a good day. He rode his bicycle to work and dressed in jeans and corduroy most of the time. His students loved him.

As Christopher walked along Lexington Avenue, he noticed that TV cameras were poised up and down Lexington Avenue near 65th Street to catch a glimpse of the mogul who swindled people out of millions of dollars. They were all there – CBS News, Eyewitness News, News 4 –to photograph a man who wallowed in ill-gotten excess, while many people were losing their jobs, homes, and sense of hope. Christopher had a lovely apartment on the Upper East Side of Manhattan, and he was happy. Life was all about happiness. For Christopher, happiness was not a fleeting notion. He had been happy most of his life, before the untimely death of his father, that is. Be that as it may, happiness was a gift, and Christopher accepted it with relish. Friends suggested that he could attribute his happiness to the fact that he had never married. What was the point? He was happy as a single, and that was all that mattered.

Of course, happiness meant leisure time to enjoy all of the marvelous things the city had to offer. A month's vacation in the midst of winter was certainly enviable. Most of Christopher's colleagues travelled to warm destinations and spent the time lounging on tropic beaches. That would not do. He planned to spend his leisure time writing and perusing books at the Strand, attending lectures at the MET, occupying orchestra seats at the ballet, and enjoying as many Broadway musicals as his budget would allow. In other words, Christopher was a dilettante, and no tropical beach would ever compare to a day spent in the company of the finer arts.

For some reason, Christopher's thoughts went back to the mogul under house arrest in his penthouse apartment and wondered how house arrest in a luxurious penthouse could be any type of inducement to forego further financial abuses? He wondered what works of art hung from the mogul's walls. Were there artifacts or relics in the stately home? Was there fine china upon which to enjoy a meal or a snack? Surely, the cook prepared delectable gourmet meals. Christopher wondered about the term *justice*. What did it really mean? He looked at one of the news crew rolling up a long, black cable wire into a large circle over his shoulder. It looked like a lasso. Perhaps it was a circus, after all.

"Well, it took you long enough to get here," said a woman approaching Christopher. She was shivering from the cold. Her long, black hair, which seemed to mock her pale complexion, lay lifelessly upon her shoulders; the wind blew a few strands across her face. Her pockets protected her uncovered hands from the cold, and her knee-length black boots kept her jeans-clad legs warm.

"You said two o'clock. It took a while to get through the crowds," explained Christopher.

"It's three sixteen," answered the woman with annoyance. "I'm freezing. I've been trying to phone you, but your cell phone is off. Did you know that?"

"What do you want to do now?" asked Christopher ignoring the question.

"I don't know. Let's go to *Trader Joe's*. We can get a couple of bottles of *Schloss Biebrich*," said the woman. She lifted her hand to hail a cab.

"I don't want to go all the way downtown," said Christopher gently lowering her arm. "I have a paper to write for the conference in Zurich."

"Another conference?" asked the woman. "Why are you going to so many conferences? You didn't tell me about Zurich." The wind blew more strands of hair onto her face. Her exposed ears were red from the arctic temperatures.

"It's in the fall," responded Christopher calmly. "Perhaps you would like to attend."

"Why can't you go to a conference in Hawaii or Rio? What's in Zurich?" asked the woman.

"Would you like to attend?" answered Christopher patiently. Reasoning with her was often like trying to reason with a child.

"I don't know," said the woman. "Maybe I'll go. I'll look up Zurich on *Wikipedia* to see if I would like it."

In every relationship, there comes a time when parting is inevitable. One gives the potentially aggrieved party endless opportunities to redeem himself or herself, but more often than not, the party is incognizant of the fact that he or she causes offense and cannot see the hatchet descending.

Christopher began slowly. "Alexandra, we've shared many memorable moments together."

The woman looked at Christopher intently. "What do you mean *shared*? Are you breaking up with me?"

"I wonder if we were ever really together or on one accord, so to speak," said Christopher tenderly. He held her frigid hands between his. Alexandra removed her icy hands from his warm embrace.

"*Shared* is past tense, Christopher. I didn't finish college, but I know what the past tense means. You're breaking up with me because I don't want to go to Zurich. I've seen this coming for weeks."

Christopher looked astonished. "Have you?"

"Of course I have. You think I'm stupid because I didn't finish college, but I'm not stupid. I know that you have been trying to dump me. That's why you were late today. You've been putting it off, but I know what you're trying to do. Just like when you spilled that plate of spaghetti on my new dress in the restaurant, and I had to go home to change."

"That was an accident," said Christopher earnestly.

"There's no such thing as an accident," insisted Alexandra. "I've studied psychology, you know. Freud said that there's no such thing as an accident. Your subconscious wanted me to leave."

"I can assure you that it was an accident," said Christopher reasonably. "Besides, I left with you, so your reasoning is illogical." Perhaps she was right. It was entirely possible that there was a subconscious motive behind the *accident*, but Christopher was certain that it had to do with the subsequent evening of passion they shared as she attempted to change into a new dress.

"Go ahead and leave," said Alexandra. "See if I care. You're not the only man in New York. Get one of those fickle, starry-eyed girls in your class to go with you to Zurich. I see the way they look at you, like you're some kind of Adonis with a brain."

"Now you're being silly," said Christopher. It was true. His female students did gaze at him as he lectured, and they seemed to become tense and flustered when he walked near their desks or made eye contact with them.

"Go ahead, see if I care," responded Alexandra. "Go to Zurich, or Hong Kong, or where ever. See if I care!" Alexandra left him and crossed the busy street without looking back.

"That was awkward," said Christopher.

The scholar tightened his scarf around his neck and entered the Lexington Avenue subway station. He drank the sparkling wine from *Trader Joe's* at ambient temperature. Christopher was uncertain as to what to do with the extra ticket he now possessed for the American Ballet's production of *Le Corsaire*. It was to be a surprise. He placed his MetroCard in his satchel beside the tickets and the small box from *Tiffany's*, which included the modest diamond engagement ring he had been carrying around for weeks. There never seemed to be a perfect time. For one reason or another, Alexandra derailed any attempt he made to present her with an engagement ring. Perhaps his subconscious *was* trying to warn him that she was not the one upon whom he should bestow such a treasure. The truth of the matter was, Christopher had been carrying the ring around in his satchel for over two years. Originally, he purchased it for Megan, who made an unseasonable remark about the benefits of global warming. How could he marry a person who believed that global warming should be encouraged in order to increase commerce? Then there was Noa, who wanted to move to New Hampshire to begin a lucrative nail salon. For some unfathomable reason, she felt that the women of New Hampshire were neglecting their nails and had to be rescued. Alexandra eliminated herself with her ghastly dependence upon *Wikipedia*. There was neither a day nor an hour when *Wikipedia* did not figure prominently within their conversations. At first, Christopher kept his silence hoping that her dependence would wane; lamentably, it did not. How could an accomplished scholar marry a woman with such a fetish? Perhaps a more important question was why an accomplished scholar would date women who were clearly beneath his required standards of erudition. The answer did not require the machinations of Freud. Christopher liked beautiful women with youthful, unimaginative convictions.

Christopher was not without his faults. He loved cracking walnuts from their shells and munching them at all hours of the day and night. The sound irritated Alexandra immensely. One evening, she gathered her clothes and left while still dressing in order to remove herself from the objectionable sound. Christopher tried to satisfy his quota of walnuts before she came over to spend the weekend; lamentably, he could not. He carried a nutcracker around in his satchel and a supply of walnuts. Alexandra suggested that he see a therapist. Surely, Freud would have something to say about a man consumed with walnuts and cracking them endlessly. Perhaps she was right, but the walnuts were comfort food. As long as he had them, he could stave off life's adversities.

Upon arriving at home, Christopher settled himself in the wing chair before the fireplace. The fire crackled, and its warmth cast a welcoming glow throughout the living room. Christopher called one of his colleagues to ascertain whether or not she was free to see *Le Corsaire* later in the evening. She was not. He phoned six colleagues, none of whom had any interest in venturing out in the arctic air in order to see the musical. "philistines," thought Christopher. All right, he would do the unthinkable. He called his mother.

Mrs. Lindlend lived on the sixteenth floor of his building. When a condo on the second floor became vacant, she provided the down payment for him to assume occupancy. It was a small price to pay to have her dear child in such close proximity. Although Christopher's condo was on the second floor facing the back, and his mother's was on the sixteenth floor facing the front, he always had the idea that his mother was watching him or having his movements watched. From the doorman to the polite neighbor next door, Christopher was certain that each person in the building was providing a full report of his comings and goings to his mother. She never interfered nor did she frequent his condo. Mrs. Lindlend remained out of sight, but she was always present in the very air that he breathed. He thought of moving out, but where would he go on his salary? At least the building was populated by intelligent professionals. What would happen if he moved into a building of *Wikipedia* lovers? Christopher convinced himself that he would move out in two years, but now the economy was unstable, and his options were becoming increasingly limited.

Mrs. Lindlend was unable to attend the production of *Le Corsaire* that evening, but she did the next best thing. She found a suitable companion for her son. Christopher was not optimistic, but he did not want to see the musical alone. Surely one evening with a stranger approved by his mother would not hurt. Irene Glassborough lived in Queens. Christopher's mother met her at one of her charity events. The name did not sound especially appealing, but Christopher agreed to meet Irene at the box office at 7:30. It would be dark, and no one would see them; in point of fact, if he kept silent, no one would even know that they were together. He did not try to conjure up images of Irene Glassborough from Queens. What was the point? A single woman living in Queens agreeing to go on a blind date at a moment's notice did not leave room for optimism. The chance that Irene might be beautiful, talented, and intellectually gifted was implausible, but beautiful, talented, and intellectually gifted she was. Christopher could hardly contain himself when they met. He had envisioned a petite, pudgy, somber woman wearing a black overcoat and sensible shoes, but Irene was tall, long-limbed, and slender. She wore high-heeled gray boots, a navy blue blazer, a gray mini-skirt, and a white blouse that showed just enough cleavage to let him know that she had all of the expected accoutrements. Irene's hair was hidden by a gray woolen hat that clung to one side of her head, but Christopher could see that she had soft, reddish brown hair. Christopher shook her hand and noticed that her fingernails were adorned with a tasteful French manicure. Was she really from Queens? He meant no offense, but the women he had occasion to meet from Queens were not quite as subtle in appearance or speech. There must be some flaw. Perhaps her voice and manner of speaking would be an indication.

"Would you like something to eat or drink before the curtain?" asked Christopher. "I apologize for such short notice. I can assure you that this is not normally my custom." He was correct. Dinner always preceded a play or a ballet.

"No, thank you. I'm fine," said Irene. Her voice was melodious, and her face was pleasant to behold. Her eyes sparkled, and she seemed to be genuinely agreeable.

Christopher led her to their seats. As the ballet ensued, he observed everything he could about her, from the gentle scent of her perfume to her posture as she walked to the ladies room during intermission. There were no perceptible flaws. He wondered what she did for a living, but he did not want to begin an in-depth conversation before curtain. Perhaps there would be time during intermission. He waited, but she did not return. Christopher had not noticed before, but she took her coat with her. Did she not enjoy the ballet? Surely, the problem could not have been him. He always imagined that he was the perfect date. Christopher checked the lobby and the refreshment area. He even stood outside the ladies room waiting, but she did not appear. Irene was gone.

While in the taxi on the way home, Christopher phoned his mother for Irene's number. His mother would not provide it. If Irene was not happy with his company, then so be it. She advised him to let the matter drop, but Christopher could not. He had to know why she left in the middle of the production without a word. Surely, her behavior was rude, but he was willing to accept an apology, if one were offered, in order to see her again.

Weeks passed, and Christopher could not stop thinking of the matter. It consumed his thoughts. Why would a person simply leave without an explanation? He hired a private investigator to provide information about Irene Glassborough. The investigator returned with more curious details. There was no such person as Irene Glassborough from Queens or anywhere else. The name was fictitious. Christopher was livid. Was it some type of cruel joke? Angrily, he pressed the elevator button to the sixteenth floor and knocked on his mother's door. The housekeeper opened the door and admitted him. His mother sat on a white sofa watching *CNN News*. She offered Christopher a glass of wine. They sat together in silence for what seemed to be fifteen or twenty minutes.

"You want to know about Irene?" asked Mrs. Lindlend.

"Yes," said Christopher simply.

"Why?" asked Mrs. Lindlend. "Did she appeal to you?"

"How would I know? She left during intermission," said Christopher.

"Did you say anything to offend her?" asked Mrs. Lindlend.

"Of course not," assured Christopher.

"Then, I advise you to leave the matter as it stands. You cannot force a person to appreciate your fine traits."

"I cannot leave the matter," said Christopher, "particularly when there is no Irene Glassborough from Queens."

"How do you know that?" asked his mother still watching the news.

"I hired an investigator," said Christopher. "Who is this woman? Where did you find her? Why did you deceive me?"

"Calm yourself," said Mrs. Lindlend. "Have another glass of wine. I did not deceive you. I know her to be Irene Glassborough from Queens. If she has another identity, then that is no concern of mine. Would you really like to resume an acquaintance with such a person?"

"Where did you meet her?" asked Christopher.

"That is no concern of yours," said Mrs. Lindlend taking

her eyes off of the television for the first time and looking at her son directly. "Now, I do not know why Irene left the theatre."

"But surely you can provide some information about her. Why is it necessary to be secretive?" asked Christopher.

Mrs. Lindlend returned her focus to the television. "Would you like to stay for supper?"

"No, I would not," said Christopher angrily. He stood and walked to the door. "I will find the answers without your help."

"Many answers are better left undisclosed," said Mrs. Lindlend.

Christopher shut the door a little too harshly and summoned the elevator down to the second floor. It was all too bewildering.

Weeks passed, and the frigid temperatures gave way to warmth and frivolity within the city. Street fairs began to appear on weekends, and Christopher's daily run in Central Park became even more agreeable with the budding trees. He walked past his favorite news stand and obtained a copy of *The Economist* before going home to work on his paper for the Zurich conference. Classes were over, and he could finally enjoy a day of unlimited leisure. His running shorts and tee shirt were filled with perspiration from his run, but he felt invigorated, as he always felt after his daily run. He walked slowly enjoying the whiff of spring in the air and turning the pages of the magazine. As he approached his building, he noticed a young woman standing on the carpet before the entrance.

"Here he comes," said the doorman. "You have a visitor, Mr. Lindlend."

It was Irene. He had not thought of her in months, four to be exact.

"So I see," said Christopher closing the magazine.

"May I speak with you?" asked Irene. Christopher could smell her perfume, and without her hat, he noticed that her reddish hair was silky and rested pleasantly upon her shoulders. She wore a blue-plaid dress that clung to her genteel frame.

"Of course," said Christopher, "come upstairs."

"No," said Irene. "Can we go somewhere to talk?"

"Yes, of course," said Christopher. He was covered with perspiration, but he did not feel the need to impress her. They stopped at a café that served breakfast outdoors. She ordered a bagel and coffee; he ordered orange juice and a croissant. They sat at a table watching passersby.

"You left without a word," said Christopher.

"I am sorry; indeed, I am," said Irene.

"I don't even know your name," said Christopher.

"It is Millicent - Millicent Ansbury."

Christopher extended his hand. "I am happy to make your acquaintance, Miss Ansbury. Now, why all the mystery?"

"You do not recognize me," said Millicent.

"Should I?" asked Christopher.

"Perhaps not," said Millicent.

"Why did you leave?" asked Christopher. "Why did you lie about your name?"

"I thought that it might be easier," said Millicent. "I like meeting normal people."

Christopher looked at her curiously. "Normal people?"

"Your mother is a gem. I really like her. How is she?"

"I think that you should explain. How do you know my mother?" asked Christopher.

"I promised that I would not tell you," said Millicent.

Christopher became irritated. "To whom did you make such a promise?"

"I cannot say, but it is for the best," said Millicent nibbling her bagel and sipping her coffee.

Christopher reached into his sneaker for the spare cash he carried when he went out for a run. He placed a ten dollar bill on the table and stood up. "I don't like playing games, Ms.

Ansbury. Perhaps we can meet again when you are ready to have an earnest conversation."

Millicent continued to nibble on her bagel and sip her coffee as Chrisopher walked away. A black limousine pulled up, and she entered. The limousine merged into the steady stream of traffic and headed downtown.

The upcoming conference in Zurich occupied most of Christopher's free time. He worked endlessly on his paper and spent several hours a day researching at a private library on the Upper East Side. He sat in a small tastefully decorated room with a comfortable leather chair, a small desk, and an antique table lamp that peered over his laptop. The room afforded the privacy he needed to focus upon his work and assured him of the sense of style and privilege that he needed to formulate his ideas. The library was closed to the general public and had been recently renovated. It was an idyllic place to work. A small knock on the door distracted him from his train of thought. Christopher looked through the door window and saw a man of indeterminate years smiling pleasantly. Christopher opened the door.

"Hello," said the man, "I don't suppose you would have a battery charger with you. I notice that we share the same style of laptop, and I am completely without an energy source."

"Of course," said Christopher. He unplugged his laptop from the wall and disconnected the charger. "Here you are."

"I shan't be a moment. I'm right next door in the adjoining room. Arlington Smythers," said the man extending his hand.

"Christopher Lindlend," answered Christopher shaking the man's hand. The gentleman exited the room with the charger and returned some fifteen minutes later with the charger in hand.

"Thank you, ever so much," said Arlington. "I'm working on the last chapter of my book, and it is proving to be a challenge.

This charge should keep me going for another hour or so. Thank you again."

"My pleasure," said Christopher.

"I don't suppose you have a copy of *The Times*," said Arlington noting a folded newspaper on the desk.

Christopher unfolded his paper and gave it to Arlington.

"I'm sorry to be such a bother, but someone steals my paper before I can get to it most mornings. I call and complain, but it doesn't seem to yield any positive results. The day is not complete without *The Times*, don't you agree?"

"Of course," said Christopher. "Why don't you keep it? I have already read it."

"Thank you," said Arlington. "Now I will not trouble you any further. Working on a novel?"

"A conference paper," said Christopher.

"Really? May I ask the topic?" asked Arlington politely.

"I am examining the impact of commodity culture in Eliot's *Daniel Deronda*."

"Fine author, Eliot. I must admit, I have never read *Daniel Deronda*," said Arlington. "Perhaps I'll add it to my must read list. Don't think me inquisitive, but may I ask where the conference is being held?"

"Zurich," said Christopher.

"Fabulous!" exclaimed Arlington. "I love Zurich. You're going in the fall, I hope. Zurich is spectacular in the fall."

"Yes, it is in the fall. I've never been, but I'm looking forward to it. You say that you're a writer? Would I know any of your works?"

"Work," answered Arlington. "I have had one book published. I doubt you've ever heard of it. It is rather obscure— *Middle Road Vistas?*"

"No, I haven't read that one," said Christopher.

"Then you're one of the lucky ones," assured Arlington. He folded the paper under his arm. "Thank you again for your help."

"No problem," said Christopher.

Arlington exited and entered the adjoining room. Christopher was pleased to meet another library patron. His routine was normally quite solitary, though he did not miss the distraction of another voice. Scholarship was a solitary pursuit, but it was quite fulfilling. Thoughts of Zurich were paramount at present. Christopher settled into the cozy leather chair and pondered an idea. It was a rather strange idea. He thought of Millicent and wondered where he might have met her before. She asked if he recognized her. What a strange thing to ask unless she was famed for something or other. She couldn't be an academic. He would have recognized her, and most academics are not diffident when it comes to discussing their research or scholarly texts. Perhaps she was a model or an actress, but why would she presume that he would know her. He neither frequented runways nor watched television. Surely, he would recognize a Broadway talent, but her face was unknown to him. She knew his mother. Where on earth would she have met his mother, and why wasn't she at liberty to discuss it? Christopher abhored conundrums; this was irritatingly intriguing. It was as though his mother and Millicent shared some secret life to which he was not privy. He would not waste any more money on detective agencies. Obviously, Millicent wanted to see him or else she would not have appeared on his doorstep. He would wait until she appeared again. Perhaps he would be able to obtain another clue as to her identity. At present, he would focus upon his paper and forget any distracting thoughts. There was another knock on the door. Christopher sighed and allowed Arlington to enter.

"I wondered if you might enjoy a bite to eat. It is approaching the noon hour," said Arlington.

"I haven't completed enough of my research to take a break," said Christopher, "but thanks for asking."

"Right," said Arlington. "I don't suppose you would like to go out for a bite to eat after you complete your research."

Christopher looked askance at his new acquaintance.

"I don't mean to impose," said Arlington.

Christopher's silence was revealing.

"Right," said Arlington, "sorry for the imposition." He closed the door quietly.

Would the interruptions never cease? Christopher thought of returning to his condo in order to find the quiet, tranquil environment that he needed to compose his thoughts. He did not mean to be abrupt, but if he wanted distractions, he would have settled for the public library or his cluttered university office. Now two things occupied his mind - Millicent and the stranger next door. He could not concentrate. He knocked on the adjoining room door. There were papers scattered across the wooden desk, the floor, and the cozy reading chair. Arlington sat at the desk before his laptop pounding the keys. He smiled when he saw Christopher at the door.

"Finished already, have you?" asked Arlington. There was a pencil behind his ear, and upon close inspection, Christopher noticed that his clothes were a bit disheveled. Arlington felt self-conscious. "You must excuse the mess, but when I work, I throw myself into it, quite literally. Do, come in." Arlington brushed the papers covering the chair onto the floor so that Christopher would be able to sit. Christopher entered the cluttered room and sat in the easy chair.

"Having any luck with that last chapter?" asked Christopher.

"Indeed," said Arlington. "I will complete it today and present it to my publisher this evening."

"I seem to be terribly distracted," said Christopher. "I can't think of a thing to write."

"I hope that I'm not the cause of the distraction," said Arlington. "I tend to be quite loquacious when I complete a novel. I hope that I haven't hindered your work."

"I was distracted before you knocked on the door. What's your book about?" asked Christopher.

"It chronicles rudimentary economic sanctions imposed after World War II," said Arlington. "I'm a bit of a history buff. Writing gives me an excuse to travel and research important historical events in some of the world's finest libraries."

"What made you come here," asked Christopher. "The research facilities here aren't exemplary."

"I live down the block," said Arlington. "My research was completed in Denmark a couple of months ago. I find the atmosphere here conducive to writing. I can scatter papers all around without having my wife complain about them. I don't suppose you have that problem."

"What do you mean?" asked Christopher.

"You look like a bachelor," said Arlington.

Christopher wondered how a bachelor looked. For some reason, the statement was troublesome. "Yes, I am single. I don't really consider myself a bachelor. The term is a bit antiquated, don't you think?"

"Of course," said Arlington. "I meant no offense. I simply meant that you appeared to be a person who relished the solitary life."

"Really?" asked Christopher.

"Oh yes," said Arlington. "There is something about your person that suggests that you are neither approachable nor available for intimate relationships."

"My person suggests all of that?" asked Christopher amused.

"Yes," assured Arlington. "Observations are crucial to my line of work. Take, for example, your shirt. I can tell by your shirt - buttoned collar, pressed to precision, long-sleeved with cuff turned up at the wrist on one of the hottest days we've had all season – outside of your trousers. Your hair, a bit longish, suggests that you are employed in a place where longish hair is not out of the ordinary and where boat shoes on sockless feet are the norm. The shirt on the outside of your khakis indicates that you vacillate between liberalism and conservatism. I would wager that you are wearing a leather belt under that shirt."

Christopher was impressed with the analysis and was glad that his shirt covered his leather belt in order to thwart the smugness, which seemed to fill the room.

"I find your assessment intriguing," said Christopher.

"Most importantly, you said that you were writing a paper to present at a conference in Zurich on George Eliot's *Daniel Deronda*. It is one of Eliot's more obscure texts. Only an academic would read it. You are, undoubtably, an English professor. That part is easy. Now, why you choose to work in a private library is a mystery to me. I work here because of the distractions at home, which are to be expected with a new wife. Why do you do it?"

"My home is too cozy," said Christopher, who was rather surprised that he was revealing so much about himself to a perfect stranger. "I find myself distracted with all of the comforts of home."

"Poor fellow," said Arlington. "Come, we can have lunch and allow ourselves to be distracted for an hour or so. When we return, you will be able to work on your research, and I will complete this final chapter."

The newfound friends exited the library and walked amiably down the street to a small café. As they dined, Christopher discovered that Arlington led a double life, so to speak. As his wife is allergic to dogs, Arlington lodges his dog with his dog walker. He goes to visit the dog, Hector, daily and takes him for walks around the park. His wife makes him shower and leave his clothes at the entrance before he enters the apartment. Arlington misses his former life with Hector, but he cherishes his wife.

"Enjoy your bachelor life," said Arlington. "You have total freedom, but there is something to be said for married life."

"Really?" asked Christopher. "What?"

"You have a solid base," said Arlington. "Marriage is an

institution that perpetuates the social order. Without marriage, we'd all be running around looking for something or someone to give us hope and to help us dream."

"I think that marriage is overrated," said Christopher. "Marriage seems to dash hopes and creates chaos. Look at your situation. Why shouldn't you have Hector with you? Without marriage, you and your dog would be united, and you wouldn't have to wash away any trace of him before entering the house."

"I suppose that's one way to view it," said Arlington. "On the other hand, my wife provides what Hector cannot. We are a family."

"Nonsense," said Christopher. "You and Hector were a family before you got married weren't you? I've often heard it said that a man's dog is family. A dog is a part of the family, just like a human being, and by George, I know who she is."

Arlington looked at Christopher curiously. "I beg your pardon?"

"Millicent Ansbury! I know who she is. I know where I met her," shrieked Christopher.

"I'm sorry, but I'm not following you. Who is Millicent?" asked Arlington.

"Years ago, my family lived in Queens. I was just a kid. I had a dog - a chocolate lab. I was the happiest kid in the world."

"So, what happened?" asked Arlington.

"Gladys Johannson happened," said Christopher with annoyance. "Gladys Johannson destroyed my life. Gladys Johannson is the reason I remain a bachelor. Gladys Johannson from Queens is the bane of my existence! She may call herself Irene Glassborough or Millicent Ansbury, but she will always be that demon - Gladys Johannson."

"Calm down, old boy," said Arlington. "Perhaps you would like to explain."

"She calls herself Millicent Ansbury now, but I'm certain it is the same person."

"Millicent Ansbury? Isn't she the journalist who reports for *CNN?*" inquired Arlington.

"What are you talking about?" asked Christopher.

"Millicent Ansbury is a world renown journalist. Just last week she gave a spectacular report on the Middle East conflict. Don't you watch the news?"

"I read the paper. You say she is on *CNN?*" asked Christopher.

"If it is the same woman," said Arlington. "What does she look like?"

"Tall, willowy, reddish-brown hair that clings to her shoulders," said Christopher.

"That certainly sounds like her. You know Millicent Ansbury?" asked Arlington.

"I knew her as Gladys Johannson. She was a neighbor in Queens. I don't know how I could have forgotten that face. The hair is different. It was dingy brown then and a bit frizzy. She was heavier also, but I'm certain that it is the same person. It appears that she also uses the name Irene Glassborough. I can't imagine why."

"And you say she stole your dog?" asked Arlington with great interest.

"She stole more than my dog. She destroyed my family," said Christopher.

It was a crisp autumn day, and ten-year-old Christopher Lindlend sat anxiously by the window peering out. It was the big day; the most important day of his life. Today, he would be the proud owner of the beautiful chocolate lab that he picked himself from a litter in Central New Jersey. The house of the lab's owner was situated within a mountain region, which seemed unusual for New Jersey, but Christopher was certain that he saw a mountain in the distance. The houses were secluded, upscale, and much more spacious than the homes in

Queens. When they entered the home, a middle-aged woman with a pleasant smile led Christopher and his father to the litter. Each pup had a small yellow tag around the bottom portion of its leg. The mother lay contented and sniffed Christopher's leg as it approached the pups. One pup did not have a tag. It was the last one to be sold.

"I want that one," said Christopher.

"Maybe we should look at some others also," said Mr. Lindlend. "We can always come back for this one."

"But he may be gone!" wailed Christopher. "I want this one."

Mr. Lindlend gave the woman a deposit, and she instructed him to return in two weeks, when the pup would be weaned. Christopher gave the pup a last look as they started for the door.

"Why did you want that one?" asked Mr. Lindlend. "There's probably a reason why he wasn't sold."

"I like him," answered Christopher calmly and confidently. Even at an early age, Christopher knew his own mind. If he wanted something, nothing could dissuade him.

Now it was the big day. Two weeks had passed, and Mr. Lindlend went to get the dog. Christopher was not permitted to take a day off from school for the event, so Mr. Lindlend went alone. Christopher's books lay on the floor near the window. He did not bother to go to his room. He was too excited. Shortly, his father's Suburu pulled into the driveway of the modest home. The puppy was on a leash, and he followed Mr. Lindlend into the house. Diffidently, he sniffed his way around as Christopher watched him. His coat was a shiny dark brown, and his eyes sparkled with anticipation. Christopher took him out for his first walk. Proudly, he led the puppy down the street. The neighborhood kids gathered around, which made the puppy nervous. Christopher ordered them away from his new treasure and decided upon the name Paris. Having completed *The Iliad*, Christopher developed a fondness for Paris, the young, foolish

Trojan. As life mirrors art, Christopher had no idea that the selection of the name would seal his new friend's fate, and like Paris in *The Iliad*, would be responsible for catastrophe.

Housebreaking Paris was a formidable task. Christopher was no match for the willful puppy. The enamoured boy provided Paris with treats even when he piddled on the living room carpet, much to the chagrin of Mrs. Lindlend. Finally, Mr. Lindlend took responsibility for housebreaking Paris. Each evening when he returned home from work, he would take Paris out two, three, sometimes four times. During the day, Paris was not allowed to roam the house freely. Mrs. Lindlend kept him in a makeshift pen near the kitchen's basement door. It was a while before Mr. Lindlend's efforts met with success. By that time, he had grown accustomed to taking Paris for evening walks and looked forward to the daily routine as Christopher completed his homework. It pleased Christopher and Mrs. Lindlend that Mr. Lindlend took such a fancy to the dog and his care. Mr. Lindlend brushed Paris's coat and shepherded him into the Suburu for rides to the local park, sometimes without Christopher. It was clear that Mr. Lindlend loved Paris.

When baseball season began in the spring, Christopher's enthusiasm for Paris waned, although he loved him. While Christopher practiced his swing at the park, Mr. Lindlend and Paris watched and cheered him on. When the season began, Mr. Lindlend and Paris attended every game and rooted for Christopher's team. Christopher was developing into quite a third baseman, and his pitching arm was improving dramatically. All was sublime until one day after the game, Paris broke free from Christopher and ran to a spectator in the stands. She was a young woman, and Christopher recognized her as the sister of Arnold, a friend from down the block. She petted Paris's head and hugged him smiling. Paris licked her face. How curious. Paris did not relish strangers and usually barked when they approached. He did not bark, nor did he show any signs of agitation. This woman was not a stranger.

Arnold, who played second base position approached his sister. Paris barked furiously. The young woman quieted him. What manner of intrigue was this? Christopher approached and reached for Paris's leash. The woman smiled and presented it to him as though Paris was her dog and she was lending him to Christopher.

Mr. Lindlend approached from the rear and called to Christopher and Paris. He did not walk near Arnold and his sister. He kept his distance.

"Ready to go?" asked Mr. Lindlend as they walked towards the car.

"How does she know Paris?" asked Christopher. Paris frolicked in front of them. Mr. Lindlend threw a small red ball, and Paris retrieved it.

"What makes you think he knows her?" asked Mr. Lindlend.

"He ran to her," answered Christopher. Paris returned with the ball. Mr. Lindlend threw it again.

"Some people just have a way with dogs," said Mr. Lindlend matter-of-factly. "She probably has a dog, and he could smell the dog on her clothing."

"From across the field?" asked Christopher. "A lot of people have dogs. Why would he run to her?"

"I don't know, Son," said Mr. Lindlend. "He's your nutty dog. Ask him."

They walked quietly to the car. Paris entered the back and placed his head out of the window in anticipation of the breezy ride home. Mr. Lindlend said something which disturbed Christopher, and from that moment, they seemed to embark upon a different relationship.

"It's probably best if you don't mention what happened to your mother," said Mr. Lindlend as he parked the car in the driveway.

Christopher did not ask "Why not?" He seemed to know, and from that moment on, he was no longer the son but the accomplice with secrets to be kept from his mother. Christopher understood perfectly. He was eleven now, but he understood such things as best he could. Mr. Lindlend's explanation was not plausible, but it didn't seem to matter. If Paris was attracted to the smell of other dogs on people, why didn't he respond favorably to Arnold? Perhaps it was just his imagination. Perhaps Arnold didn't like dogs, and Paris could tell. People always said that dogs could tell whether or not people liked them. Of course, that was it. Christopher convinced himself that all was well, but the knowledge that Arnold did not have a dog caused him great anxiety.

Mrs. Lindlend sat quietly watching television as Mr. Lindlend continued his routine of taking Paris out for nightly walks two, three, sometimes four times. Then one day, it all ended. A policeman brought Paris to the door without Mr. Lindlend. The flashing lights outside the house were alarming. Christopher watched from his bedroom window upstairs. He heard his mother's mournful sob. Somehow he knew that his father would not return.

The funeral was an awkward experience. Everyone knew. They looked at the grieving widow and her young son with pity and remorse. They all knew. Gladys and Arnold Johannson's family sat towards the left of the church. Christopher could see them out of his peripheral vision. He dared not look. Everyone waited for him or his mother to look. Gladys sat next to her mother, and Arnold sat next to his father. Gladys wore a black dress and a black hat atop her thick, frizzy brown hair. Her arms looked plump in the sleeveless black dress that could not conceal her full figure. Mrs. Johannson held her daughter as Gladys lay her head on her mother's shoulder. Mr. Johannson, Arnold, and his older brothers sat stoically. If anyone dared say anything, they would make certain that it would be the last comment uttered about Gladys and the middle-aged man old enough to be her father, who died in her arms in the dead of night under the tall oak tree in the park. She was sixteen. It was speculated that his father and Gladys had been involved for two or three years. Gladys was always around older people and did not seem to have any friends her own age. There was something sad in her eyes. She seemed to be absent from her own body. Christopher wished that he had Paris's sense of smell and that he could have smelled Gladys on his father all of those years. The thought of them together doing unmentionable things that the neighborhood kids whispered about made Christopher wish that he had Paris's teeth. Mrs. Lindlend seemed to blame the dog. She had to blame someone, so she took Paris to the animal shelter, and Christopher never saw him again.

Mrs. Lindlend and Christopher moved to Manhattan, where people go to forget and to begin anew. New York offered many distractions; Christopher was able to put the heartbreaking incident behind him. He had not thought of it in years. It did not haunt him. Christopher lived a pleasing life of quiet solitude, unending travel, and intellectual stimulation. It was an idyllic existence free from entanglements. He did not worry about betrayals, for he did not let anyone into his life. People constellated around Christopher's world, but he did not permit anyone to alight upon his utopian existence. Never again did he assert with assurance that he wanted this, that, or the other thing. No longer did he seem to know his own mind. Something was taken from him as intangible as the morning sunlight. He did not know what it was, but it was gone, and he made no effort to retrieve it.

"And you think that this is the same woman?" asked Arlington. "Millicent Ansbury. It's hard to believe, isn't it? What do you plan to do?"

"I don't know yet," said Christopher. "I'm just glad that the mystery is over."

"What I don't understand is why your mother would arrange a blind date with her if what you say is true." reasoned Arlington. "It doesn't really make sense, does it?"

"No, it doesn't make any sense," answered Christopher. "But then, none of it ever made any sense."

Millicent Ansbury checked her BlackBerry. The flashing red light never stopped reminding her of the endless array of appointments, flights, and deadlines. She checked her bags in at the check-in counter and paid the fee for overweight luggage. Millicent never seemed to travel lightly. In all honestly, one never knew how much clothing to take to Brussels. The assignment was for a week, but sometimes the assignments lingered on for longer periods of time. With the economy in such a state of flux, it was difficult to speculate how long she would cover the emergency summit meeting of the European Union. She needed a vacation and determined to take a few days off at the end of the assignment. Millicent opened a message on her BlackBerry. It was from Mrs. Lindlend. *Christopher knows. Contact me immediately.* Millicent's bag moved slowly on the baggage transport along with the other bags to be boarded onto the plane. It was too late to cancel the flight, and she had a deadline. The plane would not leave for another hour. Should she risk it? The entire matter would wait until she returned to New York in a week or two. Perhaps Christopher needed time to ponder all of the details. It would be better to face him after he had time to think things through. She sent a message to Mrs. Lindlend, *I will meet with him when I return. Fondly, Millicent.*

Mrs. Lindlend sipped her sparkling water and gazed admiringly at the friendly daisies that adorned the coffee table.

"Mr. Lindlend is here," announced the housekeeper softly.

"Tell him I've gone out," said Mrs. Lindlend. Her nerves were frazzled. What would she say to him?

"But I've already let him in," said the housekeeper. "He's in the kitchen getting the nutcracker."

"The impertinence!" said Mrs. Lindlend as Christopher entered the living room with a handful of walnuts, a nutcracker, and a paper towel. "Who told you that you could ransack my kitchen and abscond with my nutcracker?"

Christopher sat beside his mother on the sofa. He cracked a walnut and filled his mouth with its contents. He quickly cracked another.

"Stop that infernal racket!" ordered Mrs. Lindlend.

"It all comes back to me now," said Christopher cracking another walnut. "This is Dad's nutcracker. I'm surprised you kept it. The sound of his incessant nut cracking annoyed you to the point of your threatening to throw him and his nutcracker out. I remember that. Funny how the floodgates open when one small memory surfaces." Christopher cracked another walnut.

"What do you want, Christopher?" asked Mrs. Lindlend trying to ignore the sound of the cracking walnuts.

"Why did you arrange for me to meet Gladys Johannson?" asked Christopher cracking yet another walnut. "After what she did…"

Mrs. Lindlend walked gracefully to the window and looked down at the street. "I would appreciate it if you would not crack anymore walnuts, Christopher."

"Why did you do it?" asked Christopher calmly. "She destroyed our lives."

Mrs. Lindlend did not turn from the window. She continued to look down at the moving traffic.

"Well?" asked Christopher placing the nutcracker on the coffee table. "Why did you do it? Hasn't she hurt us enough?"

"Yes," said Mrs. Lindlend, "and I wanted the pain to end."

She turned from the window and faced her son. "I know that she is the reason why you remain so aloof and alone and why you have not been able to have one serious relationship. Your father hurt you, and you will not allow yourself to trust anyone. I thought that it would help if you and Gladys met to sort it out." Mrs. Lindlend sat next to her son. "I called her at the CNN offices, and she agreed to come to New York to meet with you. We thought it best if we did not force the memory upon you."

"We?" asked Christopher. "You are 'we' now? How did this happen? Are you saying that you called her at CNN and reminded her that she killed your husband and you wanted her to help your son overcome the psychological scars?"

"That's it in a nutshell," said Mrs. Lindlend removing the nutcracker from the coffee table.

"This is no time to be droll, Mother," said Christopher. "The idea is appalling. How can you forgive her?"

"Gladys was a mere child when she became involved with your father," said Mrs. Lindlend. "It is I who should be asking her forgiveness. Don't you realize what your father did to that girl? He might have been sent to prison if anyone discovered the truth? Gladys was too young to know any better, but your father knew what he was doing. She wasn't old enough to know how that ill-fated decision would affect her life. Your father didn't care. Do you not realize what her family has had to endure? Your friend Arnold killed himself a few years ago. She has been in therapy for over fifteen years, and nothing seems to help. Even a name change and a successful career have not helped. So you see, by helping you, she helps herself."

Christopher had no idea about Arnold. He hadn't kept track of his old friends.

"It had to be done," said Mrs. Lindlend. "You both need each other. Somehow, we will sort all of this out, but for now, trust that it is all for the best."

Christopher returned to his condo and sat in silence. It was all quite unsavory. Did his mother really expect him to make friends with such a creature? Gladys Johannson killed his father and destroyed his family. He would never forgive her. She was a wretch, and he would let her know that he would never forget her offense. Christopher felt that it was justice that Gladys could find no peace, and with regard to his own lack of intimate relationships, well, he would simply live with the knowledge of it. It was fine with him. Now that he knew the cause, he was more than willing to accept his plight. There would be no forgiveness. Gladys Johannson could rot in hell for all he cared.

Christopher cracked another walnut and munched it slowly. He did not realize how vindictive and bitter he had become. Was his mother right? Was that unfathomable creature responsible for all of his failed relationships? It was all the more reason to curse her. Christopher remembered his idyllic family life. His was the perfect American family. There was the white picket fence that surrounded their modest Cape, traditional American values, and the family dog, Paris. Then, Gladys destroyed it all. Christopher remembered her on the school bus flirting with all of the older athletes. His father was no athlete. Christopher became more confused whenever he thought of her. He must focus upon the Zurich conference at present. He tried to remove the unpleasant thoughts from his mind, but he could not. Gladys Johannson destroyed his father, her brother, his dog, and now the *daughter of Eve* was standing at the *gate* of his utopian existence like a *Trojan Horse* waiting to annihilate all that was good and decent in his life.

***

It was a smooth landing. A car waited for Millicent to take her to the hotel. A few people asked for her autograph. How did they recognize her? Were journalists celebrities in Brussels? Perhaps she looked like someone else. Millicent entered the limousine. In it she found Jake Torbourne, an Australian director, who had taken refuge in her waiting limo.

"I hope you don't mind," said the limousine driver. "They were mobbing him, and his chauffer had not yet arrived."

"I'll be out of your hair in a moment," said the beleaguered director. "My man should be here momentarily."

"Well, this is a surprise," said Millicent. "It certainly

explains why people wanted my autograph. No, I don't mind at all. Where are you going? We can drop you off."

"If it won't put you out," said Jake. "You're the news anchor, aren't you?"

"I am a journalist," said Millicent with condescension.

"I can't quite place the accent," said Jake calling his chauffer on his cell phone. "It's not Brooklyn, but it isn't New York either."

"Where are you staying?" asked Millicent.

"One of the other boroughs, no doubt. I pride myself on being able to place people by their accents. I must admit, yours is a mystery," said Jake. "Reginald, I am in a car on my way to the hotel. No need to go to the airport. I will meet you in an hour or so. I've got that thing at the studio at two, so don't be late." Jake placed his cell phone in his pocket. "Now, back to the mystery."

"If you don't mind, Mr. Torbourne," said Millicent huffily. It made her nervous when people questioned her background. There was always the fear. "Are you working on a movie in Brussels?"

"No, I'm on holiday. My girlfriend lives here. Thought I'd scout a few locations for my next film while I'm here. What about you? What world event are you covering? I always watch your reports," said Jake. "You tell the news in language that people can understand. I like that. We seem to be stuck in traffic. Look across the lane. That's my driver, Reginald, over there facing the airport. Traffic is abysmal. What's causing this jam?" asked Jake to the chauffer. "Do you know?"

"There's some sort of economic conference," said the chauffer.

"Aha!" exclaimed Jake. "So, you're covering the conference. Of course, that's it. Mind if I tag along?"

Millicent was taken aback. "No, I'm afraid security is tight; only registered guests and the press are allowed."

"Pity," said Jake. "I've always wanted to see what goes

on behind closed doors at those conferences. Are you sure you couldn't get a pass for me? You could say that I am your assistant."

"No, I'm sorry. Look, traffic is moving," said Millicent. Jake was making her exceedingly nervous. She wondered if his presence in her limousine was quite by accident. The limousine glided unobstructed down the highway. Jake poured himself a glass of wine from the limousine's bar.

"The news has always fascinated me," said Jake sipping the wine. "I'm a real news buff. There's nothing like real life as a backdrop for film. Did you know that I get most of the ideas for my films from the news? People like real-life drama. My last film *Coming up Empty* won a Golden Globe."

"Yes, I know," said Millicent patiently. She wondered how long she would be obliged to listen to the show business chatter. "It was a great film."

"Of course," said Jake, "and do you know why? It was based on a real life event. People like story lines that they can identify with. This conference you're attending, for example, I'll bet there are a million stories behind those closed doors that don't have anything to do with the world economy. Do you know what I mean?" He sipped his wine and pondered.

"Yes, but like I said," said Millicent, "security is tight, and only invited guests and journalists are allowed."

"There!" said Jake excitedly pointing to Millicent. "Expressions like that."

"What expressions?" asked Millicent in utter confusion.

"You said *but like I said*. I'm going to take a wild guess and say that you're from Queens," said Jake proudly. "Am I right?"

Millicent was perplexed and did not know how to answer.

"It's there," said Jake, "carefully hidden under mainstream media gloss, but it's there. You're from Queens."

"I think our conversation is over, Mr. Torbourne," said Millicent taking her notes from her briefcase.

"There's nothing to be ashamed of," said Jake. "I like

Queens. I shot *The Green Fairground* there. Did you see it? It was my first film with Gloria Plenny. Whatever happened to her anyway?"

"If you don't mind, Mr. Torbourne, I would like to review my notes," said Millicent impatiently.

"Of course, of course," said Jake. He looked out of the window, and Millicent read her notes. "There was a park," continued Jake after a few minutes. "We were supposed to shoot there, but production was shut down while they investigated a death. It seems some old guy died under a tree in the arms of his lover – a teenager young enough to be his kid. There was a big scandal. I followed it thinking that it would make a great story someday."

Millicent's hands trembled as she read her notes.

"I don't ask for much," said Jake, "but if you could get me into that meeting, I would greatly appreciate it." Jake gave Millicent his card. "Call me if you reconsider. You can let me out here," called Jake to the driver. The car pulled over on the side of the road. "I would greatly appreciate it," said Jake as he exited the car and closed the door.

Millicent's entire body trembled. She looked through the closed glass at the back of the chauffer's head and wondered how much Jake had paid him to enter the car. She didn't dare report it. So this is where it begins—or ends. She changed her name, her appearance, her manner of speaking, her place of residence, and her entire existence; yet, her past caught up with her in Brussels. First, there was the call from Mrs. Lindlend, and now this. Millicent envisioned the CNN nightly news with her picture plastered on the screen beside that of Mr. Lindlend, a horrid picture that showed her with big, mousy-brown hair, blotchy adolescent skin, and twenty pounds overweight. She envisioned her entire professional and social life falling apart, as surely they would, if the affair re-emerged. Millicent needed help, but where could she turn? No one knew of the ghastly secret, only Mrs. Lindlend and her son. She called her therapist;

he tried to counsel her by phone but provided no insight as to what she should do.

Millicent arrived at the hotel. A porter took her bags to her room as she signed in at the front desk. There, in the lobby sat Jake Torbourne in an easy chair reading a newspaper. He approached Millicent at the desk. "I forgot to mention that I'm staying at your hotel right down the hall from your room. Isn't that a coincidence?"

"No, I do not think that it is a coincidence," said Millicent taking the keys from the receptionist with a smile. Jake and Millicent walked towards the elevator, which was filled with journalists. Most of them exchanged pleasantries with Millicent, but when they recognized Jake, a barrage of questions were hurled at him regarding his latest film project, leading lady, and girlfriend. Jake smiled amiably but answered no questions.

"Come on, Millicent," said one of the journalists, "You can't keep him to yourself. Give us something."

"Mr. Torbourne is not with me," said Millicent politely. "He recognized me and wanted to say hello, that's all. Now, this is my floor." Millicent exited with Jake. The journalists followed them down the hall to their respective rooms asking questions along the way. Millicent entered her room and closed the door. She could hear the reporters following Jake to his room. How was she supposed to concentrate on the conference with this new development? Millicent pulled the drapes and let the sun enter the room. She sat on the bed, which was covered with a quaint green spread, and looked out of the window. Pedestrians and motorists went about their business on the busy street below. How fortunate to be able to go about one's affairs unencumbered. Millicent envied them, the nondescript, everyday people who keep the world afloat while the privileged tried to keep themselves from drowning. Life was much simpler when she was Gladys Johannson from Queens, but she would not want to return to that life. Privilege had its drawbacks, but they were superior to the mundane undertakings of the working classes. She took Jake's card from her purse and called the number he had scribbled over the contact numbers on the card. He was not surprised to hear from her and offered to meet her for drinks in the hotel bar before meeting his girlfriend.

Millicent met with a few of her colleagues in one of the hotel conference rooms to discuss the upcoming conference. She declined invitations to accompany them for an evening of entertainment and returned to her room to dress for her meeting with Jake. She phoned him again. The hotel bar would, undoubtedly, be packed with journalists. Perhaps they should meet at a place *far from the madding crowd.* Jake knew of a place near his girlfriend's flat. They would be able to speak without interruption. Millicent arranged for a taxi to take her to the location. It was a pleasant restaurant with a sidewalk café. Hanging flowering baskets encircled the patrons engaging in polite conversation while eating festive meals on tables adorned with pristine white tablecloths. Millicent entered the restaurant and looked for Jake. He sat at a corner table towards the back. The area was dimly lit with candles. It was a perfect meeting place for people desirous of privacy. Jake rose from his seat and held her chair. A waiter appeared. His smile was pleasant and the tone of his voice was soothing. He was the perfect waiter for such a clandestine seating arrangement, almost out of a movie. A small vase with a red rose sat romantically in the center of the table. The silverware shone even in the dark.

"Wine?" asked Jake.

"Please," said Millicent.

Jake checked the wine list and ordered a bottle of their best house wine. Millicent waited for Jake to speak.

"Have you reconsidered?" asked Jake.

"Yes," said Millicent. "I can get you a pass."

"Tremendous!" replied Jake.

"You do realize that this is blackmail," said Millicent.

"On the contrary," said Jake, "it is an arrangement between friends. I hope that we will become friends."

"There is no chance of that," assured Millicent. "I want your word that you will not trouble me again or use the information you have attained in any way."

"You have my word," said Jake.

"How do I know if I can trust you?" asked Millicent.

"I am a man of my word," said Jake.

Millicent gave him a journalist pass to the conference. Jake placed it inside his jacket.

"No one must ever know that I gave that to you," said Millicent.

"Of course," said Jake. "I am a man of discretion."

"How will you manage it?" asked Millicent. "Everyone will recognize you."

"My makeup artist will take care of that," said Jake. "No one will be the wiser. Even you won't be able to recognize me."

The waiter placed the wine on the table. Millicent sipped the wine and touched the rose gingerly. "Why is the conference so important to you? What do you hope to accomplish?"

Jake tasted the wine. It was to his liking. "I'm afraid that must remain a secret, but I can assure you that my motives are strictly above-board. May I ask a personal question?"

"No, you may not," said Millicent. "You know enough about my personal life."

"Why did you do it? He was twice your age, and judging from the photos, he wasn't particularly attractive. What happened out there?" asked Jake.

Millicent searched her innermost thoughts. No one had ever asked her why. Before she knew it, she began speaking candidly about the affair. "He looked twice my age, but he was very young inside. He knew about everything that interested me, and he taught me many things about life. I miss him. I miss the way he looked at me when I told him about my day. I miss the way he just held me in his arms, very secure arms, without saying a word. He never judged me or told me that I was too fat, too ugly, or too stupid. "

"He treated you as a daughter, but it was much more than that, wasn't it? You were, what twelve or thirteen, when you began the affair, if *affair* if the right word. The old codger should have been thrown in jail. Was he your first?" asked Jake.

"I've answered enough questions," said Milllicent.

"It must have been something in the water," said Jake.

"Or something in my head," said Millicent. "I believe it was a need for acceptance—a need to be loved. It's a common response."

"Yes, it certainly was common," said Jake.

"Now, you're judging me," said Millicent.

"No, but you are making it more difficult for me to keep my word. Your story is fascinating. You were a little *Lolita* from Queens. Would you agree?"

"I don't know what that means," said Millicent. "I must go."

Jake reached out and touched her hand. "I want to know more. How did you become Millicent Ansbury? How were you able to make that transformation without detection? You work for one of the pillars of the news world. Why weren't they aware? The old codger must have had some pretty powerful connections. Did you ever meet any of his friends? Did he ever mention anybody important?"

Before Millicent could answer, a flash went off, and a photographer exited the restaurant quickly. Millicent panicked and stood. "I was afraid this would happen."

"Wait," said Jake. "It's just some celebrity gossip photographer trying to get a picture of me. Don't let it disturb you."

"You cannot use that pass now," whispered Millicent. "If you are caught, I will be blamed."

"Nonsense," said Jake. "No one will be able to detect my presence."

"Do not contact me again," said Millicent. "It would be disastrous."

Millicent hurried out of the restaurant and entered a waiting taxi. She paid the driver extra to leave his appointed fare and to take her back to her hotel. Millicent did not know that she was the appointed fare. Jake hired the cab to wait outside of the restaurant, and he hired the photographer. Millicent had no idea of the manipulative mind that now ensnared her within its grasp. Jake Torbourne was a master director, and he knew how to get the performances he wanted from his cast and crew. Research made all the difference. Jake researched his projects thoroughly, and his films were larger than life because of his efforts. He delved into the psyche of his characters and portrayed them with the utmost precision. He sat at the table sipping his wine and pondering which leading lady would play the part of Gladys Johannson from Queens.

Christopher sat uneasily in his chair. He hoped that Arlington would not be present in the library. There was always some reason for dropping by Christopher's study room, and the distractions were endless. Arlington's chit chat did lead to some important revelations, however. It was because of Arlington that Christopher remembered his dog, Paris, which he had repressed, and that fiendish she-wolf from Queens, Gladys Johannson. His mind was beginning to wander again. The sun on the window sill made it difficult to focus upon the task at hand. It was the first time Christopher had seen the morning sun rays resting gently upon the sill and the burgundy brocade drapes. The study room was much to his liking. The ambience was conducive to scholarly endeavors, much more so than his office on campus. It was difficult to get any work accomplished there with the endless stream of students in the halls and outside enjoying the campus. The study room was a great benefit and well-worth the subscription to the private library. A gentle knock on the door, and Christopher knew that his early morning retreat was soon to be disturbed.

"Mind if I pop in for a quick word?" asked Arlington opening the door. His initial diffidence was no longer a part of his character. Arlington felt at ease with Christopher since his new friend confided the information about his dog, his father, and the young woman from Queens. "Thought that you might want to see this," said Christopher as he produced a gossip newspaper. On page two was a picture of the famous director, Jake Torbourne, flanked by pictures of two beautiful women. The picture on the left displayed a jubilant Jake with his tall, lanky, girlfriend from Brussels. They were quite an item and seemed very happy together. The picture on the right showed a reserved, serious Jake leaning over a candlelit table and showing much attention to the attractive, demure journalist, Millicent Ansbury. The caption suggested that Jake was in the midst of a tortuous triangle.

Christopher glanced at the photos and returned back to his laptop screen.

"Why did you think this would interest me?"

Arlington looked confused. "I seem to remember that you had some connection with this Millicent Ansbury woman. You remember, don't you? You thought that she was the same woman who destroyed your dog and your family?"

"I fail to see how any of this would interest me," persisted Christopher.

Arlington placed the paper on the desk. "Of course, it's just idle gossip. I'll be going to my study chambers now. Stop by when you want to go out for lunch." Arlington closed the door softly. Christopher picked up the paper and read the article. A feeling of disconcertion swept over him. He knocked on the door adjoining his room to Arlington's study chambers.

"This Islonia looks a lot like your wife," said Christopher holding the paper next to the framed photograph of Arlington's wife on his desk.

"Sister-in-law," said Arlington with a smile. "They're both quite stunning, aren't they?"

Christopher sat in the chair near Arlington's desk. "Did you happen to mention what I told you to your wife?"

"It may have come up in passing," said Arlington. "Why, is there something wrong?"

"Your wife is close to her sister, no doubt," reasoned Christopher.

"Of course," said Arlington. "They phone each other every day. It's a very close-knit family."

"Were you aware that your sister-in-law was involved with this Jake Torbourne character?" asked Christopher.

"He's quite accomplished," said Arlington. "Have you seen any of his films?"

"Don't you see what's happened?" asked Christopher shrilly. "You told your wife, she told her sister, and her sister told her director boyfriend. Of course, that's it. He researched the story, found it to be true, and is trying to make a film of it."

Arlington seemed astounded. "That seems quite far-fetched, don't you think?"

"What other explanation could there be?" asked Christopher.

"Is it at all possible that this Millicent is keen on Jake? She's there covering a conference, and he's there visiting my sister-in-law. They meet in some small café, and the rest is, as they say, *Kismet*," announced Arlington.

"I don't believe in *Kismet*. Something is off-center here," said Christopher anxiously.

"What do you mean?" asked Arlington.

"I mean that something is *rotten in the state of Brussels*," said Christopher. Arlington laughed heartily.

"That's a good one. *Methinks* you're reading too many dramas," said Arlington with affectation. "I can do it as well."

"When one's life is a drama, there's no need to read others. I want you to do something for me. I want you to arrange a meeting with Jake Torbourne."

"Why?" asked Arlington.

"He's obviously looking for information. I can give him all of the information that he needs."

"You can't be serious," said Arlington. "Would you really expose Millicent Ansbury's secret past? It might ruin her career."

Christopher placed the newspaper on Arlington's cluttered desk.

"With any luck," said Christopher. He exited Arlington's study chambers and returned to his room. Arlington followed him holding the newspaper.

"There must be a better way to resolve this," said Arlington. "If Jake produces a film of the incident, won't you and your family be involved?"

Christopher remained silent. Arlington continued. "By destroying one person's life, you may destroy your own and others as well. Is your revenge worth so many casualties?"

"Will you arrange the meeting?" asked Christopher.

"It is against my better judgment," sighed Arlington, "but I will try to arrange the meeting. I can't see what good it will do."

Arlington left Christopher to revel in his newly-formed scheme. The sun's rays crept onto the papers covering his desk. Christopher smiled and felt a tremendous weight removed from his shoulders. At last, he would find relief. The end of Millicent Ansbury would be the beginning of his new life. He felt the new life enveloping him. It seemed to have blossomed and cast a sweet aura throughout his entire body. Christopher's vision seemed a bit clearer, and his thoughts were sharper. He sat taller in his chair and felt the newness of life coursing through his being. People said that vengeance destroyed one's inner-being, but his inner-being seemed uplifted. Christopher didn't know how long the feeling would last, but for now, it was creating a euphoria that had never been present in his life, and he did not want the feeling to end.

Meanwhile in the adjoining room, Arlington texted a message to Jake Torbourne.

Mission accomplished. Wants meeting.

It would be two months before Jake Torbourne would return to New York. The director was immersed in directing his new film off the coast of the Italian Riviera. His girlfriend, Islonia, accompanied him, and the Queens story was put on the back burner until he had more time to explore the possibilities. Christopher was deeply disappointed. He thought of traveling to Italy to speak with Jake, but the director had no interest in such a meeting. Christopher was thwarted at every turn. To make matters worse, he had neither written nor researched anything that would make his paper distinctive. He was totally consumed with the Gladys Johannson story and would not rest until he had exposed every detail. It was then that the thought occurred to him that he should write the story himself. Christopher would write it from the perspective of an injured adolescent preparing to enter manhood. He would chronicle Gladys's relationships in school, at home, and divulge information of her new identity as a respected *CNN* journalist. He would expose the suicide of her brother. He would write the story, and it would be to his liking. He would exonerate every young person who sat in the wings as a parent committed unspeakable acts and somehow felt that it was his or her own fault.

Christopher checked his watch. It was time for Millicent's report on *CNN*. He turned on the television and sat on his sofa nursing a cup of tea. The phone rang. It was Jake Torbourne. Christopher watched Millicent as he spoke with Jake. He did not need Jake's help anymore. He would do the job himself. Curiously, Jake had not phoned to discuss the Queens story. He was planning a surprise one-year anniversary party for Arlington and his wife, and he needed Christopher's help in planning the event. This request surprised Christopher, for he knew very little about Arlington. They met in the library, but he knew none of his friends and had never met his wife. He had only viewed her picture on Arlington's desk.

"I'm afraid I can't help," said Christopher.

"You're the only one they talk about in New York," said Jake. "You made quite an impression on Arlington."

"I find that difficult to believe," said Christopher. "I haven't even met his wife."

"He's told her everything about you. I don't know any of their friends. Somebody has to attend this shindig," said Jake. "See if you can find out the names of any of their acquaintances."

"Wouldn't your girlfriend know these things? I understand the family is quite close," said Christopher.

"That's just the point," said Jake. "We've had a spat. I'm trying to do this to win her back. I don't have time for this nonsense, but I want to get back into her good graces. If I tell her that I'm arranging this affair for her sister and brother-in-law, she'll take me back, get it?"

"I'm quite busy with my own life," said Christopher.

"I'll make it worth your while," said Jake. "I'm going to see Millicent Ansbury next week. I only have a weekend, and I'm taking time to make this happen. I've decided to make the Queens Lolita movie. My staff is researching it as we speak. It's a fascinating story. Did you know that the old geezer left her a ton of money?"

"That *old geezer* was my father, and we didn't have a lot of money," said Christopher defensively.

"Your father left Gladys Johannson a substantial sum of money. That's why her family didn't pursue any legal action. Where would he get that kind of money? This just keeps getting better. By the way, I understand you and your mother live in the same building."

Christopher felt uncomfortable. Jake continued. "I may need to speak with both of you. My staff has tried to interview

Millicent's family, but they won't cooperate. Maybe you can help."

Suddenly, the ramifications of Christopher's plans began to unfold before his eyes. The tawdry affair would be splattered across every newspaper in the city. Millicent's family would relive the horror of Arnold's death and the shame of the illicit affair. The new life his mother had forged in the city would be destroyed when friends and neighbors begin to look at them with eyes of pity. His students, the most incurious crop he had ever taught, would suddenly be overcome with curiosity of his flawed family. What had he been thinking? Jake was still speaking, but Christopher had not heard a word.

"I'm glad that you're all right with all of this," said Jake. "I may have to depend on you and your mother for an inside perspective. My people will contact you next week or sooner. Now that your problem is solved, you can help me with mine. How soon do you think that you will be able to get the information for the party?"

"When is the party?" asked Christopher cheerlessly.

"Three weeks," said Jake. "I know that isn't much time, but that's all we've got."

"How can I contact you," asked Christopher.

Jake gave Christopher his direct number.

"The party must be a surprise," said Jake. "Somehow, you've got to do everything without Arlington and Islonia suspecting. I know this is a lot to ask, but you will be rewarded. I'm going to make a blockbuster of this Queens affair. You won't be disappointed."

When Christopher ended the call, he felt sleazy and compromised. He did not want vengeance if it meant hurting the people closest to him. Gladys Johannson must go free if he was to save his mother and Gladys's family from unnecessary strife. They all had suffered enough. Another tragedy at the hand of his family would be too much for the Johannson family to bear. He could not allow them to watch Glady's life go up in smoke again, no matter how evil and selfish he thought she was.

Millicent was no longer reporting. Another anchor was pontificating about the immigration problem. Christopher pressed the off button on his remote. Twilight cast a grayish pall over the city. As the room darkened, he sat immobilized. It was not a time to plan; it was a time to sit still and let his mind wander, and wander it did. Curiously, his thoughts did not dwell upon the Queens affair or Arlington's party. His thoughts seemed to focus upon a larger-than-life floral representation of a giant puppy by Jeff Koons. Christopher saw the statue a few years ago at the MET. For some strange reason, the statue entered his mind and would not release him. What was the connection? Freud would have a field day with the imagery. City lights outside his window began to flicker like fireflies. Slowly, the entire neighborhood was a maze of twinkling lights as people turned their lights on or off. Then, without warning, the lights stabilized. The entire city was lit, and it was a work of beauty.

Christopher let his mobile phone ring without answering. It was his mother; she could leave a message. He did not want to speak with anyone. The phone continued to ring. Christopher grew annoyed. Why wouldn't she just leave a message? He answered the phone and told his mother that he did not want to be disturbed. Within minutes, there was a knock on his door.

"I do not want to be disturbed," said Christopher impatiently.

"Open the door this instance!" demanded Mrs. Lindlend.

"Can't you respect any of my wishes?" asked Christopher opening the door.

"I just thought of something," said Mrs. Lindlend entering the apartment. She sat on the sofa removing an array of magazines and journals from the cushions. "This is important. Sit down." She patted the cushion next to her. Christopher sat obediently.

"All right, what is it?"

"Your father bequeathed a large sum of money to a charitable organization, which was to provide funding for Gladys's education should anything happen to him," said Mrs. Lindlend.

"You know about it," said Christopher. "Aren't you the least bothered? Don't you care that Dad left her any money at all? If anything, it makes me more incensed with her. Where did he get money, anyway? He was always complaining about not having enough money."

'Why aren't I holding a cup of tea?" asked Mrs. Lindlend. "Haven't you a cup of tea for your mother?"

Christopher put the kettle on begrudgingly and made his mother a brisk cup of tea. Mrs. Lindlend sipped calmly.

"You didn't answer my question," said Christopher. "Where did Dad get that kind of money?"

"Your father had powerful friends in high places. He worked for them from time to time," said Mrs. Lindlend sipping her tea.

"What do you mean? Was he in the Mafia or something?" asked Christopher.

"Don't be ridiculous," said Mrs. Lindlend. "He made investments, and some of them were quite lucrative."

"I don't understand," said Christopher. "What sort of investments, and why didn't we see any of the proceeds from these investments?"

"It had something to do with the stock exchange," said Mrs. Lindlend. "I'm not certain how it all worked."

Christopher recalled the mogul barricaded within his apartment. Were there other people involved in disreputable schemes that destroyed the lives of others? Was his father one of those people?

"I would like to be alone," said Christopher. He felt that his entire world was collapsing around him. "We could be held accountable. You could lose this condo and every penny you have."

"Don't be absurd," said Mrs. Lindlend. "Your father would never do anything illegal."

Christopher looked at his mother intently. "What was the affair with Gladys if not illegal? If he could do that right under our very noses…"

"I won't have you speak of your father that way," said Mrs. Lindlend adamantly.

Christopher tried to clear his mind of any negative thoughts, but he could not.

"I hate her with a passion," said Christopher, "and I will not forgive her. I am going to do all I can to retrieve any shred of dignity I can for this family, even if you won't. In the days to come, all of this will be exposed. It will be on every front page of every newspaper. It will be a feature-length movie, and our lives will be shattered."

"What are you talking about?" asked Mrs. Lindlend sipping her tea.

"They're going to make a movie about Gladys's life, and all of this will be exposed."

"Who's going to make a movie? Explain yourself," demanded Mrs. Lindlend.

Christopher sighed. "*The sins of the father…*"

"Talk sensibly," said Mrs. Lindlend irritably. "If your father committed any sins, they were his and not ours. He took them to his grave, and we are left to press onward. Here, I thought you might need these."

Mrs. Lindlend placed a small bag of walnuts and her husband's old nutcracker on the coffee table.

"Your father was a good man," said Mrs. Lindlend. "All of this will sort itself out. Stop worrying."

Millicent Ansbury packed the last of her bags. This would be her last assignment, of that she was certain. There was no way she would be able to retain her position when the corporate news organization heard her story. It was quite an unbelievable story. There were times when she didn't believe it herself. The position at *CNN* was a long-shot and more than she had hoped for, but Harold Lindlend's tentacles seemed to be interwoven with many prestigious firms and corporations. He knew many influential people, and she was only one of his tawdry affairs. What hold did he have over those people? Millicent did not know, but she had a little money saved, and there were the residences in London and Rome.

The residences were arranged by Harold Lindlend's investment firm. She was told that there was enough money in the account to supplement her mortgage payments to the bank. It was a mystery. There always seemed to be enough money in the account to take care of everything she wanted. It was doubtful that Mrs. Lindlend knew how extensive her husband's investments were in ensuring a life of comfort for Gladys Johannson, but the truth always surfaced.

Millicent knew that the bubble would burst someday, but she never imagined being the topic of a feature film. She had also grown quite fond of Mrs. Lindlend. Millicent did not have any answers, but she was content not to know the answers to life's perplexing questions. For the first time in many years, Millicent searched for her Rosary.

"You did all of this for us?" gushed Arlington as he and Islonia entered their apartment to find a few of their closest friends standing under lavish decorations. Christopher had a difficult time finding their closest friends, but with the help of Arlington's doorman, it was not as formidable a task as once imagined. Arlington was truly surprised, and tears welled in his wife's eyes. The word *soiree* was really an exaggeration, but

Christopher liked to imagine that he had arranged a spectacular event. He could not help but wonder why Jake's staff could research every tidbit of information about the Queens affair but could not stage a small gathering for Arlington and his wife's anniversary. He maneuvered his way to Jake Torbourne, who stood proudly with his model girlfriend, Islonia. She was quite tall with legs that seemed to consume her entire body. Every portion of her body was toned and well-manicured. Even her eyelashes were lavish. She held Jake's arm in her electric blue stiletto heels with matching mini-skirt. Her black sequined halter top announced the arrival of a *fashionista*.

"I'd like a word, if you aren't too busy," said Christopher.

"Of course," said Jake. "You have really outdone yourself, Christopher. I can call you Christopher, can't I? I feel that we're such good friends now. This little shindig is more than I imagined. It must have consumed a lot of your time. You won't be disappointed, I can assure you. Islonia and I are very grateful; in fact, she's prepared to introduce you to a couple of her friends. They're models." Jake nodded towards the door, where two beautiful women held court. They were surrounded by young men, all with admiring eyes. Jake took Christopher's arm and led him to the divas.

"This is Christopher," said Jake. "Islonia said that you would make him feel right at home." The two models left their admirers and flanked both sides of the timorous academic. They walked arm in arm to the center of the room, where they could be observed by all. They were at Christopher's side for the entire evening. He was not a fashion expert, but Christopher recognized beauty when he saw it. Even without the makeup and designer clothing, the two women on his arm were stunning.

Arlington approached the trio. His smile was more of an indefatigable grin, and his joy was contagious. Christopher returned the smile with the two beauties still clinging to his arms.

"I couldn't believe it when Isolonia said that you arranged

all of this," said Arlington with incredulity. "How did you know how to find these people? I never mentioned them."

Music began to play loudly. Christopher spoke over the music.

"That is one of those secrets that remain with the other superheroes," said Christopher with a smile as wide as Arlington's. "It must be thrilling to have a sister-in-law who can fill the room with such grace and beauty." More super models began to fill the room. Lamentably, they brought dates with them, but they brought a spirit of liveliness that Christopher had not experienced. He was not a person known for his festive spirit. Suddenly, with the arrival of these glamorous people, the room and the people in it were transformed into another species. Even the ordinary, mundane people seemed to make an Ovidian transformation and joined the ranks of the sublime. These were the party people, and they seemed to bring their party with them. It was attached to their aura. Wherever they went, the festive atmosphere evolved.

Arlington and his wife stood hand-in-hand beside the celebratory anniversary cake that seemed larger than their sedated personalities required. Christopher felt happy. It wasn't the champagne. He was certain that it was the idea of living life without the repressed troubles and cares that made him feel less than euphoric. He felt like a new man in this congenial company, and Christopher wanted one or both of the beautiful women on his arm to be a part of his new life. That was what it would be—a new life. An invisible weight, which he had been carrying for years, had been lifted from his shoulders. Now, with the advent of the beautiful, everything seemed different. He would begin again without the trauma of his father's indiscretions. He was a new man, and this new man would begin his new life by toasting it with his lovely companions, who were determined not to let him out of their sight.

In a far corner, Jake Torbourne smiled as he sipped his champagne and watched Islonia's friends lavish attention and affection upon the scholarly being. It would make a great screen play, and it would be quite an ending for the new movie.

⸻

The article in the newspaper was rather small. It was doubtful that anyone, apart from aspiring actors, noticed the ad. There was a casting call for Jake Torbourne's new movie, *Bayside Lolita*. Jake wanted an unknown to play the role of the young Lolita from Queens, and the young women were lined up for blocks. An established actor would play the role of the wayward husband.

Christopher had not thought of the affair in weeks. His new life was keeping him busy. No longer did he frequent the library to work on his paper; in point of fact, Zurich was no longer a priority. There were far too many important things to consider. Rachel, the model he decided would be most compatible with his eccentric ways, wanted him to accompany her to a *Vogue* photo shoot in Prague. Christopher had never been to Prague. He also accompanied her to Brazil, Paris, and Rome on other modeling assignments. It was an exciting life. He traveled on private planes, ate expensive meals, and spent a great deal of time sipping champagne while telling Rachel how beautiful she looked. He was not exaggerating. She *was* beautiful. What surprised him was that he did not seem to mind reassuring her with unrelenting frequency.

Christopher considered taking a sabbatical in the fall so that he would be able to spend more time with Rachel. She seemed to require his presence and approval, and he was not averse to lavishing it upon her.

The inseparable couple moved into her loft in Soho and spent many hours discussing her photo shoots and his books. Rachel was astounded by the number of books Christopher had read and longed to hear more of the intricate plots of the great writers. Each night, he read to her from Shakespeare, Tolstoy, Milton, and Trollope. She was especially enamoured with the works of the great master of English culture, Henry James. They lay under the covers sipping champagne and nibbling walnuts as Christopher's melodic voice read *The Wings of the Dove* with perfection. Rachel was in tears when he completed the last chapter.

"It's so beautiful," cried Rachel. "We started reading it in school, but I had to go to Barcelona for a photo shoot, and I never got to finish it."

"You read it in college?" asked Christopher placing his fingers in the champagne and gently rubbing them across her lips. Rachel kissed her lover's fingers and aroused great passion within the academic.

"No, of course not," whispered Rachel kissing his eyelids. "I read it a couple of years ago before I started modeling. Maybe someday when I'm too old to model, I'll go back to school and finish it, like when I'm seventeen or something. Here, use your nutcracker. Why are you trying to crack that nut with your bare fingers?

The End

THE COMMITMENT

It was six o'clock, and there were no messages on the BlackBerry. Perhaps he was lost. It was easy to get lost in Rome. Some people have difficulty maneuvering through any city and are unaccustomed to navigating subways and buses. Yesterday, she told him her name, and they agreed to meet. Opal wished that she had been blessed with a more interesting name. Who names a kid Opal? What were her parents thinking? A young man with a camera approached Opal as she pondered amidst the crowds surrounding her at the Trevi Fountain.

"Pardon me, but would you mind taking our picture?" asked a tall, slender man with closely-cropped sandy hair. He was accompanied by an older woman, no doubt his mother, wearing white Capri pants and a flowered blouse.

"Of course," said Opal taking the camera from his hand. "Which button should I press?"

"This one," said the man indicating a button to the right of the flash. He and the matronly woman positioned themselves in front of the gurgling fountain.

"Say 'cheese,'" said Opal peeking through the camera's small view-finder.

"We can do better than that," said the younger man. Instantly, before Opal could press the button, he swept the woman into his arms and kissed her ardently. The shutter went off, and the picture was displayed on the camera's small screen.

"Oh, Peter," whispered the woman trying to rearrange her hair and blouse, which had become disheveled after the rather provocative kiss. "What will people think?"

"They will think that we are madly in love," proclaimed the impulsive man retrieving his camera from Opal. "Thank you. You are an excellent photographer. Are we ready for dinner, Minifred?"

The couple walked hand-in-hand down the congested walkway and seemed eager to imbibe the textures and aromas of Rome. They kissed and laughed the laugh of young lovers enthralled with life and with one another. Soon they were out of view. A hand touched Opal's shoulder.

"Someday, maybe we'll take a picture like that," said Roger Paisley.

Opal looked at the hand that touched her shoulder, and she sighed unconsciously. Roger was a *golden* man. Light brown golden hairs illuminated his arms. The golden hairs were the first thing Opal noticed about Roger.

"A penny for your thoughts," said Roger.

"My thoughts are of gold," responded Opal wistfully.

"Perhaps you'll settle for a Euro," said Roger producing a coin. "Come, let's toss one in and make a wish." He prepared to toss the coin into the ebullient fountain.

"Wait!" cried Opal. "I haven't thought of my wish yet."

After a few moments, she smiled and signaled that he should toss the coin.

"Wait!" cried Opal again. "You can't just toss it. You're supposed to stand with your back to the fountain and toss it over your shoulder."

"Perhaps I should dance a jig as well," said Roger impatiently. "Here we go, then." He tossed the coin over his shoulder; it splashed into the fountain. "That should do it. Wait here, I'll get you a sorbet."

Before Opal could respond, Roger bounded over the rail and entered the sorbet shop across the walkway to the fountain. Opal sat in the Trevi Fountain's cement seating area observing the tourists toss coins into the majestic fountain. Some were tossing coins over their shoulders; others were throwing randomly and missing the fountain completely. Roger returned with a cup filled with raspberry sorbet and a small cone-shaped waffle *spoon*.

"You're going to spoil me," said Opal accepting the sorbet gratefully. "I must admit, this is the best sorbet I've ever tasted. We don't have anything like this back in New York."

"There's nothing like this anywhere," said Roger. "I think that the Italians invented it."

"No, I think *sorbet* is French," corrected Opal scooping out a delicious mouthful with the cone.

"Whichever country is responsible," said Roger, "I am most appreciative. Shall we move out of the sun?"

"We won't be able to see the fountain," protested Opal.

"The fountain will be here this evening," said Roger, "and it is even more beautiful in the evening light. I hope that you haven't made other plans."

"No, but let's stay here awhile," said Opal. "We don't have anything like this in New York."

Roger's countenance changed suddenly. "It may surprise you to know that New York is not the center of the universe. There are many grand spectacles in the world that are not found in the city of New York." Roger was annoyed. Opal's frequent references to New York were irritating. She seemed to measure everything against the fineries of New York City. Opal sensed his irritation. It amused her, and she continued to *bait* him.

"Oh, really?" asked Opal. "Name one thing that New York doesn't have. I challenge you to name just one thing."

"Me, for starters," said Roger finishing his sorbet cup. "I

have never been to New York, and I do not intend to go to New York. There are far more interesting places to see."

Opal laughed. "Are you suggesting that you are a grand spectacle, Roger?"

"Not at all," answered Roger indignantly.

"I suppose you're thinking of the Eiffel Tower, Big Ben, or the Taj Mahal," said Opal. "What about the intricate design of the Chrysler Building or the towering majesty of the Empire State Building?"

"You would compare those beastly edifices to the *dreaming spires* of Oxford or the lush landscape of the Scottish Moors when the stars cascade over the heavens like droplets of shimmering dew?" asked Roger. "In point of fact, you would be hard-pressed to find evidence of one feeble star over the entire New York metropolis."

"How would you know?" asked Opal suppressing a smile. "You say you've never been to New York."

"I lied," confessed Roger. "I accompanied my parents there when I was a boy of eight or ten. It was the most horrific experience of my life. I was pleased to leave your *golden* city."

The word *golden* reminded Opal of her current reality. She was in Rome on holiday, and she had met a wonderfully attractive *golden* man, who was not only thoughtful and considerate but also culturally adept. This was no time for *baiting* or arguing. She wasn't writing a paper, for heaven's sake. For some reason, the scholar within always found its way to the surface and produced an agonistic environment whenever she began a new friendship.

"*All right, idiot,*" thought Opal to herself, "*What are you going to do, alienate him because he's not as enamoured with New York as you? Get a grip!*"

Roger was now standing and glancing at his watch.

"*Uh-oh,*" thought Opal, "*Fix this before he leaves.*"

"Let's agree to disagree," said Opal standing next to Roger,

"Besides, I'd much rather hear about that cup you're so anxious to win. It's the World's Cup, isn't it?"

Roger took Opal's empty sorbet cup as she nibbled on the tiny cone. "Let's throw this away, shall we?" He placed the empty cup into the nearest trash receptacle and then took Opal's hand. They stepped over the rail and walked slowly down the walkway towards the sidewalk cafes that lined the cobblestone streets near the fountain. "It's the European Cup," said Roger at last. "Manchester will prevail over Barcelona."

"And you're rooting for Manchester?" asked Opal.

Roger looked at her incredulously but answered with a sigh, "Yes."

"I can't imagine that you came all the way from Great Britain to Rome just to watch a soccer game," said Opal.

Roger clenched his hand, the one that was not caressing Opal's hand.

"It is football," said Roger calmly.

"It's just a game, isn't it?" asked Opal in earnest. "I don't understand why you and your friends would travel all the way to Rome just to watch a game? You could watch it on TV. It's all the same, isn't it?"

Roger stopped walking. It appeared that his bottom lip was beginning to quiver. He released Opal's hand.

"I'm sorry," said Opal, "I've hurt your feelings. I do this all the time. I visit a new and exciting part of the world, and I always end up offending someone. I'm really sorry. We don't seem to take sports as seriously in the US as you do here in Europe."

"I don't think that those United States of yours take *anything* as seriously as we do in this part of the world," said Roger resuming his calm, casual gait. He reached for Opal's hand again, obviously remembering that she was from what he considered to be a backward, indifferent, and oftentimes vulgar country. "There is much that you must learn. The United States has only been in existence a couple of hundred years, while the

British can boast over a thousand years of establishing culture and civilization. Fear not, I plan to enlighten you."

How condescending, thought Opal. *Does he really think that I don't know that he's patronizing me? What is he trying to say about America, anyway?*

"This seems to be an agreeable place," said Roger stopping in front of a café with, seemingly, acres of cascading vines and lavender flowers overhanging the roof.

"It's lovely," said Opal relaxing and gaining control of her breath. "How beautiful. We don't have anything like..." She stopped in mid-sentence. Roger smiled. He was making progress. He would enlighten her if it killed him.

Trying to cross the street in Rome was taxing. Were cars really expected to stop when a pedestrian left the curb? What if someone were having a difficult day and did not want to comply with the rules of road etiquette, or if someone decided that he didn't like the looks of the person leaving the curb? The Romans Opal met were a friendly lot, but there were others who didn't seem very gracious; specifically, the man waiting at a different bus stop who muttered audibly, "Spanish bastards," when a group of noisy Barcelonan revelers passed cheering and singing. Perhaps it was the bus people and not the motorists who could not be trusted to comply with the rules of etiquette. Be that as it may, Opal was not prepared to step out into the busy street hoping that the cars would stop. She waited on the curb until two or three other people, all Romans, crossed, and she accompanied them like a little girl waiting for an adult to help her navigate the crosswalk.

The streets were not the only perplexing thing about Rome. The relationship between the tourists and the natives seemed complex. The tourists always placed a metrocard into the machine that registered metrocards on the bus. The natives simply climbed aboard using both the front and the back doors and did not pay any fare at all. Opal considered riding free but changed her mind when informed by the hotel clerk that if the driver asked for a metrocard and the passenger did not produce one, the fee was one-hundred Euros. The thought of not paying a fine or breaking any law in Italy was most distressing, so Opal purchased a metrocard each day, although the drivers did not stop anyone, to her knowledge.

The subways were the cleanest, most efficient trains that Opal had ever encountered. They were certainly a far cry from the dirty, gritty New York subways. Each station was well-lit, immaculate, and wonderfully colored with bright, cheerful paint; the maps on the wall were easy to navigate. People were polite and allowed entrance to cars without pushing, but the tourists and the natives seemed to part company where petty theft was concerned. The natives looked away when an elderly crone tried to pick a tourist's pocket while he boarded the train. The crone, who favored the witch in *Snow White*, had long, straggly hair and a protracted nose. The tourist grasped the crone's hand and held onto his wallet. The determined crone stood in the subway door and clung to the wallet trying to pull it from his pocket. Even though the Roman natives were witnessing this disconcerting event, no one tried to assist the tourist, who was yelling, "Get away from my wallet!" He managed to retrieve the wallet before the train doors closed, leaving his assailant on the platform foiled. Inside the subway car, the tourist said with amusement and surprise, "Pickpocket!" He seemed to consider it a part of the Roman adventure, but the scene was etched in Opal's consciousness, and she clung to her purse realizing that she could not expect any help from the Roman natives if she were to encounter a determined thief or assailant.

The subway continued on its route without further incident. People read newspapers, unfolded maps, or viewed the monitor, which was showing a public service video. Opal disembarked at the Coliseum stop, where Roger would meet her at noon with a surprise.

Opal loved surprises and wondered what would await her at the Coliseum. It was her second visit to the Coliseum, which was her first tourist stop when she arrived a week ago. The view of the Coliseum was splendorous from the subway exit. As soon as one left the station, the Coliseum was right there like a three-dimensional photo. It overwhelmed and took onlookers quite by surprise with its majestic aura and its 3D proximity. Opal stopped to take another picture. As she walked across the street, this time with a crossing guard and a traffic light directing the hordes of tourists, Opal realized that the remaining days of Roman splendor were dwindling down. In a few days, she would pack and return to New York for summer session. She maneuvered herself through the crowds of people and *Roman centurions* dressed in costumes complete with shields and swords, and looked for Roger on the grounds adjacent to the Coliseum entrance. He was late, as usual.

Opal liked the idea of saying, "Roger is late, as usual." It gave the illusion that she really knew him; in truth, she knew little about him. She had only known him three days, but in those three days, he knew almost everything about her. Roger seemed to be on a mission, of sorts, to elevate her out of the lamentable state of intellectual lethargy into the ethereal air of his classical education - all in three days. He wanted to know what she read and what she thought about her readings. He wanted to know her ideas of politics and social conditions around the world. He wanted to know her worldview before he decided how much time he would invest in her and whether or not he would be able to tailor her to suit himself, if he found her to be worthy of his time and effort. Opal was happy just to catch a glimpse of the golden hairs that glistened on his legs in the Roman sun, which seemed to prove his assertion that Americans did not take many things seriously. What did he expect? She was on vacation; it was not the time to think of intellectual conundrums. Despite her efforts to relinquish all thoughts of the intellectual life from her mind, thoughts of summer session commanded her attention.

Summer classes were a misery, but Opal wanted to graduate with her Master's Degree at the end of fall semester; hence, summer session was required. She was also expected back at work next week. Opal worked part-time at The Strand Bookstore, which was conveniently located near the university. Her roommate, Heather, would expect her half of the rent next week. Opal had already made two withdrawals from her emergency fund - the fund for home expenses that she vowed she would not touch while on vacation. It could not be helped. Rome was frightfully expensive, and she might not be able to return until she completed her Ph.D. in comparative literature, provided she gained acceptance into the program the following spring semester. Surely, Jim would help her replenish her funds. He always helped her when she went *bankrupt*, which was every two months or so.

Jim and Opal had been dating for over a year. They met at a seafood restaurant, where Jim was employed part-time. He was a student also, only he was a proud student of the City University of New York. He often teased her of her privileged private university existence. Jim was completing work on his Bachelor's Degree and had been doing so for the past six years. Even at the public university, his financial resources were exceedingly limited, but he was diligent and could foresee the culmination of his efforts. He would graduate in June and planned to attend law school while Opal pursued her doctorate. It seemed like a match made in heaven, but there were problems. Opal's worldview clashed vehemently with Jim's. He could not fathom why she would spend money on a trip to Rome when she should be preparing for summer session, but Opal was adventurous and believed that *the world was her oyster*. Oysters, for Jim, had a strictly utilitarian purpose. People ate them and then paid their checks at the restaurant leaving him a nice tip. For Opal, the world was an entire metaphor. The oyster, in particular, was her favorite metaphor, for it emblematized her worldview as an aesthete. Jim accompanied Opal to art galleries, the ballet, the Metropolitan Opera's free outdoor performances at Lincoln Center, the New York Philharmonic's free concerts in Central Park, and her favorite—the Metropolitan Museum of Art; he was always bored and listless. Jim liked to bowl or play baseball with his cronies, who travelled to Montreal each summer to play other teams of cronies. The thought that Opal would travel to Rome to gaze at the Sistine Chapel, Michelangelo's *Pietà*, or the flowing fountains of Rome adorned with beautiful sculptures was incomprehensible to Jim, and these activities commanded an intolerable financial expenditure; yet, he saved his tips from the restaurant and gave her two hundred dollars for spending money in Rome. Of course, the two-hundred dollars was gone before Opal left JFK Airport. There were so many things that she needed for the trip – little things like flip-flops, makeup, a new travel journal, books to read on the plane, a hat (the sun was merciless in Rome), and a host of other things that travelers require. She did not tell Jim about her expenditures, and she knew that she would be forced to dip into her household fund, but Rome awaited.

Opal rationalized that airfare was a bargain. The entire roundtrip ticket cost a mere $349 on Alitalia Airlines. It was an unbelievable offer. The airlines cut fares in January, and the advertisement appeared in *The New York Times* one cold, sunny Tuesday afternoon. Opal had $500 in savings for emergencies. This was an emergency. When would she ever be able to travel to Rome roundtrip for $349? Of course, she would purchase a ticket and travel at the end of spring semester. It was a glorious vacation, but it was drawing to a close. Today, she would meet the *golden* man at the Coliseum, who waited with a surprise. She hoped that Roger would wear his Bermuda shorts so that she could glimpse the golden hairs that gently covered his well-toned, well-formed legs. She had no hope of viewing the hair on his arms, for he always wore an Oxford shirt with the cuffs turned up. Roger carried himself with the utmost dignity and refinement, but he was also quite whimsical and had a wonderful sense of humor. Opal would miss him. She wondered what Jim, with the heart of gold, rough hands, and pale legs covered with unseemly dark hair, would think of Roger, with the golden hairs springing from his arms and legs, winsome smile, and education based upon a thousand years of civility and elite erudition.

On the day they met, Roger stood behind Opal on a crowded bus and began a polite conversation with his friends about the upcoming game. He was close enough to smell her hair and accidently graze her hand as they shared the rail overhead with the multitudinous commuters on the hot, sticky bus. He could sense that Opal was aware of his presence, even without the accidental touch. He could feel her eyes gazing upon the *golden* hair on the lower part of his arm as it clutched the overhead rail. The bus careened through the heavily trafficked thoroughfare filled with motor scooters, smart cars, and fearless pedestrians. Roger and his friends disagreed mildly about the game and sought the opinion of an innocent bystander, who was, of course, his prey – Opal. It was a clever but predictable way for singles to meet. Roger's group had employed the use of this scheme many times with moderate success. The Roman women were savvy and refused to cooperate. Opal, the American, seemed oblivious to the game plan. There was something refreshingly naive about Opal that endeared her to Roger. Most of the women he knew were pragmatic to a fault. He marveled at the literal texture which seemed to envelop Opal and was surprised to learn that she was a graduate student. Of course, she was a graduate student at an American university, which would explain the absence of depth and abstraction. Roger found most Americans to be rather one-dimensional. Opal did not contradict the assumption. His friends were gratified that their scheme worked at least once in Rome. Roger and Opal made plans to meet at the Trevi Fountain the next day. Roger exited the bus with Opal and walked her to her hotel.

Roger Paisley was a man of few words. He revered words and did not waste them. Roger was a journalist and worked for a rather large publishing firm twenty minutes from London. He was an Oxford graduate and was working on his first novel. In point of fact, Roger was gathering material for his novel with the trip to Rome. Meeting Opal was as deliberate as any of Roger's actions. He heard her speak as she ordered a sorbet in the sorbet shop near the Trevi Fountain and determined that she was a tourist worth following. She seemed to be travelling alone, and there was something intriguing about her. She interested him, and he followed her most of her first day in Rome, unbeknownst to Opal. That was the way Roger obtained material for his novels. He studied the habits, speaking patterns, and movements of people. If possible, he engaged them in conversation to ascertain their viewpoints on various subjects. Opal loved Trevi Fountain and spent most of her first day in Rome admiring its sublime beauty. Watching from a distance, Roger observed the young American enjoying the crisp sounds of the water cascading into the fountain. He knew where she liked to sit and the type of sorbet that she seemed to enjoy. Roger watched her check her BlackBerry numerous times and noted the look of disappointment on her face when the messages were not as she had hoped. He observed her willingness to photograph happy couples when they approached her and asked if she would photograph them by the fountain, and he wondered why there was no one to take a photo with her before the festive fountain. The American carried no bags of souvenirs, which was unusual. It suggested her funds might be limited. Opal passed the first portion of her *exam* admirably. She was congenial. After meeting her and reaching a certain comfort level, Roger said things that were blatantly not in keeping with his value system in order to ascertain her belief systems and to test her ability to present a viable argument to examine them. Very few things seemed to inspire Opal's passion. She had no interest in social or political issues, but she had a keen sense of responsibility for endangered species. It was a start. They had one more day in Rome together, and Roger would use it to his best advantage. Opal would remain for four more days, and he wanted to be certain that she would spend the valuable time learning things that he considered important to her travel experience, if she was going to become a part of his life. There were places that she must see and places where she should not traverse. There were people she must meet and others she must avoid. There was only one day, but one day would be sufficient.

Roger called to Opal from a long line surrounding a showcase of some sort. He waved so that she would see him. Opal joined him in the line and felt disappointed that he was wearing his khakis and not his shorts. Apart from his exposed wrists, which were visible beneath his oxford shirt turned up at the cuff, his entire body was covered.

"There it is," said Roger nodding towards the showcase. Opal glimpsed a large silver trophy behind a glass enclosure. Guards surrounded it, and a line encircled it.

"What is that?" asked Opal noticing people taking pictures beside it when the line progressed.

"It's the European Cup," said Roger proudly. "We'll take a picture before it and then make our way to Trevi Fountain for the final pre-game cheering session."

Opal was less than enthused. "Is this the surprise?"

"Yes," said Roger beaming enthusiastically. "I knew that you would like it." Roger placed a Manchester banner around his shoulders. Behind Opal and Roger were four or five men with identical Manchester banners draped over their bodies. Roger introduced Opal to his friends. They all looked like young bankers, pale, bookish, and rather out of place beneath Rome's sun-drenched skies. Roger was the only one who brought a female companion. The others were looking over the crowds for kindred spirits who might want to spend one last afternoon with them. Of course, there would be many opportunities for new friendships at the post-game party. Roger's friends seemed harmless, and they were exceedingly well-mannered. To Opal's surprise, they asked many questions about the United States, particularly about the film industry.

"It's all a myth," assured Opal. "Most Americans do not live like that. We're pretty much like everyone else."

"Well, you are," said Roger. "She lives in New York. They're speaking about the people in California."

"New York, really?" asked Noel. His hair was pleasantly brown. "I would love to visit New York. Do you live near Wall Street?"

"No, but you should visit some time," said Opal. "You should all visit. I would love to show you around."

The invitation heightened the already elevated spirits of the group. George, another member of the group, stood directly behind Roger and seemed to evaluate Opal's appearance and demeanor.

"Did everyone hear that?" asked George. "Opal has invited us to New York. I hope that she won't change her mind after getting to know Roger. Some people find him a bit redundant and somewhat of an anachronism, but we love him." George pinched Roger's cheeks playfully. Roger seemed less than amused and brushed George's hand away.

Roger led Opal to the encased silver cup. A man dressed in black took their cameras and snapped their photos. He ushered them off of the platform and reached for the cameras of Roger's friends. Roger hurried back onto the platform and took pictures with his friends. They stood as stoic gladiators ready to do battle, and the Manchester banners draped over their shoulders transformed the *Clark Kent six-pack* into a curious form of nimble superheroes ready to pounce upon the limp-kneed Barcelonans.

The group accompanied Roger and Opal around the

Coliseum and sat with them on the grass talking and sharing strategies on how the Manchester team would defeat the Barcelonans. It surprised Opal to know that they would be returning to various parts of the UK the next day. They had been in Rome for a week and a half. There was only one day left, and it seemed as though Opal would not have any free time with Roger. It was just as well. He viewed anything outside of the realm of Great Britain to be more than marginally inferior. Roger was lovely to gaze upon, but almost every word that emitted from his lips was sweetly condescending.

The Barcelonans were in town. How could anyone ignore them? They swarmed through the streets of Rome waving their Barcelonan flags through the air and singing boisterously. Interestingly, there were many women, children, and babies in attendance. Opal had not noticed a preponderance of British women and children attending the games, but the Barcelonans brought everyone – aunts, uncles, cousins, the entire city, or so it seemed. Festive Barcelonans were everywhere. There was not a space on a bus or a train that was not occupied by Barcelonans. They outnumbered the Romans in their own city. Commuter lines became unbearably long. Most Romans and tourists seemed to endure the infusion of Barcelonan pride and revelry with great patience. On the cheerful, festive subways, Barcelonans packed into the cars like sardines pounding the ceiling with their fists, singing, chanting, swirling banners and flags, and most importantly, smiling. They were a happy group, and they did not seem to mind sharing their joy with everyone.

The Roman police were out in full-force, but if the truth be known, it would have been difficult to prevent any outbursts of disagreeable behavior by the sheer number of the revelers. In such a crowd, one could easily become lost, and that is, precisely, what happened to Opal and Roger. There were too many Barcelonans streaming into and out of the subway cars. The noise level was a few decimals louder than Opal could bear. She tried to hold onto the rail and protect her ears as well. When the *army* of revelers poured out of the subway car, Opal got swept up in the midst of them. Roger yelled to her as she stood on the platform engulfed by the enthusiasts.

"Meet me at Trevi!!" yelled Roger as the subway doors closed. Opal could barely see him as she tried to move through the crowds. The train rumbled down the clean, cheerful tracks. Barcelonan revelers continued to sing happily and seemed to include Opal in their festivities. They sung and spoke in Spanish. Opal knew a little Spanish, but she didn't know enough to say, "Be quiet, why don't you. I'm lost!" She disentangled herself from the group and tried to catch her breath as they trudged up the stairs to the exit and another group descended the stairs singing, dancing, and cheering.

Opal had no idea where she was, and it was difficult to see the maps on the subway walls. The Barcelonans' lyrical *walls* replaced the subway walls. She looked around, but none of them seemed to be singing in English. Where was she, and how would she get to the Trevi Fountain? It was frustrating, to say the least. Suddenly, an idea occurred to her. There was a cheering session scheduled at the Trevi Fountain. The Barcelonans must be attending the session. She would follow them - not that she had a choice. The next train pulled up, and once again, Opal was swept up in the crowd and back onto the subway. The festivities continued in the subway car, only the singing and chanting grew more fervent, if that was possible. Remarkably, something else occurred to Opal. She remembered Roger's affirmation that Europeans took their games seriously. Here was the proof. It was not just a game, as Opal had imagined. The teams seemed to be fighting for the championship of nations. She remembered a news article that she read some time ago about the problems David Beckham faced when he insisted upon playing part of the season with his European compatriots. Many American soccer fans considered him a traitor, but he was being loyal. Americans knew little of this type of loyalty. When had they ever been given the opportunity to learn this peculiar mindset? Each American state was connected (apart from Hawaii and Alaska). Although each state embraced a different lifestyle and regional culture, all were a part of one country - the United States of America. The Europeans were connected also, but they were not states – they were independent nations, and they guarded their national identities with the same fervor that the Barcelonans were exemplifying in Rome.

Opal exited the train again at the next stop, or rather, she was whisked away with the crowd. This time, she climbed the stairs to the exit with the frolickers with hopes of obtaining directions from passersby to the Trevi Fountain. There was a brown, wooden sign with three or four yellow-trimmed arrows, each pointing in a different direction. One arrow read the Fountain of Trevi. Opal did not need to follow the arrow. She followed the festive chanters raising flags and banners over their heads. She could hear the deafening sound of more chanters in the distance. As she approached the glorious fountain, Opal was amazed. The area was a sea of blue and yellow – colors of the Barcelonan banners and flags. Barcelonans flooded the seating area and all of the entryways. There, on the right-hand side of the fountain, stood the Manchester revelers. Their red and white flags and banners were unfurled civilly over the rail. They stood seventy-five strong, and they cheered with great diction and impeccable English, as it were; lamentably, the five-hundred or so Barcelonans outnumbered, out-sang, and out-cheered them. Not to be undone, the Manchester group began taking off their shirts and swirling them over their heads. One member even climbed upon a rock within the Trevi Fountain and placed a Manchester banner near the statue of Neptune. The Roman police quickly removed the banner and led him away. Roger stood with his friends near the rail, and the *golden* hairs on his chest glistened in the hot, happy sunshine. He swung his shirt over his head along with the other Manchester supporters. Here was a man, who declined to show any portion of his trim, well-toned body beyond the knee or wrist during normal times; yet, here he was, standing in the blazing sun baring his savory chest for the honour of Britain. The Barcelonan's answered the bare British chests with thunderous chants, which were in Spanish, so Opal had no idea what they were responding. She was filled with glee at this spectacle, but she wondered how she would ever reach Roger before the game. She had no ticket, and the event was, of course, sold out. It was a quandary.

Much to Opal's surprise, the stadium where the final game was to be played was only a block or so from her hotel. Oddly, she hadn't noticed a stadium during her stay. There were many strange occurrences. When she returned to the hotel, the desk clerk presented her with a bouquet of red roses. They were from Roger. Why would Roger send roses? Why wouldn't he simply give them to her after the game? Opal surmised that it must have been a final farewell gesture. Opal reasoned that if Manchester won, Roger would celebrate with the team and the other Brits. If Manchester lost, he would not be in the mood to celebrate or to discuss the devastating blow with a woman who could not understand why he hadn't remained in England to watch the game on television. As he swung his shirt over his head at the fountain, there was a certain look about Roger that Opal found disconcerting. She hadn't known him long, but she had never seen that expression on his face. It was not a look of revelry; it was a bombastic look that indicated that the Barcelonans manifested sheer gall to chant at the glory of Britain. They were not within the same echelon of humanity. Opal saw this in his eyes at a distance. What had Barcelona ever done for civilization? Europe should have simply presented the cup to Manchester out of gratitude. It would have been the same response had the opposing team been from France or

Brazil or the United States of America. England was superior and did not require a silver cup to prove its mettle. It had done so since time immemorial. Perhaps this attitude was engrained within its citizenry from birth. Opal, for some reason, felt sorry for the Barcelonans. If they lost, they would return home with, seemingly, nothing – neither pride nor dignity. It did not matter whether Manchester won or lost. Either way, the British would return home with pride and dignity intact.

Opal carried her roses into the lounge, which was filled with Barcelonans watching the game on television. As usual, they were cheering and creating a festive scene of optimistic enthusiasm. Opal sat in the midst of them and watched the game on the rather small television. They were smiling and seemed to welcome her. Opal wondered if they would be upset if they knew that despite Manchester's condescending attitude, she was rooting for them. Perhaps it was the English connection. It was difficult to root for a team that did not share the English language—a beautiful language. Were it not for England, Opal wondered what language Americans would speak. Language was of the utmost importance. She would cheer for Manchester in gratitude for the English language. Of course, her cheers were silent, and she tried not to let the Barcelonans see the gleam in her eye whenever Manchester scored. The Barcelonans continued to smile and to welcome her, the traitor in their midst.

The thought occurred to Opal that she may never see Roger again. She pressed her nose against one of the rose petals. A Barcelonan woman sitting next to her smiled broadly and said that the roses were beautiful in Spanish. Opal thanked her in English. It was the least she could do to support her team. Yes, the roses were a parting gesture. Opal was certain that she would neither see nor hear from Roger again. They were two ships that passed under the beautiful Roman sky. Roger would be gone tomorrow, with or without the European Cup, and Opal would enjoy the remaining days of her vacation in gratitude that she had spent three lovely days with a handsome, *golden* man, who loved his country and cared enough to send her red roses before he parted. She left the lounge carrying her roses and did not bother to turn the game on in her room. What was the point? She had no interest in soccer or football – whatever it was called. She prepared for bed and went to sleep. It had been an exhausting day.

Later in the evening, her hotel phone rang. It was Roger. Opal rubbed the sleep from her eyes and thanked him for the roses. There were muted voices in the background. Barcelona won the European Cup, which surprised Opal. She expected unimaginable noise and revelry if they won, but all was silent. Opal looked out of the window; she was astounded that all was still and quiet. Even the revelers in the hotel had not made a sound. What kind of netherworld was this? After all the cheering and chanting, the Barcelonans were, seemingly, speechless after winning the cup. Had she slept through it all? It was too late to meet, but Roger wondered whether she would like to meet him at the Trevi Fountain before his afternoon flight to England. Opal accepted with great pleasure. The voices in the background were becoming clearer, as though they were closer to the phone. The voices urged Roger to hang up and return to the festive gathering. One voice was particularly disconcerting. It was a man's voice, and it seemed to be speaking right next to the phone's mouthpiece. Roger said goodbye and hung up quickly.

Why was she spending so much time thinking about Roger? Opal was in Rome, a glorious city with so much beauty to behold. How did Roger creep into her thoughts with such constancy? She wasn't void of friends or a love interest. Why was this man always in her thoughts? Opal decided to change her thoughts. Roger and his friends would be gone by the end of the day, and she would probably never see or hear from him again. Opal determined to focus upon the intoxicating beauty of Rome and let her thoughts marvel at its wonders.

Everything was back to normal on the streets. There was room on the buses and subways again. It appeared that the Barcelonans had taken their cup and left *en masse*. The streets were placid once more, apart from the buzz of the motor scooters zigzagging through traffic. Tourists filled the seating area of the Trevi Fountain taking pictures or simply sitting listening to the water splashing against the rocks. Roger was not present. He was late, as usual. Opal settled into her seat and gazed into the tremulous waters.

"So, what will you do for four days?" asked a voice behind her. It was Roger. He was wearing an oxford button-down shirt, blue this time, and a pair of seersucker pants. He wore a gentleman's straw hat and a pair of dark sunglasses. All that was missing was a walking cane and a pair of lambskin gloves. He did not sit, so Opal rose and stood beside him.

"I'm sorry about the game," said Opal earnestly.

"You didn't answer my question," said Roger. He seemed serious, more serious than she had observed in the past three days. He seemed sad somehow or deep in thought and in a different mode. No longer was it the vacation, anticipatory mode. He reminded her of an Oxford don. Of course, Opal had never met an Oxford don, but this was how she thought one might look. She felt like the student who had left her homework and had to explain her carelessness to the teacher or Don, in this instance.

"I don't know," said Opal. "There's so much to see. I guess I'll just wander around soaking up the environment. I'll enjoy whatever comes across my path."

"I've prepared this for you," said Roger presenting her with a list of places to visit. The list included things she should observe at each site. The list was quite extensive. Opal felt as though there would be a quiz after her observations. "I also brought these for you."

Roger gave Opal a bag from a local bookstore with three books inside. The books were new and seemed to be rather obscure English literature. Opal took one of the books from the bag.

"*The Good Soldier?* I've never heard of Ford Madox Ford. What a strange name," said Opal leafing through the book. It wasn't too long. Perhaps she could read it on the plane ride home. Surely, he did not expect her to read it while on vacation.

"The others are Trollope," said Roger. "There wasn't much of a selection at the book store, but I will send you subsequent texts when you return home. You must read everything I send you."

Opal looked at Roger curiously. Was this his farewell – books? Had he forgotten that she was a graduate student specializing in English literature? Apparently not. All of the books were English literature, but none of them were books that were a part of her university's curriculum – and it was a respected American university. He was doing it again. Somehow, Roger considered the United States to be patently inferior to England.

"Thank you," said Opal, "and thank you for the roses. They were beautiful."

"I did not send the roses," said Roger. Opal could not see his eyes beneath the dark glasses. She wondered if they were, indeed, brown. Why was he wearing dark glasses anyway? The sun shone at the same intensity it had for the past three days, and Roger did not wear dark glasses then. It was all very strange.

"Really? Your name was on the card," said Opal.

"George sent them to you from me," said Roger. "I'm afraid I was not myself after the party celebrating our victory."

"But you lost," said Opal confusedly. Roger smiled.

"Britain never loses," said Roger. "You will learn that."

"Well, thanks anyway for the roses. I suppose it's the thought that counts," said Opal trying to ignore Roger's smug, condescending demeanor. *Who do these people think they are?* wondered Opal.

"I will need an address so that I can send the parcels," said Roger matter-of-factly. He gave her a pen and a small white pad, knowing that she had neither pen nor paper in her large, white purse. Opal wrote her address and included her phone number and email address, in the event he wanted to contact her. She presented the pad to him smiling, but Roger did not smile. He placed the pad in his pocket. Opal wished that she could see his eyes; the glasses were too dark.

"I must prepare for my flight," said Roger somberly, "but I have one more request."

Opal looked at him; rather, she looked at his dark glasses.

"I would like to meet you here next year, right at this spot," said Roger. Opal looked down at the pavement under her feet.

Roger sighed impatiently. "I have never known anyone who takes everything so literally. What I mean is that I would like to meet you here at the Trevi Fountain in a year's time. Do you agree?"

"Will I have to read more books?" asked Opal. It was supposed to be a joke, but Roger did not smile. She wondered why he seemed so sad.

"Will you return?" asked Roger emphatically.

"I will try," said Opal.

"That is not a commitment," said Roger. "You must commit yourself to me."

Opal was taken aback. Whatever did he mean? She had only known him three days. She hadn't even committed herself to Jim, and she had known him for over a year.

"I don't know what you mean," said Opal.

"Yes, you do," said Roger. "I want to hear you say it. Say that you will commit yourself to me and return here next year."

Opal stood silently. This was awkward. "You don't know me, and I don't know you. I have a boyfriend in New York," said Opal experiencing a great amount of disconcertion.

"Has he asked you to commit yourself to him?" asked Roger.

Opal thought of Jim. Their relationship was understood. They got along beautifully and loved being together, but neither of them had made a formal declaration of commitment. Was this some type of British tradition? Americans declare love. They don't declare commitment until the wedding vows, if they ever progress that far. Was Roger asking for her hand in marriage? Opal's American brain could not comprehend this turn of events. It would require deep reflection, and she was on vacation. There could be no deep reflection while on vacation. That was what vacations were all about - removing oneself from deep thought. Before she realized it, Opal heard herself saying, "I commit, and I will return next year to this spot."

She felt like a zombie muttering words that seemed to escape from her mouth without her control. Most people throw coins over their shoulders into the Trevi Fountain to ensure a return to Rome, but on this day in May, Opal Featherton uttered, "I commit" and destined her return to Rome and her commitment to Roger Paisley.

Opal tried to relive the moments before she uttered, "I commit," as she stood on the unending line to enter St. Peter's Basilica. The sun shone so brightly that it seemed to sear her skin. Opal's white sunhat offered a small degree of relief, but the rest of her body was soaked with perspiration. After an hour's wait, the line progressed closer to the entrance, where the clothing police inspected each person's attire in order to determine whether or not he or she was fit to enter the Basilica. Signs were posted everywhere, some of which had stick figure drawings for those who could not read. Entrance was denied to anyone wearing shorts, halters, or sleeveless shirts. A large red line crossed the stick figures of those clad in inappropriate attire. Opal wore a sleeveless, navy blue sundress with flouncy ripples on the bottom that moved festively when she walked. She carried a navy and white polka dot shawl and draped it over her shoulders as she approached the guards. She gained permission to proceed to the next group of clothing police, who stood four yards from the metal detectors. This section was engaged in discord, for a woman managed to pass to the second clothing check wearing paper napkins placed under her sleeveless shirt. She argued that her shoulders were covered, but the clothing police ejected her from the line.

Upon entering the Basilica, Opal was drawn to the resplendent light to the right of the Basilica. There, behind a glass encasement was Michelangelo's *Pietá*. Opal felt as though she wanted to kneel down to pray before this sublime statue of the Madonna holding the crucified Christ across her lap. The *Pietá* was one of Opal's main reasons for traveling to Rome, the seat of the Roman Catholic faith. She wanted to study the beautiful artwork and architecture, and now, she stood before Michelangelo's masterpiece. It did not wind her and make her feel as though she would collapse to the floor, as did the genteel ferocity of the plaster cast of Michelangelo's *David* at the Victoria and Albert Museum in London. Quite the contrary, this statue compelled a graceful gentleness that urged commitment on a higher realm. There was that word again, *commitment*. For some reason, Opal could not get the word out of her mind, even while standing before the splendiferous *Pietá*. She quickly moved from the magnanimous statue and proceeded towards the breathtaking High Altar. Opal had never seen an altar so high, and the swirling, brown columns that stood on each side made her mouth open with wonder. She approached the High Altar slowly, but something to her right seemed to beckon her. It was a chapel for praying and not sightseeing.

A heavy red curtain hid the chapel from the sightseers. Opal entered the chapel and sat in one of the chairs near the altar. Several people were praying silently. Opal took her Rosary from her purse and held it as the words, *I commit* swirled through her mind. What did it mean? Why couldn't she forget these words? They were just words. Why did they seem to be entangled with every fiber of her being? What had Roger done? Was it some type of British spell? Opal thought of Harry Potter waving his wand through the air pronouncing some unpronounceable word and making people and things change. Had she been reading too many books? Opal did not know what had happened at the Trevi Fountain, but she could feel that her life was changing. She made a commitment, and the glorious *Pietá*, the small, unassuming chapel, and the imperious High Altar seemed to work in tandem to ensure that her commitment was officially sanctioned. Roger was on a plane back to England, but he had left an indelible mark within her. It was not a mark *upon* her, it was a mark *within* her. Opal began to feel a sense of trepidation. Something was different. It was something otherworldly, and it seemed to grasp hold of her.

Nervously, Opal left the Basilica and entered St. Peter's Square. She sat in a shady area on the steps to the right of the Basilica, where all of the tourists sat to rest or sip cool beverages or nibble Italian ice treats from the nearby stand. She told herself to relax. The heat was getting the better of her. Her imagination was running away with her. There was no call for disconcertion. Opal nibbled on the lemon-lime Italian ice treat. Slowly, she began to relax and enjoy the surroundings of St. Peter's Square. What a wonderful vacation. Rome truly was an *eternal* city. Three young priests sauntered along the Square near the shady steps. The surroundings seemed new to them, for their expressions almost mirrored the tourists' expressions of amazement, wonder, and appreciation. One of the priests looked directly at Opal, almost as though he recognized some intangible essence. He smiled at her; his glance seemed to congratulate her. *He knows*, thought Opal, *he knows about the commitment.* Opal watched the priests as they walked along the shady area to the end of the Square and onto the tourist-filled street. *What the heck is going on here?* thought Opal. *No, you're imagining it. You stood in the sun too long this afternoon, that's all. What you need is a good nap. Go back to the hotel and take a nap.*

Opal could not finish her ice. She discarded it in a nearby trash bin and hurried to the nearest bus stop, but the list that Roger gave her flashed upon her memory. She removed it from her purse. According to the list, she should visit the *Sistine Chapel* next. Opal realized that she was in Vatican City. The Vatican was its own sovereign state, even though it was located in the heart of Rome. The Vatican was right next door, so Opal began her trek to the winding line of tourists waiting to enter the stone-wall fortress that surrounded The *Vaticano*.

The protective walls surrounding the Vatican reminded Opal of the Alamo. Swiss Guards manned their posts surrounding the area. The ones near the entrance wore blue and white uniforms, but the closer one got to the sacred area, the Swiss Guard wore yellow and blue uniforms that made Opal think of the festive attire of clowns, but these guards were far from being clowns. From their icy expressions to their blue stockings, they gave the impression that they were ready to defend the Vatican at any cost. Certainly, they were not people with whom one should trifle. Opal could feel her BlackBerry vibrating from within her purse. She checked her messages. There was a message from Jim. Strange, she had not really thought of Jim during her trip. How easy it was to forget him, after all he had done for her. How easy it was to remember a man she had only known three days. *Call me,* the message said. Opal knew that she would not. What could she say? Perhaps Roger was just an excuse to end her relationship with Jim. If they had not made any type of commitment in a year, then perhaps it was time for both of them to move on. There was that word again. Life was less complicated before she met Roger. Now, she had books to read, a vacation to plan, and a commitment to fulfill.

The line proceeded slowly into the Vatican. Opal purchased a ticket and followed the signs to the Sistine Chapel. After walking through numerous hallways filled with artwork, some of which was on the ceiling, Opal entered a small passageway with the other tourists. Immediately, the atmosphere changed. It was darker and less festive. There were benches alongside the walls of the Sistine Chapel, and to Opal's surprise, it was an actual chapel with an altar, candles, and a Crucifix. Behind the altar was Michelangelo's floor to ceiling painting of *The Judgment*. Such blues and greens Opal had never seen. They were the most vivid colors that had ever entered her consciousness. The images were frightening, as was to be expected. It was, after all, a time of judgment. Up above were the famous paintings that made the chapel renown. There was nothing frightening up there. Opal was familiar with the paintings of the Sistine Chapel. She had seen them in many books and on many posters. She tried to imagine Michelangelo lying on his back on a scaffold painting the sublime masterpiece. The sounds of the guards' voices pierced the chapel. "Silence!" they demanded. People calmed their excited spirits in the presence of such splendor and quieted their voices. It did not last long, however. Within minutes, the uproar began again. One could not help it. The "oohs" and "ahhs" were not only audible, but they were also amplified with each moment they spent before the inexpressible beauty of the magnificent artwork. The guards began to clap their hands to ensure silence. "No pictures!" they yelled when tourists tried to sneak a photo. They were insistent that people respect the chapel as a place of reverence and prayer. A space opened up on one of the benches. Opal sat on the bench and perused the darkened room. The vivid colors of the paintings were striking, and they pierced the darkness. Opal tried to find the painting of God's finger touching Adam's finger. There it was! Opal could not believe that she was actually sitting beneath Michelangelo's jewel. There was more clapping and pronouncements of "Silence!" It did not matter. The Sistine Chapel was a place to forget about clapping and pronouncements. For some reason, she wanted to cry, and so she did. Tears began to stream down her face. Such beauty deserved tears. Opal looked at *The Judgment* again behind the altar. It garnered her attention even more than the beautiful works upon the ceiling. It seemed to want to relay a message. She would be held accountable. She made a vow. Vows were not to be taken lightly. What was she thinking? Why did she do it? It did not matter. The die was cast. She made a commitment, and she would have to honor it. Were the tears for the glorious works of art, or were they for herself? Perhaps Roger would break his vow, but as Opal recalled, he did not vow. He did not make a commitment. How unfair. He demanded a commitment, but he did not commit in any way. Surely, this was a loophole - perhaps not. Why was she surrounded with religious things? Why was she in the Vatican? It felt as though the walls and the ceiling were closing in on her. Why was this *commitment* occupying so much of her thoughts? She was on vacation, for heaven's sake. People say all sorts of foolish things on vacation. Why was she crying? She could not extricate herself from the *commitment*. Opal wiped her eyes with her handkerchief and took several yoga breaths. When she felt calm, she stood up and walked slowly to the exit. She would feel better in the bright, golden sunshine.

The sun was bright and golden, but the feeling of unease did not cease. Opal seemed to be at war within herself, and she was losing the battle. She argued with herself that it made no difference, but it did make a difference. Somehow, she was inextricably entwined with Roger Paisley. Opal took her BlackBerry from her purse and checked her messages again. There were voice mail messages from her mother, her roommate, and Jim. She wished that she was back in New York. Life wasn't so serious there. No one expected commitments or vows. She could light a candle at St. Patrick's and then go on her merry way. Rome was different. With every step in the *eternal city*, she was held accountable. There were Swiss Guards and ceilings and judgments. Perhaps the *commitment* was not the problem at all.

Opal had read many stories where people announced that they met themselves in Paris. She did not know why they always discovered some great revelation about themselves in Paris, but they always seemed to find themselves or their true nature in Paris. Perhaps Rome was Opal's Paris. "I met myself in Rome," said Opal audibly. It sounded romantic, sophisticated, and worldly, to be sure, but Opal wasn't certain whether she had met herself or lost herself in Rome.

The plane ride home was quite enjoyable. Alitalia Airlines had the most delectable meals Opal had ever eaten on a plane. Wine accompanied each meal, and there was no limit! It wasn't like the American airlines, where one was given a bag of peanuts. Wine was extra, and heaven forbid one should request more than one measly glass. On this airline, the passengers received small bottles of red or white, and the meals were gourmet, to be sure. Opal loved wine, and she requested the small bottles with her meals. The plane ride home was utterly enchanting. What a way to end her vacation in paradise. Yes, Rome was paradise, and she would be happy to return.

Jim and Heather waited for Opal at the airport. They remarked upon her tan and relaxed demeanor. She seemed different, they said. She *was* different; in point of fact, they were different also. They did not seem the same as when she left them. Perhaps it was the way in which Heather took Jim's arm as he lifted Opal's suitcase, or the way he looked into Heather's eyes as he held the door open for them to exit the airport. Jim rented a car; he did not want Opal to feel exhausted taking the train back to the city. He was thoughtful that way. Opal sat in the front next to him. He touched her hand and said that he was glad that she was home, but his touch was different. Perhaps her touch was different also, for he seemed to recoil slightly and avert his eyes at the warmth of her hand. He could feel it, Opal was sure. He could feel the *commitment*.

Jim pulled out of the JFK parking lot. Heather talked incessantly in the back seat relaying information about their friends and their antics in Opal's absence. Jim was silent, as was Opal. There it was between them. The *commitment* shared the front seat with them. It quietly divided them. It spoke a language that neither of them heard but both of them understood. Jim's eyes did not leave the road. Opal's eyes did not leave the view from the side window. Heather continued laughing and talking, oblivious to the painful scene that was being enacted in the front seat.

"I thought that we'd go out to dinner," said Jim at last. "Are you too tired?"

"No," said Opal. "I feel fine. It's a great idea."

"You can drop me off on campus," said Heather. "I must finish this paper today. Professor Isles won't give extensions. Who does he think he is, anyway? So, we're all going out to dinner then? I hope that you took lots of pictures, Opal. I can't wait to see them. So where are we going to eat – Balthazar's?"

"Yes," said Jim simply. "I thought that we'd celebrate Opal's return in style."

"All right," said Heather, "I'll tell everyone. We should get there before the dinner crowd arrives, or we won't get a table. Just let me out here at the corner."

Jim pulled up to the curb, and Heather exited on West 4th Street near campus. The car entered traffic again.

"You seem subdued," said Jim. "How was your flight?"

"Wonderful," said Opal. "It was one of the best flights I've ever taken. You wouldn't believe the food and the unlimited wine."

Jim smiled. "So that's it. You've had how many glasses of wine?'

"Not glasses – small bottles," said Opal with enthusiasm. "I think I may have had three or four. It was unlimited, so I didn't really count."

"Then that explains it," said Jim somewhat relieved. "You

seem preoccupied, but it's probably just the wine. You know that it makes you sleepy."

"I'm not the least bit sleepy," said Opal. "In fact, I feel full of life and energy. You, on the other hand, seem rather reckless."

"What do you mean?" asked Jim nervously.

"Balthazar's? Won't that break your budget? It's not like you to do anything so extravagant," said Opal.

"Maybe I'm changing," said Jim.

"Yes," said Opal looking out of the window again, "maybe you are."

They rode in silence to Opal's apartment. Jim carried her suitcases upstairs and then went to return the Zip rental car. The apartment looked different. There was a different air about it. Everything was still in place, but there was something different. There was an uncomfortable aura that Opal had not felt before. Jim had not asked about her trip. He had not asked to see her pictures and did not make mention of the souvenirs that he gave her money to purchase. She would return the money to him when she returned to work, for she did not purchase any souvenirs. Her room was just as she had left it. The bed was strewn with clothing that would not fit into her suitcases and was left behind. The clothing seemed to mock her. *So, you chose to leave us behind, did you? We weren't good enough to make the cut, eh? Just try wearing us again - we dare you!*

Opal placed her suitcases near the window and glanced out at the people walking down the block. It was a quiet, tree-lined block. The building was especially quiet, which was unusual for this time of day. Usually, she could hear people going up and down the stairs. Most of the building's occupants were graduate students and young professionals. Opal liked the apartment, but today, there was something eerie about it. Things do not remain the same when people leave. Upon returning, everything has changed, whether it be the expression on the face of a friend or the way the sun hits the curtains. The changes are ever so slight, but they are evident. Opal lay on her bed and pushed the clothing to the floor. She closed her eyes and fell asleep almost immediately, courtesy of the five small bottles of wine that she consumed on the plane.

Balthazar's was crowded with festive diners and drinkers. Jim's party of six was escorted to a booth, where they sipped wine and nibbled on bread until the dinner arrived. Opal felt radiant in her navy, flouncy sundress. She wore a gray pashmina over her shoulders. The dress always made her feel lively and full of glee. Jim wore a white short-sleeved shirt and jeans. The chatter was incessant as the friends imbibed more wine gregariously and began eating their meals. A waiter dressed in black and white brought a bottle of champagne to the table.

"We didn't order champagne," said Jim.

"Compliments of the gentleman at that table," said the waiter.

Everyone looked at a rather middle-aged man seated near the door.

"Who's he?" asked Heather.

"I don't know," said Jim. "Does anyone know that guy? Is he anyone's father or uncle?"

No one knew the gentleman with the distinguished, graying temples dressed in a stylish blue suit.

"Maybe the waiter brought it to the wrong table," said Opal, "but I think that we should drink it, since it's already open."

"You are so devious," laughed Heather, "but I think that you are right. We are celebrating Opal's return, so let's celebrate."

"I'll go over and see what this is all about," said Jim.

As he approached the table, Jim was aware of his informal attire in comparison to the stylish gentleman's. He wished that he had foregone the sandals and worn something more professional. The gentleman smiled as Jim approached.

"Did you send us champagne?" asked Jim.

"Yes," said the gentleman. "I hope that you don't mind. It seemed as though you were celebrating a special occasion."

"Do we know you?" asked Jim.

"No," said the gentleman. "I just like to see people enjoying themselves."

"Well, thanks," said Jim. He returned to the table with a queasy feeling in his stomach.

"Well?" asked Heather's boyfriend, Hank.

"He said that he just wanted to help us celebrate," said Jim.

"That's weird," said Heather.

"This is New York," said Richard, another friend. "Nothing is weird."

"Quite right," said Opal. "Nothing is weird in New York."

"My, you sound very British," intoned Paula, Richard's girlfriend.

A tremor raced through Opal. *Where did that come from? Quite right? Since when do you say 'quite' anything.*

"Did you go to London or Rome?" laughed Heather. The entire group laughed. Opal joined them, but it was not amusing. Was she beginning to speak like Roger now? It was disconcerting. Roger seemed to be present at the table. Opal couldn't explain it, but he seemed to be hovering over the table watching them. Her eyes shifted to the gentleman seated near the door. He was reading his newspaper and was no longer watching the festive group. Opal tried to clear her mind.

"Let me taste some of your skate," said Opal. Jim placed a rather large portion of his fish onto Opal's plate. It was delectable.

"Glasses up, everyone," said Richard. "To Opal, who looks fetching in that dress, I might add. May you return to Rome and live your dreams!"

"Hear, Hear!" said Hank mocking Opal's recent foray into a British intonation. Everyone raised their glasses. Opal smiled.

The smile faded when she noticed the gentleman seated near the door lift his glass as well and smile at her.

"What's wrong?" asked Jim.

"Nothing," said Opal. "I'm going to the ladies room."

"We'll go with you," said Heather and Paula.

The three friends walked swiftly to the stairwell leading to the lower level. They laughed and giggled as they passed the gentleman near the door. When they entered the ladies room, the laughter ended.

"All right, what's going on?" asked Heather.

"Yes, you're like a zombie from another planet," said Paula. "What happened back there? Do you know that man?"

"I've never seen him before," said Opal.

"Well, he seems to know you," said Heather. "I saw him looking at you during dinner."

"I tell you, I've never seen him," reiterated Opal. "This is quite odd, isn't it?"

"Stop saying 'quite'!" insisted Heather. "You sound like the soundtrack of a Hugh Grant movie. What's happened to you? You're all – weird."

"Nothing has happened to me," said Opal. She placed a dollar onto the attendant's plate. "Let's go back upstairs."

"Wait," said Paula. "I really need to use the rest room. You two go ahead."

Opal and Heather walked up the stairs. "I notice that you and Jim seem to have become chummy," said Opal.

"I didn't tell you this; I didn't want to spoil your return, but Hank and I broke up last week. Jim has been a real friend trying to get us back together," said Heather.

"I didn't know," said Opal with much concern.

"We're trying to make it work," said Heather, "but you notice that he hasn't said two words to me this evening. I think that it's really over."

They reached the top of the landing. The gentleman seated near the door was gone. Opal felt relieved.

"You're lucky to have Jim," said Heather. "You don't find too many men like him. He's really devoted to you."

"I know," said Opal. Heather was right, of course, but something had changed. Everything was changing and changing rapidly.

After the festive evening, the couples walked to their various apartments near campus. Summer was beginning to make its presence felt. After weeks of cool, drizzly weather, at last it was warm enough to go out at night without a wrap or jacket. Opal removed her gray shawl and walked with Jim hand-in-hand in front of Richard and Paula. Hank and Heather walked towards the rear. They did not hold hands, and they seemed to be arguing quietly.

"What a perfect evening," said Opal looking up at the darkened sky.

"So," said Jim. "Tell me all about your trip. Did you get to see all of the sights of Rome?"

"Yes," sighed Opal. "Rome is a feast for the eyes. There are so many wondrous sights. I was there for the European Cup. Did I tell you?"

"No," said Jim. "You haven't told me anything, and you didn't return any of my calls. I assumed that you were having a great time and didn't check your messages. What about the European Cup?"

"It was a soccer game, or I should say football game between Manchester and Barcelona. Was it on the news over here?"

"No," answered Jim feigning interest.

"Well, it was quite a spectacle over there. I have never seen such revelry," replied Opal.

"I didn't know that you were interested in sports," said Jim. "I can't get you go anywhere near a Mets game. Why the sudden interest?"

"Everyone was interested. One had no choice. The entire city was overwhelmed with anticipation," responded Opal.

"I notice a change in your vocabulary," said Jim. "Words like 'one' and 'rather' and 'quite.' I like it. You sound international. What else did you do?"

"I just walked around enjoying the sights, but it sounds as though you had a handful with Hank and Heather. Why didn't you tell me that they had broken up?"

"You're evading my question. What else did you do in Rome?" asked Jim. "Did you meet any people?"

"You meet people here and there," said Opal. "People are everywhere."

"Anyone from Manchester?" asked Jim.

"From Manchester? No," said Opal with assuredness.

"From any of the British Isles?" asked Jim.

"What are you really asking?" asked Opal.

"I think that you met someone," said Jim. "I can hear it in your voice, and I can see it on your face; in fact, I can feel his presence when I'm near you."

Opal laughed. "You mean like a ghost or something? How can you feel someone's presence when you're near me? Are you suggesting that I can have someone else's essence? That's absurd."

"Is it?" asked Jim. "I can smell him on you, Opal."

Opal laughed again, only this time more heartily. "Are you a dog now, sniffing people?" She turned around to the couples behind her. "Listen to this. Jim says that he can smell someone's essence on me."

"What do you mean, Jim?" asked Paula.

"He says that he can feel another man's essence when he's near me, and he can smell him on me. Have you ever heard of anything more ridiculous?" laughed Opal.

"I don't think it's ridiculous at all," said Hank. "Why don't you ask Jim if he leaves his essence behind as well, 'cause I can sure smell it on Heather."

The group became silent. They walked along the street in stony silence, and it was awkward.

"I think that we should talk about it," said Richard at last. "There is tension. We can all feel it."

"All right," said Jim. "I'm willing to talk about it. I only tried to help Heather, and I tried to help you too, Hank."

"Well, stop helping me so much," said Hank angrily. "I don't need your help. The farther away you stay from Heather, the better off we'll be. There, I've said it."

Once again, there was silence.

"Fine," said Jim. "I won't help."

"What about Opal?" asked Heather.

Opal cast a derisive look at her roommate.

"Since we're being honest," said Paula, "I have noticed a change also. You *are* different, Opal. I don't know whether it's because of someone's *essence*, but I think that someone has influenced you or maybe is still influencing you through some type of mental telepathy."

"This is really getting bizarre," said Richard. "Do any of us really believe that people have essences – that we're born with a certain biological proclivity that cannot be altered? Do you realize what you're suggesting?"

"I think that it's true to an extent," said Heather.

"Then, no matter what we do, we are designed to behave a certain way? Is that what you're suggesting?" asked Richard.

"Well, yes," said Heather, "to a degree. For example, I like to ski. My ancestors are Scandinavian. They skied; therefore, generations later, I still like to ski."

"That's preposterous," said Hank. "So, in other words, education and culture have no bearing on a person's *essence*, if there is such a thing? Let's say a person is Scandinavian and is reared in the tropics. Will that person still like to ski?"

"The person may not know it, but yes, I believe the person will have a natural proclivity to ski, and as soon as he or she sees a ski slope, the person will ski like a natural. It is in the blood," said Heather.

"Interesting," said Hank. He spoke loudly to the group. "Do you see why this relationship is doomed?!"

"Just a moment," said Opal. "Maybe Heather's statement has some validity.

"Now, don't you start," said Jim.

"What if, and this is strictly for the sake of argument, I met a person from another country. He has one essence, and I have another. In order to be compatible, wouldn't our *essences* have to combine?" asked Opal.

"Don't tell me that you believe in this essence nonsense," said Richard.

"There may be something to it," said Opal. "I believe that a person's *essence* may be fused with another person's *essence*."

"This is getting more ludicrous by the minute," said Richard.

"Not really," interjected Heather. "Plants do it all the time. Over time, when a plant adapts to a new environment, its essence changes, doesn't it?"

"So are we arguing some Darwinian type of theory whereby people can somehow infuse other people with their *essences* and create hybrid people?" asked Hank. "Should we call Spielberg for the movie rights?"

"Mock if you wish," said Heather, "but I believe it is entirely possible to become so close to a person that you can read his or her mind and almost feel the person's presence, maybe even feel the person's essence inside of your body."

"Is that what happened, Opal?" asked Hank sardonically. "Did someone in Rome leave you with his *essence*, the same *essence* that Jim can feel and smell? Are you under someone's spell? Tell us, Opal, for the sake of science, tell us all."

Opal remained silent.

"That's enough," said Jim. "Leave her alone."

"I was only kidding," said Hank. "At least we're all back to normal now."

Hank was right. The tension was no longer present. The

group laughed and chatted again in an harmonious bond, but each knew that the bond had been altered, and it was quite possible that a foreign *essence* had entered into their midst and was undeniably present.

"I made a commitment!" blurted Opal. The words poured out of her mouth before she could contain them in that small section of her heart that retained secrets. The group stopped walking at the intensity of her response. "I made a commitment. I committed myself to another man. I'm going to meet him next year in Rome, and I can no longer be with you, Jim."

No one uttered a word. Opal walked away from the group, quite boldly. They stood in silence watching her.

"Go after her, Jim," said Richard. "Find out what it's all about."

"You go after her, if you're so interested," said Jim. He walked away in the opposite direction.

"Don't tell me there's no such thing as *essences*," said Heather. "That wasn't Opal speaking – that was her new *essence*. She shares the person's *essence* now, and she speaks for both of them."

"I've had enough of this," said Hank impatiently. "Heather, if you have any of my *essence*, please forward it to my mailing address. This just isn't going to work." Hank followed Jim down the street.

"Well," said Richard, "I guess I'll escort you ladies home. This was a fun evening, wasn't it?"

"Great fun," uttered Paula. "Great fun, indeed."

Summer passed too quickly. The signs of autumn were undeniable. The skies seemed darker and more melancholy. The sun's rays were weak though bright, and it began to get dark sooner. The fall semester was well underway. Opal felt awkward passing Jim on campus with his new girlfriend. They seemed to be happy, despite the difference in their ages. Her name was

Molly; she seemed sensible and mature. She could not possibly fit in with the group, but she seemed to be a perfect match for Jim. One did not hear the name Molly often. Clearly, it was of a different generation. For some reason, Opal's thoughts returned to the Trevi Fountain and the couple she photographed. The woman seemed old enough to be the young man's mother, but they were a couple. Molly wasn't old enough to be Jim's mother, but she could certainly pass for an older sister – a much older sister. What was the attraction of these older women? Opal did not know. She hoped that she would be appealing when she became older. Jim nodded as he passed her. Opal smiled and nodded as well. Molly did not seem to notice her.

There was a chill in the air, signaling that it was time to pack the shorts away and pull out the cardigans. It was only the beginning of September. Surely, summer cheated New York this year. There were the usual fun activities: Shakespeare in the Park, the NY Philharmonic Concert in Central Park, Summer Stage, Broadway in Bryant Park, and a host of other free activities that Opal attended with Heather and Paula, but they were enthralled within a cloak of chilly air and half-hearted sunbeams. The thought of Roger was ever-present. Opal thought of him at work, in class, and while walking through the brisk, nippy breeze that encircled pedestrians.

Roger's correspondence consisted of brief notes attached to books and DVDs that he thought would be of interest. There were comedies, dramas, mysteries, and historical documentaries. They were all set in England. It was as though he was helping her to acquire a taste for all things British. It occurred to her, more than once, that if she and Roger ever became one, she would be required to place the USA in a neat little box and store it away in an attic or cupboard in order to make way for all things British. Oddly, it was becoming easier as the weeks progressed. Her bookshelves increasingly reflected British culture, compliments of the steady stream of books that Roger sent, and her taste in music and movies reflected the same penchant. It was as though the more she absorbed, the more she developed a proclivity for the UK. Heather and Paula ceased to tease her; in point of fact, they found themselves enamoured with the selection of DVDs. Heather even asked to borrow one of the books Roger selected for Opal. Opal was taken aback when an elegant silver service arrived. It was charming. The teapot stood guard over a silver creamer, sugar bowl, and tray. The tea service was quite a conversation piece when friends visited from class. They drank Rose tea from Harrods with ever so much enjoyment. Everyone indulged themselves in the little slice of England in Apartment 3B.

Opal had not spoken to Roger since their meeting in Rome. He did not call nor did he email. There was always sent a small card with a brief note within each parcel. The communication was neither romantic nor inquisitive. Roger did not inquire about her activities, health, or state of mind. His only interest seemed to be how she was progressing with her readings and whether the DVDs were to her liking. It really did not seem to matter if they were not. The important thing was that she read everything he sent her and watched all of the DVDs. Curiously, they did not discuss religion. Opal made it a point to mention her Rosary and her weekly prayers at St. Patrick's as an indication, but Roger was not lured into theological discourse. He did not address the issue in any of his notes. Her assumption was that he was a member of the Church of England. Opal wondered what they were like. She visited St. Paul's Cathedral once when her high school class visited London, but that was years ago. The only thing Opal remembered about the service was the choir director and the magnificent choir. The director was comically animated. Opal and her classmates tried not to giggle at his eccentric movements.

Was this an actual relationship? Opal could not say, but it was quite intriguing. She wondered what they would do when they met in Rome. Opal imagined herself in a silky, floral dress and Roger in his khaki shorts, Oxford shirt, and sandals. He would present her with a glittering piece of jewelry – perhaps a brooch that belonged to his grandmother. Wouldn't that be grand? They would sit and gaze at the cascading fountain in the cool of the evening. She would rest her head upon his shoulder, and he would caress her. This was a dream that was, quite frankly, unrealistic. Opal knew that Roger would question her about her readings, provide her with sorbet, and suggest that they visit the Keats and Shelley Museum, since she did not have time to visit it before she left Rome. It was the only place on his list that she omitted, as there was no time. This revelation was unacceptable to Roger, and Opal was certain that a trip to the Keats and Shelley Museum would be of primary importance when they met again on May 24th, one year to the day when they stood at the Trevi Fountain, where Roger asked her to commit herself to him. There was something utterly romantic and wondrous about the plan; it was a great adventure – this commitment business. An exercise in frivolity was the pronouncement Jim made on the matter, according to Richard. Be that as it may, Opal was happy with the dream and the commitment, for she was a dreamer by nature. The Dreamer and the Scholar - what an agreeable combination. Without dreams, there would be no scholarship. Man must dream in order to view the world and to write about it. They seemed like the oddest of couples, but they were ideally matched, or so Opal thought.

A strange communication awaited Opal. It was not within her mailbox; it was taped to the outside of the mailbox, where anyone could see it. The writing was different. It was quite bold and elegant at the same time. Opal removed the beige, stationary envelope and searched for a return address or a name. There was neither. The missive was addressed to Opal. Curiosity filled Opal's thoughts, and she tore open the envelope without waiting to walk up the stairs. Inside, there was a photograph. Opal examined it carefully. It was taken in front of the Trevi Fountain. Roger stood beside a rather attractive young man. They seemed much younger in the photo and stood with arms around one another's shoulders. There was a gleam in Roger's eyes that she had not seen before. The young man smiled blissfully at the camera. Were they brothers? Opal turned the photo over. There were no words. She continued to stare at the photo as she climbed the stairs. What did it mean, and who taped it to her mailbox? She wanted to write Roger immediately, but something made her refrain. Upon entering the apartment, Opal placed her books on a kitchen chair and walked to the living room without taking her eyes off of the photo. Heather sat in the living room reading.

"What's that?" asked Heather.

Opal did not speak. She presented the photo to Heather and awaited a response. Heather looked at the photo and then up at Opal's confused countenance.

"Where did you get this?" asked Heather.

"It was taped to the mailbox in an envelope," said Opal.

"It wasn't there when I checked the mail. Someone must have just placed it there," said Heather.

"What do you think it means?" asked Opal.

"I think that someone is trying to tell you something about Roger," said Heather, "and he's concerned enough to place this on our mailbox. For all we know, he may live in the building."

"But why?" asked Opal.

"Perhaps he doesn't want to share Roger's *essence* with you," said Heather seriously. "I think that we should call Hank and Richard. They'll know what to do."

"So then, you think that Roger may be…" Opal could not bring herself to say the word.

"I don't know what to think," said Heather. "What rotten luck. I was just beginning to enjoy those tea biscuits that Roger sends you."

"Do you really believe that Roger and this man are involved in that way?" asked Opal.

"What else can you believe?" asked Heather. "Didn't you say that you met him at the Trevi Fountain? Isn't that the Trevi Fountain in the background? Do the math, Opal. This Roger likes to travel to Italy and pick up people at the Trevi Fountain."

"That's ridiculous!" exclaimed Opal. "If that were true, he could pick up people anywhere, couldn't he? No, it's something else, I'm certain."

"All right then, why don't you call him and tell him about the photo?" asked Heather.

"I don't want to jump to conclusions," responded Opal. "Let's talk to Richard and Hank. They can advise us. Besides, Roger never gave me his phone number. I only have his mailing address, and it's a P.O. Box."

"So, for all you know, this guy could be married with ten children or gay with a series of extremely cute, jealous lovers," said Heather looking at the photo. Opal snatched the photo from Heather's hand.

"I'll call Richard and Hank," said Opal softly looking at the photo one last time before placing it in her desk drawer.

Richard and Hank seated themselves on the sofa that evening and viewed the photo.

"What does your *essence* say about this?" asked Hank.

"Come on, Hank," said Richard. "This is serious. It sounds like Opal has herself a stalker, and a stalker who doesn't want her around this Roger guy. The fact that he attached the envelope to the mailbox is troubling. He obviously knows your address. Why place it on the outside of the mailbox?"

"He's trying to intimidate her," said Hank. "He wants to frighten you and make you think that he's watching your every move. I say we call the police."

"And tell them what?" asked Heather. "Placing a photo on a mailbox is not against the law. We don't even know if the guy in the photo placed it there."

"There's something askew about this," said Richard. "You should contact this Roger right away and find out what he knows. He can tell you who this guy is and whether or not you should be concerned. He might be a relative or an ex-lover, but one thing's for certain, he has qualms about you and Roger and wants to cause a rift."

"I agree," said Hank. "Call Roger. What time is it in England?"

"She doesn't have his phone number," said Heather. "She only has his P.O. Box address."

"Are you insane?" asked Hank. "This guy could be anywhere with a P.O. box in England. You're too naive, Opal. You should have gone with her to Italy, Heather."

"With what?" asked Heather. "I can barely pay the rent."

"All right," said Richard. "We'll handle this. I think that we should notify the police, just in case we have some idiot on our hands who wants to cause trouble. Meanwhile, write to this Roger creep and tell him about this photo. Get his phone number and real address. You need to ask the hard questions, Opal, like are you married or gay. You live in a dream world, but everyone isn't a dreamer. There are some real creeps out there who will make minced meat of you if you give them the opportunity."

Opal was close to tears. It felt that her entire world was crumbling around her feet. She knew that they were right. She hadn't asked the hard questions, and he hadn't asked any of her. It was an idyllic *relationship*, but Opal could not bring herself to believe that Roger would do anything untoward. She couldn't account for the person who left the missive attached to the mailbox, though, and determined to follow Hank and Richard's advice.

Hank and Richard remained close to Jim and relayed the

information about Opal to him. Jim was not surprised, for he knew that Opal was too trusting of people. He considered calling her but thought better of it. It would be unwise to trouble his new relationship with his old one, so he left Hank and Richard to sort out the problem. Secretly, he felt a sense of pleasure that Opal's *commitment* wasn't worth a farthing. Now, perhaps she would realize what a treasure he was and how foolish she was to let him go. Knowing Opal, though, Jim knew that she would not feel that way at all. She would feel no remorse, and she would continue to prefer the stranger to him, her trusted friend for many years. They hadn't been lovers, but he was waiting to do the right thing. He wanted to marry her and take care of her, but Opal had other plans. She would rather attach herself to a foreign stranger, of whom she knew nothing, and cast him adrift. Jim still felt hurt and betrayed. A part of him wanted to help Opal, as he always did, and tell her that all would be fine – that he would make everything better. It was too late for that. Nothing would make it better. The stranger had a commitment, and he had nothing to show for his loyalty, devotion, and love. Perhaps love could not survive without some sort of commitment. Perhaps the foreign stranger got it right. What if love could only survive with everything spread out, as it were, on the table of life – a sort of this is what I want for us, and this is what I need from you posture. Jim had never stated it in quite that way. He assumed that Opal knew how he felt and that she felt the same. Life had other plans. From out of the blue comes a foreign stranger bearing nothing more than a desire to have her commit to him. "Commit what?" wondered Jim. This was new terrain – putting one's feelings out there for all to see. The stranger saw Opal and knew right away that she was what he wanted. Jim saw her every day and was still waiting to decide whether or not they would be committed for life. There was that word again, and the impact of it hit Jim like a boulder. The stranger wanted and needed a commitment; he did not. The truth of the matter was that Jim could not commit to anything apart from his educational goals. Those goals must come first. And there it was - his goals were his commitment. He wanted to become a lawyer, and nothing would prevent him from attaining his goal. Life stepped in and sorted out the debris with a trip to Rome and a commitment at the Trevi Fountain.

Roger Paisley looked at his schedule for the day. His assistant brought him a cup of coffee and a croissant. He nibbled the croissant thoughtfully and sipped the coffee as he looked out of the window onto the metropolis. New York was cooler than he had anticipated. His meeting would consume most of the day, and then he was off to Denver. The Colorado branch was having difficulty meeting deadlines. He was sent to place everything in order. Undoubtedly, it meant releasing the aged CEO. Roger did not like using a heavy hand, but he would if necessary. The parent company was losing money, and the Colorado branch was a particularly troublesome drain – troublesome in that the CEO was Roger's mentor and once future father-in-law. Harding Cromwell was a top-notch executive in his day, and the widower was quite the ladies man for much of his youth. In his younger days, after a particularly nasty scandal involving a young woman in the office, Cromwell placed his young son, George, in boarding school and removed himself from the London imbroglio. He took residence in the United States branch of his company, with hopes that his British charm would work wonders in Denver. He married a young American woman and produced an offspring – Emily. Emily was twenty-five now and quite winsome. She graduated from an American college and returned to England, where she met her step-brother's friend, Roger. It wasn't long before Roger asked her to be his wife. Harding Cromwell was tortured by this news and refused to give his blessing. Roger was devastated, for he always felt close to the old man. Now, the dreadful truth emerged. Roger was not a part of the *manor born*. Marriage to Emily Cromwell was out of the question. To soften the blow, Harding Cromwell gave the industrious and personable Roger Paisley a prominent position within the corporation, where he worked side-by-side with George Cromwell, his best friend. Emily returned to the US vowing never to return to England. Now Harding Cromwell was beginning to manifest signs of dementia. Emily, living in California and thoroughly "Americanized," lived a life of privilege near the ocean with a young man named Max. Max was barely out of high school. How does one put one's mentor "out to pasture"? Roger could have refused the task, but he wanted to handle the matter personally. George and his father were never on the best of terms. Roger would handle the matter with the required delicacy. Then there was the Opal affair, if one could call it an affair. Roger had no doubts that he would marry her.

Opal and Emily were similar in many ways. Both were impulsive and seemed averse to logical, rational thought. Both lived in dream worlds. A commitment seemed the best solution to keep Opal's fanciful yearnings in check. The world was not a dream. It could be an horrific place for dreamers. With a commitment in the back of her mind, he knew that Opal would not stray into pastures that were not conducive to the musings of an idyllic dreamer. The commitment would keep her safe until he could plight his trough to her. She needed to be taught how to live in his world, a much more agreeable place than the world which she currently inhabited. She belonged with him in the English countryside, where she could read, write poetry, and learn of her English countrymen. She would not break the commitment, of that he was certain. Once he got her onto English soil, all would be well.

Roger was convinced that America ruined civilized people. There were too few traditions to hold people in check. Anything goes and every man for himself seemed to be the mantra; lamentably, money was a motivating factor, but money could not replace good old-fashioned traditions and heritage. Opal would share his traditions and his heritage, but that would come later. At present, Roger's thoughts went to the ailing Cromwell, and he pondered how he would get him to return to England without making him feel that he was no longer a useful part of the company he established.

Opal's missive came as a complete surprise. *Are you married? Are you gay? What is your home address and phone number?* Clearly, she was being prompted. Roger could not determine who was prompting her nor did he know why she was being prompted to interrogate him. There was trouble brewing, and he determined to get to the bottom of it. His response was in the manner in which they had been accustomed to communicating. He wrote her a missive and asked the reason for her inquisitiveness. He wanted her trust; completing a *questionnaire* did not elicit feelings of trust. He would answer none of the questions; rather, he would continue to trust her as he expected her to trust him.

Hank and Richard were furious with the response.

"You've got to end it, Opal," said Hank impatiently. "I don't know why you haven't done it already. What are you waiting for?"

"Hank's right," said Richard. "Are you waiting to get hurt? He's not answering your questions for a reason. Can't you see that? Open your eyes, Opal. Get out of it before you get hurt."

Opal was hurt already, but she did not respond. She continued to look out at the colored leaves as they sprinkled the sidewalk. "I'm going out for a walk," said Opal. She took her jacket from the coat rack and closed the door softly.

Crimson and gold leaves crunched beneath her feet. Opal did not know where she was going nor did she care. She simply wanted a charge of fresh air throughout her body in order to clear her mind. It was best to think of something else and to put all thoughts of Roger behind her. She entered a bagel shop, purchased a bagel with Swiss cheese and ham, a bottle of sparkling water, and sat down at a small round table near the window. She peered out of the window as she nibbled the Swiss cheese that extended over the side of the bagel. The fresh air and the change of scenery did her an inexpressible amount of good, for an idea occurred to her. She would travel to London. Yes, that was the best thing. She would visit London with hopes of arranging a meeting with Roger. If they could just talk things through, she was certain that all would be well.

Opal was certain that she could work extra hours; it was approaching the holiday season. New York always began the holiday season early – sometimes before Halloween. Her studies would suffer, to be sure, but she had no alternative. A gentle knock on the window brought her focus back to the present. Jim stood outside the bagel shop smiling at her. She waved and took a bite of her bagel sandwich as Jim entered and sat at the table. He looked surprisingly well. There was a different air about him. It was an air with which Opal was unfamiliar. He seemed more confident, settled, and mature, if that was possible.

"I'm surprised to see you here," said Jim. "Don't you have a class?"

"I am on holiday," said Opal, "or I soon shall be."

"Going away?" asked Jim.

"I don't want to talk about it," said Opal.

"You don't need to. I hear there's trouble in paradise," said Jim. He walked to the counter, ordered a cup of coffee, and returned to the table. "Do you want my advice?"

"Not really," said Opal. "You agree with Richard and Hank."

"I'll give it to you anyway," said Jim. "You know that you can't afford the expense of travel right now, and if you work extra hours, you will not be able to keep up with your studies. You're a dreamer, Opal, and you believe that everything will work out, but it won't. You have everything to lose and nothing to gain."

"Maybe I'm not trying to gain anything," said Opal petulantly. "Does everything have to be about gain?"

"Let me help you think it through," said Jim calmly sipping his coffee.

"I don't need your help thinking," said Opal unconvincingly.

"I'll give it to you anyway," said Jim. He took a napkin from the dispenser on the table and began to draw a time line. "Here you are today." He placed a star on the line. "This is where you want to be in five years," said Jim extending the line five inches and placing another star. "You will have your doctorate and a lucrative career will loom before you." Jim drew another line under the line he had drawn. "Here you are today, and here you are in September." He extended the line one inch. "You will be unable to enter the doctoral program, for you will not be able to obtain the fellowship. Your plummeting grades will be the reason, which means that you will spend another year or two applying to doctoral programs of lesser quality hoping that they will overlook your poor academic performance. They will accept you, but you will not receive the financial resources that you need, which means that you will work even longer hours at the bookstore and forego a full-time doctoral program." Jim opened the napkin and extended the line eight inches. "Here you are in the six or seven years that it will take you to complete your degree. You are exhausted and completely disillusioned." Jim looked at Opal firmly. "Is this what you want? Does it make more sense now that I have spelled everything out for you?"

Opal smiled and took the pencil and napkin from Jim. She drew an intersecting line on his timeline. She placed a star and the words "Rome – Trevi Fountain" near the star. She drew two smiley faces and encircled them with a heart. "This is me in seven months," said Opal. "I will return to Rome, meet Roger, and all will be well."

"Opal, you're a fool!" shouted Jim balling the napkin up in his hand. "Don't say that I didn't try to help you." He pushed his chair away from the table vigorously and exited the bagel shop. Opal smiled as she watched his feet trod heavily down the street. Charts, graphs, and diagrams were Jim's approach to life. Opal shuddered thinking of the discontentment they would have experienced as a married couple. Her every thought would be charted out on a bar graph until she came to reason or agreed with him. He would chart out when they would marry, have children, purchase their first home, and die. Jim would even have the cemetery on the chart. Opal did not want to be a cipher on a graph or a chart. She wanted a man with a heart not a pencil poised to draw a time line or a flow chart at the least provocation. She made the right decision; Jim was not the man for her. Opal didn't need to think it through any further. Sometimes the heart provides answers when one is not looking for them. There was a reason why Jim and Opal had never committed or had the serious talk. Opal's heart felt it for over a year; Jim's graph displayed it in less than a minute. For the first time in weeks, Opal felt happy and contented. She didn't have all of the answers, but one thing was certain. The answer would not manifest itself on a graph.

The trip to England would be a secret. Opal reasoned that if her life was entwined with Roger's and they shared the same essence, then surely he would feel her presence there. It did not occur to her that Roger would feel her presence, but he would feel it across the pond, as it were. Roger was in the United States trying to convince the truculent Harding Cromwell to return to England and would not return until Christmas, two months after Opal's proposed visit.

Harding Cromwell's manservant packed the last of the bags. He felt relieved that his employer would be returning to the UK. Rippleton missed his family and had wanted to return to England years ago, but he was loyal to Harding Cromwell and did not want to leave the ailing old man alone. After his wife's death, Cromwell's behavior became erratic, and he grew more and more isolated. The luxury suite that was once filled with visitors of distinction grew to be a desolate cavern of newspapers, books, and letters that went unread and invitations that elicited no reply. Roger entered Cromwell's bedroom. The old man slept peacefully.

"See to it that he's up and about before noon, Rippleton," said Roger. "We must be at the airport at 14:00."

"Yes, Sir," said Rippleton. "Sir, a missive arrived this morning."

"From whom?" asked Roger impatiently. Missives usually caused unnecessary delays.

"I believe it is from Mr. Cromwell's daughter, Emily," replied Rippleton.

"Well, read it Rippleton," said Roger with increasing annoyance. A letter from Emily to her father could not be good news. Most likely, it was an appeal for a larger allowance to support the ridiculous life she was living in California.

Rippleton opened the missive with a gold letter opener and read the contents:

Dear Father,

I hope that this letter finds you in good health and spirits. Since you will not answer the phone and refuse to reply to my emails, I am writing with hopes that you will at least read my letter. George informs me that he has dispatched Roger Paisley to take you back to England. Of course, this is against your wishes. I hope that this letter reaches you before Roger arrives. I know how inflexible he can be. You have not been in the best of health, but I do not believe that England will benefit you or lift your spirits in any way; therefore, I propose that you move to California and live with me and Max. We have more than enough room. You will love it out

here, Father. The ocean is right at our doorstep, and you will
adore the evening sunset. Do not return to England, Father.
It will not suit you at this stage of your life. If you receive this
letter after Roger Paisley arrives, then all is lost. He will not
rest until you return to England. I will await word from you
as to your decision. I can come and escort you personally, if
you decide to honor us with your presence.

> *Yours faithfully,*
> *Emily*

Rippleton folded the missive, placed it within the envelope, and presented it to Roger.

Roger placed the envelope into his jacket's breast pocket. "Thank you, Rippleton. I'll respond to this missive. There is no need to trouble Mr. Cromwell with regard to its contents. It would only upset him."

"As you wish, Sir," said Rippleton.

"Oh, and Rippleton, I don't suppose you could make me a cup of tea," requested Roger.

"Yes, Sir," said Rippleton exiting the bedroom.

Roger opened the envelope and read the missive again. He smiled a wry smile as he read it. Emily had a penchant for dramatics, which he found both annoying and irresistible. He would respond to the missive upon Harding Cromwell's return to England. Better yet, he would let George respond. That would infuriate Emily immeasurably.

George Cromwell had little regard for his sister. Her ill-fated engagement to his best friend, Roger, was her only redeeming quality. George did not understand why his father insisted upon observing the old-fashioned feudal customs with regard to class distinctions. Be that as it may, George kept Roger nearby and grew to depend upon his business acumen and friendship. Whenever it seemed that Roger might venture forth without the Cromwell dynasty in mind, George would find a way to reel him back. George encouraged Roger's trip to Denver in order to remove him from Opal's thrall.

George realized that Opal would be a threat when he noticed Roger's attentiveness in Rome. It was George who insisted that Roger send Opal flowers on their last day in Rome to divert any suspicions that he had inclinations to oppose the union. George and Roger had been friends since their days at Eton. Eton was nestled in a tranquil community just over the bridge from Windsor Castle. It was the perfect place in which to solidify friendships. After class, George and Roger would walk through the town in their uniforms of tails, pin-striped trousers, and crisp white shirts with bow ties. It was important to establish such friendships when one was away from the comforts of home. Roger's home, of course, was far from what one would call a comfort. There were endless rows with his father, and his mother was powerless to help him. Nothing was ever good enough for Richard Paisley, and he made certain that his son knew of the shortcomings that he observed in him. Roger spent most holidays with the Cromwells, where the Cromwell children frolicked in an idyllic setting of stables, lush landscapes. Roger and George emerged from Eton's cocoon all too soon. Roger proceeded to Oxford, and George established himself at Cambridge. Still, they remained close friends through the years, and one rarely made a move without the other's approval.

Roger's plan to meet Opal at the Trevi Fountain in May came as a complete surprise. George could not imagine what Roger saw in Opal. She was a hopeless lunatic, in George's estimation, who would not be able to supply even a modicum of Roger's needs and would prevent his advancement socially. The woman spoke like an imbecile, and what woman in her right mind would make a commitment to a total stranger? The union had to be thwarted for Roger's benefit, and George would ensure that it was before the scheduled reunion in Italy. Roger, cognizant of George's inimitable propensity to interfere in his personal life, tried to maintain a reasonable distance from Opal in order to avert any such interference. He took the precaution of not providing his address, email, or phone number so as to thwart any possibility of his dearest friend's involvement. Lamentably, Roger was unaware that George was very much involved in Opal's day to day activities. He knew where she liked to dine, where she liked to purchase her sparkling wine, and when she attended classes. George knew her movements to the minutest detail. He even knew when she retrieved her mail from her mailbox. George would end the unseemly affair before Roger made a serious mistake, which would compromise his position within the firm and within the hearts of the Cromwell family. Opal would not mar their indestructible union.

The London sky was overcast, and Opal was pleased that she remembered to pack her umbrella and leather gloves. The wind was a bit nippy and refused to let her hair rest peaceably upon her shoulders. The scarf Jim bought her for her birthday came in handy and provided much warmth. Opal walked to the Piccadilly Line station and purchased a one-week ticket. Surely, a week would be sufficient. Roger would be able to meet her, and they would enjoy an early reunion. Jim's words, "Opal, you're a fool," came to mind frequently as she walked around London enjoying the sights, sounds, and the people. The trains were particularly crowded, as there was no service on the entire Central Line. People packed onto the subway cars in close proximity. It reminded Opal of the Roman subway cars just before the Barcelona/Manchester games for the European Cup. This time, there was absolute civility. People stood politely awaiting their stops in a hushed atmosphere. As she rode, it occurred to her that she should visit The National Portrait Gallery. Opal found this idea to be less than appealing. She did not want to view portraits; she wanted to find Roger, but she ventured forth to the gallery. There was an exhibit featuring musicians from the 60s to the 80s from Bowie to the many transformative stages of the Beatles' career. The pictures were impressive, but Opal felt bored and wanted to do something more intriguing. London had much to offer. Surely, there was something better to do apart from gazing at the angelic faces of The Rolling Stones before they became the bad boys of rock. It was a holiday weekend in America but not so here. Naturally, the English did not celebrate Thanksgiving. Opal felt particularly out of sorts, on the one hand, and very much relieved, on the other. Had she remained at home, she would have been obliged to join her family in New Jersey for the annual Thanksgiving meal of stress, strife, and turkey. She made the right decision. Home was where one felt truly at peace, loved, and welcomed. For some reason, Opal felt more peace, more love, and more welcomed in London than in New Jersey. The reason was unclear, but the feeling was not a new one. Since her first visit when she was fourteen, England seemed to open its royal arms to her. There was a feeling of connection that was not present in the state of New Jersey. Of course, New York was another matter. Not only did New York open its arms to her, but it also enveloped her in a warm, tender embrace. There was no conflict or lack of communication. Opal was loved on both shores, and it made travel between the two destinations feasible and desirable. She thought nothing of taking a weekend in London and the surrounding areas. It was home, of sorts. It was not quite like New York, but it came close, and close was good enough. Opal realized that with or without Roger's presence, she would be happy in London for the weekend or forever.

The red light flashed on her BlackBerry. There was an instant message from Heather. A parcel arrived with a London postmark. Opal instructed Heather to open it and view the contents. She pressed the send key; the reply was immediate. Heather informed Opal that there were books, as usual, but this time there was a ticket to The Royal Ballet's performance of *The Nutcracker* at The Royal Opera House, November 30th.

How odd. Why would Roger send a ticket to The Royal Ballet's performance without knowing whether or not she would be able to go to England? He did not forward an airline ticket, so the idea that she would be able to drop everything and fly to England was presumptuous, and Heather expressed her chagrin at the effrontery. Strangely, she was in England and would be able to attend the performance before her return to New York. This was an otherworldly coincidence, or was it? It was the *essence* again. Somehow, they shared an inexplicable connection, but why would he send the ticket to New York? It was perplexing. Opal requested that Heather send the ticket to her hotel using the quickest express mail possible. If she was to attend the performance, then she would need to receive the ticket the next day. Heather complied with reservations. She would be obliged to relay this new endeavor on to the group, who would, surely, be outraged at such cheek. Perhaps that was the point. Roger, obviously, wanted the group to know of their plans and the strength of his involvement in her life – in all of their lives.

Opal realized that she would need a dress, shoes, and a purse. One could not show up at the Royal Opera House in loafers and jeans. If she delved into her savings, she would be penniless when she returned to New York, but what choice did she have? She was already in London, and Roger thought enough of her to send the ticket. Opal surmised that he would appear at the performance and take an adjoining seat. Opal wondered about her hair, but it was too late for that. There was no way her budget could withstand a trip to a stylist. She would pin it up and hope for the best.

A quick trip to the flagship store, *Top Shop*, gained priority on Opal's agenda. The trendy dresses were quite reasonable, and Opal was able to find shoes, a purse, and a sparkly hair ornament as well. The dress was royal blue taffeta with a wide black belt. It was rather short, but she could always take a cab rather than brave the elements. The dress flounced out three inches above the knee and was sleeveless. The scooped neck made the purchase of a necklace imperative. She also purchased a pair of long, black gloves that reached the top of her upper arm. Black satin pumps and a black frilly clutch made the ensemble complete. Opal toyed with the idea of purchasing a festive jacket but vetoed the idea. She would wear her old standby navy peacoat and remove it as soon as she entered the theater. Excitement filled her breasts as she walked around the dressing room in her new dress. It would be a glorious vacation after all.

The ticket arrived the next day, as expected. The thought of seeing Roger filled Opal's every thought. What a romantic way to arrange a meeting. She still wondered how he knew she would be able to fly to England. Her finances, being what they were, provided no guarantee from month to month what she would be able to afford, and that included her half of the rent. Be that as it may, she would not let the mundane things of the world dampen her spirits. She was enroute to a performance of The Royal Ballet, arguably, the best ballet group in the world, and she would sit beside the man of her dreams.

Unable to contain her excitement, Opal arrived early. There were a few people on line waiting for the doors to open. Opal stood on line oblivious to the icy wind blowing through her taffeta dress and nipping at her legs. She wrapped her scarf around her neck and tried to imagine the wonderful treat that would await her inside. Soon, the doors opened. It was early. A few people walked around preparing to have dinner before the program. Opal's budget did not permit dinner, but they would probably go out for dinner after the performance. Opal nibbled on a snack and sipped a glass of wine in the café. Several people had the same idea. They waited patiently at small circular tables and sipped their beverages. The ambience was casual, and Opal felt relaxed. Her dress was splendidly elegant and festive. Opal looked around for Roger. There was no sign of him yet, but she was certain that he would appear. Why else would he send the ticket?

Opal ventured to her seat. It was a moderately-priced seat in the center area. The Royal Opera House was rather staid, in Opal's estimation. Of course, she was accustomed to the *MET* with the winding staircases and sparkling, ascending crystal chandeliers. She was impressed, however, with the royal insignia on the curtain that bedecked the stage. It reminded her that she was in England, where understatement was of the utmost importance. Most assuredly, Roger would detest the opulence of the *MET* and render it an example of American ostentation and gaudiness. Whatever - Opal liked the shiny, ascending chandeliers and luxurious ambience of the *MET*. The seats began to fill. The one next to her was conspicuously empty. Almost all of the seats were occupied by couples. Opal had never seen so many couples in one place. In New York, singles and couples lived in harmonious bliss enjoying the treasures of the city, but London was different. Everyone was paired, and Opal felt like an outsider. The lights dimmed, and the seat beside her was still empty. Opal sighed forcing herself to think positively. He would come; he would not disappoint her.

Her attention focused upon the stage, where instead of children frolicking about attending a Christmas party, there was on old man sitting at a kitchen table staring at a painting of a soldier. Was this *The Nutcracker*? Where were the kids and the toys? To Opal's surprise, the principle dancers were not children but adults. What kind of *Nutcracker* was this? The music was mesmerizingly beautiful, but the action on the stage was truly foreign. Where was the huge, expanding Christmas tree? The soldier mice were not comically rotund; they seemed sleek, vicious, and militaristic. It was beautiful yet disconcerting. This version of *The Nutcracker* had a plot, which seemed diametrically opposed to the one emanating from Lincoln Center each holiday season. The New York City Ballet's rendition was geared towards children, who comprised most of the audience, and preteen dancers danced with the professional dancers onstage. The Royal Ballet's interpretation of the classic was a far cry from anything Opal had ever witnessed. There was a story line which did not involve festive, dancing children. These dancers were as serious as death, but they were ever so beautiful and poised. It was a grown-up's *Nutcracker,* and there were few children in the audience. Opal became so involved with the ballet that she did not notice that the seat next to her was now occupied.

"What are you doing here?" asked Opal impolitely as lights brightened the theater at intermission.

"I am enjoying the ballet," said the gentleman with a smile. "Are you enjoying it? Roger thought that you might."

Opal gasped uncontrollably. She wanted to appear poised, but that was not possible now. "I know you," said Opal trying to regulate her breathing. "You're Roger's friend. You were with him in Rome."

The gentleman smiled again. "Roger and I are dear friends. Would you like a glass of champagne?"

"No, thank you," said Opal anxiously. "Where is Roger? Isn't he coming?"

"Lamentably, Roger is in Colorado," affirmed the gentleman. "He had an unexpected business appointment, but he sent me in his stead. I hope that you are not too disappointed."

"Roger isn't coming?" asked the crestfallen woman.

"No, but he wants you to enjoy the performance and hopes that you won't be too disappointed by his absence. I can see that you are devastated. Come now, it isn't quite that bad. Let me offer you a glass of champagne before the next act. You will feel better. Roger certainly wouldn't want you to be dispirited."

Opal fought off the tears. Her voice quivered. "I'm not dispirited."

"Of course, you are, but it is to be expected," said the

gentleman extending a handkerchief towards her nose. "Roger forgets how fragile people can be."

Opal took the handkerchief and wiped her eyes and nose. She held it firmly in her hand.

"Would it surprise you to know that it was I who first noticed you on that bus in Rome and selected you out of all of the beautiful tourists"? asked George Cromwell. "Roger won the coin toss. Had it been tails, perhaps we two would be here enjoying the ballet. As it turns out, we are here enjoying the ballet. I suppose the Universe has a way of working things out for the best."

"I don't understand," said Opal. "You and Roger tossed a coin for me?"

"How clumsy and indelicate of me," said George. "Let's begin again. My name is George Cromwell, and I am Roger's dearest friend. Won't you permit me to offer you a glass of champagne before the curtain?"

Visions of Roger and George Cromwell tossing a coin on a bus filled Opal's mind with derisive thoughts.

"Excuse me," said Opal rising from her seat and hastening down the stairs in tears.

Opal's new clutch and her jacket remained on the seat. George reasoned that she wouldn't get very far without them. She would be forced to return. Why were women so impulsive and emotional? The wretch should have been grateful that she had been selected. Did it really matter if a coin were tossed? George opened the clutch and found a perfumed handkerchief, a hotel key, three £20 notes, a lipstick, and the ticket stub to the performance. He waited patiently for her return, but Opal did not return. The curtain ascended, and the seat remained empty. Where had the foolish woman gone without her purse and jacket? How would she return to the hotel without any money? George waited until the end of the performance reasoning that Opal was probably watching the remainder of the program from another location and would return for her belongings when he left. After the ovations, George placed the clutch under the jacket on the seat and entered the throngs of people exiting the theater. He made a discreet detour and watched from a distance. The jacket and clutch remained unclaimed. Was she upset enough to do something foolish? George began to panic. He searched the theater, but Opal was not there. Beads of perspiration began to cover his forehead. Perhaps he had gone too far this time. Opal was not like Roger's other lady friends. There was a vulnerability about her that seemed to dictate her impulsive behavior. Just as George was about to approach the seat to retrieve Opal's jacket and clutch, a young man walked deliberately to the seat and carried them down the stairway. George followed from a distance. He wasn't certain whether he should intercede or wait to ascertain whether the young man would lead him to Opal. The young man left the theater and entered the back of a black automobile, which quickly turned the corner and disappeared into the night.

The plane ride home was uneventful. Opal tried to read her book, *How Milton Works*, in order to prepare for Monday's Milton class. She had done little reading on the trip, and she would be unprepared for the rigorous discussion period. Be that as it may, the damage was done. She was unprepared for class, and she was equally unprepared for life, so it seemed. What kind of idiot drops everything and goes traipsing about England on a whim? She had spent a fortune – a fortune which she did not have. *Yes, Opal, you really are the fool everyone believes you to be,* she heard herself say aloud. The gentleman sitting next to her looked askance at her then closed his eyes to nap. Opal closed her book and retrieved her journal from her carry-on bag under the seat. She began to write a new entry with tremulous hands.

2 December 2009

Cold, Cloudy Flight from London to NY

Well, you've done it again. You should be preparing for a career as a jester. Step up one and all and take heed. The fool has struck again – big time! Picture this—a struggling student spends her last cent to fly to London with hopes of meeting a man she met briefly while vacationing in Rome. The man does not know that she is coming, mind you, and she does not know how to contact him. She is convinced that he will know where she is and will, quite miraculously, turn up. Here comes the clincher. The mystery man sends a ticket to The Royal Ballet's performance of The Nutcracker to her New York apartment. She spends her last cent on, you won't believe this, clothing for the performance. She believes that he will sit beside her in a tuxedo with a crisp, white shirt and a white, silk scarf draped around his neck. What the heck, he will also carry a walking cane with a gold handle. Instead of this dapper creature, a cruel man in a coarse, black suit parks himself in the seat next to her and informs her that not only is he a friend of the mystery man, but that he is also the man who vied for her attention while in Rome with the mystery man and tossed a coin to see which one would woo her. Said girl leaves her seat distraught and cries in the ladies room for an indeterminate amount of time before she realizes that she has left her purse and her jacket on the seat. She asks the help of a fellow patron in the ladies room. The patron's husband retrieves the purse and the jacket, and they provide her with a ride back to her hotel. One cannot make up such nonsensical events.

Now, I, the foolish girl, find myself on a plane to New York, and I am having an epiphany, of sorts. The man in the seat, I think he said that his name was George something or other, and I believe that he is the same man in the picture with Roger that was taped to my mailbox. Yes, I am certain that it was him. Something is askew. This man is stalking

me. Good grief, what if he was the one who sent me the ticket?
What if he has been sending me things all along? What if
it wasn't Roger at all? Everyone was right. I have placed
myself in a dangerous situation. I have been acting like a fool.
I won't belabor it. Tomorrow is another day, and I am on
my way home. Will I be safe at home? This man knows no
boundaries. What is his connection to Roger? What should
I do? I thought that writing would help, but it hasn't. I am
more confused than ever.

Opal ended the entry with the squiggly line that she always used to mark the end of an entry and closed her journal. She tried to close her eyes to sleep through the flight, but she could not rest. The events of the past few days swirled around in her head like an unrelenting whirlwind.

The posh environs were just as Harding Cromwell had left them. George had not interfered with his father's home the way he interfered with his father's business. Harding could not remember how long he had been away from his English country home, the home of the ancestral line. Perhaps that was why George had not dared to touch anything. The family portraits hung solidly upon the walls with the ancestors peering into every crevice of the house. Harding felt a sense of comfort now that he was within his element. Colorado had its pleasures, but it was good to be home. He sat comfortably in his green leather wing chair that provided an impressive view of the east side of the estate.

"Hand me my binoculars, will you, Roger?" asked Cromwell extending his hand while keeping his sights on the pheasant in the far distance. Roger placed the binoculars into the elderly man's slightly tremulous hand. Harding placed the binoculars in front of his eyes and smiled. The pheasant had scurried beneath the thicket, but the view of the grounds was mesmerizing. Harding sat for a long time looking over the grounds.

"I think I'll take a walk this afternoon," said Harding comfortably. Rippleton brought a glass of warm sherry on a silver tray lined with a white linen cloth and placed it on a small table near Harding's chair. The old man lifted the glass to his lips while still viewing the grounds. "I feel like a young man again," said Harding. "Rippleton, bring me my walking stick. I want to walk around the estate."

Rippleton complied and returned with Harding's walking stick and heavy winter coat and hat. The weather was clement, but cold set into the elder's bones quickly these days. "Coming Roger?" asked Harding while Rippleton helped him button the coat.

"Yes, of course," said Roger gathering his coat and hat from the hands of one of the servants.

The duo walked steadily down the stairs and onto the grounds of the estate. Of course, they would not be able to walk the entire length of the estate, as it was fifty-three acres, but a small walk would suffice. Harding wrapped his scarf tightly across his neck. They walked in silence for a while before Harding spoke.

"How's your family, Roger?" asked Harding.

"My father's well, so I'm told" said Roger. "I don't see them often. I hear my sister is planning to marry a promising young architect."

"Your father must be pleased," said Harding. "An architect, you say? Well, that's fine news. I believe in work, Roger. There's nothing like it. It keeps one strong, alert, and healthy. You *do* know what I'm saying to you, don't you, Roger?"

"I believe so," said Roger.

"If my son thinks that I will hibernate within this estate and forego my responsibilities within the company, he is sadly mistaken," said Harding emitting a slight cough. "I plan to return to work tomorrow morning. I want you to arrange everything, Roger. See to it that my office is in order, and I want to meet with all of the staff. I will, in all probability, work part-time, but I will work. Nothing will prevent it. Relay that message to my son, won't you? Why wasn't he at the airport to meet us?"

"I believe George is in London," said Roger. "He's entertaining a friend of mine from New York, since I could not meet her."

"Still, one would think that he would have taken the time to meet us. He could have brought the friend along," said Harding.

"I'm told that she flew back to New York rather despondent," said Roger.

"Well, that's George," said Harding. "He's never had much luck with women. They despise him. He has only to open his mouth, and they are aghast with his cruelty and stupidity. "

Roger remained silent, but his silence was a tacit agreement. George alienated most people – men and women. He had an acidic nature that repelled most people. Were it not for Roger's company, George would be utterly alone.

"I feel invigorated, Roger. This place is like a warm balm soothing my spirits," said Harding. "I think I'll go back now. No need to over-extend my faculties on the first day. The old place will be here tomorrow."

They turned to walk back to the estate. "You're very quiet, Roger," said Harding. "What is troubling you?"

"I'm concerned about my friend's state of mind," confided Roger. "She may have misconstrued George's intent."

"Well, why don't you call her and tell her that George is a blithering idiot"? asked Harding.

"We have sort of an agreement," said Roger. "I don't want to speak with her personally until May."

Harding stopped walking and peered into Roger's face. "Are you daft? What does this mean? I don't understand."

Roger attempted to explain his unusual relationship with

Opal. The old man listened intently then spoke before they entered the house.

"I don't want to interfere," said Harding, "but my advice is to go to her, if you care about her and sort things out. Communication is essential."

"We communicate," said Roger. "She can sense what I'm feeling."

"Nonsense!" uttered Harding as Roger helped him up the stairs. "Go to your young lady and make things right; otherwise, you will lose her. I feel responsible that you were tending to my needs while that imbecile son of mine acted in your stead. Leave her name and address with Rippleton before you leave. I'll handle things. It is the least I can do."

"I would rather you did not intercede," said Roger. "We have a commitment. It is important that she follows through without any prodding. This is the way I want to handle it, Sir."

"Very well," said Harding. "I will leave it to you, then. Let me know how it all works out." The old man laughed. It had been years since he laughed heartily, and it felt good.

Opal poured tea from her silver teapot into a white, china cup. She sipped the tea and looked out of the window. The leaves were all gone now, and the trees were bare. Without the luxuriant leaves, sunlight streamed through the windows, although the temperatures outside were arctic.

"I can't believe that you're still using that teapot," said Heather. "I would have thrown away all of his little gifts."

"It wasn't his fault," said Opal.

"I've given up trying to convince you," said Heather. "We're going ice skating before they light the tree tomorrow. There will be so many tourists tomorrow that we won't be able to get near the rink. Are you coming?"

"No, I think I'll just sit here and enjoy my tea and my book," said Opal

"You'd better enjoy your books for the Milton class. You're really beginning to irritate Professor Langley. You don't know a thing about Milton and Republicanism. Paula told me what happened in class. He almost threw the book at you. Paula said that his hands grasped the book so hard that they were turning pale, and his face was so contorted after your response that she thought that he was going to have a stroke or something," said Heather. "I'll bet that he retires next semester."

Opal smiled as she remembered her untimely response and her professor's reaction.

"As well he should," said Opal. "He must be a hundred years old. The whole world doesn't revolve around Milton."

"Nor does it revolve around Roger Paisley," said Heather resting her ice skates over her shoulder.

"Touché," said Opal sipping her tea thoughtfully.

She would see it through to the end. Five months left and she would receive a reward for her faithfulness. Opal felt comforted as she sipped her tea. All was well. After days of discomfort and tears, she emerged unscathed with feelings of tranquility. She did not know how, nor did she try to analyze her feelings. Somehow, her entire being was forged with Roger's presence. He was in the very blood that coursed through her system and gave life to her beating heart. Her eyes saw with his vision. She felt his presence in an unobtrusive manner. She was free to choose her course of action, but each setback drew her closer to him and strengthened the commitment. It made no sense to try to explain it to other people. It was an ethereal experience.

"And so, it has been decided that Roger Paisley will head the New York branch," said Harding Cromwell lifting his glass of champagne at the staff meeting.

Roger looked askance at the CEO. Hearty congratulations were hurled, some sincere, others not, in the young executive's direction. This was not the promotion that he was seeking, and he had no intention of living in that urban metropolis.

"With all due respect," said Roger, "I'm afraid I will have to decline."

"Nonsense!" shouted Harding with a wink. "It's all settled."

The office cheered; Roger was taken aback. This turn of events would ruin everything. There would be no life for him in New York. It was not a place where he could ever call home, and the thought of overseeing a branch populated with boorish Americans was unfathomable. He had visited the New York branch on several occasions and found it to be poorly managed and grievously over-endowed with painted, aggressive women in tight dresses that revealed too much cleavage and muscle-bound men who spent more time at the gym and prowling the clubs than creating an infusion of life and creativity within the company. If the truth be told, Roger was just what the New York branch needed. He would get them in order or bring in transports from the steady English labor force.

"Don't worry," whispered George, "I'll handle everything."

"I'll resign before I accept this assignment, George," said Roger quietly.

"It won't be necessary," said George confidently. "Leave it to me."

"As you are aware, three additional junior executive positions are available within the New York division," said George. "We will be notifying the fortunate applicants within the week."

The staff meeting vacated with the respondents hastening to their respective offices. Most of the hopefuls were women, for whom an assignment in New York under Roger Paisley would be most agreeable. George smiled. Everything was to his liking. With a number of English beauties accompanying Roger to New York, the dim-witted Opal would not stand a chance. Yes, everything was to George's liking.

"It may be for a month or two," assured George, "no longer."

"Are you insane? I will not accept the assignment for a day," said Roger. "I am submitting my resignation today."

"Wait!" resounded George excitedly. "You can't do that. I told you that I would handle it."

"Well, you haven't done a very good job of it, have you?" asked Roger. "There are three hundred applicants, male and female, for three New York positions. May I ask how you have handled it?"

"Out of the three hundred applicants, is there no one to your liking?" asked George.

"Damn you!" asserted Roger. "I should have known that you would be up to your usual tricks."

"All right," said George. "I confess. I had hoped that you would find suitable English applicants to accompany you, but since you are adamant, I concede. Opal it is, and there will be no further 'tricks' as you call them. You are becoming more American as we speak."

Roger smirked and started for the door. "I once considered you a friend, but now, I don't know what you are."

"I am always on your side, Roger," said George. "You can believe that."

"I believe nothing," said Roger. "I no longer consider you a friend. Goodbye, George."

Roger Paisley closed the door and walked to the tubes. He rode in silence contemplating his next move without his dearest friend. If he had to venture to the United States, it would only be to bring Opal back with him. Why was this foolish woman so important to him? He did not know. Somehow, she had gotten under his skin, as it were, and he had to have her with him. It was incomprehensible, but it was a reality. Opal was his; they were bound together for life. They had a commitment. He knew it, and she knew it as well. Whatever happened, it would happen to both of them. They were forever.

Jim opened the email attachment that Heather forwarded with an in-depth description of Opal's actions during the month of November and pleaded with Jim to reason with her before the Christmas holidays brought on more troublesome events. Heather had a special concern about George Cromwell, whom she surmised was trying to interfere with Roger and Opal for reasons unknown. Jim, progressing nicely within a relationship with Molly, viewed the matter cautiously. He did not want to interfere in Opal's relationship with Roger; yet, he concurred that the events of November were, indeed, perplexing and decided that the best thing to do would be to meet with George Cromwell to get the matter out in the open. Obviously, George Cromwell had some interest in Opal and George's relationship. The group would meet with him in order to ascertain the nature of his interest. In truth, the group, Hank, Richard, Paula, and Heather, believed that the relationship would fizzle out before the May meeting in Rome, but the George Cromwell addition was problematic. They distrusted him and feared for Opal's safety. It was determined that Opal should know nothing of their plans. Hank, a top-notch computer expert, had no difficulty in finding George Cromwell through the Google network and was able to research a great deal of information about the Cromwell family. Curiously, there was nothing about Roger Paisley on Google, but through the George Cromwell link, the group was able to discover many interesting facts about the family. The project occupied much of their time, and they were careful to conceal their endeavors from Opal. Hank composed a letter to George Cromwell requesting a meeting at the New York branch of Cromwell Publishers on 58th Street. George readily complied. The request was intriguing. George checked his calendar. He would be able to attend a meeting in New York mid-December.

George liked New York in December and was especially enamoured with Rockefeller Center's elaborate Christmas tree. English tree decorations were subdued, but the American

Christmas tree decorations were jubilant. He loved the fervor of the crowds that enveloped New York society during the Christmas season. Of course, Roger found it garish and wanted no part of it. George could never get Roger to visit New York during the Christmas season. Now, there was an opportunity to participate in the festivities with Americans. Perhaps he would have an opportunity to share some of them with Opal along with her friends, who obviously cared deeply about her well-being. George would not inform Roger of the meeting. The less he knew, the better it would be for all concerned. Yes, George would meet with the group, and a new beginning would unfold for each of them.

Opal, thoroughly immersed within her studies, put the holiday season far from her mind. She had missed a considerable amount of work during her mini-vacation in London, and her professors were less than sympathetic. In point of fact, they seemed determined to penalize her for the untimely excursion. The Milton class was of particular concern. If she did not attain an "A," her nearly-perfect GPA would plummet, and she would risk losing the fellowship she worked so hard to attain.

The streets were brightly lit with Christmas lights that swung from one side of the street to the other, but Opal had no time to marvel at their radiance. There was the research paper and then the myriad of finals that filled every crevice of her thoughts and her being. She barely spoke a word to Heather, who also seemed occupied with her own studies and projects. This preoccupation facilitated the deception that was necessary in order to meet with George Cromwell.

The day of the meeting finally arrived. Everyone dressed in business attire, apart from Hank, who wore jeans and a sweater over a tee shirt as a means of demonstrating antipathy towards George Cromwell. The latter's behavior deserved no respect, and Hank would make his feelings clear, in the event his attire did not convey the message. The group took the elevator to the thirtieth floor and was shown to a rather modest, yet impressively decorated, conference room. They sat in the over-stuffed upholstered chairs that surrounded the highly-polished, cherry oak table. Bookshelves lined the walls, and flowers with interesting arrangements, adorned the conference table. A portrait of a rather austere-looking man hung above a cozy fireplace at the far end of the room. It seemed to be a working fireplace.

"How cliché," observed Hank. "Are we supposed to be impressed?"

A sparkling silver tea service rested unobtrusively on the table.

"We should have met at Star Bucks," continued Hank. "We are in his element, and it should be the other way around. He is in our country; we should be the ones in charge."

"Look around you, Hank" said Richard. "Even if we met at Star Bucks, do you really think that we would be in charge? This is old money, and we are out of our league. The best we can do is to state our case and hope that he is a man of reason. We are here for Opal, and we want to protect her from all of this. What are your thoughts, Jim?"

Jim surveyed the room. His eyes rested on the law volumes within the bookcases. The room was not intimidating, although a modest crystal chandelier hung above the table.

"I think that he's making an effort," said Jim. "He didn't have to come all the way to New York to meet with us. He could have had someone else handle it. I say we give him the benefit of the doubt. Let's hear what he has to say before we judge."

George Cromwell entered the room. He wore a gray herringbone suit, a white shirt, and an olive green and red-striped tie. He seemed younger than they had imagined, though there were flecks of gray in his dark brown hair. George wore glasses with a black frame, which made his cheerful face seem rather businesslike. It was difficult not to notice the cufflinks that adorned the cuffs of his shirt. The group viewed this as a line of demarcation, of sorts. In their world, people did not wear cufflinks. They were entering a different realm and realized that they would need to tread carefully.

"Sorry to keep you waiting," said George taking his place at the head of the table. "Would you care for tea?"

Hank looked derisively at his friends. The thought of tea from the sparkling tea service irked him.

"No, thank you," said Richard.

"I'll have a cup of tea," said Heather. The group looked at her with annoyance.

"Cream or sugar?" asked George pouring Heather a cup of tea.

"Both," responded Heather. She was beginning to understand how Opal could fall for one of these chaps.

"We don't want to take up too much of your time," said Richard relieved that Paula could not attend the meeting and be swept off of her feet by the suave interloper. He wished that Heather would have remained home as well.

George sipped his Earl Grey tea and surveyed the group one at a time. He formed his impressions carefully and quickly, as he was wont to do whenever he made a new contact. At a glance, he could tell that Jim was the man of compassion, Richard was the most intelligent, and Hank, although wearing the attire of a poor working-class rebel, was of a higher socio-economic status than any of his compatriots. The gleam in Heather's eye indicated that she was impressed with him, and he would give her an opportunity to become chums when the others were out of his tightly-controlled environs.

"How can I help you?" asked George calmly.

"As I expressed in my email," said Hank, "we are friends of Opal, and we are concerned about her. We don't know much about her friend, Roger, and we know little about you; yet, she tells us that it was you who showed up at the Royal Ballet and had the effrontery to tell her that you and Roger tossed a coin for her."

George smiled. "I can understand your concern."

"Who is this Roger anyway?" asked Heather. "He's always sending her things - books and teapots."

"We are also concerned about the proposed meeting in Rome," said Jim. "Opal is not from a family of means. She can't fly off to Rome whenever she feels like it. Her studies are suffering because of her relationship with Roger, and I use the term *relationship* loosely. He hasn't called her or visited her since they met. She doesn't even know how to contact him. It's all very strange, and we want to put an end to it."

"This is distressing news," said George returning his cup to its saucer.

"Personally," said Hank, "I would like to know your involvement in this. Opal says that you are very likely the man in the photo with Roger that was taped to her mailbox. Is this true?"

"How observant Opal is," said George. "You see, you are not the only ones concerned about your friend. I, too, am concerned. Roger has been a dear friend since our school days together, and he is a very important part of this firm. I don't want to see him hurt, and I don't want his position in the company compromised. You can understand that, can't you?"

"No," said Jim. "I do not understand it. That doesn't explain your tossing a coin for her or your meeting her at the ballet instead of Roger."

"Opal was really upset," said Heather. "She spent her last cent going to London and buying clothes for the ballet. She thought that she was going to meet Roger and instead, you sit beside her. She was devastated."

"We want Roger to stop sending her things and give up this idea of meeting her in Rome," said Richard. "What does he hope to gain from all of this? Opal knows nothing about him. What if he's married? What if he is mentally unbalanced? Quite frankly, I'm beginning to question Opal's mental stability. She thinks that she has some sort of connection to him."

"What sort of connection?" asked George with interest.

"Never mind that," said Hank. "What is your part in all of this, and what are you going to do about Roger Paisley?"

"It's Hank, isn't it?" asked George. "I like to know about the people I meet before I meet them. Your concern is justified. My methods may seem draconian, but I can assure you that Opal is not in any sort of danger. Roger is the most stable person I know, and his feelings for Opal are quite legitimate. He is not married. It is my opinion that he will meet Opal in Rome and honor his commitment."

"Just what is this commitment?" asked Jim. "Opal hasn't made that clear."

"As a gentleman, Roger will honor his word. As far as the commitment, even I don't know what that is. Roger hasn't made it clear to me either. So, you see, we are both in a similar predicament. You are concerned about your friend, and I am concerned about mine," said George.

"What are we going to do?" asked Heather.

"Is there any chance Roger will meet with us?" asked Richard.

"There is as much chance of Roger meeting with you to discuss this relationship as there is of Opal meeting with me to discuss it," said George. "I'm afraid there's very little we can do. I would like to know more about this connection that you mentioned. What sort of connection is it?"

"Opal says that she can feel his presence within her – that she can feel his *essence*," said Heather.

"I felt it," said Jim. The entire group looked askance at him. "Well, I did. When she returned from Rome, I could feel a different presence about her. It was almost as if she was looking through someone else's eyes and feeling with someone else's hands. I can't explain it, but there was something."

"You never mentioned that," said Richard.

"Well, I've said it. I couldn't stand to be around her. It was as if I was around him too," said Jim. "I tell you, he was there."

"Like an apparition?" asked Hank.

"I don't know. I just sensed something. Somehow, he was right there whenever I looked at her or tried to touch her," said Jim. The group tried not to notice the tears welling in his eyes.

"It was his *essence*," said Heather. "You laughed at me when I said it before, but he filled her with his *essence*."

"*Essence?*" asked George.

"Heather believes that it is possible for people to infuse their *essences* within other people," said Hank impatiently. He was relieved to draw the attention away from Jim, whom George handed a pristine white handkerchief.

"I would like to know more about this *essence*," said George.

"It's sheer nonsense," said Richard. "I think that they are referring to one of Milton's writings, *Comus*, where the Lady cannot be touched by the external forces outside of her because she is filled with a particular *essence*, which enables her to remain unscathed."

"What?" asked Hank.

"Never mind," said Richard. "Opal has been studying Milton for two semesters. I think that it has taken its toll."

"So then you are asserting that Roger, somehow, possesses this *essence*, of which you speak?" asked George curiously. "Why haven't I seen it or heard of it?"

"It isn't available to everyone," said Richard. "According to Milton, only those who share the *essence* can access it. It is hidden from all others."

"Can we return to the Twenty-First Century?" asked Hank. "Now, I say that we confront this Roger and ask him what his intentions are towards Opal. We don't want her running off to Rome on another wild goose chase. It will destroy her."

"Confrontation will be of no use," said George. "We need a subtler approach. I think that this *essence* dynamic is just what we need. I confess, I have not read *Comus*, but you may rest assured that I will. Milton isn't my favorite author, but I think that this time, I will study his words intently. Amazing how far literature can take one, isn't it? Leave it to me, my new friends. I think that we can work together to sort this out – you on this end with Opal, and me on the other end with Roger."

"What will you do?" asked Heather.

"Leave it to me," said George. "I'm no match for John Milton, but I do know a thing or two about Roger Paisley. My hunch is that Opal is not the only one with Roger's *essence*. There must have been others before Opal. "

"What if Opal is the one with the *essence?*" asked Richard. "What if Roger is the victim here?"

"You mean that Opal may have filled Roger with her *essence?*" asked Heather.

"Precisely," said Richard.

"Have you all lost your minds?" asked Hank. "Let's, for the sake of argument, say that Opal has this mysterious *essence*. Wouldn't she have shared it with Jim?"

"Not necessarily," said Richard. "Don't take it personally, Jim, but perhaps, being a man of logic, she couldn't share it with you. Of course, that's it."

"But it doesn't make sense," said Hank. "Jim said that he felt Roger's *essence* when he was with Opal."

"Jim felt another presence when he was with Opal. Who is to say that it was Roger?" asked Richard. "It may have been Opal, the part of Opal that Jim has never seen or experienced - the part that came alive when she met Roger."

"I'm confused," said Heather.

"As am I," said George. "I think that we need to step away from this and give it thought for a few days."

"Maybe we should consult a priest," said Heather. "Maybe this *essence* thing is something unwholesome."

"Stop it!" yelled Jim. "This is ridiculous."

"I agree," said George. "In light of what we have discussed today, I think that it would be wise if we kept our communications clandestine. I won't return to New York until mid-March, but we can remain in touch online or by phone, if you feel something urgent has transpired. I can generally be reached at this number," said George handing Richard a business card. "My assistant knows how to reach me at all hours. Now, how about dinner and a show? It is my treat. My assistant will handle the arrangements."

Opal opened her latest package. There were white roses and what appeared to be baby's breath. A picture from a magazine was included. A beautifully understated Christmas tree was pictured decorated with white roses and baby's breath. Atop the tree was a silver ribbon tied into a simple bow. Opal had never seen a Christmas tree decorated in such a manner, but she was willing to try envisioning Christmas decorations in a new way. Of course, there would be a fracas with Heather, who always took charge of the Christmas decorations and coordinated the annual Christmas party. It would mean substituting Heather's artificial tree with a real one – another problem. Heather had an aversion to real Christmas trees. Heather considered it a waste of a natural resource; trees were needed to clean the air. She was probably right, but the thought of an actual Christmas tree and the smell of pine filled Opal with a sense of excitement. She hadn't had a real Christmas tree since she left home. It would be a nice change.

Sidewalk vendors displayed their wares proudly. Christmas trees of all sizes filled the make-shift stalls on every corner. Some stood majestically surveying their surroundings. Others peered into the crowded pedestrian traffic and tried to catch the attention of the passers-by, particularly the children who beamed excitedly at the prospect of taking one of them home. It was an exciting time in the city. Opal was filled with a sense of vibrancy and new hope as she selected a tree. It was a medium-sized tree and light enough for her to carry home and up the stairs. She also purchased a stand, which she filled with water the moment she arrived home. She cut the cord that encircled the tree, and its branches flourished gracefully into the air. It was more beautiful than Opal imagined. The scent of fresh pine filled the apartment as she placed the tree into the stand and fastened the screws securely. She stood back and looked admirably at the new addition. The tree was gorgeous, and Opal wondered how she lived without the hands-on Christmas experience of selecting a tree, bringing it home, and watching it emerge into a sublime object of beauty. With the white roses and the baby's breath, the tree was transformed into an even greater feast for the eyes. Atop the tree, Opal tied the silver bow for the final treatment and looked on with sheer delight. It was heaven, a heaven that would soon be tested by the sound of Heather's key in the lock.

Roger Paisley signed his name on the lease. It was a quaint, yet charming flat with a view of the Thames. Opal would need to be weaned off of city living slowly. A small flat in London would help her to make the transition to the country home that she would share with him as his wife, and it would give them enough time and space to make the necessary accommodations before the wedding. Roger could not fathom how couples lived together before taking the marriage vows. It seemed absurd. Part of the thrill of newly-wedded bliss was learning of the other's living habits and foibles that were made manifest only within the close confines of those first few months of marital bliss.

The realtor handed him the keys, and the apartment was his, for a year at least. Opal would decorate it as she saw fit, but in order to ensure that their decorating styles congealed, he would send suggestions through magazine photos and various artifacts of importance in a new home, through small gifts and books for the bookshelves that he would purchase before her arrival. The Christmas tree was the latest endeavor. Opal would be the perfect English wife long before she arrived in England. The transformation had begun, and he would allow neither

George nor Harding Cromwell to interfere. The proposed transfer to New York was certainly out of the question. Opal would share his life in England; he had no intention of beginning a life together in those dreaded states, particularly New York, which, in his estimation, seemed to function as its own sovereign state.

Roger drove to the Cromwell residence and was told that Harding Cromwell was indisposed, which meant that he was napping. Before Roger could exit the driveway, George's olive-green Bentley pulled up behind him. George was pleased to see Roger.

"What a stroke of good fortune," said George exiting the car and smiling broadly. "I've been trying to reach you. You know that the family Christmas party is next week. Emily and her young man, Max, will arrive tomorrow."

"That should be a blissful occasion," said Roger sarcastically.

"Surely, you plan to attend," said George hopefully.

"I'm afraid I have other commitments," intoned Roger.

"Walk with me," said George. "There is something that I must discuss with you."

"I am not moving to New York," said Roger adamantly.

"Of course you aren't," said George taking Roger's arm. They walked onto the estate passing scurrying partridges and charming streams in the midst of acres of wintry green.

"What's so pressing?" asked Roger.

"I wanted to ask you about Milton," said George.

"Milton Prescott in accounting?" asked Roger.

"No, no," said George, "John Milton."

"What are you going on about George? What is your interest in Milton?" asked Roger.

"I didn't read *Comus*," said George.

"Why would you want to read it now?" asked Roger.

"I've contacted Lucius Graves," said George.

"I haven't heard that name since I was at Oxford. Is he still there?" asked Roger.

"Yes, and he's agreed to read with me," said George.

Roger stopped walking. "You're up to something. No one voluntarily submits to reading with Lucius Graves. Who is the woman? There must be a woman involved – someone with an interest in Milton. Opal is studying Milton." Roger peered at George. "Come now, George, you're not seriously thinking of impressing Opal with your knowledge of Milton."

"Don't be ridiculous," said George. "I know when I've been defeated. Your Opal has no interest in anyone apart from you. I suppose that is why you have rented an apartment for her. You must be very sure that she will be willing to uproot herself and move to London."

Roger remained silent.

"Opal is somewhat flighty, Roger, but I do not believe her to be stupid. This little scheme of yours is mushrooming beyond your control. Do you intend to support her?" asked George.

"Do I intend to support my wife?" asked Roger.

"Be sensible, Roger!" howled George. His face had turned a crimson color as though he were ready to explode. "You cannot consider marriage with that simple woman. If you ever had children…"

"Best left unsaid, dear friend, if we are to remain friends," said Roger earnestly.

"You would forsake our friendship for that…" George stopped speaking as he watched Roger turn and walk away from him.

"Be so kind as to allow me to move my car," said Roger opening the door of his Mini Cooper.

George moved his Bentley and watched Roger drive down the scenic road.

"Damn you," uttered George as the car turned the bend. "Damn you both."

Glasses tinkled with New York Christmas cheer as the friends toasted a new and festive season. Jim brought Molly to the party. It was the first time that she had met the entire group. Everyone seemed to like her. Molly was a sensible choice for an uncomplicated man like Jim, who felt uneasy in the transformed apartment.

"Where are the lights on the tree?" asked Jim pretending not to notice the English ambience of the room.

"No lights this year," said Heather. "Opal decorated. I must say that I'm getting used to having a live tree. I've never had one before."

Jim viewed Opal as she gazed admiringly at the winsome tree.

"Why the sudden change?" asked Jim.

"No reason," responded Opal. "I just wanted a new look this year. It's quite lovely, isn't it?"

Jim did not reply; instead, he walked to the silver tea service that bedecked the end table and observed the craftsmanship.

"William Rogers, isn't it?" asked Jim.

"Is it?" asked Opal approaching the tea service. "Who is William Rogers?"

"My mother has one," said Hank also approaching the service. "This seems like an antique, Opal. Look at the spout. My guess is that it's over ninety years old."

Paula laughed. "He's been watching 'Antiques Road Show'."

"For your information, I saw one like this at the MET, and it isn't William Rogers. I think that it's Dutch. Look, there's an inscription on the tray," said Hank observing the back of the silver tray.

"Let me see that," said Opal taking the tray and reading the inscription, "Stafford and Millicent Cromwell on Their Twenty-Fifth Wedding Anniversary, 1823."

"Cromwell," said Heather, "isn't that George's last name?"

The group froze. Opal looked startled.

"Yes, that's the name of the man I told you about who met me at the Royal Opera House, George Cromwell. I'm surprised that you remembered his name."

The group remained silent hoping that the awkward moment would pass without revealing its secret.

"Why would Roger send me a tea service that belonged to George Cromwell's family? This thing must be worth a fortune," said Opal.

"Isn't it obvious?" interjected Molly, "Roger didn't send the tea service, just as Roger didn't meet you at The Royal Opera House. This person, George, must be really smitten with you."

Opal viewed the tea service derisively with the thought that it might have been an irreplaceable gift from George Cromwell.

"You seem to have a secret admirer," said Molly amused.

"Not so secret," scoffed Jim. "He left his name or family's name on the bottom of the gift and the date that is proof that it is a valuable antique. Didn't you look at the bottom of the tray?" asked Jim.

"Of course not," said Opal, "Why would I do that?"

Richard looked askance at the silent group.

"I don't feel like celebrating anymore," said Jim. "Molly and I are leaving."

"I think we should celebrate another time," said Hank getting his jacket and hat from the coat rack.

"Where is everyone going?" asked Opal. "Don't let George Cromwell spoil our evening."

"I think that we should go," said Paula. "Something just doesn't seem right."

"I know what you mean," said Richard. "You've placed all of us in an uncomfortable position, Opal, with your 'commitment.' Now, things are spiralling out of control. We've all told you to drop this Roger affair, but you refused; as a result, we have George Cromwell to deal with. The whole thing reeks. You've allowed this guy to upset your life, your career, and now your friendships."

"My friendships?" asked Opal.

"I'm getting out of here," said Hank following Jim and Molly. Richard and Paula exited with them. Opal and Heather stood in the cheerfully decorated apartment.

"Now what?" asked Heather.

"Now, I send this tea service back to George Cromwell," said Opal.

"Are you crazy?" shrieked Heather. "You can sell it on ebay. It will probably pay for your tuition until you graduate. You won't even have to work those long hours at the book store anymore."

"Do you really think that I want George Cromwell to be responsible for my graduation from the university?" asked Opal. "What am I to do, Heather? What if Roger really did send the tea service? What if he's trying to tell me of his connection to George."

"This *connection*, as you call it is not normal behaviour," said Heather.

"Maybe it's normal English behaviour," offered Opal.

"Wake up, Opal!" shouted Heather. "I don't care if it's Russian, although it sounds a bit French, it can't be a good thing, can it?"

"I suppose not," sighed Opal.

Opal had no idea what was happening, but it was true that her life and her relationships were at odds with this new focal point within her life. She lost Jim, her studies were in peril, and her friends thought that she was out of touch with reality. Still, there was a glimmer of hope shining consistently within her heart. It was a tiny flame deep within a tall, circular candle that burned a small crevice through the center to the base. One could not see it without peering into the candle, but it was there burning steadfastly. It was a tiny, unobtrusive flame, but it lit her very soul. Each passing day drew her nearer to the final destination in Rome.

Roger Paisley selected a royal blue tie and wrapped it expertly underneath his collar. This time, he would see Harding Cromwell without fail. George was attending a conference in Switzerland for the week. There would be no interruptions. Rippleton, the butler, opened the door and led Roger to Harding's study.

"You needn't have brought a gift," said the elder Cromwell still in his dressing gown. Roger sat comfortably in the leather wing chair near the window. The expanse was lovely and green, even in the heart of winter. He placed the tastefully wrapped gift on the end table.

"One gift deserves another," said Roger watching the old man unwrap the present like an expectant child. Harding held the exquisite, porcelein figure of his favorite horse, Alastair. Every detail was impeccably replicated.

"It's a masterpiece," said the elder statesman. "Alastair was the best darned horse I ever had."

"He was the first horse I ever rode," said Roger.

"You always outdo yourself," said Cromwell.

"It's nothing in comparison to the gift that you sent Opal," said Roger.

Cromwell smiled mischievously. "You know about that, do you?" asked the patriarch.

"Of course," said Roger. "Why did you do it?"

"Someone had to," said Cromwell. "It's about time we had a wedding here, and I want to hear the sound of children's voices before I push off."

"You'll be around a long time," said Roger.

"That may be, but I won't be able to wait for Emily or George to fulfill their obligations to produce an heir. They're too selfish. Emily wants to spend my money on her young fortune hunters, and George wants to rule the world. What a sorry lot," announced Cromwell.

"They're not so bad," said Roger.

"That blasted girl called me this morning to say that she's bringing her young man here for Christmas. Do you know how old he is?" asked Cromwell.

"He's barely eighteen, so I hear," said Roger.

"That's right," said Cromwell. "If she marries him, he stands to inherit half of my fortune. It should go to you."

"We've been through this before," said Roger. "I'm not a legal heir, nor do I wish to be. That isn't important now. I came to tell you that I must return the tea service to you."

"Why?" asked Cromwell. "Didn't your young lady like it?"

"It's much too valuable," protested Roger.

"It's a priceless heirloom!" bellowed Cromwell. "Let the young lady know that you're not a pauper."

"But I am," said Roger. "She doesn't mind."

"Blasted Americans – they don't know the value of a good name or of old money. Anyone with 'a dollar and a dream' can be king over there," apprised Cromwell.

"That notwithstanding," said Roger, "I must return the tea service. It belongs with the family treasures."

"You're a part of this family," said Cromwell.

"If you're asking me whether I prefer to be the legitimate son of a well-renown author of little means or the bastard son of a wealthy landowner and publisher, whose daughter I almost married, I think you know the answer to that. No one must know of our secret. Allow me to live with a modicum of dignity, if you will," said Roger. "In any event, the tea service will be returned when Opal moves to London in the fall."

Harding's countenance brightened. "She's moving to London, is she?"

"Yes," said Roger. "I've secured a small flat for her near the offices."

"Good man," said Cromwell. "I knew that you would take matters in hand."

"I request that you send no more gifts. We don't want to frighten her away, do we?" asked Roger.

"Say no more. I'll leave it to you. Shall we have tea?" asked Cromwell.

Rippleton brought in tea, a tray of crab puffs, and biscuits. The two gentlemen enjoyed a restful afternoon before the hearth.

Christmas Day was uneventful. Opal attended Mass at St. Patrick's Cathedral; after which, she visited her family in New Jersey. New Jersey seemed desolate. There were no people walking around. There was no energy. It was like visiting death. The family was dwindling. Some preferred to remain in their own homes; others were out of town. Opal spent Christmas Day with her aging mother and a few relatives. She distributed souvenirs from her trip to London. The children wore bobby helmets and seemed quite pleased. After dinner, Opal returned to her quiet New York apartment, where she could enjoy the living Christmas tree and her amiable, English surroundings.

Across the Atlantic, the Cromwell Christmas party was well underway. The festivities had begun. Roger rang the bell, and Rippleton opened the door to the stately residence. Roger presented Rippleton with an envelope – a gift of £100. The butler was most grateful. Roger joined the other guests in the large area reserved for entertainment. There were tasteful decorations around the room. Mistletoe and holly bedecked every entranceway. Servants wearing crisp, white shirts and gloves carried refreshments on silver trays. A roaring fire provided extra warmth to the room of festive revelers.

"I hear you're getting engaged to an American," said a voice behind Roger.

He turned and saw Emily standing before him. Her

chestnut brown hair was upswept with wisps trickling over her ears and neck strategically. A small bejeweled comb rested gently in her hair behind her ear. It was a comb Roger remembered purchasing for her in Rome, at her insistence, when they were courting, before Harding Cromwell confided that he suspected that he was his father. Those days were a nightmare to Roger's remembrance, and he wanted to forget them as urgently as he wanted to forget that he might be related to the dysfunctional family.

"Hello Emily. Yes, an engagement to an American is imminent. I hear that you're living with a young man who isn't able to drink legally in his own country," said Roger derisively. Emily laughed.

"Are you jealous, Roger?" asked Emily.

"Hardly," affirmed Roger. "What you do is your affair – no pun intended."

"For the record, His name is Max, and he gets all of the alcohol he wants in our home," said Emily defensively.

"I don't doubt that," said Roger scornfully. "You'll pardon me."

Emily watched her former fiancé as he strode confidently to the fireplace and engaged in conversation with a group of Cromwell management employees.

"See here," said a middle-aged man holding a glass of champagne, "I don't much like the idea of your transfer to New York, Paisley."

"I am not transferring to New York," said Roger with finality.

"But Cromwell said..."

"Mr. Cromwell is mistaken," said Roger quietly. "You'll pardon me."

Roger left the group and stood alone near the bannister of the swirling staircase. He was ready to ask Rippleton to get his coat when a young man approached him.

"You're Roger Paisley," said the young man.

"You must be Max," said Roger extending his hand reluctantly. Max shook it with enthusiasm. He seemed older than his eighteen years. The hubristic swagger of irrepressible youth defined his presence.

"Your work is phenomenal!" gushed Max. "You implemented the XK 3000 and made a tremendous profit."

"You're familiar with the XK3000?" asked Roger impressed.

"Of course," said Max. "Someday, I hope to work with you. I know that I'm young, but I'm eager to learn. Bill Gates didn't graduate from college."

"Ah, but I read somewhere that Mr. Gates *did* graduate from high school," said Roger sardonically.

"You mock me," said Max softly, "but I'm really serious, Mr. Paisley."

"If you are really serious, you'll finish high school and enroll in a reputable college. If you're as bright and eager as you say, that should not be a problem," said Roger.

"I could attend college over here," said Max. "Maybe I could work as your intern or something."

"I don't think that Emily will want to move to England," said Roger.

"She'll help me," said Max. "She always helps me. She's like a big sister – you know?"

Roger winced.

"One step at a time," said Roger. "Complete your education, and we'll discuss an internship."

Max's face illuminated. "Thank you, Mr. Paisley. You won't regret this."

Max's long, straggly blond pony tail fluttered as he hastened to Emily's side.

Spring arrived reluctantly. Winter fought fiercely to maintain dominance for as long as possible. Eventually, the icy winds and the unrelenting frigid air gave way to bright, sun-filled days. Buds made their appearance on trees, and flowers appeared, seemingly out of nowhere. First, the pansies showed their delightful natures, and then the daffodils grasped the attention of every jogger in Central Park. The air was fragrant and delightful. Winter had been the most oppressive in Opal's memory, but she was prepared to step into a new world. It was May.

The Trevi Fountain spluttered. Tourists filled every crevice. It was time. Roger Paisley checked his watch. She was late. Would she actually come? He did not read the latest reports from his sources, who kept watch over Opal in New York. He wanted to savor every moment and enjoy the suspense. Would she come, or wouldn't she? He thought of sending her an airline ticket but checked the idea. This would have to come from her. She would have to make the sacrifice. It would prove her willingness to intertwine her life with his. The ring rested comfortably in his breast pocket. He would ask her to be his wife at the splendid Trevi Fountain.

Standing in a far corner of the fountain, Opal caught Roger's eye. There was something strange about her gaze. Even at a distance, Roger knew that she was different – more mature than when he last saw her. The woman approaching him was unrecognizable. She was sedate, sophisticated, and confident. A year ago, her gaze reflected him; now, the gaze was self-assured, and he did not see himself within her eyes. Opal's hair was pinned up. Roger had never seen her neck before. It was elegant and genteel. Her eyes worried him. Something was different about them. They connected with his but not with the shy, intimidated look that he once perceived. Her eyes engaged his; increasingly, he could feel the strength of them as she approached him. He could not look away.

Roger's heart began to tremble as Opal drew near. Her gait was steady and sure. Roger had the strange feeling that he wanted to turn and run in the other direction, but it was too late. She was standing before him, and her intoxicating eyes never left his. They stood face-to-face without uttering a word. Roger did not know what to say. He was standing in front of a stranger.

"Hello, Roger," said Opal. Even her voice was different. Roger remained silent. Opal extended her hand and held Roger's within hers.

"You've changed," said Roger at last. He did not recognize his own voice. Now, he was the one with the voice of youthful inexperience. He felt like a school boy on his first date.

"Really?" asked Opal. "I guess it was to be expected. You wanted me to change, didn't you? All of your gifts were designed to change me into a new person befitting your lifestyle and temperament. You have succeeded in your endeavor. I am what you wanted me to become."

Roger had never heard her say so many words without interjecting some thought or word that he felt compelled to correct. If this was *Pygmalion*, then he was uncertain whether the end result suited him.

"Your hair is different," said Roger. He could not control the inane remarks that spewed from his mouth without warning. Seemingly, he could not form a coherent thought. Opal smiled as she watched him gaze uneasily at her.

"I'm more like you than you imagined," said Opal confidently. "I've been a living embodiment of you since we met. I feel as though we have been breathing the same air and living with one heart between us. What you see before you is what you are."

Roger was without words. He wanted Opal and not a female version of himself. He enjoyed molding her and watching her grow, but now that the flower was in bloom, he was reluctant to pluck it from the garden. Would it continue to grow in a foreign soil? Admittedly, he liked what he saw, but something was missing. It was that childlike dependence upon him, his thoughts, and his words, which he found so endearing. He stood before Opal, who was now transformed into an English rose, as it were, but he did not know what to do with her. He could not send her back to New York. What chance did an English rose have of surviving in that churlish metropolis?

"Is anything wrong?" asked Opal noting his silence and uneasy demeanor.

"I was just thinking," said Roger holding her hand firmly and leading her from the fountain to the congested walkway. "How about a sorbet before we talk?"

Opal smiled. Roger was grateful that her effervescent smile had not changed.

"What do you think of English gardens?" asked Roger.

"I've never had a garden, English or otherwise," answered Opal candidly. "I don't think I've ever seen an English garden. Are they quite different from American gardens?"

The pall, which cast a shadow over Roger's face, suddenly lifted, and his countenance beamed in the fervent Roman sun. Yes, this English rose would bloom nicely within his garden.

The End

PIPE-DREAMS FROM THE FAR SIDE OF THE HA-HA

Chapter I

The fragrant sea breeze blew gently upon the wet brows of the sweaty passengers bearing up under the oppressive heat. The ferry to Governors Island was filled to capacity. Curious New Yorkers dressed in their finest garments and chicest broad-brimmed hats in order to view the polo match between visiting Prince Harry's team, Black Watch, and Ralph Lauren's team, Black Guard. The former team would be led by the dashing British prince, and the latter team would follow the charge of Nacho, an Argentinean model, who served as the image of Ralph Lauren's Polo line. It was a charity event; all of the proceeds would benefit Prince Harry's charity, which supported an African village. The ferry traversed the short distance in record speed, and the baked passengers hastened to the seating area in order to secure seats with vantage points.

The sun shone mercilessly upon the grounds. The 11:00 AM ferry was the first to transport visitors to the match. There would be ample opportunity to find spectacular seats. No one sat on the hot, metal bleachers. People with any knowledge of decorum knew to bring picnic blankets, umbrellas to protect themselves from the fervent sun rays, and coolers filled to the brim with icy beverages. The really savvy people also knew that the attire was semi-formal, and hats were a must. Most of the female spectators wore hats, short strapless dresses, and carried umbrellas to match their ensembles. Knowledgeable men wore seersucker pants and straw hats. The area filled quickly with blankets and umbrellas. Long lines were forming by the umbrella concession stand and the champagne stand; children flocked around the Italian ice stand.

A tall, slender woman in a ruffled, navy blue sundress and blue-stripped sunhat that covered most of her golden-brown hair, stood upon a sliver of parched land between two blankets.

She unfastened her white sandal heels and let them drop to the ground. The space seemed satisfactory. It was right at the white chalk line that separated the spectators from the field. A rather corpulent, middle-aged woman lay out-stretched on the blanket to the left, and a trio of twenty-somethings sat on the blanket to the right. Placing the unfolded program on the ground beneath her, the young woman sat down. Across the field were festive white tents, where celebrities, politicians, and models could enjoy the match in shady comfort. Waiters in white jackets served them champagne. The young woman was certain that the silver-haired gentleman standing across the field observing the grounds was Ralph Lauren, but she could not be certain. She removed her BlackBerry from her purse and asked the corpulent woman to take a picture of her. Struggling to stand up, the large woman obliged. The picture was of no use, but the young woman smiled and thanked the hefty photographer.

It would be a long wait in the hot sun. The match was scheduled to begin at 3:00 PM. The unbridled, unsaddled horses stood leisurely at the far end of the field near the Piaget scoreboard.

"Is this your first polo match?" asked a voice emitting from the rotund woman's blanket. Her slim husband had joined her. Neither of them dressed for the occasion. He wore khaki shorts and a polo shirt; his circular wife wore massive white pants and a red sleeveless tank top. They seemed friendly.

"Yes," replied the young woman.

Something caught the young woman's eye. Two blankets over, two teen-aged girls sat daintily. One was holding a *Twilight Eclipse* umbrella to shield her from the sun. A large winsome picture of Edward the vampire graced the umbrella and the area. The young woman smiled and walked over to the blanket in her bare feet. She asked the girls if she could take a picture of the *Team Edward* umbrella. They agreed smiling amiably.

"He's hot, isn't he?" asked the enthusiastic keeper of the Edward flame.

"Indeed," answered the young woman with a smile. She returned to her space in the slender expanse, which did not encompass the aura of the pale, moody vampire. She wished that she had brought an umbrella to thwart the sun's determined rays. An Italian ice would have to suffice. She returned with her lemon ice to hear a discussion between the husband and wife about the prospects of purchasing an event umbrella. The umbrellas were bright yellow and large enough to cover two people.

"They cost too much," argued the wife.

"I'm going to get one," insisted the husband. He left the blanket and joined the long concession line for event umbrellas.

"You wouldn't have a bandage, would you?" asked the wife.

"No," answered the young woman.

"I'm wearing these socks because my shoes rubbed against my heels and left a blister. It hurts," remarked the wife.

"I'm sorry," said the young woman enjoying her Italian ice. Life was filled with compromises. She could not afford an event umbrella, but she had lovely, unscarred feet, and her pedicure helped to complete the picture of a polished young lady. Yes, life was filled with compromises; yet, she always seemed to be on the winning side.

Living in New York City had its advantages. One moment, one could be reading the newspaper while eating grapefruit at the breakfast table and the next moment find oneself en route to a polo match featuring Prince Harry. Quick adjustments in the Sunday schedule were required. Sunday Mass at St. Patrick's was a must, but an early Mass would be acceptable. The young woman attended the 9:00 Mass in order to board the 11:00 ferry to Governors Island. There was also the concern about attire. Where would one find a suitable hat on such short notice?

Her striped sunhat was transformed into a stylish pleasantry with the addition of a sparkling broach on the band, and a wide, black belt brought new life to her ruffled sundress. After watching the *fashionistas* parade by, the young woman made a mental note to purchase a substantive hat for formal summer wear. The young woman's attention was directed to the blanket on the left again.

"Let's see your feet," said the husband to his wife.

The husband had returned with a bright yellow event umbrella, which his wife quickly opened in order to provide much needed shade. The husband, apparently observing the unclad feet of the other women on blankets, had a desire to see his wife's feet. She resisted. The young woman felt compassion for the pudgy wife with the blistered feet. Oftentimes, marriage brings such a feeling of complacency that one does not notice that one is falling beneath the mark, as it were, until one finds oneself on a blanket in the midst of a plethora of stylish beauty mavens, who take pains to replenish every aspect of their appearance. It matters not whether one has cared for a husband, has nurtured children, or has established a home lovingly. Quite simply, there is one question that reaches into the depths of the soul: Can one remove one's socks and display the enticing feet of a twenty-year-old as one reclines on a picnic blanket eagerly anticipating a polo match led by two male marvels? Disappointment emitted from the blanket on the left, while eyes of curiosity darted furtively from the blanket on the right. One of the twenty-somethings, a rather pale young man with a prematurely balding spot at the top of his head, had taken notice of the young woman cooling herself with spoonfuls of the tangy Italian ice on her tongue. How refreshing it was. She could feel the young man's eyes upon her but declined to notice him.

"I say, would you care to join us on the blanket?" asked the young man at last. "There's more than enough room."

"Are you English?" asked the young woman happy to hear the comforting accent.

"This isn't a trick question, is it?" asked the young man. "Have you a grievance against the English – I mean with the entire BP affair and all, one wonders."

The young woman smiled. "Look around you. All of these people have gathered and are waiting patiently in the hot sun for an opportunity to breathe the same air as Prince Harry. If anyone can put the oil spill on the Gulf out of our minds, it's Prince Harry. Speaking candidly, I'm not sure the oil spill was ever on our minds. New Yorkers can be quite self-absorbed. If it isn't happening here, it isn't happening. Do you know what I mean?"

"No, but please tell me more," said the young man smoothing the blanket in preparation for the new arrival.

"So, did he call you, or what?" asked Alyson eagerly.

"No," replied the young woman checking her weight on the health club scale. One hundred twenty-four pounds - the perfect weight for her long, lean 5'10" frame. "They were visiting the United States and returning to England on Monday. I don't really expect to hear from him. It was nice chatting, though."

"I wish I had gone to that polo match," said Alyson with remorse. "I've never met anyone from England."

They gathered their towels and approached studio one. The step class was ending, and the body toning class was entering the studio. The two women placed their mats near the front of the room as the instructor added weights to his barbell.

"You need one more weight, Hayley," said the instructor to the young woman.

Hayley took a five pound weight from the storage chest and returned to her mat next to Alyson.

"Did you tell him that your Mother is English?" asked Alyson.

"No," said Hayley, "it was superficial chatting – the weather, polo, things like that."

"I would have told him," said Alyson, "developed a connection, you know?"

"All right," barked the instructor, "put those bars on your shoulders and give me squats!"

The class followed instructions and began squatting in time to the pulsating music.

"I'm not really good at meeting new people," said Hayley squatting rhythmically.

"It takes practice," said Alyson struggling to keep pace with the class. "You don't get out there often enough. You have to really get out there, you know?"

Hayley did not know where *out there* was. She had been in New York for two years and did not wish to partake in the singles bars or clubs. She was more the museum and chamber music type. Life in Oregon had been much simpler. She lived with her father and two brothers in a sleepy hamlet near the Washington border. Hayley had reservations about leaving them. When her mother left to return to London, her father and brothers depended upon her to care for them, but she did not want to spend her life caring for her father and her brothers. It was simpler to attend college in New York, far from the tranquility and the responsibilities of home. New York was home now; she would not return to Oregon. After tasting the delights of the city, she could not return. New York was like a vampire. She had been *bitten* and now belonged with the other *undead* citizens of the metropolis. They formed a silent community that looked and carried on daily activities with a sense of normality, but New Yorkers shared a bond that was far from normal. The city had a personality, which it shared only with people who lived and breathed its essence. The honour was not bestowed randomly. New York selected its *citizens* carefully from the influx of tourists and residents and left its *bite* upon the unsuspecting honourees. Sometimes it took months or even years before the person realized that he or she shared a special bond and would always find solace and new life within the metropolis. The *undead* walked with the others but in a parallel universe, of sorts. They saw with New York eyes and felt with New York hearts. They never despaired, for as long as they resided within the city, they would have abundant life – a life of which outsiders could only dream.

"My brother wants to come to visit next week," said Hayley placing her barbell on the polished floor and picking up two hand weights for lunges. "I told him that he could stay with us."

"Sure, I'm surprised your father would let him come alone," said Alyson placing her weights on both sides of her knees and lunging to the right.

"That's where we may have a problem," confided Hayley. "He's not coming alone. He's bringing a friend. I thought that they could stay in my room, and I'll sleep on the couch."

"Who is the friend?" asked Alyson dropping to the mat and forming a weak plank position. Her wobbly arms had difficulty holding her slightly overweight body upright.

"I haven't a clue," said Hayley assuming the required plank position flawlessly. "Knowing Jordan, it could be anyone or anything. He's a little unorthodox."

"Just don't let him bring a snake," said Alyson flopping to the mat in a plank of defeat. "I hate snakes."

The financial district was oppressively hot, and the swell of tourists taking pictures with their cell phones was a source of irritation. Madison Timbrenel counted the days until his vacation. Most financial denizens dreaded taking time off, but he was different. The call of the wild was enticing, and the fledgling stock broker looked forward to the delights of the sea. Of course, there was the BP disaster going on in the Gulf. Madison wondered how far the oil had spread and if it would affect his plans to sail his father's streamlined vessel from New York to California. Peace, quiet, and the smell of pungent sea air were what he craved. He did not want to be encumbered by the smell or the sight of dirty oil covering the estuary. Madison was not a *green* person. He did not think of the environment at all. Air was air. One had no choice but to breathe it. If it was polluted, it was polluted. The cost of progress was high, but the world had to progress. What was the point of changing to energy-efficient light bulbs when a calamity like the oil spill counteracted all efforts to *go green*? Nature had a way of balancing everything out in curious, oftentimes brutal ways. It was difficult to know which side Mother Nature was on, in the final analysis. It was somewhat akin to the Tower of Babel – get too close to the source, and all hell breaks loose. The humans were nothing more than human. There were mistakes and blunders to be made. It was all a part of the human experience. One could not worry about it; it was the way of life. One point balanced or counteracted another. Even Al Gore, guru of *green*, was a victim of the act/counteract aura, which seemed to be engulfing the world and its inhabitants. If the Nobel Prize winning author and environmentalist could not rise above the turmoil of his personal life in order to help rescue the environment in its time of need, then what chance did mere uninformed, unassuming environmental sloths like Madison have?

A better global environment was not his concern. Madison was content to live in the jumbled mess humanity had made. His was a comfortable life, and now that the tax laws were enabling those of means to establish long-term, seemingly endless perpetuity trusts, his privileged life would be assured, as would the lives of future generations of Timbrenels. There was only one thing that caused Madison some degree of angst. He lamented the rising number of people who could not speak or write the English language coherently. Enunciation had suffered the fate of the relics that marked the passage of time. The American tongue had been compromised to the point of irrelevance. So few people spoke Standard English in the United States that the language would, surely, suffer the fate of Latin.The other thing that irritated the language enthusiast was the deplorable lack of manners throughout the nation. Madison doubted whether parents still instructed their children to send thank you notes when they received birthday or holiday gifts, as he had been taught. Where had it all gone? The unseemly traditions were rapidly infiltrating all levels of society. The thought produced a tremor throughout his body.

"Will you be going home for the weekend?" asked John Claybourne. Madison had almost forgotten that John was present.

"I'm going on vacation – remember?" answered Madison. "I'm having second thoughts about leaving. Perhaps I should wait until they clean up that oil spill."

"Dreamer," murmured John impatiently. "You can always take another route or go off in another direction entirely. What do you care? You'll still be sailing and enjoying the peace and tranquility of the water."

"I'm thirty-years-old," said Madison pragmatically. "I resolved to sail from New York to California when I reached thirty."

"You'll be thirty for the entire year," reasoned John. "You can put it off for a couple of months."

"Procrastination is not something that I endorse," said Madison. "Besides, I hope to visit my son, Peter, in China.

Madison had a six-year-old son, who lived in Shanghai, China with his mother. He provided for the boy substantially, but it was difficult to make a connection with him. His mother refused to allow him to visit the United States, and their relationship was fraught with the tensions one would expect when parents divorce after one year of marriage due to irreconcilable differences. There was one difference that separated Madison from his wife. He was American, and she was Chinese. Normally, that was not a problem. Madison witnessed countless American and Mandarin relationships that evolved and grew stronger with time, owing to the supposed docility of the Asian partner. His partner, obviously, was hewn from a different cloth. She was obstinate, moody, and oftentimes volatile. She wasn't like that when they met or when they courted, but things changed drastically after their clandestine wedding. Suddenly, she could not bear living in the United States and demanded that they relocate to Shanghai. Madison could not speak Mandarin and knew nothing of the culture. If the truth be known, he didn't know why he should be required to change the course of their relationship. They hadn't met in China, and she seemed willing to live a blissful life in the United States. He didn't know that she could even speak Chinese. She wasn't born in China. She was born in Buffalo, for heaven's sake. Their marriage was a living nightmare. After the wedding, she became another person, and his resentment grew more insidious with each passing day of their torrential marriage. Then came the ultimatum. Either he moved with her to Shanghai, or she would go alone. Madison thought that he would give her a little space. Let her see what life was like in China with all the pollution, and she would hasten back home. She did not return, and the news that she was expecting a child brought more disquietude. His son should have been born in the USA; instead, he was born in Shanghai. She, whose name could not be spoken without a torrent of verbal diatribes, sent him a picture of the infant, a winsome boy, by all accounts. Three months after the divorce was final, the pictures stopped coming; instead, Madison received a letter informing him that she had remarried and would prefer not to continue communication. There were tears, and there were curses, but Madison resolved to make the most of the difficult situation. He would not fight for joint custody. Why put the child through that torment? Someday, his son would come to him on his own volition. Although his reasoning was plausible, Madison knew that his reluctance stemmed from a deep-seated fear of commitment. It was better to remain free of all entanglements, at least until he figured out what he really wanted in life.

Madison's career was promising, and he was advancing at a commendable pace. What more could anyone ask? His was a life that most would envy – adoring, wealthy family; playthings like boats and single-engine planes; loyal friends; charming personality; and resplendent appearance. The pieces of life's puzzle fell into place for him, and nothing was askew. Some people wondered when it would all unravel, but Madison was not a pessimist. He had no reason to be. Life always offered the very best, and the very best was what he had come to expect. The lamentable marriage was the only flaw in his crystal.

"I wonder if you'll do me a favour while I'm away," said Madison sipping a martini at one of South Street Seaport's outdoor restaurants overlooking the East River. A cool breeze blew through his brown, tussled hair.

"What is it?" asked John.

"I tutor a kid on Fridays," said Madison. "It's only an hour, and the kid's great. I teach him intermediate French."

"A humanitarian *and* a polyglot – you never cease to amaze me. Where do you find the time?" asked John.

"His name is Noel, and I meet him at The New Society Library on 79th," said Madison. "He's pretty bright, so there shouldn't be any problems. We meet in one of the study rooms."

"I suppose I can do it for a couple of weeks, but you're going to be gone for a couple of months, aren't you?" asked John.

"The program ends in two weeks. Noel should be able to pass his exams admirably," said Madison.

"Why are you doing this, anyway?" asked John.

"Didn't I tell you?" asked Madison. "I'm planning to run for Congress in a couple of years. I must demonstrate that I am not only philanthropic but also passionate about community affairs. I volunteer at several agencies that serve the common good."

"Well, in that case, I can sign on. Congress, eh? I can see that. I'd vote for you," said John.

"Thanks, you're a pal," said Madison. "Here is the address of the library. Just tell them that you're filling in for me, and they'll give you the key to the study room. I'll alert Noel. You *do* speak French, don't you?"

"Fear not," said John, "my French literature classes at Stanford have prepared me for this monumental task."

"Great," said Madison finishing his martini. "I knew that I could count on you. I'll see you in a couple of months."

Madison paid the check and walked along the harbour. The Brooklyn Bridge, relic that it was, glimmered in the noonday sun. Finding a tutor for Noel was the last item on his To Do list before he left. Now, the difficult part would be telling Gretchen that he would be leaving for two months. Gretchen and Madison had been dating for three or four months. She moved some of her things into his apartment, including her dog, Bernie, although she kept her own apartment on E. 90th Street. Gretchen and Bernie were somewhat alike, in Madison's estimation. Both were frilly on the outside and whimsical on the inside. Madison met Gretchen and Bernie at a doggie day care center, where she worked as a part-time dog psychologist. Madison's dog, Oswald, an English Bulldog, was having separation anxiety issues. Madison was spending too much time away from home, and Oswald had become depressed. He would neither eat nor sleep. Doggie day care with a dog psychologist on the staff seemed a viable solution. Gretchen's frisky, sandy-haired, bishon friese, Bernie, was the perfect playmate for the reserved, pensive Oswald. They met for doggy play dates twice a week, and their owners became quite close in the interim. Madison did not recall when he knew that it was serious enough to request that Gretchen and Bernie move in, but the arrangement was working commendably well.

Madison's decision to sail to California was irrevocable. He had a list of resolutions. He was thirty, and at thirty, he was resolved to sail from New York to California. He didn't know why. It seemed like a feasible idea at twenty-three. Once he made a decision, it was irreversible. Madison did not accept change easily. Gretchen, Bernie, and Oswald would have to make the necessary accommodations. His resolution list could not be altered. There were many other things on the list, but they could wait until his return. He had already started taking the necessary preliminary steps for his proposed run for Congress in five years, and his family's contacts would, most assuredly, assist him in his endeavour. The world was his oyster, was it not? Everything was falling into place, and life was grand.

Chapter II

The East River seemed agitated. Sometimes, the waters were placid and at ease, but today the river moved with a restless urgency, as though a storm was brewing. Hayley eased into the far lane on the FDR Drive South. She did not like driving to work, but she was late and did not want to endure the chastising glares of her immediate supervisor. It would be necessary to park in a garage, and they were incredibly expensive in the Wall Street area. Hayley took a few deep yoga breaths to calm her frazzled nerves. She had forgotten how irritating her brother, Jordan, could be. It was wonderful to see him initially, but after a few days, the wonder wore off rapidly.

Jordan Rembrandt was an exemplary snowboarder; in point of fact, he planned to enter the qualifying competitions for the Sochi 2014 Winter Olympics in Sochi, Russia. Jordan idolised Shaun White, US gold medallist, and determined to compete against him. It was a pipe-dream as far as Hayley was concerned. She tried to convince Jordan that he should spend more time in pursuit of acceptance into a prestigious university, but Jordan had an intractable mind and would be swayed by neither rhyme nor reason. To make matters worse, Jordan's friend and trainer, Rick Mason, accompanied him. They would spend two more days in New York before travelling to Vancouver, where they would meet with a group of snowboarders, and practice in a near-perfect environment. Two more days didn't sound like a long time, but to Hayley, it was an eternity. The apartment wasn't large enough for four people, particularly when two of them filled the small space with snowboarding equipment. It was fortunate that Alyson did not mind the inconvenience. She found the exploits of Jordan and Rick exciting and expressed an interest in watching Jordan compete in Sochi. Alyson's view was that everyone should have a dream and live his or her dream. She applauded Jordan for his courage and tenacity.

Hayley, on the other hand, had no patience for dreams or dreamers. Oftentimes, she wished that she had the heart of a dreamer in order to understand their strange obsession with that which could not be grasped, organized, or controlled. Dreamers lived in a world of the unknown and the indeterminate. That world was frightening, to say the least, and not particularly encouraging within the Wall Street environment, where Hayley worked as John Claybourne's assistant. She suspected that her lack of whimsy was one of the true reasons that she had not been able to find a suitable mate. She was down-to-earth to a fault, and as hard as she tried, she could not break the tedious pattern on a personal level. She also realized that breaking the pattern would create an incongruity within her professional life, and incongruity was something Hayley Rembrandt could not envision comfortably.

John Claybourne was not in his office when Hayley slinked to her desk. Hopefully, he was meeting with a client and had not notice her tardiness. Hayley breathed a sigh of relief, but the sigh turned into a grimace when she saw the note on her desk. John Claybourne preferred paper to modern technology and had a strange fetish for hard copy. He believed that his emails, phone calls, and texts were monitored by his adversaries, and he kept a supply of carbon paper in his bottom drawer to make copies of his correspondence. Hayley did not know how he survived in a modern world driven by technology.

After reading the note, she wondered when her employer would take her position as his assistant seriously. In the two years that she worked for him, there were always assignments that had nothing to do with finance. Sometimes she wondered if she was merely window dressing. It was 2010, and things like that were no longer supposed to exist, but they did. She was an exemplary financial analyst, but it was as though she was sitting in a boat with a life preserver wrapped around her waist when everyone else was frolicking in the water. Now, she was expected to tutor some kid in French. Hayley was fluent in French, German, and Russian, which probably accounted for John's confidence that she would be up to the task, if it was, indeed, a task. She was indispensible when his clients spoke these languages, and he had no reservations about sending her to countries where the languages were spoken in order to prepare the groundwork for gaining prospective clients. Immediately upon returning to his office, John Claybourne delegated Madison's inconvenient request to his underling, Hayley Rembrandt. Tutoring a kid was a step backward, in Hayley's estimation, unless there was some practical reason, which would help John obtain a lucrative account. That must be the reason. John Claybourne was neither altruistic nor philanthropic. There must be some reason why tutoring a kid in French was to be a part of her hectic day. As usual, she would do it without complaint, but she wished that there was some other way to show her employer that she could handle at least one client on her own.

The packing was complete, and the vessel had been given a commendable assessment by the Timbrenel's resident expert in charge of boat maintenance. The Timbrenel's had three vessels, one of which could be called a luxury yacht. Jason Timbrenel, Madison's father, did not allow his sons or his wife, Marion, to *play* with his yacht. If they wanted to frolic on the high seas, the other vessel would have to suffice. Madison's *voyage* from New York to California was considered youthful *play* by the old man. He understood that young men of means needed *play toys*, *playmates*, and an ample supply of leisure time in order to enjoy the fruits of life. As Madison had reached the age of commitment and responsibility, he was allowed one more fling before divesting himself of his whimsical life. After the *voyage*, he would be expected to honour the family values, which mandated a serious investment in political life. Madison's brother, Oliver, was already ensconced within the outer edges of Mayor Bloomberg's inner circle and seemed to be making inroads with the expected alacrity. Madison was not serious about the prospects of a political life. Oftentimes, his father and brother despaired of him. He seemed destined to be the perpetual idealist always attracting the wrong associations and garnering a plethora of broken hearts, which usually required financial recompense to heal.

The sea air rubbed Madison's face and tousled his chestnut hair. As the vessel moved farther away from the port, Madison felt a sense of peace and tranquillity. There was nothing like the sea to lift one into another world, but he did not want to be transported to another world. Madison's world was to his liking. He did not need a change of scenery either. The *voyage* was on his To Do Before the Age of Thirty list, and he would accomplish his goal. Strange, but Gretchen intimated that the To Do list was Madison's way of rejecting maturity and revealed a deep-seated hostility towards his family's expectations of him. He told her to leave the *psychobabble* to qualified psychologists and concentrate on canine problems. To Gretchen, canine problems oftentimes mirrored human dilemmas.

Madison's valet, Kensington, brought him the latest edition of *The New York Times* and a glass of chilled chardonnay. There was nothing on the list that said that he had to make the voyage without his accustomed creature comforts. Kensington had been in the Timbrenel's employ since Madison was seventeen-years-old. Madison acquired him when Oliver turned twenty-six and thought that an aspiring political leader having a valet sent the wrong message to the masses. Madison harboured no such feelings. He had little concern for this aggregate of people, if the truth be told, and the farther they stayed away from him the better. He had seen *the masses* as he walked here and there in Manhattan. Most seemed surly, pedestrian, and rather insipid. Madison wondered why anyone would want to bother with them at all. They seemed happy in their *worlds*. Why not just let them be? Wasn't life perplexing enough without wondering what *the masses* would think of his actions?

Sometimes Madison wondered whether Gretchen was considered a part of *the masses*. She was always polite and civil, but he had never met her family. She avoided them like the plague. Whenever one of them ventured across the George Washington Bridge to pay her a visit, she always met them at her apartment—never his. From what Madison could gather from her scant description of them, they were simple people who had little regard for education or high culture. But then, from Madison's observations within the firm, few of the analysts regarded education or high culture as necessary accoutrements within their lives; in point of fact, the manner in which most of the *titans* of the stock market communicated made Madison wonder about the state of higher education in the United States. Be that as it may, one of the first legislative priorities he would endorse as congressman would be a return to good old-fashioned Standard English.

"What is our first port-of-call, Kensington?" asked Madison sipping the chardonnay and perusing the headlines.

"Mr. Graves informs me that we should be approaching the Maryland coastline around four-thirty, Mr. Timbrenel," said Kensington. "Will you be dining ashore? I understand that the area is particularly renowned for its crab delicacies."

"Perhaps I will," said Madison. "Do I know anyone in that area, Kensington?"

"Not to my knowledge," said Kensington, "and there aren't any contacts on the list presented by your father of people you should visit while enjoying your adventure."

"Well, then, it would probably be best to dine here. Perhaps you can go ashore and retrieve some of those crab delicacies for us to nibble on later this evening. I think I'll go below for a quick nap. No point in overdoing the sea air. Wake me if anything interesting approaches like a shark or a blue-finned dolphin," said Madison as he placed the newspaper on a side table and went below to his luxurious bedroom/den.

Two hours lapsed before Madison's restful sleep was disturbed by Kensington's gentle knock on the door.

"I'm afraid we must return to New York, Mr. Timbrenel," said Kensington sorrowfully. "Your Aunt Patrice has passed away."

"The old bird in Connecticut?" asked Madison rubbing his eyes.

"I believe so," said Kensington. "Your father called about ten minutes ago."

"I hardly knew the woman. She was his sister, wasn't she? I don't think I've seen her more than three times in my entire life. Why, on earth, should her passing bring my voyage to an untimely end?" asked Madison to no one in particular. He weighed the pros and cons of returning vs. carrying on in the invigorating sea air. Kensington remained silent.

"All right, Kensington," said Madison resignedly, "tell Graves to turn this inauspicious vessel around - wait. How far are we from the Maryland shore?

"I think that we should reach it in an hour or so," said Kensington.

"Tell Graves to head for the Maryland shore. We'll get the crab delicacies and then start back," said Madison. "Funny thing about death, isn't it, Kensington?"

Kensington looked askance at his employer.

"It disregards a person's agenda and shows up uninvited every time," said Madison.

"An apt description," said Kensington.

Hayley packed the last of Jordan and Rick's clothing into their duffle bags. She spent the entire afternoon laundering their clothing before their trek to Canada. It seemed that when her family came within two feet near her, she was relegated the task of cleaning up or laundering or cooking for them. Rick was not a family member, but he had acquired the ethos of the Rembrandt family – women belonged in the domestic sphere. Oddly, she was sorry to see them leave. As irritating as it was to dust off her caretaker skills, she had to admit that it was good to see Jordan and Rick. It also pleased her to know that Jordan was accomplishing his dream. She did not approve of his truancy, but he had talent, and the Olympics waited for no one.

"You had a call from a Noel something or other," said Alyson entering Hayley's bedroom. "He said that he won't be able to meet with you for tutoring today."

"Thank goodness," said Hayley. "I really don't want to spend the afternoon conjugating French verbs. You know, Alyson, I'm thinking of leaving the firm."

"Are you insane?" asked Alyson. "Have you forgotten how difficult it was to get that position?"

"I'm a non-entity there. No one really needs me, and I can count the number of hands-on experiences I've had while in John Claybourne's employ. This last assignment, tutoring the kid for Madison Timbrenel, was really the last straw. I've had enough," said Hayley.

"Before you do anything hasty," said Alyson, "You'd better read the newspapers. No one is hiring. Would you rather be unemployed? We're in a recession."

"Jordan has really inspired me, Alyson. He's following his dream of becoming an Olympic snowboarder. When will I be able to follow my dreams? Is this all there is to life?" asked Hayley reflectively.

"Jordan is a kid," said Alyson, "and if you weren't here providing him with a place to live, he wouldn't be able to follow his dream. There are dreamers and there are providers in this world. You are a provider."

Hayley remembered the middle-aged woman on the blanket next to her at the polo match. The woman was a provider, and her husband was insensitive, callous, and he could not keep his eyes off of the beautiful feet surrounding him.

"I don't want to be a provider," said Hayley.

"We don't always get what we want," countered Alyson. "We are what we are, and we're stuck with it."

"No," said Hayley adamantly. "We don't have to be stuck with anything. We can be anything we want to be."

"Who are you, Mr. Rogers? This is not the 1970s, Hayley," assured Alyson. "The American Dream has changed, in case you haven't noticed. We're all fighting to belong to a society where everyone is equal and has the right to do anything and everything, Well, that's only true in New York. The rest of the country is in a sorry state."

"We live in New York, don't we?" argued Hayley. "Since we live here, why not do what we really want to do?"

"You *are* doing what you want to do," said Alyson. "You have dreamed of becoming a financial analyst on Wall Street since undergraduate school, and you are a financial analyst. You are accomplishing your dream in one of the top firms in the country. Why throw it all away on a pipe-dream? What do you want to do, anyway?"

"I haven't figured that out yet," admitted Hayley.

"Fine," said Alyson. "Until you decide upon an alternate career, you'd better stay where you are. Besides, if you quit, how will you pay your half of the rent? Stay within your realm, Hayley. You are not a dreamer born of the dreamer *tribe*; you are a provider."

Alyson's words irritated Hayley, but she knew that she was right. Surely, a dreamer would have some sort of vision. Hayley had no right brain vision of art or poetry or prose. There was no great novel within her waiting to be written. She was all left brain – facts and figures. She longed to be a right brain person, but it was too late for that. Hayley was who she was, but she was not happy with both feet planted securely on the ground. How she longed for one great whimsical experience – just one, which would entitle her to say, "I dreamed a dream and lived it, if only for a day."

———

The funeral parlour was bleak. No one expected a festive environ, but this was absurd. The thickly-curtained room for mourners was an elaborate spectacle of purple and black. The mourners sat quietly in antique upholstered chairs. All was silent, save for the whining strings of recorded violin music. Madison and Gretchen sat in the comfortable chairs and observed the pictures surrounding the closed casket. Madison had never seen any of the pictures before. Aunt Patrice was quite attractive in her younger days. He had always known his aunt as a small, shrivelled, humourless woman. It was hard to imagine that she was ever young and vibrant. It was said that she was quite wealthy, but she never spent money on pleasurable things. What was the point of having money if one could not enjoy it?

Madison credited his parents with living life fully. They travelled, enjoyed fine foods, and were generous with their children. It was the kind of life Madison hoped to pass on to his children someday. He looked at Gretchen in her crushable, black, velvet cloche hat with a maroon flower on the front band. She wore black boots that stopped at the ankle and black tights. Madison was glad that she had not removed her jacket. From what he could see, she had elected to wear the black and white check dress that screamed *Target*. Madison concluded that this was final proof that, although a psychologist, Gretchen was definitely one with *the masses*.

"Thanks for coming," he whispered into her ear.

"Of course," said Gretchen. "I've wanted to meet your family for a long time."

"These aren't the best circumstances," said Madison. "They may not be themselves."

Gretchen gave his arm an extra squeeze.

"Relax, everything will be fine," said Gretchen. "Which ones are your parents? Everyone kind of looks the same."

It was true. The front chairs were occupied by gray-haired matrons and elderly statesmen types. He observed his mother looking at the floral arrangements with a discordant look upon her face. His father spoke quietly to a gentleman in the far corner of the room – exchanging stock tips, no doubt. Oliver, Madison's brother, checked an endless array of messages on his BlackBerry as he sat beside his wife, Lois. Lois and Oliver were a handsome couple. They received endless invitations to dinner parties and couples vacations. Oliver and Lois had many friends and were the most envied couple at any gathering. If ever there was an example of the *beautiful people,* they were it. Lois placed her hand over the BlackBerry in an effort to encourage her husband to be less mindful of the day's political turmoil and more funereal. Oliver brushed her hand away gently. He had to keep abreast of things. The Ground Zero mosque debate was raging, and his BlackBerry was flooded with emails that required his constant attention – not to mention keeping up with news of the latest person to *weigh-in* on the crisis.

"Donald Trump just opposed its location," said Oliver hyperventilating. "The Muslim Miss America is against it too."

Oliver switched to *The New York Times* website to garner further information. He hoped that no one would interrupt by offering sympathy or anything of the sort. It was a wake, granted, but there was a time and a place for everything. Now was the time for all political aides to be fully engaged in whatever debate or crisis clouded the city's golden, majestic image.

"Pardon me," said a gentleman sitting behind Madison and Gretchen, "aren't you Madison?"

Madison turned around and found his cousin Elmore smiling broadly. Elmore was Aunt Patrice's son. He was an artist living in Paris. Aunt Patrice never forgave him for leaving a congressional seat to become an artist in what she deemed a decadent city. Elmore looked the same as Madison remembered him as a young adult – longish brown hair, which was now clasped in a ponytail, large almond eyes that seemed to be filled with wonder, and a grin that could be either mischievous or malevolent.

"Elmore, how nice to see you," said Madison. "So sorry about Aunt Patrice. She was a treasure."

Elmore's smile seemed mischievous at present. "Still the diplomat, aren't you? If I recall correctly, she telephoned the police when you and the neighbourhood children had a grape fight pulling her precious grapes from their lascivious vines," said Elmore. "That was some summer visit. How I wished that you would visit more often to put some life into the old place."

"Speaking of which," said Madison, "what are you going to do with it?"

"Put it up for sale, I imagine," said Elmore. "I leave for Paris after the funeral tomorrow. I'll let the realtors handle it. Who is your friend?"

"Gretchen, this is my cousin Elmore," said Madison. "You've heard me mention him."

"Pleasure to meet you," said Gretchen. She had never heard Madison speak of his cousin, Elmore.

"*Enchanté*," said Elmore suavely as he kissed her hand. "Madison always selects the best desserts but never indulges his sweet tooth. I, on the other hand, enjoy nothing more than the crumbs from his dessert table. Forgive my musings, Gretchen, but I hope that you will retain the thought for future reference. Oh well, I suppose I must sit with the family mourners in the front - coming Madison?"

"I'll be there in a moment," said Madison as Elmore walked to the front of the staid room. Many mourners hugged him and provided sympathy kisses.

"That was weird," said Gretchen with a slight shiver.

"There's something that I must tell you about my family," said Madison. "They can be rather odd at times."

"They seem normal enough," said Gretchen watching the mourners in the front row, "except for your cousin, Elmore."

"It's a wake," countered Madison. "Of course they *appear* normal, but trust me, there are many loose screws in the Timbrenel toolbox."

"What do you mean?" asked Gretchen remembering the time Madison insisted upon standing atop the *Alice in Wonderland* monument in Central Park with his arms folded across his chest during a thunderstorm. He said that it was something he had always wanted to do as a child, but no one would let him, owing to the fact that the monument was bronze and would probably attract lightning. There he stood straddling Alice's shoulders, drenched from head to toe beaming broadly, as Gretchen gazed up at him struggling to hold onto the dogs' leashes and the umbrella, while the tumultuous thunderstorm wreaked havoc. That notwithstanding, she admired his boyish charm and adventurous spirit.

"You must promise that nothing they do or say will prevent you from remaining as close to me as you are today," said Madison.

"Of course," said Gretchen. "What do you think they will do or say?"

"Why do you think I am still single?" asked Madison. "Everyone I bring to meet them becomes offended and blames me."

"Don't worry about that," said Gretchen. "I don't offend easily; besides, we won't be here long. We'll be back in the city in a couple of hours. I can bear it for a couple of hours."

Madison took a deep breath as he approached his mother, who watched them as they walked down the aisle and envisioned the young woman beside her son in a wedding dress of polyester and spandex.

"Hello Mother," said Madison kissing his mother's cheek. She smiled and directed her gaze towards Gretchen.

"You need a haircut, Madison, and you must be Gretchen,"

said Mrs. Timbrenel. "Madison tells me that you are a dog psychologist. How curious. I must say that I'm intrigued. You must take a look at Herbert, our faithful hound. He is quite eccentric. Madison, you must invite Gretchen to spend the weekend so that she can render an opinion about Herbert."

"We can only attend the wake this evening," said Madison.

"Nonsense, Gretchen can observe Herbert this evening, and you two can return to New York after the service tomorrow," said Mrs. Timbrenel decisively.

"Mother's right," said Madison without hesitation. "It would be best if we returned tomorrow."

Gretchen looked askance at Madison. How quickly he acquiesced to his mother's demands.

"Of course, you're right," said Gretchen. "I would be happy to spend the night at your home, Mrs. Timbrenel. Thank you."

A bemused Elmore sat silently in his chair watching Madison crumble under the powerful gaze of Mrs. Timbrenel. He glanced at the closed casket and felt relieved that his own mother's formidable gaze was enclosed with her.

The Timbrenel home was lavish, to say the least. There were original works of art, sculptures, and a vast library the size of a football stadium. Gretchen felt like Belle in *Beauty and the Beast*. She gazed with wonder at the books, which lined shelves from the ceiling to the marble inlaid floors. There were sliding ladders on the bookshelves. For a moment, Gretchen lost control of her breath. Madison conducted the tour with little relish or interest.

"This is the library," said Madison without looking up at the ascending treasures of literature.

"Just bury me here," said Gretchen looking up in wonder. "How can you be so nonchalant?"

"They're just books," said Madison.

"Just books?" shrieked Gretchen. "I'll bet there are some first editions in this literary utopia."

"Most of the books are rare first editions," said Madison looking at the books with a sense of boredom and fatigue.

"What I really want is to make love to you amongst all of these words of wisdom," said Gretchen, "pressed against the books, like in the movie *Atonement*."

Madison winced. "You *do* remember the consequence of that. I can assure you that my mother's retribution will be on a grander scale if we were to pursue your proposed course of action. Besides, there are cameras all over the place to thwart theft of any kind. In addition, I do believe that these masterpieces would take umbrage with our using them as a mere backdrop to a passionate encounter. Come, we'd better find Herbert before he finds us. My mother wasn't kidding when she said that he was eccentric."

Gretchen looked once more at the towering treasures and thought how fortunate Madison was to be an integral part of such a literary fortune, unaware that Herbert sat comfortably beneath one of the sliding ladders in a far corner observing them carefully and determining his course of action.

"At what hour would you like Kensington to draw your bath?" asked Madison earnestly.

"You've got to be kidding," remarked Gretchen. "Draw my bath? Since when do we take baths? We take showers, remember? My apartment doesn't even have a bathtub. I've made my peace with the shower stall."

"You'll have to bathe here," said Madison. "There aren't any showers."

Gretchen searched Madison's face to ascertain the beginnings of a smile or some other indication that he was jesting.

"My father loathes showers. He refuses to permit them anywhere on the premises. I think it has something to do with the war."

"What war?" asked Gretchen with incredulity.

"I don't know, some war or battle he either witnessed or fought. He doesn't like to dwell upon it. Would you like a glass of wine before you go to bed?" asked Madison.

"Bed?" asked Gretchen. "It's only eight o'clock."

"We turn in early around here - lights out at nine. It has always been that way," said Madison grimly.

It was becoming clear that Madison's warning that his family was a bit odd was not an exaggeration. Be that as it may, Gretchen determined to make the most of it. They searched for Herbert, but he would not allow himself to be found. Madison kissed Gretchen tepidly and led her into her room.

"If you need anything, Kensington will provide it. Just ring this bell," said Madison drawing Gretchen's attention to a silver bell on the night stand.

"How will he hear the bell if the door is closed?" asked Gretchen.

"Kensington always hears, fear not. Now, I'll leave you to get comfortable. We have a wonderful claret that you must try. Everyone loves it. Kensington will bring you a glass," said Madison pulling the door closed. It made only the slightest sound, but Gretchen felt as though she was sealed within a tomb.

The room was candlelit; it was a nice touch. As the room was lit dimly, it was impossible to see the paintings which adorned the walls, but they seemed to be portraits of ancestors. The canopy bed had a white curtain overhanging it elegantly. The bed linens were pulled back to reveal white, silk sheets. Gretchen placed her hand upon them timidly. How she would be able to sleep upon them was in question.

Gretchen looked for a closet or a wardrobe but did not see anything resembling one. She opened the chest of drawers, which was filled with lingerie and an assortment of female garments, all of which were new with the tags still on them. Gretchen looked for a light switch to brighten the room enough to find the closet. There were no light switches anywhere on the walls. After a quick perusal of the room, Gretchen realized that the only source of light was emitting from a beautiful crystal candelabra, which graced the mantel of the fireplace. A soft, amber fire burned unobtrusively and provided the room with a pleasing sunset hue. Gretchen tried to open the door, but it would not open. It seemed to be locked from the outside. She bang on the door and called for Madison. Kensington opened the door and stood in the doorway with a glass of claret sitting atop a white doily on a silver tray.

"May I be of assistance?" asked Kensington.

"The door was locked. Why was the door locked?" asked Gretchen anxiously.

"All of the doors are locked at precisely eight-thirty," said Kensington entering the room and placing the glass of claret on the night stand.

"What for?" asked Gretchen.

"Perhaps you would like to discuss that with Mr. Timbrenel in the morning," said Kensington.

"I would like to discuss it with him now," insisted Gretchen. "Where is Madison's room?"

"I fear Mr. Timbrenel has retired for the evening," said Kensington.

"That's impossible," said Gretchen. "I was just speaking with him five minutes ago."

"Within the closet, you will find suitable attire to wear to the service tomorrow." Kensington opened the closet door. The wallpaper covering it was so impeccably matched that it was difficult to discern that a closet existed within the room. "Will there be anything else?" asked Kensington patiently.

Gretchen was agog. She stood silently.

"Very well," said Kensington, "goodnight."

Gretchen fumbled through her purse for her cell phone. There was no service. She hastened to the window. Perhaps she was close enough to climb out of the window. Her room was on the second floor. It wouldn't be that much of a drop. The first thing that caught Gretchen's attention when she pulled the drapes open was a sky filled with bright, flickering stars. The view was hypnotic. Never before had she seen such a sparkling array of twinkling celestial bodies. For a fleeting moment, Gretchen forgot about climbing out of the window. The scented air smelled of evening mist mixed with flowers from the extensive gardens that surrounded the house. Gretchen felt content to simply stare into the heavens and inhale the intoxicating aroma of the lush grounds. Her attention shifted to another bright light under her window. Herbert's sparkling teeth adorned the evening landscape, and they appeared to be quite sharp. He bared them ominously towards her open window. Gretchen knew that even if she survived the fall, Herbert would tear her to shreds. She closed the window and the drapes. This turn of events was most disconcerting. Gretchen gulped down the claret and flopped down upon the bed.

The ride to the mortuary was sombre and almost macabre. Gretchen sat between Madison and Elmore, who was crying inconsolably. The scene was a far-cry from the informal, nonchalant atmosphere of the wake. It was apparent that reality had set in, and Elmore realized that he would no longer see his mother's caustic face. He was alone in the world, and he wept on the black Chanel suit Gretchen selected from the items in the closet.

"I must speak with you about last night," whispered Gretchen to Madison.

"We can talk after the funeral," said Madison. "This isn't an appropriate time.

Elmore's sobs became more audible. He was now crying into his hands, which were on his knees.

"We're here, Elmore," said Madison opening the limousine door and stepping out. He extended his hand to Gretchen, who took it and exited the car. Madison reached in for Elmore's hand. It was wet with tears. The entire funeral party was small. It appeared that Aunt Patrice had few friends. The sparse group of relatives entered the mortuary and prepared for the final service. Aunt Patrice was to be cremated, and she requested that her ashes be strewn over her rose garden in her back lawn. The family questioned the legality of the request, but Elmore was intractable. He would spread her ashes over the rose garden.

There was a brief meal after the service and before the cremation. The Timbrenels hosted the meal at their estate. Gretchen was fascinated by the seemingly endless array of specialized rooms within the elaborate house. The funeral luncheon was held in a small room outside of the chapel, which occupied a separate wing of the house. Gretchen had never seen a chapel within a home. She wanted to inspect it further, but it was not the time to request a tour. Madison had never discussed his religion, and Gretchen was becoming increasingly curious. This Madison was nothing like the Madison, with whom she shared her life in New York. That Madison was adventurous and unencumbered. This Madison seemed bound by silent, illusive forces. Gretchen watched him standing beside Elmore, who had gained control of his emotions. They spoke quietly near the window. Gretchen thought she recognized one of the mourners. The mourner was not present at the wake, and Gretchen had not noticed her at the funeral; she approached her.

"Pardon me, but don't I know you?" asked Gretchen. "You look so familiar."

The young woman extended her hand.

"I'm Hayley Rembrandt, and this is my brother, Jordan. Patrice Butterfield was my godmother. I missed the wake, and we almost missed the funeral. There was a crisis at the office, and everyone had to try to help avert it. Jordan drove like Phaeton trying to make it here in time."

Mrs. Timbrenel approached the pair smiling. "Hayley Rembrandt. I haven't seen you since your Confirmation. That was ages ago. How are things going at the firm? Who is this handsome young man accompanying you?"

"Hello Mrs. Timbrenel." Hayley kissed the matron's cheek. "This is my brother, Jordan. He was to leave for Canada this morning, but he unselfishly agreed to accompany me to Madame Butterfield's funeral. I didn't want to come alone. Madame Butterfield has been like a mother to me."

"Have you seen Elmore? Come, I'll take you to him. He will be comforted by the sight of you," said Mrs. Timbrenel.

Mrs. Timbrenel led Hayley away from Gretchen to Elmore and Madison. They were both elated to see Hayley and embraced her. Gretchen remembered Hayley from Madison's office, though she had no idea that they were acquainted. Madison did not introduce her to his associates when she visited.

"Did you know Mrs. Butterfield well?" asked Jordan.

Gretchen had forgotten that he was standing there.

"I didn't know her at all," said Gretchen. "Why is she called Madame Butterfield?"

"I don't know. I never met her," said Jordan. "I live in Oregon with my dad and brother. I was on my way to Vancouver when my father called and said that Madame Butterfield died. He never met her either. She was a friend of my mother's."

"Oh," said Gretchen. "Your mother is deceased also?"

"No," said Jordan. "She lives in England. I'll probably visit her on my way to Sochi for the 2014 Olympics. I'm going for the snowboarding gold."

"How impressive," said Gretchen. "Where is Sochi?"

"Russia," answered Jordan. "Excuse me, my sister wants me. Nice talking to you."

"Yes," said Gretchen, "Good luck with the Olympics."

"It's not about luck," said Jordan adamantly. "It's all about skill and determination."

"Yes, of course," said Gretchen. "Well, have a safe trip."

"Thanks," responded Jordan.

There was a bounce in the young snowboarder's step; his brown hair moved rhythmically on his shoulders as he walked. Gretchen watched the trio near the window. She was pleased that she had selected the Chanel suit from the closet. It made her feel elegant. Madison's father approached Gretchen.

"So, you live with my son," said the meticulously attired patriarch.

Gretchen blushed and was at a loss for words. She stood silently trying to think of something to say.

"You're wondering how I know about your relationship with my son," said Mr. Timbrenel. "Very little happens in this family about which I do not know. Fear not, his mother knows nothing of it. If she did, you can rest assured that you would not have been allowed to attend this funeral. My wife is conservative where these things are concerned. I'm told that you have a thriving practice. New York is a dog-friendly city. People pay more attention to their canines than they do to one another. They think that it's perfectly normal to invest in a dog psychologist, when the problem probably has more to do with them than their dogs. What do you think of my layman's analysis?"

"It's simplistic, but there is some truth in what you say," said Gretchen. "I met Herbert last night. Well, it wasn't actually a meeting. He stood outside barring his teeth at me as I gazed out of the window. He seemed agitated."

"Herbert is always agitated," said Mr. Timbrenel. "That's a part of his character. He's like a grumpy old man who wants his way and is unaccustomed to change. You represent change, and Herbert doesn't like it. He's protective of the family. That's normal, isn't it?"

"Yes," answered Gretchen.

"Herbert couldn't stand my sister, Patrice. He tried to take a plug out of her every time he saw her," said Mr. Timbrenel.

"I've been curious about your sister," said Gretchen.

"You want to know why she was called Madame Butterfield," answered Mr. Timbrenel.

"Yes," said Gretchen.

"My sister married a Frenchman and lived in Paris most of her life. His name was *Beurre* something or other. No one could pronounce it over here, so when he died and she moved back to Connecticut, she changed it to Butterfield, like the syrup," said Mr. Timbrenel."She instructed all of the French servants that she brought with her from Paris to call her Madame Butterfield. I guess the name stuck. Patrice viewed most people as her personal servants. Poor Elmore called her Madame Butterfield until he was eight-years-old..."

Mr. Timbrenel left Gretchen as abruptly as he approached her, seemingly, in mid-sentence. At least he shed light upon many of the questions that were swirling within Gretchen's mind. Madame Butterfield's god-daughter was leaving to return to the office. Madison walked Hayley and Jordan to their car. Interestingly, he did not introduce Gretchen to Hayley in this environ either. Gretchen made a mental note to observe Hayley Rembrandt more carefully the next time she visited Madison at the office. Madison returned and placed his arm around Gretchen's shoulder. His smile was reassuring.

"It won't be much longer," said Madison. "We should be able to leave in another forty-five minutes or so."

"I've been learning a lot about your family," said Gretchen. "Who is Hayley? I've seen her at the office."

"Don't mind her," said Madison. "She's like a sister to me. My aunt was her godmother. We've spent a lot of time together. I wouldn't be surprised if Aunt Patrice leaves her something in her will. It's going to be read next Thursday. Would you like to attend the reading?"

"Yes, I would really like that," said Gretchen. "I've never attended a will reading before."

"Come on, let's get something to eat before the cremation," said Madison. "Elmore is anxious to spread the ashes over Aunt Patrice's rose garden. I think it will be a semblance of closure for the poor soul. I don't know what he will do with himself now that Aunt Patrice is gone."

"I thought you said that he lived in Paris," said Gretchen. "There must be loads of things to do in Paris."

"Elmore was close to his mother, although she did not regard him favourably," said Madison. "We're a strange family, Gretchen. I hope that you won't hold it against us."

Strange was an understatement. From what Gretchen could observe, the entire family seemed to be in need of psychiatric care. Be that as it may, her only concern was Madison. The sooner she could get him away from his family, the better.

Gretchen's assessment was simplistic. The fact that Madison had been married before and had a young son came as a revelation. Elmore assumed that she knew all about it. How wrong he was. The ride back to the metropolis was frigid. Gretchen answered Madison's questions with simple "yes" or "no" answers. She was swirling from the news that her loved one did not mention his previous marriage or child, so much so that she did not mention the locked door or Herbert's snarling teeth beneath her window. What kind of person keeps such secrets? To hear it from the likes of Elmore was even more disconcerting. Elmore planned to sell his mother's house at a substantial profit after the will-reading and return to Paris, where he would live on the proceeds comfortably.

"How do you feel?" asked Madison turning onto the New York exit.

"How do you think I feel?" asked Gretchen. "I feel as though I've been duped."

"Duped?" asked Madison indignantly.

"Don't you dare correct my English," warned Gretchen. "I'll get out of this car and walk home if you do."

'How have I deceived you?" asked Madison.

"How can you ask that question?" asked Gretchen shrilly. "You have an ex-wife and a son."

"Yes," responded Madison, "but the key word is *ex*."

"A child can never be an *ex*, Madison," said Gretchen. "Sooner or later, he will appear and inhabit our lives."

Madison tried to be as delicate as possible. "We've only been living together three months. We haven't made any sort of commitment, have we?"

"Don't be stupid, Madison," said Gretchen. "When a woman moves in with a man, it is a commitment. Are you telling me that you are not sure of this relationship?"

"I'm merely suggesting that we have not been together long enough to decide whether or not we want to commit," said Madison earnestly.

"That does it," said Gretchen. "I'm moving back to my apartment as soon as we return New York."

"Don't be hasty," said Madison. "We can discuss this rationally."

"No, you discuss it rationally with your mother. And you can give her this suit back as soon as I have it cleaned," said Gretchen. "Was this your wife's suit? Was she my size?"

"Now you're being ridiculous," said Madison changing to another lane.

"Why is it ridiculous?" asked Gretchen. "Why didn't you tell me about your wife and your son?"

"Ex-wife and son," said Madison. "I suppose I didn't want a scene like this."

"Well, you have one. I will be moving out as soon as we return to the city," said Gretchen.

"Fine," said Madison.

"Fine," said Gretchen. "Now you can see Hayley. Why

didn't you introduce me to her at the funeral? I've seen her at the office too, but you've never bothered to introduce me. Are you involved with her? Is she an old girlfriend or something?"

Madison sighed. "I can't do this. Let's just be as amicable as possible so that I can drive this vehicle safely."

"It's true, isn't it?" asked Gretchen. "You've been involved with her."

"Yes," admitted Madison, "Hayley and I were once involved for a brief period of time, but it didn't work. None of my relationships work. I thought that you would be different. I was wrong."

Gretchen collected her wits. She was destroying their relationship for no reason at all, if concealing a wife, son, and girlfriend were unimportant reasons. In her heart, she forgave Madison and determined to endure with him. He wasn't perfect, but neither was she; however, she had not lied or concealed anything from him, apart from the churlishness of her family. She was certain that in time, they would be able to work things out.

"Let's go home," said Gretchen resting her head against the seat. Madison smiled and proceeded down the expressway. Heaven preserve us.

Things were not proceeding well at the office. The moon shone brightly as the youthful executives attempted to solve the latest crisis, which showed no signs of relenting. The light of the moon joined company with the lights of the metropolis, and the people seated around the conference table seemed entranced.

"Can we just focus?" asked John Claybourne. "Surely, there must be some way we can make this palatable before I make my report to Mr. Bradley. Come on, people, think or we're doomed! Does anyone have any ideas?"

The light of the full moon continued to beam brilliantly into the conference room. Its radiant reflection graced the walls and cast a lethargic ambience within the room. Everyone seemed piteously resigned to whatever fate had in store for them. For now, the moon rendered everyone insensible, at least as far as John Claybourne was concerned. The door opened, and Hayley entered sheepishly and sat at the far end of the table.

"Oh, Ms. Rembrandt," said John Claybourne, "you've returned from the funeral. How gracious of you to lend your invaluable assistance. The team comes first, Rembrandt! Death is not a priority."

"It's not Hayley's fault," said a mild voice at the far end of the table. John Claybourne swirled around in his swivel chair menacingly.

"What? Who said that!" demanded John.

The gentle hand of Gregory Plaitsburg extended into the tension-filled air. Gregory was a pale, slender account executive. He said little to anyone during the course of the day, but his work was always submitted on time in the most meticulous fashion.

"Oh, it's you *Bartleby*," said John sarcastically. "You would like to protest my utterance to Ms. Rembrandt?"

"It wasn't Hayley's fault that her godmother died," said Gregory softly. "We all have families. Sometimes death *is* a priority."

The team nodded in agreement. There was strength in numbers. John Claybourne did not pursue his verbal diatribe. He changed the subject quickly but made a mental note that Gregory Plaitsburg could be a hindrance to a productive team, for he spoke the truth in and out of season.

Hayley smiled and cast an appreciative glance in Gregory's direction. Gregory was not adept in picking up social clues; hence, the nickname *Bartleby*. Like the scrivener, Gregory seemed to live in isolation. His interactions were curt, direct, and emotionless. He did not enjoy speaking or listening to others speak. Gregory was in his own insular world most of the time, and any attempt to engage him in conversation was construed as a source of irritation, which he remedied quickly by walking away and avoiding eye contact. John wished that the others on his team were more like Gregory but without the irritating ethical proclivities. Most of his team had little regard for ethics and chatted incessantly about the most inane topics when they were not interacting with clients.

John wished that he had Madison's team of sharp-shooters - an amiable, professional lot. Adding Hayley Rembrandt to John's aggregate team of losers was, surely, the last straw, but John could not complain. Madison's family was formidable, and his father was an imperious shareholder within the firm. If that were not enough, Jason Timbrenel was a close friend of Mr. Bradley, CEO. When Madison's unseasonable affair with Hayley Rembrandt disintegrated, John had no recourse. He had to accept Madison's request to allow Hayley to work with his team, for Hayley was not only Madison's ex-lover, she was also god-daughter to his aunt, who would be incensed at any wrong-doing to the god-daughter, for whom she secured the position as intern. Be that as it may, John accepted Hayley with a smile, with hopes that the Butterfield woman would take note of his cooperative endeavours. But now the old fossil had the temerity to die; thus, there would be no one to offer gratitude for his sacrifice.

The meeting resumed, but it was clear that the reluctant *think tank* had no ideas which would salvage a financial merger on the brink of collapse. John adjourned the meeting. He would face Mr. Bradley with the troublesome statistics and hope for the best.

"Hayley, I have an assignment for you," said John placidly. "You know that kid you were tutoring in French?"

"Noel?" asked Hayley.

"Yes, Noel. He's Madison's protégé, isn't he?" asked John.

"I wouldn't say that he's his protégé. I think that he was just a part of an agency where Madison volunteers as a financial consultant," said Hayley.

"What's this group like? I mean, is it in a poor area? Are they a non-profit organization?" asked John.

"I believe so," said Hayley.

"I want you to get all of the information you can about the agency right away," said John.

"Why don't you just ask Madison? I'm certain that he knows all about it," said Hayley.

"If I ask Madison, he'll want to take credit for my idea," said John. "I want to use the organization to butter up old man Bradley. Besides, Madison has no interest in non-profit organizations. He's just using them to enter the political arena next year. Get as much information as you can about the organization and report back to me tomorrow morning. There may be a bonus in this for both of us, Rembrandt."

"I don't understand," said Hayley perplexed.

"You will in time," said John. "By the way, don't mention this to Madison. I don't want him to derail our efforts before we have an opportunity to put them into action."

"Our efforts?" asked Hayley.

"Don't stand there parroting me, Rembrandt," ordered John. "Try to be useful, for once, and get the information I requested."

It was disconcerting that John used her last name. This seemed to be a new tactic to make her feel more detached. Hayley tried to remain calm and civil. She was not a confrontational person, and insults usually did not blemish her tranquil character in any way, but for some reason, John Claybourne's remarks were intolerable. Perhaps it was because of the hectic pace trying to get to the funeral and back before it had officially ended, or it might have been the brief conversation with Madison's new girlfriend. Whatever the reason, Hayley Rembrandt heard herself uttering, "Mr. Claybourne, I resign, effectively immediately" and walked out of his office with a new sense of dignity. That was it. John Claybourne had been eroding her sense of dignity since she first arrived. It wasn't his fault. How could he be expected to respect her? She was Madison Timbrenel's castoff and was not expected to do anything significant. That was why John never gave her an assignment directly related to her financial abilities, which were impressive. He only saw Madison's stamp of rejection upon her forehead. Leaving would be the most merciful thing she could do for herself. It was strange how answers oftentimes appeared when one least expected them. The answers are ever-present but remain invisible until the strategic moment arrives when they make their presence felt, and one has no recourse other than full-disclosure and soul-searching honesty. Hayley left her belongings in her desk. She wanted no part of them. It was time to begin anew.

The next few days were tortuous. Alyson's ranting was understandable. There was enough in savings for three months rent. After that, Hayley had no knowledge of how she would survive. New York was an expensive place. It was possible to spend a hundred dollars on the bare necessities like laundry, food, and items from Duane Reade. She would have to cut back on her spending until she secured another position, which would not be easy in the lamentable economic environment. It would be necessary to ask Madison for a reference. Surely, John Claybourne could not be trusted to provide a positive reference when he had not allowed her to work up to her full potential. The future looked bleak, indeed. Her BlackBerry rang. Hayley looked at it and wondered how long she would be able to keep it. To her surprise, the caller was the man with whom she shared a blanket at the polo match. That was three months ago. Had he lost her number? Why the sudden interest? His name was Rupert, and he would be in New York for the next two weeks attending a conference. He wondered whether or not she would like to join him for dinner. Of course, she would be delighted. The buzzer rang as soon as her conversation ended. Hayley pressed the button.

"Who is it?" asked Hayley.

"It's Elmore. May I come up?" asked Elmore.

"Elmore? Of course," said Hayley.

Hayley pressed the buzzer again. Within minutes, Elmore was standing on the threshold. He looked haggard, as though he hadn't slept or shaved in days.

"Elmore, come in. Have a seat," said Hayley. "You look awful. What is it – jet lag? I thought that you were in Paris."

"I was," said Elmore sitting on the worn, plaid sofa. "I came as soon as I heard the news."

"What news?" asked Hayley hoping that there was not another death with which to cope. Her nerves were already strained. At least there would be no scheduling conflicts if she had to attend another funeral. She had all the time in the world.

"My solicitor phoned me. I sent him to the will reading and gave him proxy to sign any papers so that I wouldn't have to make another trip back to Connecticut," said Elmore accepting the glass of wine that Hayley was offering him.

"Was there a problem? Madame Butterfield left you the house, didn't she?" asked Hayley.

"She left me the house, all right," said Elmore. "She owed so much in back taxes that I won't be able to salvage much when I sell it."

"I'm sorry to hear that," said Hayley earnestly. She had no idea that her godmother was in such dire straits financially. "Poor Madame Butterfield."

"Not so poor," said Elmore finishing the glass of wine. He placed the delicate stemware on the end table. "It seems that my stepfather left her a vineyard in Tuscany. It's worth millions. I knew nothing of it. All of these years, she kept it a secret. Uncle Jason didn't know anything about it either."

"Well, it's a blessing in disguise, isn't it?" asked Hayley. "You can sell the vineyard and pay the back taxes on the house."

"I wish it were that simple," said Elmore. "You see, my mother left the vineyard to you."

Chapter III

Alyson's words resounded unceasingly, *There are dreamers, and there are providers. You are a provider. We are what we are.*

Hayley never dreamed of owning anything of value. It was enough to have a nice place to live, food in the refrigerator, and a little money for impulse shopping. She allowed herself that tiny extravagance. When one lives in New York, impulse shopping is a necessity and a part of the lifestyle one acquires when one moves to the metropolis. A vineyard in Tuscany was quite another matter. Perhaps Madame Butterfield saw the provider in her god-daughter and the dreamer in her son, which precipitated the decision to leave Elmore the house and bequeath the vineyard to her. Be that as it may, it was quite a dilemma.

Hayley did not know what to say to Elmore. If Madame Butterfield wanted her to have the vineyard, surely, she could not give it to Elmore. The financial aspects of the generous gift did not enter Hayley's consciousness. She loved Madame Butterfield, and she wanted to honour her request. Hayley was not surprised when Elmore threw a tantrum in her living room. Elmore was always throwing tantrums to get his way. Madame Butterfield often relented in order to maintain a peaceful existence with her only child, but Hayley was not Madame Butterfield. She ordered her cousin to leave her apartment, or she would call the police. Elmore left immediately. Bad publicity for a struggling artist was not an acceptable idea. Hayley phoned Madison Timbrenel in order to discuss the turn of events and to assess the family's general attitude. They agreed to meet at Hayley's favourite restaurant on East 72nd Street. Madison was not enamoured with the location.

"If you wanted seafood," said Madison, "I was able to obtain the most succulent crabs from Maryland. Why are we here?"

"Don't be such a snob," said Hayley. "I don't want to dine on your boat."

"It's not a mere boat," corrected Madison, "besides, you are an heiress now. You can afford finer dining establishments."

"I'm not an heiress yet," said Hayley. "That is why I phoned you. I don't know what to do about this vineyard business."

"There's nothing to do," said Madison. "Obviously, the vineyard is turning a profit. It's worth millions. My father is livid. He had no idea that his sister was in possession of such wealth. She was constantly borrowing from him. Apparently, she was saving the vineyard for you. There is no need for concern. In a couple of months, you will be financially secure for life and beyond."

"I'm not really interested in the financial profits of the vineyard," said Hayley. "I simply want to ensure that it will continue to prosper under my guidance. I don't want to disappoint Madame Butterfield."

Madison laughed. "Madame Butterfield, as you call her, is not in a position to care about whether or not you will disappoint her."

"I mean, I don't want the vineyard to fail under my leadership," said Hayley anxiously.

"What leadership?" asked Madison. "How much leadership did Madame Butterfield render all of these years? She must have a team of professional advisors working for her here and in Tuscany in order to continue to profit. These people now work for you."

"I don't know anything about the wine business," said Hayley.

"You don't have to. It's an investment," said Madison. "The vineyard in Tuscany is a source of revenue for you, but it is also a way of life for the people who worked for my aunt. If you want my advice, here it is. Go to Tuscany and meet with the people who work for you. Let them know that you are interested in the vineyard and that you are not just an investor in New York.

You'll win them over. You are charming to a fault. I must say, Hayley, I would rather not dine here. Let me take you to one of my favourite places."

With that, the twosome exited the modest seafood restaurant on the upper eastside and had a marvellous crab dinner on the Timbrenel vessel on Long Island Sound.

The details of Hayley's *rags to riches* American fable fascinated Rupert. Surely, America was the land of opportunity. Hayley suggested the same seafood restaurant on East 72nd, which pleased Rupert. He was of average build and wore a pin-striped suit with a white handkerchief protruding from his suit jacket. Rupert's hair was auburn and exceedingly straight. Most of the men in New York preferred a wind-blown, carefree look about their hair, but he was not a New Yorker. For some reason, Hayley was fixated upon Rupert's hair, which seemed to refuse to be blown in any direction and clung steadfastly to his head. Hayley wished that at least one hair would move when he turned his head. Hair should move. Why was his hair so straight and stiff? Why was she being so critical and shallow? Did everyone have to look like Madison Timbrenel?

"You aren't going off to Tuscany in the immediate future, are you?" asked Rupert politely.

"Probably not," said Hayley, "My inheritance isn't finalized yet, and you do recall that I am unemployed. I am not able to go to Tuscany or anywhere else at present. Why do you ask?"

"Well, I am having a small gathering with a few friends next week, and I wondered if you might like to attend," said Rupert tasting the succulent salmon.

"I suppose I could attend," said Hayley. "Yes, I will attend. In fact, I look forward to attending!"

"My, that was a spirited response," said Rupert. "I hope that you won't be disappointed. It's just a small gathering. I must say, the food in this establishment is superb."

Hayley looked at Rupert with interest. Perhaps she could learn to like his hair.

"What do you do, Rupert?" asked Hayley tasting her swordfish.

"It fascinates me that Americans place such a high regard on careers or professions. That is the first question I am asked when I meet someone from the United States," said Rupert.

"Well, what do you respond?" asked Hayley.

"I would like to tell them that it is none of their concern, but I try to maintain a modicum of civility," said Rupert.

Hayley realized that he was not going to answer her question. It was then that she began to take an interest in him. The fact that he would not reveal his profession was of keen interest to her. It demonstrated character. In point of fact, Rupert consumed an entire meal without divulging much personal information; however, he knew everything there was to know about Hayley before the waiter brought dessert. What was it about Americans that prompted them to reveal so much personal information about themselves to total strangers? Rupert noticed this unseemly trait as he made his way through the valleys and canyons of the USA.

"We're not far from the MET," said Hayley touching the pristine white napkin to her lips. "Perhaps you'd like to go there. It's really lovely in the evening. The sculptures seem to come alive."

"All right, that sounds like a marvellous idea," said Rupert not mentioning that he had tickets for *Phantom of the Opera*.

Gretchen belaboured the task of trying to ascertain Madison's preferences. After meeting his family, everything changed. He was of aristocratic blood; she was *of the people*. It simply would not work. For some unfathomable reason, she could not reconcile the vast difference between her family and his. When would they ever meet? The thought of such a meeting filled her with an excruciating dread. If they were to marry, there would be no family members on her side of the church. Marriage seemed a remote possibility. Madison had made no indication that marriage was in their near or distant future, so what was she doing with him? She wanted marriage, children, and a home, not an estate inhabited with strange relations. It would probably be better if she broke it off first. The thought of an estranged ex-wife and son showing up on their doorstep in the future was too much to bear, and they always showed up, didn't they? Gretchen could picture it – she and Madison would be in their pajamas bouncing their cuddly baby boy on their laps when the doorbell rings and in walks the ex-wife and son in need of a place to stay. Madison places them in a hotel and visits every day. Soon, the visits turn into more time spent with the first family than the second. Then comes the revelation that he still wants to be with his first wife and son but will make more than adequate accommodations for his new family. That simply would not do. Gretchen worked all of it out in her mind, and it simply would not do. She would break it off and start anew.

Madison entered the apartment with a cheerful smile and a cone-shaped wrapping filled with red roses. He kissed Gretchen's cheek and presented her with the roses before he entered the shower. Once again, Gretchen's plans were foiled by nothing less than love for the man bearing flowers and a problematic history of relationships. She was in again, but she had no idea for how long. When Madison exited the shower with a white towel draped over his exquisitely toned body, he asked a question, for which Gretchen was not prepared.

"Would you mind if Hayley and a friend dropped over for dinner Friday?" asked Madison leafing through the mail on the coffee table.

"I suppose not," said Gretchen. "Why is she coming here?"

"As I told you, she has inherited a vast amount of money, and she has no idea what to do with it," said Madison. "I fear that some gold digger will try to extricate her from her inheritance."

"And you think that this friend is a gold digger?" asked Hayley.

"Of course," answered Madison.

"It is possible that he actually likes Hayley," said Gretchen.

"Oh, that is not possible. I understand that he is from England," said Madison.

"So?" asked Gretchen.

"So, English people don't just like other people," explained Madison. "They expect a dowry or something."

Gretchen looked askance at Madison. "Why is this your concern?"

"Hayley is a friend, and I don't want to see her hurt or fleeced," explained Madison.

"Hayley is an adult and capable of managing her own affairs," responded Gretchen shrilly. "I don't see why you are so interested in Hayley's personal life. You are not involved with her anymore, or have you forgotten that we are now in a relationship."

"Don't do this, Gretchen," said Madison with exasperation. "I really cannot take another scene like the one on the way home from the funeral."

"Then you need to make a decision, Madison," said Gretchen in tears. "Will it be Hayley or me? Will it be the ex or me?"

"What are you talking about?" asked Madison. "Where is this coming from?"

"I don't know," said Gretchen as the tears streamed down her cheeks. "You have an ex-wife and son. You were involved with Hayley. All of this is news to me, so forgive me if I take time to absorb all of it. You never mentioned any of it. That is not what people do when they are in a relationship."

"You're right," said Madison. "I didn't want to take a chance of losing you or making you doubt me. This always happens to me."

"It's not about you, Madison!" yelled Gretchen. "Don't you dare try to turn it around to reflect your feelings. I'm hurting. Can't you see that?"

"Of course I can see it," said Madison with grief etched upon his unlined face. "What would you like me to do? I can't change the past."

"I need time to think this through," said Gretchen. "I think that I should move back into my apartment and give you space."

"I don't want space," said Madison.

"Then I want space for myself. I need to clear my head," said Gretchen. "I'll move out in the morning."

"Don't do this, Gretchen," said Madison.

"I must. If we are to survive, then I must," said Gretchen.

"Fine," said Madison, "then go back to your apartment and take all of the time you need to sort things out."

Gretchen waited for the final part of the speech - the part in which he stated that he would be there waiting for her return, but it did not come. Madison entered the bedroom, dropped the towel on the floor, and nestled between the warm, cotton sheets. He slept the sleep of the just. When he awoke the next morning, he found the apartment emptied of Gretchen, Bernie, and all of her belongings. The Chanel suit that Gretchen wore to the funeral was placed neatly over the sofa. There was no time to have it cleaned. Gretchen wanted to make a clean break. Oswald sat on the sofa with a look of bewilderment upon his face. Madison sat beside him and rubbed his neck.

"I know what you're thinking, boy," said Madison, "but this time, it wasn't my fault. They always leave, don't they? Oh well, it's just the two of us again. I guess we'll need to find another doggie day care program for you. It would be awkward to meet them every day, wouldn't it? The irony is, I really liked this one. Come on, boy, let's go out for a walk in the park. Don't start feeling depressed again, or you will make me feel sad as well. They never think of how their departure affects you, do they? Selfish wenches, the lot of them. They never think of how their absence affects you. I almost hate them for that. They enter our lives, and then they go without thought of how they hurt both of us. We're better off without them," said Madison rubbing Oswald's stomach. "We don't need any of them. Good riddance. Selfish wenches, the lot of them."

Hayley perused the mail and placed it carelessly onto an old wing chair that Alyson retrieved from her grandmother's attic. The stately chair held court in the living room over an aggregate of lowly furniture of wicker and plastic from Ikea. The chair was an elegant blend of beige and white leather. Although the arms showed signs of wear, it was the most comfortable chair in the entire apartment, and it never let the inhabitants forget it. The lineage was Basset, and the structure was impeccable. Hayley and Alyson resolved to have the graceful embodiment of culture upholstered but could not arrange for the exorbitant expense. Perhaps now with the vineyard, it could be reinstated to its illustrious form. Hayley stopped herself from thinking about the vineyard. It was still a pipe-dream, and she would not allow her future financial status to depend upon it until things were settled. She left the mail in the chair and trudged to her closet. There wasn't much there for social gatherings. All of her money was spent on tasteful business attire. Hayley realized that she hadn't a thing to wear to Rupert's gathering, and purchasing a new garment was out of the question. She entered Alyson's room and looked for something appropriate in the closet. Hayley removed a black and grey dress with black flounce around the lower hip. For some reason, the dress appealed to her. It was rather provocative, but she thought that Rupert would appreciate seeing her in something apart from a business suit. It occurred to her that the first time she met him, she was wearing a dress with flounce as well. Oh well, flounce added just the right amount of perkiness to keep a gentleman interested, and Hayley wanted to keep him interested.

The front door opened and closed. Alyson had arrived home. She dropped her purse on the coffee table.

"Hayley, did you check the mail?" called Alyson.

"It's on the chair," said Hayley entering the living room with the grey and black dress. "I hope that you don't mind, but I want to borrow this for Rupert's affair on Friday."

"Never mind that," said Alyson. "Did you notice that there is a letter here from your mother?"

Hayley's face clouded. "No, I just placed the mail onto the chair." She took the letter from Alyson and read it.

"Well" said Alyson," what does she say?"

"She wants me to come for a visit," said Hayley holding the letter as though it were poison tinged. "She requests that I spend the Christmas holidays with her. Can you imagine? I haven't heard from her in two years, and now she wants me to come and spend Christmas with her."

"What do you think?" asked Alyson.

"*Methinks* that dear old mom has heard about the vineyard and would like to re-establish a connection. She even sends a round trip ticket, first class, mind you. This must have set her back a few hundred."

"What are you going to do?" asked Alyson. "You know that a letter from your mother always means trouble. The last time she visited, it took you three months to recover."

Hayley smiled. "Well, I think that I shall visit dear old mom and see what she's up to. Elmore has probably been in touch with her, or it might have been Jordan. There are no secrets with him."

"Was the vineyard a secret?" asked Alyson.

"From my family – of course it was a secret," lamented Hayley. "They'll be coming out of the woodwork requesting loans, which I shall never see again."

"Well, they are your family," said Alyson. "I advise you to visit your mother for Christmas. Why shouldn't you be miserable? I'm visiting my family as well. You only have to stay a week or so, and you're not working, so there are no time constraints. Go and visit her. When you return, the vineyard affair will probably be finalized."

"I agree," said Hayley. "There's nothing to keep me here for the holidays. I will go to London and spend Christmas with my mother." Hayley genuflected and looked solemnly towards heaven.

Rupert's apartment was furnished exquisitely. Hayley was not certain that it was actually Rupert's apartment. She was greeted at the front door by a young man wearing an ascot and a smoking jacket. He held a pipe between his lips and smiled when he saw Hayley.

"You must be Hayley," said the young man. "Rupert said that you were attractive, but my brother is a master of understatement. You are more than attractive. You are quite lovely, actually. Do come in and make yourself at home."

Hayley entered the apartment and presented the young man with her coat. She could not remember the last time she had seen anyone smoking a pipe or wearing a smoking jacket. They were usually reserved for men of considerable age or men wanting to make an erudite impression or men in Noel Coward's entourage. Rupert entered the room wearing a monocle against his eye. Hayley was taken aback. Were these people presenting caricatures of how they thought Americans viewed the English?

"I realize that I have been remiss," said Rupert. "I neglected to tell you that we would be in costume; I didn't want to frighten you away."

"A monocle isn't much of a costume," said Hayley smiling.

"For me it is," said Rupert. "I have a top hat and tails in the other room."

Hayley looked around the room. Everyone was in costume. For some reason, a monocle, top hat, and tails did not seem out of character for Rupert at all; in point of fact, they seemed quite appropriate.

"I trust my brother, Julian, hasn't been too familiar," said Rupert. "He's been living in New York for some time, and he seems to have adopted the peculiar American custom of familiarity with perfect strangers."

"He was quite hospitable," assured Hayley. "This is a very nice apartment. Do you live here?"

"When I am in town, I live here," said Rupert. "The apartment belongs to my family. Our business interests bring us to New York several times a year."

"You never said what it is that you do," said Hayley remembering his reticence at the restaurant.

"Didn't I?" asked Rupert. "Come, there are people I would like you to meet."

Rupert led Hayley towards a small gathering near a white, grand piano in the corner of the room. One of the young men was playing a quiet, festive tune while the other people around the piano spoke quietly and sipped their drinks. Rupert made the obligatory introductions to "Joan of Arc," "Henry the VIII," "Batman," and the "Lady of Shallot." A bearded "Alfred Lord Tennyson" held court near the bar. It was amusing to see "Alfred Lord Tennyson" and "William Shakespeare" discussing the severe austerity budget cuts in Britain. Rupert introduced Hayley and briefly excused himself to rescue another guest from Julian's imitation of Cary Grant.

After an hour of chit chat, Rupert took a break from his duties as host and led Hayley to a comfortably overstuffed armchair near the working fireplace. It was time for the entertainment. Each character was to recite a passage, sing a song, or render some other offering that was emblematic of his or her selected character. Hayley was relieved to know that since she was not dressed, she would not be expected to perform. The other guests eagerly anticipated the renderings of their fellow guests. Hayley had to admit, it was the most fun she had had in ages. She couldn't remember when she had laughed so hard or nearly cried from the beauty of the poetic recitations.

"So, if Julian is Cary Grant," said Hayley inspecting Rupert's monocle at close range, "who are you supposed to be?"

Rupert smiled slyly and directed her attention to a rather cumbersome framed portrait hanging over the fireplace. To Hayley's astonishment, Rupert and Julian bore a remarkable resemblance to the man's portrait. Hayley could not decide which brother favoured the elder in the portrait more. The sturdy man wore a stiff, black woollen suit. He sat in an uncomfortable-looking wooden chair with a docile brown-furred dog at his heels. The dog's eyes were downcast and exceedingly tame. The gentleman's eyes displayed an inward passion for order, decorum, physical strength, and civility. He was not a man with whom one could trifle, and his demeanour was illustrative of his stance. The portrait reminded Hayley of Theodore Roosevelt, but what would Roosevelt be doing on Rupert's wall?

"He was a distant relation," said Rupert. "I believe he was your twenty-sixth president."

"That's Theodore Roosevelt!" shrieked Hayley observing the monocled eye. "Good grief! I had no idea."

"He was not on the best of terms with our small branch of the family," said Rupert, " but there he is in all of his glory. I'm writing a book about his life within the illustrious Roosevelt family."

"You're related to the Roosevelts - how exciting. I suppose that would include Franklin Delano Roosevelt as well," said Hayley resuming her composure.

"We refer to him as 'the other president.' Once again, the blood lines were not amicable." said Rupert.

"I feel as though I'm in the company of royalty," said Hayley.

"You are, my dear," said Julian joining them. "Rupert, you have allowed our guest to be deprived of our best champagne." Julian exchanged Hayley's empty glass with a new one filled to the brim with golden champagne.

"Thank you," said Hayley. "I'm beginning to feel like royalty myself."

"That cannot be avoided," said Julian, "when you are the honoured guest of the Chesterfield brothers."

"I didn't realize that I was honoured," said Hayley.

"Enlighten her, Rupert," said Julian as he took his leave sauntering across the room leaving a small trail of refined smoke from his pipe.

"Your brother is quite a character," said Hayley. "Is he always like that?"

"It's vintage Julian," said Rupert. "What are you doing tomorrow? I thought that you might like to see an art exhibit in Soho. The artist is an old childhood friend."

"That sounds wonderful," said Hayley, "but I'm afraid I'm on my way to London to spend Christmas with my mother."

"Your mother lives in London?" asked Rupert.

"Yes. It's a long, boring story," said Hayley.

"I'm a writer. I like long, boring stories," said Rupert.

"Perhaps another time," said Hayley. "I don't like to think of unpleasant things. I'm having such a nice time."

The last thing Hayley wanted to do was think about her troublous family relationships. Rupert was not the only one with less than amicable familial blood lines. She tried to distance herself from thoughts of her family. The nearest thing to family that Hayley experienced since moving to New York was the Timbrenels and her godmother, Patrice Butterfield. For a moment, she reflected that she was fortunate in that many people living in New York lived single lives flitting through many relationships; her relationships were all inclusive of people with families to share. A few months ago, Rupert was the name of a stranger with whom she shared a blanket on Governor's Island. Today, she met his brother, his closest friends, and she felt that somehow she was a small part of the Roosevelt legacy. Only in New York. Hayley could feel the BlackBerry vibrating within her small, black clutch. A quick look revealed that Madison had sent a text, a very disturbing text.

"Anything wrong?" asked Rupert.

"A friend seems to be in distress," said Hayley. "He wants me to meet him as soon as possible. I think it can wait a couple of hours. He is always in some sort of distress."

Hayley returned the BlackBerry to her clutch without responding to the text. All evening, she thought of the message and could not enjoy the rest of the festivities. Rupert noticed her lack of engagement.

"Perhaps you should respond to that text. You seem preoccupied with its contents," said Rupert.

"No, I'd rather not respond," said Hayley. "This is the most enjoyable evening I have had in years, and I will not spoil it with messages from the past."

Hayley's life with Madison was a part of the past and refusing to respond to the text was emblematic of her break with the past. Now, if only she could do something about her mother. She, too, was a part of the past – a past that Hayley did not want to relive. Why should she go traipsing all over London to visit her mother, when she would much rather visit the art exhibit in Soho with Rupert. Rupert was a part of the future. Even if the relationship did not amount to anything, at least she would make a start at a new and better life. Down with the past and onward with the future.

"Is it too late to change my mind about visiting the art exhibit in Soho?" asked Hayley.

"Of course not," said Rupert. "Are you not going to visit your mother for Christmas?"

"Not," said Hayley emphatically. "I'd much rather spend time with you."

Each Christmas, Hayley travelled to Oregon to be with her father and her brothers. She always returned depleted. This Christmas would be different. She would spend it in New York and, for once, enjoy the holiday season without a care in the world, apart from visions of a vineyard in Tuscany.

Chapter IV

Bedtime stories were not Madison's forte. Visions of the restless sea filled his mind. He could smell the briny breeze penetrate his nostrils. His brother Oliver's son, Branford, slept peacefully after listening to his uncle Madison's bedtime story. The child seemed like a cherub as he slept. Timbrenel children always seemed like cherubs when night fell and the moon shone wistfully over the estate. Daylight brought about another aspect of the Timbrenel character. Timbrenel children during the daylight hours were, without exception, cunning, mischievous, and implacable. The shift in generation did not alter the perspective. During the course of the day, Branford placed a paste-like substance over Mrs. Timbrenel's finest porcelain vase. It was his attempt to replicate the priceless object with a papier mâché rendition and present it to the *lower-orders*, who had found entry, through some sort of philanthropic endeavours, into his primary class. After a play date in the home of a less-fortunate classmate, who lived on the Upper West Side and shared a bedroom with his sister, Branford found it difficult to recuperate from the horror. There were no priceless antiques in the comparatively small apartment, no domestic help, and the thought of sharing a bedroom with one's sister was unfathomable. Still, the Timbrenel's were nothing if not philanthropic altruists. When his mother and grandmother refused to part with any of their priceless artefacts, the young lad determined to help the *deprived* family by presenting them with a suitable representation of exquisite art. The thought that any household could be without fine art was more than the young dilettante could bear. Lamentably, neither his grandparents nor his parents agreed with his world-view. In their estimation, there were people who adored art and could not live without it, and there were philistines who did not care for art in the least. The philistines could not be altered, nor should they be altered. The world was divided into Philistines and people of culture and fine breeding. It was not always easy to detect which side of the ha-ha people belonged, particularly in New York, where the philistines and the *others* oftentimes shared common spaces in close proximity. Usually, it was the lack of appreciation for the arts that exposed the chasm. Art could not be forced upon such people. There were laws in place that prohibited drawing, quartering, and parading aesthetically-challenged people through the streets. Adding insult to injury, Branford's *less fortunate* friend berated him for trying to present him with a gift that looked like it should belong to a girl. What had boys to do with vases – porcelain or otherwise? Branford learned a valuable lesson. No longer would he try to inflict his values upon the *lower-orders*. He learned to view them as inhabitants of the far-side of the ha-ha and would decline all future play dates outside of his established set.

Madison turned off the light and let the sleeping cherub rest. Herbert stood guard over the little boy. Madison rubbed Herbert's chin and exited the room. Herbert looked around the room. All was clear on the home front, so he assumed a position of rest as well. A light snow covered the estate grounds. Madison's thoughts returned to the sea and to his To Do list. The waters would be cold and unpleasant. It would be best to resume the nautical adventure in the spring. Madison liked to walk the grounds at night when he visited the estate. Christmas visitations were particularly festive and enjoyable. There were twinkling lights glowing from the trees. Madison could hear sleigh bells jingling from the horses pulling an antique sleigh. Oliver and his wife, Lois, sat in the Victorian sleigh wrapped in a tartan blanket. They were all smiles and enjoyed the whimsical delights of an evening sleigh ride. Oliver relinquished the reins to the waiting groom and assisted Lois out of the sleigh.

"What happened to your friend, Gretchen?" asked Lois. "It's a lovely evening for a sleigh ride under the stars, Madison."

"I'm afraid she had another commitment," said Madison. He hadn't thought of Gretchen in weeks.

"Call her and invite her to the Christmas celebration Friday," said Lois. "I'll bet she would love to attend."

"You've lost another one," said Oliver resignedly. "What was it this time – your rendition of *Jingle Bells* on the lyre?"

"Mock if you must," said Madison. "Everyone cannot have your good fortune of an exemplary mate."

"Be patient, Madison," reassured Lois. "There is someone out there for you. You'll find her in due course."

"I don't think you'll find a wife on my brother's To Do list," said Oliver. "I hope you know that your days as a carefree bachelor are numbered. I've secured a place for you on Cuomo's junior staff; you will need a wife."

"Why? He hasn't got one, nor does Bloomberg. Why can't I follow their example?" asked Madison.

"You are not a billionaire, and our father has not won any bid to become governor of New York or any other state. It is up to us to carry on and prepare the way for Branford and any children you might have in the future," said Oliver.

"I know just the person for him," said Lois. "I don't know why I didn't think of it before. We could invite Melissa Kendrickson to the Christmas celebration. She's still single, and her father has most of the Vermont constituents in his pocket. It would be a match made in heaven."

"I'm going to invite Hayley," said Madison.

"Neither Hayley nor Gretchen are acceptable candidates," assured Oliver. "Father will agree with me. It is time that you started thinking sensibly about your future. You want someone with connections who can survive on this side of the ha-ha."

"We don't have a ha-ha," said Madison.

"Don't kid yourself," answered Oliver leading Lois towards the stairs through the delicately-fallen snow.

Gretchen Miller pressed the speed dial key and disconnected for the third time. If Madison did not want to contact her, why should she bother contacting him? She had enough in her life to occupy her time and thoughts. Her practice was growing, and she was beginning to meet an assortment of eligible bachelors with moody dogs in need of her expertise. For some reason, she could not rid herself of the image of Madison with a wife and a child. Every Asian person she encountered on the street or on the subway triggered thoughts of Madison and the family that left him behind. Gretchen pressed the key again and disconnected for the fourth time. Bernie looked at her and then at the phone intermittently. Gretchen rubbed his neck and placed her phone on the coffee table next to a half-eaten pear. Gretchen stared at the phone while rubbing Bernie's neck, hoping that it would ring. The silence was woefully heart-breaking. It was over. The tune from *The Nutcracker* sounded as the phone glistened on the coffee table. The number revealed a recent client. Yes, she would try to assist with a dog that refused to go outdoors. As it was a weekend and the holiday season, she would require an additional fee. Fine, she would be there within the hour.

Gretchen opened the door of her minivan, and Bernie jumped into the back area, where his toys and favourite blanket rested peacefully upon a half-eaten pizza crust. Gretchen reminded herself to take the minivan to the car wash and have them give it a thorough cleaning. She drove to Soho and searched for a parking space. Fortuitously, one presented itself a few blocks from the client's apartment building. Bernie jumped out when Gretchen opened the door. Another dog greeted him at the end of the leash of a disgruntled man. The man looked vaguely familiar. Bernie and the dog, a long-haired dachshund with a striking coat of auburn hair, sniffed one another. The man pulled the dog along impatiently.

"Don't I know you?" asked Gretchen looking at Bernie and the dog as they exchanged greetings.

"Are you speaking to me or to Gavin?" asked the man drawing his attention to Gretchen.

"I suppose I am speaking to both of you. I never forget a face – a dog's face, that is. Weren't you in my office with Gavin a couple of years ago?" asked Gretchen keeping her gaze upon Gavin and Bernie.

"Oh yes, of course," said the man. "You're Dr. Miller. How are you?"

"Quite well," said Gretchen redirecting her gaze towards him. "How is Gavin getting along? As I recall, he had a fear of birds."

"He has his days, just like a person, I suppose," said the man. "Sometimes we can be in the park, and he will be fine when a pigeon walks by; other times, just the sight of a bird flying by will give him spasms. He'll just crumble and shudder until he's spent. I have to carry him home. You were a big help, though. He's better than he was before I took him to see you."

"I'm glad to hear it," said Gretchen. "Well, I have an appointment. It was good to see both of you. Come on, Bernie."

"Wait," said the man. "Those two seem to get along. Why don't we arrange a play date? I know that Bernie probably gets to see many dogs, but Gavin spends all of his time cooped up with me. It would be good for him to have a buddy."

"As a matter of fact," said Gretchen, "I'm hosting a small get-together next week with a couple of dogs that get along well together. It's a celebration. One is celebrating two years without snarling at my client's cook, and the other is celebrating four months of the complete absence of shredding pillows. I am most proud of that accomplishment. I can't tell you how many pillows I've lost in the waiting room."

"Sounds great!" said the man. "I'll have my secretary phone your office for the details. Should Gavin bring anything?"

"I think the other dogs will bring some sort of treat or toy for the celebrants," said Gretchen.

"All right," said the man. "We'll bring something festive. It was great seeing you. We're really looking forward to this."

The man proceeded down the street with a smile upon his face. New York is the most "dog-friendly" city in the world. It is not unusual to see dogs dressed with accessories like their owners or riding in dog carriages. Gretchen was pleased to see a dog in a pearl necklace and a mink doggie coat in a restaurant on the upper west side. People in New York take their dogs everywhere, and most establishments welcome them. Dogs are like children to solitary New Yorkers; some reside in their own residences, when their owners marry and the dog cannot abide the new spouse or subsequent children. Yes, the dog party would be a most welcomed event. Just talking about it lifted Gretchen's spirits tremendously. Where but in New York would a practice such as hers flourish? Gretchen and Bernie walked cheerfully down the street to the home of her client. It was a rather tall apartment building with an agreeable doorman clad in a black uniform with gold cord trim and matching hat. The doorman phoned the client and announced the visitor with dog.

"You can go up," said the doorman petting Bernie's head.

Gretchen and Bernie entered the mirrored elevator with oak panelling. Thoughts of Madison started to creep back into her consciousness. She wondered if there were any messages on her BlackBerry. The client opened the door. A grey sheepdog stood reluctantly behind his owner and peered at Bernie. As the client explained the perplexing behaviour, which prevented his companion from exiting the building, Bernie made himself comfortable beside Gretchen's feet. Slowly, the sheepdog inched near him and began to sniff him.

"I don't understand it," said the client. "Cyril enjoys other dogs and used to enjoy romping around in the park. But now, he won't go outside at all. It's as though he's afraid of the sidewalk or something. The moment he smells fresh air, he balks. I make him go potty on newspaper on the terrace. How long can that go on? We need help. What do you think is wrong with him?"

"I will need to spend some time with Cyril," said Gretchen placing her hands under Cyril's chin. "How long has he been behaving this way?"

"For about a month," said the client.

"Has there been any change in his routine?" asked Gretchen checking Cyril's ears.

"Well, my wife returned from Beijing last month," said the client. "We've been separated for a few months, but she likes Cyril, and they get along just fine."

"I see," said Gretchen. "I would like to schedule a counselling session with the three of you. Would that be possible?"

"Sure, I don't see why not," said the client. "Do you think that it has something to do with Sylvia's return?"

"Let's schedule the appointment and proceed from there," said Gretchen.

Gretchen was always amazed that people could not see the answers to their problems when they were right before them. Of course the behaviour had something to do with the wife's return, but she would wait to meet with them before she diagnosed the condition. The word "Bejing" made Gretchen think of Madison. When would his wife and son return? It was becoming an obsession. Somehow, Gretchen had to rid herself of these thoughts that robbed her of her sense of well-being. Were it not for the wife and son, she would still be with Madison. *Physician, heal thyself*, thought Gretchen. She tried to focus upon the upcoming canine celebration and made a deliberate attempt to expunge Madison from her thoughts.

It was the Christmas season, but Madison felt less than festive. The thought of enduring the family Christmas party was more than he could reconcile. There was the office Christmas party, the community organization where he did volunteer work's Christmas party, and the condo Christmas party. He felt empty and alone. It was the first time he had ever felt depleted during the Christmas season. Perhaps he was getting older. The To Do List flashed before his eyes. He was thirty, and he had not accomplished a substantial number of items on his list. The most pressing was the voyage from New York to California on the vessel. It would have to wait for spring, but he would turn thirty before spring. If it must be done, then it would be better to do it now before the weather turned warm. Madison resolved to take the journey after the Christmas holidays. It would not be as enjoyable in the cold, but the voyage was not about enjoyment. It was about a sense of accomplishment.

No doubt, his family would pressure him to marry any suitable person. He could feel their tentacles encircling him and their choice of the moment, Melissa Kendrickson, the most insipid female he had ever encountered. Melissa was beautiful and unquestionably suitable for a man of his description, but Madison could not envision evenings curled up in front of a warm fire with her. Melissa was from Vermont, and her family was well-connected politically. It was his impression that the people from Vermont were singularly boring and lethally formidable where family honour was concerned. He couldn't imagine an evening of passion with Melissa without the engagement ring box visibly extending out of his breast pocket. Their children would be beautiful and well-mannered. Their home would contain masterpieces of art, and they would attend the smartest social engagements, where he would mingle with people who could advance his political career. The problem was that Madison Timbrenel did not want a political career. If anyone would have asked him two months ago what he wanted, he would have been at a loss to provide a plausible answer. Today, for some inexplicable reason, he knew precisely what he wanted. He phoned Hayley's number again and left another message. Why wasn't she returning his calls? Madison determined to see her before the dreaded Christmas party.

Madison took a glass of champagne from the silver tray Kensington extended. He took a glass for Melissa as well.

"Thank you, Kensington," said Madison cheerfully. Kensington nodded and proceeded to walk through the festive throng with his silver tray of cheer.

"You look ravishing this evening," said Madison with an ethereal tone. It was his third glass of champagne. He reasoned that it would take at least three glasses of champagne to enable him to make polite conversation with Melissa, and he was correct. After completion of the third glass, Melissa did look ravishing.

Melissa wore a crimson, velvet gown with a scooped neck and sparkling earrings that dangled playfully near her shoulders.

"I do believe that those are the longest earrings I have ever seen," said Madison flicking them with his fingers.

"And I do believe that you have had more than enough champagne," said Melissa laughing joyously. It was the first time that he had heard her laugh without thinking that it was a most irritating sound. Everything pleased him this evening. Perhaps it was the champagne, but Madison felt that it was more than that. There was something in the air – something wonderful. Perhaps it was the Christmas spirit, which was finally beginning to make an impact upon him. This was the way Christmas should be – happy and festive.

"Melissa, will you marry me?" Madison heard himself say.

Melissa looked at him thoughtfully. "The champagne has gone to your head."

"No, it hasn't," said Madison taking her hand.

"You're joking," said Melissa incredulously.

"I have never been more serious," said Madison earnestly. "Will you be my wife?"

"I don't know what to say," said Melissa. She was in a state of feigned disbelief. "Are you really serious?"

"Of course," said Madison.

"Then, I accept," said Melissa with a smile that brightened the room and everything in it. She wondered about the ring but felt that it would be more appropriate to wait until he brought up the subject. Melissa had selected her engagement ring and her wedding dress when she was thirteen years old. She knew that she wanted a round-shaped diamond with four baguettes, and her dress would have a bodice of lace and yards of satiny fabric cascading around her slender hips and down to the floor. There would be a train of three to six feet following her down the aisle of her family's Episcopal church. She knew what the bridesmaids would wear down to the bows on their shoes and in their hair. Her flowers would be an extensive arrangement of calla lilies that flowed gracefully from her fingertips. Yes, the wedding had been planned since she was old enough to dream. The groom was always in question, but she knew that one would present himself in due course. Due course had just arrived.

"I'm speechless," said Melissa. "You've made me the happiest person in the world."

Madison smiled as he drank another glass of champagne. "Shall we make the announcement to everyone?" asked Madison.

"Oh, yes, let's do it while everyone is jubilant," said Melissa straightening the front of her dress and feeling her hair to make certain that every strand was in place.

Madison took Melissa's hand, and they walked to the center of the room.

"We have an announcement to make," said Madison over the gregarious revellers. The guests looked at the pair and guessed their news before Madison could announce it with a slight slur in his speech, compliments of the champagne. Everyone's eyes were fixed upon the couple awaiting the transcendent words.

"Melissa has consented to become my wife," said Madison. Euphoria filled the room. Even Elmore Butterfield, still brooding about his mother's neglectful will, cheered the young couple. The well-wishers surrounded the blissful pair with words of elation. Herbert, sitting quietly near the front door, allowed Hayley to pet him as she entered with her Christmas gift for the Timbrenel family.

"I didn't forget you, Herbert," said Hayley presenting him with a rubber chew toy in the shape of a bone. Herbert accepted it graciously and trotted to the center of the room, where he placed it near Madison's feet.

"What do you have there, Herbert?" asked Madison observing the toy.

"It's just my Christmas present to him," said Hayley cheerfully approaching the couple.

Madison's eyes were transfixed upon Hayley. She looked spectacularly embraceable in a pale blue taffeta skirt that displayed her dimpled knees and a black knit bodice that illuminated her trim breasts, which seemed to press menacingly against the knit fabric. Madison did not know whether his look was a result of the champagne or a desire to revisit the familiar territory. Melissa noticed the lingering gaze and intercepted it with a wry comment about the change in atmosphere. Melissa and Hayley had never met, but Hayley surmised that she was the woman from Vermont – the future Mrs. Madison Timbrenel.

"Hayley, may I present Melissa Kinnerson," said Madison holding Melissa's hand.

"That's Melissa Kendrickson," said Melissa amiably. "How do you do?"

"Where's Kensington?" asked Madison impatiently. "I need another glass of the bubbly for Hayley."

Kensington appeared as he usually did, out of nowhere. He placed the silver tray before Hayley, who took a frosted champagne flute from the tray. Madison helped himself to another glass.

"Where were you today?" asked Madison. His eyes seemed glassy. "I was calling and calling and calling, but you didn't… you didn't…Is the room spinning, or is it me?"

"I'd better get you to a chair," said Melissa leading Madison to a large, comfy upholstered chair near the window. "Perhaps we'll meet again, Hayley. Come along Madison."

Melissa whispered into Madison's ear as he walked unsteadily towards the chair. He seemed to giggle while still sipping another glass of champagne.

"Lovely couple, aren't they?" asked Elmore standing near Hayley. She hadn't noticed him.

"Yes," said Hayley. "They are lovely. So, how are you, Elmore? I haven't seen you since Madame Butterfield's funeral. Are you still living in Paris?"

"Don't make small talk with me, Hayley," said Elmore. "My lawyers are working to contest that will. The vineyard belongs to me."

"Let's not argue, Elmore. It's Christmas," said Hayley. "I really can't see Madison marrying that woman."

"She's loaded, and her family can help him," said Elmore.

"Does she love him?" asked Hayley.

"I have no ample supply of clairvoyance, Hayley, but they seem happy," said Elmore

"He's drunk or soon will be," said Hayley wishing that she had returned his calls. "I think that he will regret his decision in the morning."

"What has it to do with you?" asked Elmore. "He threw you aside for that dog psychiatrist, or have you forgotten? Madison has a short memory where women are concerned. He'll marry Melissa, no doubt. He wouldn't dare back out now that they have made their announcement, but he'll be the same hubristic, self-absorbed philanderer he has always been. She'll add a sense of respectability to him and his political aspirations, but don't harbour any illusions that he's pining for you or any other woman. Madison is in love with Madison. Madison and Madison make the most endearing couple one could ever imagine."

Elmore left Hayley standing in the centre of the room. She touched the rim of the champagne flute. The bubbles tickled her fingers. She felt numb and wanted to go off alone and sort things out, but she could not. There were greetings to be exchanged and presents to be opened. It was Christmas. Why was every Christmas a catastrophe? Was she never to enjoy the heart-felt sentiments of the season? To make matters worse, she promised the Timbrenel's that she would spend a few days with them. How was she supposed to accomplish this feat now? The thought of spending a few days with Madison and Melissa was more that she could tolerate. Hayley remembered that she had been invited to spend a portion of the holiday with Rupert. As she recalled, it was an invitation to an art exhibit in Soho. Perhaps the Timbrenel's would not mind if Rupert came to visit. After all, the Timbrenel's were the closest thing to family that she had in the New York area, and one wanted to be near family or some semblance of family during the Christmas season. While in New York, one tended to make one's own family from friends and acquaintances. It was a unique lifestyle, but it suited her. Her new plan rested peacefully within Hayley's consciousness, and it eased the pain of Madison's announcement. She would put on a cloak of gaiety and circulate around the room as though her heart was not breaking, but truly, it was.

"I suppose you would like your usual room, Miss Rembrandt?" asked Kensington opening the door to a bedroom in the east wing of the historic mansion. "The fire is newly lit, so I brought a few blankets."

"Thank you, Kensington," said Hayley. "That's very kind of you."

"Will there be anything else?" asked Kensington.

"No, thank you, Kensington, unless you wouldn't mind bringing me a cup of warm cocoa," said Hayley. The room was almost frigid as the fire in the fireplace got underway.

"Very good," said Kensington departing with a smile.

Hayley blew into her hands to keep them warm. She sat on

the rug near the fire and wrapped two of the blankets around her. She remembered that the room, her favourite, was a delight in summer when the temperatures were ascending, but she forgot how intemperate it could be in the winter. The fire cast a warming glow around the room creating an amber environ. The room was small and cosy, which was the reason she liked it. It offered a mesmerizing view of the lake, which was ever so pleasing during the early morning hours of summer. A steamy haze seemed to emit from it welcoming the summer sunrise, but in winter, the lake was frozen and cast an uneasy shadow against the light of winter's moon. The bed, covered with a white satin comforter, seemed luxuriously inappropriate in winter. She would much rather have a patchwork quilt that offered warmth rather than the smoothness of the satin comforter.

A pair of blue satin pyjamas lay across the bed. Hayley smiled. Mrs. Timbrenel loved dressing her visitors and providing attire that would befit the estate and the room. She opened the closet door to see the "goodies" Mrs. Timbrenel placed there. Good grief! There were riding breeches in the closet. Surely, Mrs. Timbrenel did not expect her to ride in the winter. There were two gowns, quite lovely, that were to be worn to dinner. The Timbrenels always dressed for dinner. Hayley pulled the blanket around her as she surveyed the room, which had a large vase of white flowers. Hayley did not know the name of flowers, but they were beautiful. As usual, there was neither television set nor radio. Guests were expected to read. There were three Trollopes on the nightstand, all from the *Barchester Chronicles*. The door opened without a knock. Branford, Madison's youthful nephew, sauntered in and dived atop the bed.

"It's freezing in here," remarked Branford. "May I have one of your blankets?"

Hayley tossed a blanket over him.

"They say you're crestfallen," said Branford snuggling under the blanket.

"Who says?" asked Hayley.

"Everyone downstairs says that you're crestfallen because Madison is going to marry Melissa," said Branford. "What's crestfallen?"

"I think that it means extremely disappointed," said Hayley.

"Are you crestfallen?" asked Branford.

"What are you doing up at this hour?" asked Hayley. "Shouldn't you be in bed?"

"They think that I am in bed, but I waited until they left my room and came to see you," said Branford. "Shall I spend the night with you?"

Hayley laughed in spite of herself. "Why would you want to do that?" asked Hayley.

"Because I believe that you are crestfallen, and crestfallen people should not be alone. I can make you laugh. I know many jokes and funny stories. I can help cheer you," assured the cherubic youth.

Hayley bent over the bed and kissed Branford's cheek.

"Branford, you are sweet, and you have the most generous heart that I have ever known, but you must return to your room. Believe me, I am not crestfallen. I am fine. Off to bed with you," said Hayley shooing him from under the blankets and out of the door.

There was another knock on the door. Kensington brought the hot cocoa in and placed it on the nightstand. There were three marshmallows floating in the cocoa. Hayley smiled. Suddenly the room seemed warmer. Yes, the Timbrenels were like family – better than family. Hayley would miss these precious moments when Madison married Melissa.

"Thank you, Kensington," said Hayley. "This is perfect."

Kensington smiled and exited the room. The Timbrenel's home was truly a home. The little touches that provided comfort made one feel wanted, respected, valued, and loved. This was living. Someday, when she had a family of her own, Hayley would emulate the Timbrenels and provide her family with the same loving care they always provided to her. For some inexplicable reason, the vineyard in Tuscany crossed her mind, and for the first time, Hayley realized that she was a lady of means – perhaps on par with the Timbrenels. The thought had not occurred to her before. The vineyard was an abstraction, but now it felt like a reality. She was no longer Madame Butterfield's charming but poor godchild. She was a woman of position. Hayley cast off the blankets. The room was beginning to warm. As she sipped the cocoa on the rug before the fireplace, Hayley realized that she would now be required to conduct herself as a lady of means. She would require a new residence, new clothing, and new ideals. She had not received any money from the vineyard yet, but she would plan her course before it arrived. A smile crossed her face. She wondered if Kensington might like to come and work for her, once she was established. Money isn't everything, but it does have the propensity to change one, oftentimes for the better.

A third knock on the door made Hayley sigh with fatigue. Madison popped his head in first, then he swung the door open and stumbled onto the rumpled satin comforter.

"I'm not drunk," said Madison incoherently. "I thought that I should…should…I wanted to see you before Vermont."

"You *are* drunk, Madison, and you are not making any sense," said Hayley sitting before the fire on the rug. Suddenly, the room seemed cold again, even though the fire in the fireplace roared with heat and festivity.

"I always love the smell of wood burning in the fireplace. It really makes me think of Christmas," said Hayley as she stared into the fire. It cackled and fragranced the room with an aroma of woodsy pleasure. Madison slept peacefully atop the satin comforter. Somehow, it did not seem out of place beneath him. Madison *was* satin and elegance. Perhaps Mrs. Timbrenel's sense of style and fashion was not off the mark after all. Perhaps she knew that the decor of Hayley's room should first and foremost suit her son. Hayley wondered if she had drank one glass of champagne too many, for she was emerging into a philosopher this evening making connections and seeing the intricacies of life as she had never seen them. Champagne was a marvellous gift from above. It was festive and revelatory. Hayley watched Madison sleep calmly as though he hadn't a care in the world. In all truthfulness, he hadn't. He would marry Melissa, and they would live an idyllic life together somewhere between Vermont and New York, while Hayley would become the next Madame Butterfield, perhaps marrying a European aristocrat and returning home without him to live a life of grace and ease. That was Madame Butterfield's plan, and it was coming to fruition. Perhaps she would have a son, quite unlike Elmore, of course, and he would play with Madison and Melissa's son when they visited. It was all beginning to make sense. Finally, the vineyard was beginning to make sense. Hayley rang the bell for Kensington. He appeared with calm alacrity. Hayley motioned to Madison lying on the satin comforter as though embraced within a cloud of heavenly bliss.

"Mr. Timbrenel entered and collapsed on the bed," said Hayley in a business-like manner. "Can you assist, Kensington?"

Kensington nodded and smiled, but rather than attempting to awaken Madison and get him onto his feet, Kensington quietly closed the door and locked it from the outside. Hayley was agog. What was the meaning of this turn of events? Was she expected to spend the evening with Madison, who was stretched out on the satin comforter in a drunken stupor? Hayley was familiar with the locked doors in the Timbrenel house. She had heard many rumours, but the family had never locked her into a room. The Timbrenels were a strange family, to say the least. Kensington would never enact such a plan on his own accord. He was acting according to instructions from some member of the family – Mrs. Timbrenel, no doubt. But what did it mean? She did not ring the bell or try to exit the room. Madison was asleep and would sleep until dawn. Someone wanted to give the impression of a tryst between the two former lovers – but why? The entire family applauded Madison's engagement to Melissa. Hayley saw them smiling and cheering the announcement. From a far corner of the room, Hayley heard a muffled growl. Herbert emerged and lay before the door.

"*Et tu*, Herbert?" asked Hayley.

Herbert was always the final touch. He either frightened guests with his fang-like teeth under their windows if they attempted to exit the house by window, or he prevented them from entering the house at all.

"Don't worry, I'll play along," said Hayley. "But I warn you, Herbert, even your teeth won't prevent me from leaving this asylum in the morning. I'd forgotten how odd this family was." Hayley rubbed Herbert between the ears. He lay contentedly in front of the door. "They are crazy, but they are still family to me. I must say, I am elated that at least one of them thinks so highly of me as to want me to remain."

Hayley threw a blanket over Madison and snuggled in a chair beside the fireplace. The room was warm and friendly again. Upon reflection, Hayley realized that this was the best Christmas present she had ever received – the gift of being wanted.

The pungent aroma of coffee filled the room as Hayley awakened in the comfy chair by the fireplace. Madison had gone. A large indentation remained upon the satin comforter where he had lain. There was a small note atop the satin pillow case. Hayley read it with interest.

> *Hayley,*
> *You deserve so much better, but I can't help wonder how you will ever find it without me. I wish you the very best.*
> *Madison*

Hayley smirked. Madison was condescending to the end. Of course, he could not imagine that she could find true happiness with anyone apart from himself. The man with the massive ego was in for a rude awakening. She would not sit in the shadows pining for him. He was right in that she deserved better than Madison Timbrenel. Pity filled her heart for Melissa, who would now be the one feeling crestfallen when Madison lapsed into his philandering ways. Hayley perused the closet for the designer attire so generously contributed by Mrs. Trimbrenel. Soon, she would not need a couture contribution. She would be able to afford her own designer clothes. Kensington knocked gently on the door. Hayley granted him admittance.

"Good morning, Ms. Rembrandt," said Kensington. "I hope that you slept well. Mrs. Timbrenel requests you presence in the parlour before breakfast, if that is pleasing to you."

"Thank you, Kensington," said Hayley. "Has Madison left for Vermont?"

"Yes, he left early this morning," said Kensington.

"Good," said Hayley. "Please tell Mrs. Timbrenel that I shall be down as soon as I am dressed."

"Very good," said Kensington departing the room.

Herbert sauntered down the corridor past Hayley's room without looking in. Hayley wondered what mission the neurotic dog had embarked upon so early in the morning.

After dressing, Hayley found Mrs. Timbrenel in the parlour sipping a glass of sherry. Mrs. Timbrenel sipped sherry all day from the moment she awoke to the moment her head rested upon her pillow in the evening.

"Good morning, my dear child. Did you sleep well?" asked Mrs. Timbrenel.

"Yes, thank you," said Hayley.

"Sit down here," said Mrs. Timbrenel patting a cushion on the sofa. Hayley obliged and sat next to the matriarch.

"Hayley, you know my affection for you – the entire family adores you," said Mrs. Timbrenel.

"Thank you," said Hayley.

"Madison adores you as well. His will be a marriage of convenience – you do know that, don't you?" asked Mrs. Timbrenel.

"No, I didn't know," said Hayley. On some level, she knew quite well that any marriage Madison undertook would be a marriage of convenience – his convenience.

"Of course, in politics, one must marry a suitable partner. I mean, one must marry within the correct political sphere. Melissa's family is well-connected. They can do Madison a world of good when he embarks upon his political career," said Mrs. Timbrenel.

"I wasn't aware that Madison aspired to embrace a political career," said Hayley. Madison did not like politics, and his one regret in life was that he would be required to realize the dreams of his family.

"He has no choice in the matter," said Mrs. Timbrenel. "Madison knows what is expected of him. Politics is in his blood. He will run for national office after a brief stint working in local government. It has all been arranged."

Suddenly, Hayley felt remorse at her dismissive attitude towards Madison. The family was not only strange but demanding and unyielding as well. Madison's life was not his own. It was a sorry state of affairs.

"May I inquire as to whether or not you arranged for Madison to spend the night in my room last night?" asked Hayley.

Mrs. Timbrenel smiled. "Of course, it was the only way to test Melissa's resolve to marry him. Madison is a thoughtless young man and self-absorbed. He is also prone to indulge himself in the affections of beautiful women. Melissa will need to be aware of this if she is to marry him and bear my grandchildren. It is one of the givens within the political sphere."

"Givens?" asked Hayley.

"Men of prestige, power, position, and wealth will digress. Oh, the wives pretend that it is not the case, but they are aware of it. In fact, most expect it at some point, but the men must be discreet so that the wives do not look like fools. I always thought that you would understand that," said Mrs. Timbrenel sipping her sherry. "My husband has two mistresses. Most people know it, but no one says anything. Most people know that I am aware of it, but no one is indiscreet. Do you understand, Hayley?"

"I'm not sure that I understand at all," said Hayley.

"Let us speak plainly," said Mrs. Timbrenel. "Madison's infidelities will be many. She knows it and expects it. Of course, she will never admit it. She must play according to the rules. My son is one of the most indiscreet young men I know. I cannot tell you the miscreants he has brought into this house, and his liaisons within the city have gained unwanted notoriety. Did you meet that dog psychiatrist? Have you ever seen anyone so ridiculous – ridiculous for Madison, that is? His first wife was no better. My happiest day was when she removed herself from our presence and went to China. It was the most desirous place for her. I want to know that Madison is in a secure relationship. I know that he will be happy with you. I want you to remain a part of my son's life," said Mrs. Timbrenel. "He loves you, as much as it is within him to love anyone, and knowing this about him, you love him as well. Don't try to deny it. I saw it in your face last night when you heard of the engagement. Fear not, all is not lost. You two can still be together. I will arrange everything. He will have his life with Melissa, and he will have his life with you. You will find the Timbrenels to be a very generous family."

Hayley looked incredulously at Mrs. Timbrenel. "Are you asking me to become Madison's mistress after he marries Melissa?"

"That's a crude way of putting it, but I suppose it amounts to the same thing," said Mrs. Timbrenel. "I want you to remain an integral part of Madison's life. You are a practical young woman. There aren't many around like you. You will bring stability to this family, and I know that you will see to it that Madison is well-cared for."

"Like a provider," said Hayley.

"Yes, that is the word I'm searching for," said Mrs. Timbrenel agreeably. "You will encourage him to cut his hair."

"Does Madison know that you are making this request?" asked Hayley.

"Of course not," said Mrs. Timbrenel. "It has to be your idea."

"My idea?" asked Hayley.

"You must help Madison to see the sense of this type of relationship rather than involving himself with strangers who will destroy his political career and his family," said Mrs. Timbrenel calmly sipping her sherry. "My sister left you a sizable fortune, Hayley. I am aware that you do not need our money, but I do believe that you need Madison, and he needs you. Do this for Madison. Do this for your country. Do we really need any more scandals in Washington? I don't expect you to answer now. Take some time to think it over. I realize that it is a big decision."

"I can answer you now, Mrs. Timbrenel," said Hayley. "As much as I love and respect this family, I cannot do as you ask. I want a different sort of life, and Madison cannot be a part of it. Marriage is a sacrament to me, Mrs. Timbrenel."

"The Pope will never know," whispered Mrs. Timbrenel.

"The Pope has nothing to do with it," said Hayley. "Madison will have to grow up and uphold his responsibilities to his wife, to his family, and to his country, should he run for office. That is my decision, and I'm afraid it is irrevocable."

"Very well," said Mrs. Timbrenel, "but the offer remains. Go and have your breakfast. Take the horses and go sledding. I understand you have a friend you would like to invite to spend time with you while you are here."

"How did you know that?" asked Hayley.

Mrs. Timbrenel smiled and sipped her sherry. "My dear child, it is my duty to know all that concerns my son. Invite your friend. Ask him to stay a few days. We would love to meet him and get to know him. He's English, isn't he?"

"Yes?" answered Hayley.

"A descendant of Theodore Roosevelt - quite nice. Invite him," said Mrs. Timbrenel. "You'll find that we are a welcoming family to all of your friends, Hayley. Now, I must prepare for an engagement this afternoon. I will look forward to seeing you at dinner. What did you think of the gowns?"

"They are beautiful," said Hayley.

"Wonderful," said Mrs. Timbrenel. "I knew that they would be to your liking."

Hayley exited the parlour. She felt as though she had been hit with a massive boulder.

The horses clip-clopped through the wooded area of the estate. Gentle mounds of snow covered the ground. Fragments of snow brushed across Hayley's face as the horses kicked up the lightly adorned flakes. The gentle mist felt therapeutic as they sprinkled themselves upon Hayley's face and neck. The Timbrenel estate was, indeed, beautiful in winter. The groom led the horses out of the wooded area and around the lake, which was frozen and glassy in appearance. Tree branches covered with shimmering snow made the scenic spectacle a delight to behold. Hayley tried to clear her mind and digest her breakfast as she sat in the antique sled covered with a Tartan blanket. If she understood the chain of events correctly, she was to be offered as fodder to Madison's sexual impulses so that he would not involve himself with disreputable or unsuitable women as he cheated on his wife. Hayley shivered. The very thought of such opprobrium chilled her blood. She reminded herself that it was not Madison's idea but that of his meddling mother. Another thought occurred to Hayley. The Timbrenel family would not approve a marriage between their son and the lowly daughter of the Rembrandt family. While she and Madison were dating, they were tolerating her presence with him. No doubt, they reminded Madison of his familial responsibilities. Were they responsible for the demise of his first marriage? Were they to blame for the untimely end of their relationship as well? It all made sense. Madison and Madame Butterfield did what they could to elevate her in their esteem using their connections and finally the vineyard in order to remove the taint of the populace from her essence, but it was useless. Money could not provide what Melissa's *good blood* ensured. Hayley looked across the expanse and wondered how she had ever managed to cross the ha-ha in the first place.

The horses stopped in front of the stables. The groom helped Hayley out of the sled. It was an exhilarating ride, which did much to open her senses and her consciousness. One thought stood out above the others – even with money, Hayley would not be able to penetrate the *caste* system the Timbrenels had erected for people beyond their orb. She would always be in the lower echelons – not quite an *untouchable*, but certainly not fit for marriage within such an illustrious family. Hayley returned to the house and began to pack her suitcases. She hoped that there would not be a confrontation with Herbert. He did not seem to be anywhere in sight. Hayley checked the grounds outside of her window. The coast was clear.

"Are you leaving, Ms. Rembrandt?" asked Kensington. As usual, he appeared from out of nowhere. Nothing happened within the Timbrenel home that escaped his notice. "I was given to understand that you would be remaining a few days and would be inviting a friend to join you."

"There has been a change of plans, Kensington," said Hayley. "I must leave now."

"Very well, shall I bring your car to the front?" asked Kensington.

"No, thank you, Kensington," said Hayley. "I'll leave by the back door, if you don't mind. I don't want a confrontation with Herbert or anyone else."

Kensington nodded and carried Hayley's suitcase to her car in the garage. He placed the suitcase in the trunk and watched her back out of the garage and embark upon the meandering driveway, which led to the exit of the estate. Soon, the car disappeared from view.

Christmas in the city assured festivities beyond measure. Whether the festivities were related to the true meaning of Christmas was not even a point of contention. Most people realized that there was a formidable economic plan in place throughout the country. Christmas meant, hopefully, economic gain and a boost within the economy. Nothing was spared. The hanging lights were placed around lamp posts and strung across streets long before the official start of the season. One could observe the decorations as early as September. Fifth Avenue was ablaze with crystalline, twinkling lights. Saks Fifth Avenue was a monument of Yule Tide splendour. Lights in the form of snowflakes adorned the front of the building twinkling to the tune of *Christmas Bells*. *Cartier* was wrapped in a tremendous red ribbon, and the tree at Rockefeller Center remained unparalleled. It was the Christmas season, and the tree held court over the entire city with its festive lights and enormous crystal star. No one could be immune to the Christmas season in New York. It enveloped everyone in its midst and cast a mesmerizing glow over the entire city.

Madison Timbrenel gazed upward at the tree. His fixated stance paralleled the look of awe upon the faces of the other onlookers. Young or old, no one escaped the majesty of the twinkling tree. Madison was a kid at heart. He wasn't one to dream of taking his children to see sights that enthralled the young, for he *was* the young – in spirit and at heart. As he gazed upward, a plan evolved within his consciousness. His son, Peter, would adore the sight of the tree at Christmas. Did Peter celebrate Christmas, or had his Asian family replaced Christmas with a new religious observance? Madison shuddered at how little he knew about his flesh and blood across the seas. Did Peter bear any resemblance to him? Were there days when his mother secretly observed some expression or action which reminded her of her discarded American husband? It had been years since he had communicated with his ex-wife and his son. Now that his own marriage was imminent, Madison felt the need to incorporate Peter within his new family. He and Melissa would have children, and he wanted Peter to visit from time to time. It was a bold and daring idea, an idea that might disrupt his entire future with Melissa, but he dared not broach the subject before the wedding. Peter was just one of many issues Madison would place before his new bride after the wedding. There was still the To Do list. Would he be able to accomplish his goals with Melissa in tow? Marriage was a big step, and Madison was beginning to realize the seriousness of his endeavour. He crossed the street and looked at the rings in the *Cartier* window. He entered the establishment and indicated his interest in a ring that sparkled brilliantly in the window. Fifteen minutes later, Madison walked onto the crowded streets of Fifth Avenue with the engagement ring in an elegant, red box. He would present the ring to Melissa the next time he saw her, though he did not know when he would venture to Vermont. Melissa waited for him the day after the Christmas party, but Madison went directly to his New York apartment after he awoke in Hayley's room. He needed time to think about the engagement. It was quite a surprise. He did not expect to hear the words *Will you marry me* spew from his lips. The champagne was the culprit, but Madison wondered why Melissa would accept an engagement under such indeterminate circumstances. She must have been aware that he was under the influence of the intoxicating nectar. Was it entrapment?

Could he sever the binding entanglement? That would not be fair to Melissa. If he had to marry anyone, she was an acceptable choice. Madison wasn't certain whether he loved her or not, but then, he wasn't certain whether he knew what love was, so why should he expect it. He had involvements with a plethora of beautiful women. Did he love any of them? He loved one's hair, and he loved another's mouth. He was smitten with the eyes of yet another, and he loved the dulcet tones of one maiden's voice. To find a woman with all of the attributes that he loved would be an awe-inspiring task and perhaps an unrealistic one. There were no thunder bolts when he looked at Melissa, but there were not thunder bolts when he looked at any of the other women he had known. There was no spark, no flash, or any special sign from above, but shouldn't there have been? The male gaze faltered when he looked at any of the women in his life. None of them reflected the best of him. Perhaps it was his fault. He was unique. Should he expect any woman to measure up to his flawless standard? Hayley came remarkably close, but even she lacked that certain something that would drive a man to distraction and alert him that she was the one. Madison felt the ring box within his pocket. He would present Melissa with the ring and marry her. It had been arranged, and everyone would be happy; nonetheless, there was a gnawing feeling within his body that alerted him that he was embarking upon a course that might, quite possibly, extinguish his youthful, exuberant spirit and cast him within the realm of the old and depleted.

A message voice message awaited. Voice messages were becoming obsolete. Everyone was texting. Madison intuited that the message would be from someone who was not enamoured with the texting craze. Truthfully, he did not like to text and preferred to leave a spoken message to the recipient. Speech was important to Madison, and he enjoyed listening to the speech patterns of people, particularly if they had a firm command of the English language.

If it isn't too much trouble, would you please ask your friend, the dog psychiatrist, to contact me? Herbert is beside himself. He seems to be grieving and will not eat or harken to any of our commands. She may be able to help him. You need a haircut.

As usual, there was no greeting or closing. His mother always left him suspended in mid-air. Herbert was not a griever, so something else must be bothering him. Herbert was more than the family dog. He was a member of the family in the fullest sense of the word. Very little was done without some type of consideration to Herbert. Madison's own dog, Oswald, did not gain Herbert's approval, and for that reason, Madison was unable to bring him to the family homestead.

The thought of contacting Gretchen was not pleasant. She was quite upset when they last spoke. Madison decided to text her, for he did not want to hear her voice. When Gretchen received the text, she was elated. Everything was beginning to fall into place. The festive celebration for the doggie playgroup promised to be a thrilling experience. Of course, Herbert could not be a part of such a festive group. It would be necessary to meet with Madison and Herbert in order to render an initial evaluation before assigning him to a group with similar needs, but she would be pleased if Madison would attend the celebration in order to see how the playgroups worked and to ascertain whether or not Herbert should be a part of one. Madison sighed heavily when he received Gretchen's text and was filled with trepidation. He would be forced to tell her about the engagement. It would not be a pleasant affair. Madison imagined Gretchen becoming shrill and inconsolable, as she was in the car when they were last together. Madison did not want another scene, but he would tell her as soon as possible so that she could not accuse him of keeping secrets from her – like the existence of an ex-wife and son. Perhaps in the presence of the dogs and their owners she would be more accepting of the news.

Be that as it may, Madison was certain that Gretchen would not agree to treat Herbert once she learned of his engagement to Melissa.

"I brought Oswald," said Madison. "I didn't think you would mind. Oswald gets along with everyone."

Gretchen smiled and welcomed Madison and Oswald into her living room, where the other dogs and their owners were enjoying the festivities. There were doggie presents yet to be opened, and all of the dogs, seven in number, looked anxiously at their expected treats. Gretchen introduced Madison and Oswald to the group. Oswald was pleased to be in the company of so many friendly canine companions. He sniffed them, and they sniffed him and welcomed him within their midst.

"I didn't realize there would be presents," said Madison. "Oswald didn't bring anything. I could run out and get something."

The gaiety of the event lifted Madison's spirits. It was remarkable how dogs brought such a feeling of well-being.

"That won't be necessary," said Gretchen. "We have extras, so Oswald can receive a present also."

Madison enjoyed watching Gretchen work with the dogs and their owners. She was quite exceptional, and for the first time in many months, Madison remembered why he found her so intriguing. As long as there were dogs around, Gretchen was vibrant. Madison found himself smiling in such festive surroundings. If only Gretchen could be as pleasing to humans as she was to dogs.

"How long have you had Oswald?" asked one of the owners.

"About six years," said Madison. "Which dog is yours?"

"Cyril is mine. He's the sheep dog opening his present now. Good boy, Cyril," said the man. "That's a good boy."

Cyril bit the wrappings off of his present and found a rubber chew toy.

"I haven't seen him this happy for quite some time. My wife and I are separated. She just returned from Beijing, and Cyril refuses to go outdoors. I had a time trying to get him here," said the man.

"China?" asked Madison? "I think my son lives in Shanghai."

"Don't you know?" asked the man.

"I'm divorced, and his mother remarried," said Madison. "I haven't been in touch with them for six years."

"I'm sorry," said the man. "At least Oswald seems to be good company. He seems so well-adjusted. Was he upset when they left?"

"He has never met them," said Madison. "If they were to return tomorrow, he would be upset, no doubt. It's just been the two of us for six years."

The man looked as though he had an epiphany.

"By gosh, I'll bet that's it," said the man.

"What is it?" asked Madison.

"Cyril is troubled by Sylvia's return," said the man. "That *has* to be it."

"Perhaps," said Madison. "What does Gretchen say about it?"

"Dr. Miller is meeting with us tomorrow," said the man, "but I think I have the answer. Cyril and I will find a new residence, something temporary to establish whether or not the problem persists."

"What if it doesn't?" asked Madison.

"Then the new residence may become permanent," said the man. "After all, Cyril has never left me or caused me any chagrin. He deserves to be able to live comfortably."

"What about your wife?" asked Madison.

"If she loves me, she will understand," said the man. "A man can't simply disregard his dog. Anyway, Cyril has been with me longer than Sylvia, and he has never let me down. Thank you. You have helped me to figure this out."

"I didn't do anything," said Madison.

"Oh, but you have," said the man. "You have helped me to realize what I must do. I will tell Dr. Miller. Thank you again."

As the man spoke privately with Gretchen, her glance shifted to Madison. The joy had left her eyes, and her face indicated that she was not pleased. The man and Cyril left immediately. He was filled with an elation that seemed to transcend to Cyril. They left the celebration with sprightly step and gleeful exuberance.

"I'd like to speak with you when everyone has left," said Gretchen smiling. The smile was forced. Madison was well familiar with it. This was the Gretchen he knew. For some reason, he seemed to bring out the worst in her gregarious nature.

"It wasn't my fault," said Madison quietly. "He jumped to conclusions."

Gretchen joined the dog owners and their well-behaved dogs as they attempted to play a game. Madison sat despondently. Oswald nestled close to him sensing his mood.

At the conclusion of the affair, Madison helped Gretchen clear the living room of any remnants of the festivities. There was little to clear. The dogs and their owners were perfect guests – so perfect that Gretchen scheduled another play session in the spring. Gretchen sat on the sofa and rubbed Oswald's stomach.

"So, why are you here, Madison?" asked Gretchen calmly.

"It's Herbert. My mother phoned and requested that you meet with him. She seems to think that he is grieving," said Madison.

"Has anything happened of late out of the ordinary that might disrupt his routine?" asked Gretchen.

Madison pondered how to respond. "We had a Christmas celebration a couple of days ago."

"Your family gives parties all of the time. Was there anything unusual or different about this celebration?" asked Gretchen.

He couldn't put it off any longer. "I became engaged," said Madison.

Gretchen sat still. "I see," she said at last.

"Her name is Melissa. She's a friend of the family. Everyone is pleased. I hadn't planned to tell you like this," said Madison.

"Congratulations, Madison," said Gretchen. "I hope that you and Melissa will be very happy."

Bernie sat beside Gretchen on the sofa and licked her wrist.

"I would like you to meet her," said Madison dishonestly. "I think that you two will be great friends."

"I doubt that," said Gretchen. "Regarding Herbert, I may have an opening coming up soon. If Cyril's problem is solved, then Herbert can fill his slot. Would Thursdays at two be all right?"

"That's all?" asked Madison. "You aren't going to say anything else...about the engagement, I mean?"

"What is there to say?" asked Gretchen. "I had hoped that we might be able to work things out, but I see that it is not going to happen, so I wish you every happiness." Bernie licked Gretchen's taunt face.

Madison breathed a sigh of relief. "I thought that you might be upset. I can't tell you how relieved I am. So, you're willing to see Herbert?"

"Providing Cyril is no longer in need of my services," said Gretchen. "I will phone your mother next week and inform her of my availability."

Madison stood up as Gretchen presented him with his coat. He smiled broadly.

"Wow, this is the best Christmas ever!" exclaimed Madison. "First, Hayley gives me her blessing, and now you wish me every happiness. I tell you, this is the best Christmas ever!"

Madison kissed Gretchen's cheek. Oswald placed his present, a blue ball, between his teeth and walked to the door. Madison followed. Gretchen closed the door softly and walked to the sofa, where she wept inconsolably with Bernie at her side for quite some time.

Spring arrived far too quickly. The trees were budding, and the lake's thaw produced a splendiferous haze, which seemed to envelope the entire estate. Preparations were in full-swing for the wedding of the year. The ceremony would be held within the indoor chapel, and the reception would be outdoors under a huge, white tent that was decorated with glorious bouquets of white flowers.

Elmore paced frantically. Weddings made him nervous. He could not understand why Madison would relinquish his freedom to please his family. His own mother, Madame Butterfield, wanted him to marry as well, but he rebuffed the idea, moved to Paris, and became an artist of some recognition. It was an honourable life, in his estimation. Why Madison would not exert his right to live life on his own terms was beyond him, so he paced and hoped for a rapid conclusion to the event.

Oliver Timbrenel, Madison's best man, adjusted the bow tie of his son, Branford, who fidgeted in his junior tuxedo.

"Don't forget to smile," advised Oliver.

"Why?" asked Branford. "No one else is smiling."

"Just do it," said Oliver. "There, the tie is perfect. Go and find your mother."

"What for?" asked Branford.

"Just do it," said Oliver. "She may need you."

Branford sighed and went to find his mother.

Melissa sat patiently as her attendants adjusted her veil. The gown was beautiful and everything she had hoped for all of her life. Her hair clung to her shoulders in defiance of everyone's recommendation to pin it up for the occasion. Everything was perfect. She would marry Madison, and they would live a glorious life. There would be children, of course. Madison never made advances towards Melissa. She wondered what the honeymoon would be like. She had done everything that a young woman of culture and means should do. She kept herself pure and spotless for the man she loved – her prince charming. Well, perhaps Madison Timbrenel was not her prince charming, but he came close. He had everything a prince should have – money, position, looks, and personality. He was her knight in shining armour, and this was her wedding day. The sun was shining and all was perfect.

"Oliver, are you keeping abreast of everything?" asked Mrs. Timbrenel. "Please put that gadget away and see to it that all is well.

Oliver looked at his BlackBerry in amazement. "There will be a vote on marriage equality in June."

"What are you babbling about?" asked Mrs. Timbrenel. "Would you, please put that thing away and check on your father? I want to be certain that he has not gotten his hands on the whiskey until after the ceremony. What do you mean marriage equality?"

"Never mind," said Oliver. "It will be a milestone if it passes. Cuomo is in favour and…"

Mrs. Timbrenel snatched Oliver's BlackBerry from his hands. "Go and check on your father. If he is inebriated when the ceremony begins, I am holding you accountable!"

Oliver retrieved his BlackBerry from his mother's grasp and dutifully complied with her wishes as the servants admitted a continuous stream of guests into the chapel. Two guests caught Mrs. Timbrenel's eye. They seemed out of place.

"Mildred," said Mrs. Timbrenel to one of the servants. "Who let those people in? Why are they here?"

"I don't know, Mrs. Timbrenel," said the servant. "Shall I ask Kensington?"

"Yes, please ask Kensington to find out who they are," said Mrs. Timbrenel. "I'm certain that they are not on the guest list."

"Yes, Mrs. Timbrenel," said Mildred.

Mrs. Timbrenel searched for her son, Oliver, who was in a corner texting a message to a colleague.

"Will you please put that thing away? Interlopers have intruded, and you are still preoccupied with that contraption," said Mrs. Timbrenel.

"Interlopers?" asked Oliver. "Where?"

"Over there on the groom's side of the chapel," said Mrs. Timbrenel. "I cannot believe the effrontery. Go and rectify that, Oliver."

"Of course," said Oliver.

Oliver approached the two guests and greeted them civilly. Tactfully, he inquired if they were seated on the right side of the chapel. One of the guests produced an invitation with a brief note inscribed across the bottom. Oliver read it and smiled at the guests politely. He returned to his mother, who was watching carefully.

"It's Peter," said Oliver.

"Peter?" asked Mrs. Timbrenel.

"Your grandson, Peter," said Oliver.

"Good heavens!" shrieked Mrs. Timbrenel. Some of the guests looked in her direction. "What on earth is he doing here? Who is that with him?"

"I don't know," said Oliver. "I suppose he's some sort of courtier accompanying the boy. You can hardly expect his mother to bring him."

"But what is he doing here?" asked Mrs. Timbrenel. "Find your brother. We can't have those people here. Everyone will wonder who they are. They're sitting right on the front pew as though they are family; they will spoil everything. People don't know about Madison's unfortunate first marriage. We did everything we could to keep it a secret and end it. We sent that girl back to her country where she belongs. Now that boy is sitting there in the front of the church. If Melissa sees him… This cannot be. Bring your brother to me at once. We must do something. Do you hear me, Oliver? Something must be done!"

"Calm down," said Oliver. "I agree that something must be done. Let me sort it out. I'll think of something."

Hayley Rembrandt looked out of the window at the budding flowers growing on Rupert's terrace. Spring was always delightful. Everything was fresh and new. Spring was about new beginnings. Her relationship with Rupert was growing, just like the blossoms within the planters. Hayley felt comfortable with Rupert. The more she knew of him, the more she wanted to be a permanent part of his life. Rupert slept soundly as Hayley tried to imagine life as Rupert's wife. She lay beside him and enjoyed the peaceful morning. The sun streamed into the room through the curtains. Hayley loved spring and new beginnings.

Meanwhile, further uptown, Alyson received a phone call from Hayley's father after Jordan's tragic accident during the snowboarding competitions. Jordan Rembrandt fell on his spine and was paralyzed from the neck down. Hayley's father wondered if she might come home to see him. Alyson promised to relay the message to Hayley as soon as possible. Alyson poured herself a glass of wine before she called Hayley and felt a sense of remorse, part of which was for Jordan, the promising Olympic competitor, and the other part was for Hayley, the provider.

The sea breeze filled Madison's nostrils. Kensington brought a glass of port on a silver tray and placed it beside Madison as he stretched out on a deck chair. The sun shone brightly, although it was cooler than Madison had anticipated. The nip in the air invigorated him as the vessel sailed calmly towards the Gulf of Mexico. All was blissful. There was no hurry to reach California. The important thing was that Madison Timbrenel was his own man. He did not allow his family or his career responsibilities to dissuade him. He accomplished every item on his To Do list. Yes, there were casualties, but they were to be expected. Melissa wasted no time in securing another engagement. Hayley's elopement with the young Brit, Rupert, came as a surprise, but Madison wished her every happiness. The proceeds from the vineyard were useful in securing the best medical care for Jordan, who was making a rapid recovery. The prognosis was that he would walk again after sufficient therapy, but snowboarding was no longer an option.

"Do you know what I plan to do when we reach California, Kensington?" asked Madison sipping his port.

"I have no idea," said Kensington.

"I plan to make another To Do list of things I must do before I turn forty," said Madison.

"How interesting," said Kensington.

"Have you ever been skiing on the Swiss Alps, Kensington?" asked Madison.

"No, I have not had the pleasure," said Kensington.

"Well, it is the first item on the list. We'll take the boy with us," said Madison.

"The boy?" asked Kensington.

"Yes, Peter, my son," said Madison.

Kensington's foreboding look alarmed Madison.

"What is it, Kensington?" asked Madison. "You seem troubled."

"It is not my place, Mr. Timbrenel," said Kensington.

"Not your place? What is not your place? Come on, man, out with it," demanded Madison.

"I was informed some time ago," said Kensington reluctantly, "that the young man, Peter, is the son of your cousin, Elmore. I gather your former wife has arranged for the young man to remain with his father indefinitely."

"What nonsense!" said Madison laughing. "What on earth makes you think that Peter is Elmore's son?"

"I heard your parents and Madame Butterfield speak of it before I was instructed to present your former wife with a check for passage to Shanghai. They were quite generous. I believe it was the time of your first To Do list – the tennis tournament at Wimbledon, if I recall correctly. It was number three on the list. Shall I pour you another glass of port, Sir?"

Madison tried to digest this information with the utmost civility.

"Yes, Kensington, I would like another glass of port," said Madison. "So, you are asserting that Peter is Elmore's son?"

"Yes sir," said Kensington. "The family thought that the unfortunate circumstance would derail your political endeavours if the facts were to be made public, and it also accounts for Madame Butterfield's decision to bequeath the vineyard to Ms. Rembrandt rather than her son."

Madison sipped his port. "And my wedding to Melissa…"

"The presence of the young man made concealment of your first marriage impossible. Miss Kendrickson and her family took the necessary course of action without a moment's hesitation," reasoned Kensington. "The press *was* present after all, and the cancellation was expedient before they could ascertain…"

Madison sat quietly breathing the brisk sea air for a few moments. Soon, his eyes began to sparkle with a new resolve.

"This is the best news that I have ever had," said Madison. "Things happen for a reason, Kensington. Do you believe that?"

"Undoubtedly," responded Kensington.

"This is a new beginning for me, Kensington. I am in complete control of my destiny. I can now make all of my own decisions without hindrance. It is a new day. The sun is shining, and I am free of my family's machinations. They thought that they could coerce me into marriage and life within the political arena, but little did they know that I and I alone have made the decision to enter the foray of politics. This entire fiasco was a sort of *deus ex machina*. Scratch the Swiss Alps from my new To Do list, Kensington," said Madison. "in fact, discard the list. I am no longer in need of it. It is you and I against the world, Kensington. I will forge my way into the great unknown with you by my side as my confidant. My family will no longer control me or my actions."

"Very good, sir," said Kensington. "It is a very sensible idea."

"By the way, Kensington," said Madison, "although I am happy to be enlightened by all of these events, I didn't invite Peter to the wedding. Who sent the infernal invitation?"

"I did," said Kensington. "Here is a copy of the international section of *The New York Times*, *The Washington Post*, and *The Financial Times*. Their view of world events is most invigorating and comprehensive. You might want to visit a few embassies while on our journey. I took the liberty to make the required arrangements, and if I might suggest a haircut, sir?"

The End